Nexus

Frances,

I hope you enjoy Nexus! I'd love to hear what you think...

– [illegible]

Nexus
By Jeff Dunne

Cover Artwork by Jeff Dunne

ISBN: 978-1-936033-41-6

For information, address correspondence to:

Wyrder Books, a division of
ICRL Press
P.O. Box 113
Sykesville, MD 21784

NEXUS

By Jeff Dunne

Wyrder Books

Contents

DEDICATION

This book is dedicated to the life and memory of my mother, Brenda, the woman who taught me the nature and criticality of balance. She dedicated her life to laying the groundwork for the scientific world to accept what most people appreciate at a subconscious level but often cannot remember on a day-to-day basis: that cause without purpose . . . how without why . . . entropy without syntropy . . . past without future . . . yang without yin . . . can never do more than tell half the story.

And we are, without question, creatures of story.

And we deserve more than half.

My mother showed me that peace lies in accepting others for who and what they are, and that lesson too is woven into this story. She taught me to value what is different from myself, and to realize that every flavor of person is necessary to realize the great ice cream sundae that is humanity. She gave me the space and encouragement to be true to myself, to be the person I want to be and not submit or conform to the expectations that others may try to force upon me.

And I hope that if you are reading this dedication, you too will follow that wisdom.

Prologue

Valerie Guerrero awoke to the sound of breaking glass. She sat bolt upright in her bed, little fingers clutching the flowered pink of her comforter. A moment later the other sounds came... the door of her parents' room slamming open against the wall, her father's footsteps clambering down the staircase.

Something was wrong.

Near the edge of her bed lay the pink and yellow Frombit that was her constant companion, with its worn fabrics that weren't quite a creature yet unmistakably a friend. She grabbed it, hugging it close as the door to her room slowly opened. The fair skin of her mother's face became visible, almost spectral in its paleness. The fear was unmistakable, and Valerie's knuckles whitened to match as she gripped the Frombit even tighter.

"Get under the bed, sweetheart!" Her mother's voice was a fierce whisper. Valerie was frozen in place. "Now!"

She scrambled out from beneath the covers, and a moment later was hiding between boxes in the cave beneath her big-girl bed. With a deft flick of the wrist, her mother rearranged the blankets so Valerie could only see the beige carpet. Then a fold of the blanket was lifted to reveal her mother's face again.

"Now stay there and don't make a sound. Not a sound, you understand?"

Valerie nodded, eyes wide with fear, and then her mother was gone. The door closed with the faintest of clicks, and there was only the beating of her pulse. The stillness was eerie, stifling, but only for a few breaths. A gunshot shattered the silence and her mother screamed. Then another burst of gunfire. Then everything was silent once more.

Valerie held her breath until her lungs began to burn, and then she heard something. Sirens. The wails of distant police cars, faint but growing steadily louder. Downstairs, a door slammed. She closed her eyes as tightly as she could...

"Valerie?"

She opened her eyes. The soft blue walls of the psychologist's office felt like a cartoon rendering of the afternoon sky, and Elena Harkins, the counselor she was supposed to call 'Elle' but never could, was watching her with kind eyes. The notepad was in her lap. Sometimes Val wondered whether the woman took it with her when she went to the bathroom. Elena inclined her head forward, a silent repeat of her question.

"No, ma'am," Valerie lied. "I don't really remember a lot about that night. I guess I kind of blotted it out."

Counselor Harkins smiled softly. "That's perfectly natural, Valerie. Really. Nothing to be concerned about. I just wanted to know if anything had changed since the last time we spoke."

Valerie shook her head as she pushed her hands down into the soft fabric of the couch. Elena had told her she could lie down if she wanted, but that felt too weird. Besides, she had to leave someplace for—

"Your grandparents tell me that you have a new friend." Valerie's attention snapped back to the woman. "Do you want to tell me about her?"

Involuntarily, Valerie turned to look by the office door where a little girl stood. It was hard to say how old Kelly seemed. Val didn't really care. Seven? Eight? Maybe even nine, but certainly not younger than herself. She was dressed in red, the color she nearly always chose—a simple sundress with a pattern of white, wavy lines that hugged the waist and made it unquestionably the attire of an elegant young lady.

"They said her name is Kelly." Valerie's stare returned to the psychologist. "Is that right?"

Val glanced back at her friend, who was twirling a lock of her straight, blond hair around a finger. Kelly scrunched her face, then shook her head. The way her left eye squinted a little more than the right always gave Valerie the feeling that her friend found everything just a little amusing. Kelly walked forward, passing through the couch as if it didn't exist, but then sat on it solidly next to her friend.

"Valerie?" the psychologist prompted.

"Yes. Kelly."

"Would you like to talk about her?"

Valerie shrugged. "There isn't anything to say."

"That's okay. Maybe another time."

"Maybe," she mumbled. She watched, and then . . . there it was. The little note on the pad. If she put the pen down now, Valerie knew . . . Yes. The session was over.

"I just want you to know," the counselor said, "that it is not uncommon for children who have been through severe trauma, like you have, to . . ." She struggled to find the right word. "To find a friend, like Kelly, who can help them work through the experience. There's absolutely nothing wrong with that."

Valerie endured a brief eternity in awkward, fidgety silence before Elena continued.

"I suppose that's enough for today," she finally said, and gave Val a kind, slightly-too-clinical smile. "Please keep writing or drawing in your journal, and we'll talk again next week, okay?"

Valerie mumbled a quiet "okay" in response, then slipped off the couch and walked out of the office to join her grandparents in the reception area. Kelly stayed a moment longer, smiling warmly at the psychologist.

"Thank you, Elle. She may not say it, but I know she really appreciates your help." Kelly's voice was steady, confident, and completely imperceptible to the psychologist, who had already started flipping through her notes in preparation for her next appointment.

CHAPTER ONE:

Legacy Claimed

The village of Woodhome Heights, where few if any of the innumerable, quaint little houses were actually made of wood, was a suburb for people who liked to go to bed early and sleep through quiet nights of gentle breezes and serenading crickets. The residents on Canterbury Road, however, didn't always enjoy this luxury. From time to time they would be awakened by the roar of a black Yamaha YZF-R1 sports motorbike blasting its way beneath their street's canopy of green ash. It was an unpredictable event, sometimes absent for weeks at a stretch but occasionally happening several nights in a row.

This particular evening fell into the noisy category.

Two figures were atop the sleek motorcycle as it screamed along the street before pulling a dangerously sharp turn into the driveway of a two-story Colonial that had remained all but unoccupied over the past five years. The passenger hung on tightly, one might even say desperately, to the lithe form in front. His arms remained wrapped around her waist after they skidded to a stop, at least until she peeled them away. He stumbled off the bike and inhaled deeply to calm his nerves. It didn't really work. The woman swung a leg over in an effortless motion, and before the man finished his second exhale, Valerie had removed her helmet and was pressed against him, a mischievous smile flickering in her eyes as she studied Mike's features.

He opened his mouth to speak, but then her lips were on his. He stumbled backward, nearly knocking over the bike.

"Careful," she warned, playful but with an unsettling edge. "I like that bike more than I like you."

He laughed nervously, trying to decide if he should believe the words or the smile. Before he reached a conclusion she was pulling him toward the house. He blinked in uncertainty.

"I hope the ride wasn't too rough for you," she laughed as she reached around to squeeze his backside.

"No." He swallowed, then took the lie one more step. "Not at all."

"Good, because that was the gentle part of the evening." She pulled him to her again, claiming another moment of passion, then drew away and withdrew a set of keys from her jacket pocket.

"I thought you said you lived downtown."

"I do. But this place is mine too." She opened the front door. "Sort of."

"Sort of yours?"

She pushed him into the house with an aggressive kiss. By the time the door was closed, her jacket had hit the floor and she was starting on his.

"Technically it belongs to my grandparents' est—"

"Your grandparents?" He stiffened. "What if they...?"

"Their *estate*. Trust me. No one's going to interrupt us. Unless maybe their ghosts are hanging around." She laughed, then went for another kiss.

Mike leaned back. "Their *ghosts*?"

She grabbed him by the neck, pulled him close, and whispered into his ear. "Relax. If their spirits didn't want me using the place, they've had plenty of chances to let me know." Then she was on him again, her face buried in his neck.

"Plenty of... just how many—"

She put a finger to his lips. "Shhh." Another long, grinding kiss. "You talk too much."

They marked a path through the dusty living room one article of clothing after another. It was clearly the home of an elderly couple who believed the décor of 1972 never went out of style, and who, equally clearly, had doted on their granddaughter with boundless affection. An expansive matrix of framed photographs revealed only narrow slivers of a pale green wall, and each row was organized by topic. At the top was a progression of Valerie winning Krav Maga competitions, starting around ten years old and concluding in her early twenties. Two more rows depicted family life; early photos included Valerie's parents, but most were scenes of her with her grandparents, Maria and Julio. Still another row spoke of a lifelong friendship with a short, auburn-haired girl who eventually matured into an attractive woman several inches taller than Valerie.

Shirts and belts were discarded by the time Mike and Val had reached the far end of the living room.

"Door," she warned. Before Mike could mutter 'what?' he was slammed against it. "Warned you," Valerie whispered with an impish smile.

"Ah, door." He fumbled with the handle. Her bra was on the carpet by the time he had the door open. She pushed him through into the master bedroom.

The chamber was sparsely populated with old, worn furniture. A scratched dressing table of dark wood and two matching dressers lined the walls on either side. An unmade king-sized bed—the kind with four posters intended to support some missing canopy of heavy felt or velvet—was centered on the far wall and framed by dirty windows. Mike couldn't stop himself from wondering when the sheets had last been washed, but the thought quickly evaporated as Valerie pulled him around to face her. Her jeans were crumpled on the floor and his eyes fell momentarily to her black panties, that is until she pushed him onto the bed and started pulling off his own jeans. They got as far as his shins, but she unexpectedly stopped and looked around.

"What's that sound?" Valerie twisted her head back and forth, trying to localize the source.

"What sound?"

"You can't hear that humming?"

Mike listened. He heard it, a faint buzz, rhythmically pulsing louder then diminishing. It sounded perhaps like a distant exhaust fan that was slightly out of balance.

"I...I guess I hear something. Maybe it's the A/C system?"

"With that throbbing sound?"

"If you're interested in throbbing—"

"Don't be an ass, Mitch."

"Mike," he corrected with a touch of indignation.

"Whatever. What the hell *is* that?" Valerie stepped back, leaving his jeans abandoned just above his ankles.

He sat up and pulled them off the rest of the way. "Like I said, it's probably the air conditioning. Maybe the blower's out of balance or something."

"The A/C isn't on, m—" She stopped herself at the last moment, replacing 'moron' with, "Mitch. Why would I run the A/C when I'm not living here?"

Mike opened his mouth to reply, but Valerie had already turned around, and was now crossing back and forth across the room. The humming seemed loudest near the bed, and she bent down to listen.

Definitely louder.

She grasped one of the bedposts. Mike watched her momentarily, earning him an irate glare. He stood, and she gave the bed a push. It barely budged. She gave him a second, colder glare. Its meaning was clear: *why aren't you helping?*

Together they were able to walk the bed over by several feet, and Valerie bent down to examine the carpet.

"Get the lights," she ordered without looking up.

Mike walked back to the door and flipped a switch. Nothing happened. "There's a metaphor for the evening," he muttered.

"What?"

"Nothing."

He hit a second switch and two lamps, one on each dresser, threw pale yellow light into the room. Through dusty lampshades it was only a little brighter than what the moon was casting through the uncurtained windows, but it was enough. Valerie traced the edges of a square hatch, perhaps two and a half feet across. There was no question why she hadn't seen it when she had been living in the house. With the carpet as thick as it was, the trap door would be impossible to detect without moving the bed.

She caught a glint of metal, and pushed the threads apart to reveal a small keyhole near one edge. Valerie's eyes grew wide, and she reached out with a hesitant finger. "No," she muttered.

"What's that?" Mike asked from the doorway. She ignored him.

"No. It can't be."

"Can't be what?"

But there was no doubt in her mind. *This* was the matching keyhole.

All but naked, she rushed out of the bedroom and towards the stairway off the kitchen, interrupting Mike's, "What are you—" with her own "Be right back!"

Despite an overwhelming sense of urgency, Valerie paused at the foot of the stairs. She hadn't ascended this flight for years, and it felt like a tunnel back in time. Slowly, step by step, she allowed herself the journey.

The door to her old room at the end of the hall was closed. She approached it hesitantly, running her fingers along the walls as she went. Valerie had worked very hard to leave her past behind and suddenly here it was again, standing between her and whatever secret was hidden beneath that mysterious hatch in her grandparents' bedroom.

She turned the handle and pushed gently. The door swung open, revealing a sea of adolescent clutter. Clothes covered the floor, and nearly everything else upon which a garment could be flung. Jutting out from beneath the landscape of fabric was an amalgam of old martial arts magazines, books, CDs, and rocks and shells from vacations long past. Each artifact evoked flashes of buried memories, and for the briefest of moments she was a teenager again. Her grandparents were calling, summoning her to come down for…dinner, school, to say hello to the neighbors. If one could truly forget the trauma of her parents' murder, it really wasn't a bad childhood.

And then it was gone. She was twenty-seven once more, standing in the room of the teenager left far behind, and she finally knew what mystery that key would unlock.

Val waded through the mess, nearly tripping on a set of nunchaku lurking beneath a hooded sweatshirt to ambush unwary feet. She lifted the corner of her old bed to reveal a stash of her most personal memories. Photographs, scraps of poetry, and a dozen other items that had once seemed so important all pleaded for her attention, but only one mattered.

In the center of the hoard was a small combination lockbox. Valerie quickly rotated the dials, heard the soft click as the mechanism released, and opened the case. Posters of the world's great martial artists stood in silent witness as Valerie reached in and solemnly withdrew the silver teardrop locket that contained the tiny key.

Her grandmother had given the pendant to her in the last minutes of her life. Valerie had been across town, working in the dojo when the call reached her. She had raced home at breakneck speed, and burst into the living room to find Nana on the couch. Her grandmother had weakly motioned her over, and immediately held out her hand. Val took it, and felt the locket's smooth, warm shape on her palm. Then Nana smiled. Valerie would never forget the sense of peace and pride that shone from the woman's soft brown eyes in that moment. Nothing was spoken in those final moments. In fact, it was only after her grandfather had placed a shaking hand on Valerie's shoulder that she realized her grandmother had stopped breathing.

Val returned the lock box to its hidden shrine. Once the mattress was back in place, she returned downstairs and into the master bedroom. Mike stood by the doorway, rooted in the same spot as when she had dashed out, and she trotted past him without a word.

"What's that?" he asked, nodding at the delicate silver chain draped over her fist.

Valerie didn't respond. When she reached the trap door, she opened the locket and withdrew a small brass key.

"What *is* that?" Mike repeated.

She shot the briefest of glances in his direction, but still said nothing. Valerie snapped the locket shut again and placed the chain over her head. The silver charm swung back and forth, flickering in the dim light as she knelt down in front of the trap door. With a deep breath, held in anticipation, she slipped the key into the lock. It fit perfectly, gliding into the chamber with a barely audible metallic whisper.

She twisted, the key turned, and the trapdoor sprang up a quarter of an inch. She slowly exhaled as the low, rhythmic humming became more intense.

"Holy shit," she muttered as she rocked back onto her heels, staring at the hatch. A strand of her dark hair escaped, falling in front of her eyes; she secured it behind an ear.

"What's down there?" Mike asked, suddenly right behind her. Valerie jumped at his nearness. She hadn't heard him approach, which was unusual for her.

She glanced over her shoulder, appreciating his nakedness for a fleeting moment, but the allure of what lay beyond the trapdoor was far greater.

"Let's find out."

Valerie lifted the carpeted square to reveal a steep, narrow staircase descending into the darkness. The pulsing surged in intensity, and Valerie's skin suddenly felt electrified. The teardrop locket vibrated against her chest.

She peered downwards, but the light from the bedroom lamps was too dim to reveal anything. She took a step down the stairs, then another. The darkness was complete.

"Mitch," she called back, "hand me my phone. It's in my pants pocket." She turned to see Mike buttoning his jeans. "What the hell are... You're not leaving, are you?"

"Honestly," he replied, "I don't know. But I'm pretty sure that whatever I *will* be doing, I don't need to be naked for it." He retrieved the phone from her pants and stepped over to where Valerie stood, clad in her panties like they would protect her from any danger the Underworld could dare present. He placed the phone in her outstretched hand. "You might want shoes."

• • • • •

Fully dressed, cell phone casting a stark white light before her, Valerie descended the staircase. With tall risers and treads less than half the length of her feet, it was a slow process. Mike followed a few steps behind. By the time he reached the bottom, Valerie had already made her way down a short passage and was examining a closed door. The pulsing hum had continued to grow in intensity and was now producing an unsettling sensation in the pits of their stomachs.

The door was unremarkable, but a sharp rap told Valerie that it was both wood and very thick. She waded through two decades of memories of living with her grandparents, trying desperately to recall any hint as to what lay beyond. Nothing surfaced.

"Only one way to find out," Kelly whispered in her ear.

Valerie didn't reply. She never spoke aloud to Kelly where others could hear, and certainly not a one-nighter like Mitch. An adolescent could get away with talking to imaginary friends, but that kind of thing was a big risk for a twenty-seven-year-old woman. Only her friend Amelia was privy to the relationship between Valerie and Kelly. Amelia would proclaim that she didn't truly understand it, but it was a part of Valerie, and that was enough for her. Kelly thought Amelia was tops, but then that was hardly a surprise. The minds of imaginary friends worked that way.

"Are you going to open the door at some point, or should I take a nap first?"

Kelly's sarcasm had, as usual, a calming effect on Valerie. Also not much of a surprise after twenty years. Val reached for the doorknob just as Mike came to stand behind her. She turned it and pushed. The door swung open with a creak.

The pulsed humming took another leap in magnitude, and Valerie felt her whole body quivering with it. She expected the sensation to be uncomfortable, but it was less a sense of loudness as a feeling of resonance. Her ears, like everything else in and on her, were vibrating intensely.

"It's like being strapped to a massage chair on steroids," she whispered back to Mike, but if he heard, he gave no indication.

Valerie held her phone up and stepped into the room beyond.

It was a small, cylindrical chamber, perhaps a dozen feet in diameter and with only about a foot of clearance above Valerie's head. The walls appeared to be formed out of a rough concrete, windowless and unadorned; the floor felt gritty beneath her shoes, like dirt or fine gravel. In the center was a pedestal with something upon it, although the light from her phone was too weak to reveal its nature. She had no doubt, however, that it was the source of the vibrations.

Valerie began to take a second step, but stopped as Mike's hand fell on her shoulder. She turned her head and saw the look of concern on his face. Kelly stood beside him, rolling her eyes in disapproval of his timidness. Valerie couldn't tell if Mike's expression was worry for her, fear for himself, or something else entirely, but it didn't matter. She brushed his hand away and stepped forward to the center of the chamber.

As she approached the pedestal, her phone's flashlight revealed that there were actually two items upon it. A folded piece of yellowed paper lay beneath a hemispherical crystal. The latter was vibrating so intensely that its edges were a blur.

Abandoning Mike in the doorway, Kelly strode forward to stand beside Valerie. Her customary short red sundress, a solid pattern now that the white augments of childhood had been abandoned, was muted gray in the darkness, yet her blond hair somehow kept its golden color, as if it shone of its own illumination. Did it always do that? Now that Val thought about it, yes. It did. Funny how she had never noticed before.

"Well, that's interesting," observed her lifelong companion.

"Isn't it?" Valerie whispered back.

"What do you suppose it is?"

Val shook her head. She put her hand out, palm forward, trying to see if she could feel the vibrations emanating from it. She could. She looked at Kelly, who responded with a single raised eyebrow.

"What is it?" called Mike.

"If you don't want to be part of the action, you have to wait to hear about it on the weekend news, Mitch."

"Mike." The irritation in his voice was undisguised. That's fine. Anyone who couldn't handle this definitely couldn't handle her.

Val reached towards the stone, almost touching it; she turned to look at Kelly again.

"Hell, yeah, Val. We've gotta know."

She extended her finger, touched the crystal, and everything went utterly silent.

• • ● • •

Praxis's eyes shot open as they sat bolt upright with a gasp.

"Of course she would do it when I'm sleeping." They shook their head and groaned, half to dispel that moment of transition between the worlds of dreams and wakefulness, and half in general disgust at the situation. "It would have been way too civilized to do it at a reasonable hour."

Praxis lit a slip of sethrey paper, stood up from their sleeping mat, and made their way to the Great Library of the Interstice. They could replay it later, of course, but it was never quite the same as watching while things were actually happening.

CHAPTER TWO:

Iceland Bound

The library on Montgomery Boulevard had once been a monastery, and it exuded a stately presence that was completely lost on Valerie. As she and Kelly walked through the glass doors that had replaced the original oak, a heavy silence fell over them. The custom of being quiet in libraries may have lost its luster over the years, but this building seemed a holdout to the old ways. It demanded hushed whispers, and so naturally Kelly spoke as loudly as possible. This meant nothing to the other patrons, but it made Valerie uncomfortable regardless.

"Oh, this is nice. We should have come here ages ago." Kelly ran a hand over a painting on the wall.

Why, exactly? thought Val in response.

"Just to, you know, experience the ambience."

By which you mean, to disturb the ambience.

"Naturally."

They stopped, looked at each other, and then chuckled in unison.

Where do you suppose we'll find a librarian?

"One of the desks, I guess. Maybe over there?" Kelly pointed through an archway at an array of long tables. A lone man, perhaps in his late twenties, stood behind one, sorting a stack of books.

He's cute.

"I think the librarians are complimentary. You can probably take him home."

I just might.

"If you wanted to do that, you probably should have showered before coming here."

Funny.

"Or at least changed clothes." Kelly flicked at Valerie's untucked shirt.

Guys like the disheveled look. Trust me.

Kelly looked down at her own clothes, which were as immaculately styled and pressed as always. "Is that why I never get a date?"

That, and maybe the whole 'I'm not actually real' thing, she thought back at her friend as they approached the table.

The man looked up with a smile. "Good morning. Can I help you?" He had a slight accent that Valerie couldn't place.

She flashed her own smile in return. "As a matter of fact, I believe you can."

"Maybe you can help us both," added Kelly very loudly.

You can go now. Then out loud, "I'm guessing you work here?"

"I do," replied the librarian. "Are you looking for something in particular?"

"Yes, actually," Valerie nearly purred as she leaned forward slightly.

"Ask if he has an imaginary friend."

Seriously. You can go now. Any time.

"You never let me have any fun anymore."

The man waited.

"Fine. I'm going," Kelly yielded with mock resentment. Then added as an afterthought, "Don't forget to ask him about the writing."

I'm not an idiot.

"You get forgetful when your mind turns to—"

Bye bye, now. Valerie stole a quick glance around to make certain her friend had indeed vanished, then returned her attention to the man on the other side of the table.

"I don't suppose..." She slid the folded paper from the pedestal toward him, "you might know anything about strange languages?"

• • • • •

The librarian's name was Viktor, not that Valerie remembered that. There was no point in wasting gray matter on such things, she figured, since men seemed perfectly fine being called 'babe' or 'handsome'. It's not that she minded paying attention to the little details... Okay, actually she did, so when she undertook that kind of mental investment, she preferred to focus on things that mattered.

Like the crystal.

Once Vincent...? Vinnie? It was something starting with a V... Once he had stepped away to pull some reference books from the back, she took the stone out of her jacket pocket and studied it again. It was a hemisphere, perhaps three or four inches in diameter, and perfectly smooth on the rounded top. The bottom had a rough texture with some shallow edges as if the crafter had grown tired of polishing it and said 'eh, no one will be looking at the base anyway'.

When she first saw it, blurry in its vibration, she had guessed the stone to be quartz. Now, however, she could see that it was shot through with veins of crystalline blue, green, and red, as if filaments of sapphire, emerald, and ruby had been injected through the bottom to permeate the silicon matrix. The veins refracted light into a scintillating pattern, a prismatic dance of colors as she turned the crystal to consider it from different angles.

Why would her grandparents have kept this so carefully hidden? It was certainly pretty, but it did not appear as if it would be exceptionally valuable as a gemstone. Perhaps it had to do with its vibrate-the-paint-off-the-walls property. And how did it relate to the map drawn on the piece of yellowed parchment?

The sexy librarian had recognized the outline almost instantly as that of Iceland. Val could not recall her grandparents ever mentioning a trip there, or really anything about the country at all. Hell, they didn't even like traveling. Just getting them to take a weekend trip to the shore was a battle. Surely, she would remember something like—

The librarian returned, and it was clear from the look on his face that he had found nothing helpful. *Maybe that's better*, she thought. *Now there's no excuse for not going to Iceland.*

He handed Val the folded piece of parchment with an apologetic smile.

Oh, those eyes are so *pretty. Would be a shame for my first trip to a library in the last ten years to be a total loss…*

• • ❂ • •

Valerie idly glanced down at her watch as she made her way along Saxon Avenue. It was nearly 10:45.

"Less than two hours late," noted Kelly. "We're definitely improving."

They shared a smug smile.

The street was busy with cars, and even busier with pedestrians. It was always this way on the weekend mornings when everyone and their dog felt compelled to strut about the sidewalks, asserting to the world that they were just as metropolitan as the next phony. Valerie marched in a straight, purposeful line towards the corner of Saxon and Eighth where an etched glass door would give entrance to Sally's Café. She assumed people would get out of her way, and for the most part they did. One burly stranger was an exception. He apparently had the same strategy for navigating crowds, and they came to an abrupt halt in front of each other, mere inches from a collision. After several seconds of Valerie's cold, unyielding stare, the man finally stepped aside. The irritated roll of her eyes was as close to a 'thank you' as he would receive.

Val and Amelia always ate breakfast at Sally's on Saturday mornings, ostensibly together, and always at 9:00. Of course, Valerie rarely made it there before 11:00, so typically Amelia just had a quiet meal by herself, and then the two would chat while Val wolfed down something vaguely lunch-like.

"She's at the usual table," noted Kelly as they neared the street corner.

Valerie nodded in acknowledgement and pushed the door open. She stepped inside and was about to let the door swing shut when, at the last instant, she noticed someone coming in right behind her. She shot a foot out, catching the door before it slammed into a young... Val couldn't quite tell if it was a man or a woman. Their hair was cropped short and dyed with an array of colored highlights that complimented delicate features. An interesting tattoo on the left side of the person's face caught Val's attention. It was a pattern of interwoven curves and circles, and it suddenly came to her that it was an intricately stylized yin/yang symbol.

"Thanks," the stranger nodded with a quick but genuine smile. Before Val could respond they had already walked past, targeting an empty table at the far end of the restaurant.

Valerie followed Kelly to a booth halfway along the café's large front window. Amelia was readjusting her auburn ponytail as Valerie slid in across from her.

"Look at you," Amelia said, checking her phone for the time. "Someone got out of bed early." Then she noticed that Valerie was in the same clothes she had been wearing the night before. "Or should I say someone got out of someone's bed early. So... how was he?"

"Who?"

"Didn't you leave the club with—"

"Oh, right. Mitch."

"I thought his name was Mike."

"Whatever." Valerie reached over and stole a piece of bacon from Amelia's plate.

"Hey. I was going to eat that."

"Really? You're always finished by the time I get here."

"I slept in today too."

Valerie waved at a server who gave no indication of having seen the gesture. She immediately switched to a more direct approach. "Menu at table six!" she demanded in a loud voice, and was rewarded with an irritated nod from the aproned woman.

"So how was he?" Amelia tried again.

Valerie reached for the remaining slice of bacon, but Amelia slapped her hand away and picked it up herself to make sure there wouldn't be a second attempt. She raised her eyebrows with a questioning look. "Well?"

"Let me ask you something," began Valerie. "Have you ever had a guy tell you that he's afraid of confined spaces?"

Amelia thought for a moment, then shook her head. "No. In fact, most of the men I've dated seem pretty fixated on getting into confined spaces."

"That's what I thought."

"So Mike was more of a talker?"

"Who?"

"Mitch," Amelia uncorrected herself in a bemused tone.

"Oh." Then, "No, not really. More of a cling-to-your-waist-for-dear-life type."

"Can't fault him for that. I've ridden with you."

Valerie grinned. "He actually sounded a little like you when he squealed in fear."

"He didn't!"

Val smiled impishly. "No, but I think he wanted to once or twice."

The server arrived and extended a menu at Valerie. She waved it away.

"I'll just have the Buffalo Bill burger, with a side of—"

"No," the waitress interrupted.

"You know, the..." Valerie grabbed the menu out of the woman's hand and glanced over it. "Where are the burgers?"

"That's the breakfast menu. We don't start serving lunch until 11:00."

Valerie let out a heavy sigh. "Well, that's only like twelve minutes away. Can you start early this once?"

The woman gave her a syrupy sweet smile and replied, "Let me check with the cook." She shifted as if she was about to walk away, but then immediately turned her attention back to Valerie and said, "I'm sorry, hon. No can do."

"State law or something?"

"No. It's just that all our lunch ingredients are kept in a time-locked refrigerator."

Valerie looked up at the woman, an iota of respect threatening to breach her expression. "I guess you don't store the sarcasm in there with it, do you?"

The woman just stared at her.

"Fine. I'll just have a couple of eggs over easy."

The waitress nodded and turned to leave, but Valerie grabbed a fold of her blouse.

"With some hash browns. And a side of sausage."

The woman nodded. "Okay."

"Oh, and a side of bacon." Val looked at Amelia's plate. "Better make that two."

"Right. Two eggs over, hash browns, sausage, and a double bacon."

"You know what?" Valerie continued before the waitress could escape. "Let me also have an order of pancakes and some wheat toast."

"Whatever."

"The sausages are links, right?"

"What?" the woman asked in a tone of Herculean indifference.

"The sausages. Links. Not patties."

"Right. Links."

"Oh, and I want a large orange juice. And a glass of water."

The waitress stared at her. Valerie stared back, daring her to say something. Finally the woman asked, "No tea or coffee? Maybe a vat of mimosas?"

"No, I think that'll be good for now."

The waitress smiled insincerely and began to leave.

Kelly nudged Valerie. "Get me an OJ too."

"Actually make that two large orange juices!" Valerie called out.

The woman didn't turn back, merely acknowledging the request with a curt wave of her hand as she disappeared into the kitchen.

"I didn't think you'd actually do it," noted Kelly.

"I'll drink it," replied Val with a quick glance at her imaginary friend. The look was not lost on Amelia.

"Hi, Kelly," Amelia said in Kelly's general direction.

"Hi, Mel," the imaginary friend replied.

Amelia couldn't actually see or hear Kelly, but she always made a point of including her, a gesture that meant all the world to Valerie.

"So," Amelia mused. "Where were we?"

"I—"

"Oh, right. Mitch-Mike."

Val waved her off. "Forget him. Something way more interesting happened last night."

"Oh, this should be good." Amelia put down the bacon, pushed her plate to the side, and settled in to listen. Valerie immediately snatched the slice, shoved it into her mouth, and then proceeded to share the whole story with only minor embellishments. When she reached the point of encountering the librarian, the server returned and unloaded an array of plates onto the table.

"Are you sure there isn't anything else I can get you?" she asked acerbically.

Val smiled back sweetly. "I think this will do for now. But can you put that judgmental look in a to-go bag for me? I want to enjoy it all day long."

With a withering scowl, the woman withdrew.

"Wait," said Amelia. "So did you bring the stuff here with you?" She saw the twinkle in Val's eyes. "Well, let me see!"

Valerie retrieved the crystal and parchment from her pocket, placed the pair on the table, and navigated them through the labyrinth of plates. Amelia first examined the stone, and then unfolded the map.

"And you're sure this is Iceland?"

While shoveling a forkful of runny eggs into her mouth with one hand, Val unlocked her phone with the other. She already had a map pulled up in a browser tab.

"Yep," agreed Mel. "No doubt about it. That's a match. So was this Vincent guy able to tell you anything about the writing?"

Valerie mumbled a response around a mouthful of food.

"Chew, swallow, then talk, Val. We've been through this."

After that process was complete, Valerie tried again.

"No. He said it looks very old, older than anything he's ever seen. He thought the best chance might be to talk to a bunch of researchers at some institute associated with the university there."

Amelia nodded. "Makes sense. So did you call them?"

"Nah."

"Are you *going to* call them?"

Valerie considered for a moment, then, "Nah."

"You're kidding, right? You can't just ignore this."

"Of course I can't."

"Then . . . ?"

Valerie picked up her phone, switched apps, and showed Mel a plane ticket booked for the following Tuesday.

"Oh my god, Val! This is so cool! You're going to Iceland! I've heard it's really—"

"Nooo."

"No? No what?"

"Not me. We."

"We?"

"We . . ." she paused dramatically, ". . . are going to Iceland."

Amelia blinked. "What?"

Val tapped a few times on her phone. "There. I just forwarded you your ticket."

Amelia took out her own phone, unlocked it, and read the email.

"Val," she began.

"Yes?"

"I can't just fly off to Iceland. I've got work, and—"

"Get someone to cover!"

"I've got stuff going on, Val. I can't just disappear on a whim!"

Valerie smiled devilishly. "You always have stuff going on. So do I. Blow it off."

"Val!" she pleaded.

"Come on, Mel. How often does someone hand you a ticket to Iceland?"

"Never, but that doesn't change—"

"You know you're going to go, so why not just accept it and finish the rest of your bacon?"

"Because you already ate it."

Valerie transferred a couple of slices onto the empty plate.

"Don't worry, Mel. It'll be fine. Tuesday gives you plenty of time to get someone to cover your classes."

"I have a new routine that I just started, and no one knows it but me." It was a weak excuse. Amelia chuckled softly at her own words, realizing that deep down she had already given in.

"I'm sure they'll be fine," Valerie assured her. "Stretch, hold, twist yourself into a knot. They'll figure it out."

Amelia shook her head slowly, a smile growing on her lips. "I suppose I should be thankful you didn't book a flight for tonight, huh?" Then the realization struck her. "Wait a minute. Why *didn't* you book it for tonight?"

Valerie looked up mid-chew. Kelly leaned in and whispered, "Don't tell her about Viktor."

"You have a date, don't you?" Amelia accused.

"Maybe."

"You picked up that librarian, didn't you." It wasn't really a question.

"Maybe."

"How the hell..." she began, but then thought better of it. "You really are something. How do you get all these guys to go out with you? You don't even remember their names."

"They don't know that."

"They find out, though."

"Yeah," Val smiled. "But by then, who cares?"

Amelia had that look, the squint followed by a shake of her head that simultaneously conveyed both amazement and disapproval. The gesture was all too familiar, and they both laughed. Two tables away, the stranger with the yin/yang tattoo was focused intently on their own meal, overtly oblivious to everything going on around them.

CHAPTER THREE:

Traversing Aerth

Annaphora, City of Visions. It is said that her white and gray spires stand tall over every horizon, that her citizens course along shining streets like blood through the world's heart, ebbing and swelling with the Callings of the Great Circle. It is that Great Circle, numbering nearly a billion souls, that dwells across the continents of Aerth—hunting, farming, teaching, playing... and ever listening to what the future whispers to them through the Beacons.

Gabriel, son of Marissa and child of the Circle Massaea, stood upon the deck of a sturdy trading galleon and stared eastward.

"I don't see them," he said quietly to the ship's captain. His voice was a gentle tenor.

"Who were you expecting?"

"Not who. What."

The captain considered Gabriel, her eyes taking in his slender frame clothed in a simple blue tunic of fine, homespun cloth and thick brown leggings. His eyes were a misty gray, sometimes partially obscured—as they were now—when his dark curly hair escaped the leather band that held it in place. He spoke with the accent of someone hailing from the southern continent of Jasseth, which meant he had been traveling for many months to reach this far north.

She also considered him with her *nythlen*, that inner sense by which one listens to the Beacons, and smiled at his warmth. This boy was like an ocean in still winds: beautiful, calm, yet with a depth and purpose almost frightening in its magnitude. She imagined what his mother must be like. Had Gabriel been her son, she would be very proud indeed.

"Alright, then *what* were you expecting?"

Gabriel continued to scan the horizon as he answered. "The spires."

It took a moment for the captain to piece it together, and then she gave a gentle laugh. "That's a description meant to be taken metaphorically. Annaphora is on the opposite coast, about two hundred miles to the east. With the forests you'll be traveling through, you probably won't see her spires until you're a day's travel from the city. Maybe two, if you have clear weather and a disposition for climbing trees."

Gabriel nodded thoughtfully at this. He had appreciated the captain's friendship and company over the past week, and would be sad for its ending. But he knew there wasn't time to delay, and so quieted his mind as he studied the nearby shoreline. A small cove a few hundred yards to the north presented itself as the best place to land, and he pointed to it.

"There."

The captain nodded her approval. She put a friendly hand on his shoulder, and Gabriel could feel the sentiments within the gesture. *It's been a pleasure, safe journeys, success in what draws you forward.* It carried a greater sincerity than spoken words could have expressed. And then she was off, directing her crew to make the necessary adjustments.

Gabriel went below deck to gather his things.

• • • • •

The downy birch and juniper that lined the coast gave way to the much taller, stately—almost stoic—trees of the primordial forest through which Gabriel now traveled. He was a quiet man by nature, but even if that had not been so, Gabriel doubted he would speak much in their presence. This was a place of solemness and reflection; even the animals seemed reverent in their scampering. He was surprised, therefore, when the Beacons indicated that it would not be unreasonable to hunt for food here.

On the second afternoon, Gabriel made an early camp and followed his nythlen north along a small deer trail. His inner sense, probing the immediate future, soon warned him to pause. Two more steps would alert a rabbit secreted in the bushes ahead.

Slowly, silently, he crouched low and picked up a small rock near his feet. As he set his intention to throw the stone, he sensed the imminent response of the rabbit—how it would jump, where it would try to run. He shifted his intention until he identified the optimal target, a spot approximately eight feet in front and slightly to the right of him.

He threw the rock.

The rabbit came bounding directly at him and Gabriel dove, not for where the creature was at that instant, but toward where it would dart once it became aware of his presence. With his arms extended he began to bring his hands together, shifting his focus from the future to the present. The rabbit's pre-shadow, the premonition from his nythlen that manifested as something of a visual overlay, coalesced with what his eyes were actually observing as prediction became the present. When the alignment completed, his hands had closed on either side of the rabbit's body and Gabriel quickly brought the terrified creature under him, pinning it to the ground.

"Sorry, my friend," he muttered with sincere regret as he slid his hands up to the rabbit's neck. With a sharp twist it was over. He rose to his knees and looked down at his dinner. "I know. Someday I'll be in your position. I hope I can accept it as well as you did."

As he returned to his campsite, Gabriel wondered, as he so often did when hunting, if the animals heard their own form of Beacons, and if so, why he was able to catch them at all. If the spirit of this ancient forest held the answer, however, it was not inclined to share it with him this evening. Perhaps it was a question for the Chakrava, the Council of Elders who governed all of Aerth.

This thought brought to mind the conversation he had with his family when this journey began. His father had been fussing to straighten out the fabric of his tunic under the strap of his shoulder pack when his mother had laughingly nudged her husband aside, rolling her eyes at his pampering, and then gently laid her hands on Gabriel's shoulders.

"When you are granted an audience with the Chakrava, you should keep your head bowed," she had said.

"I am certain the Beacons will guide me in the proper respect, Mother."

"*If* you remember to listen for them," she chided.

"He will, Mari," his father insisted. "He's a sensible, level-headed young man, aren't you, Gabby?"

Gabriel did not have a chance to respond.

"Except when he isn't," his sister injected playfully. Sendra was five years his elder, and already married with a child on the way. Her husband Kenth was a good man. A little too timid and much too fixated on the irrelevant details of life, in Gabriel's opinion, but a good man nonetheless.

"Maybe," Gabriel offered, "I am being called to the High Temple to tell the story of how Sendra, the unboundingly responsible, used to sneak into Pritchard's orchards in the middle of—"

"Alright," she cut him off. "That's enough of that."

"What is this?" his father asked. Reimas was not a man quick to mete out punishments, but he was an incurable gossip.

"Nothing," Sendra retorted quickly. "Nothing at all."

He turned to look at Gabriel.

"Nothing," Gabriel repeated. But when Sendra turned away a moment later he whispered, "I'll tell you when I get back."

Reimas' eyes glittered. There was a bond between father and son that had grown out of deep similarity and was profoundly cherished by both. They were not at all like Marissa, who was a dynamo of activity from the moment she woke up until her head touched her pillow. Gabriel and his father had the utmost respect and appreciation for who and what she was, but that was not them. The men of the family were truly kindred spirits—quiet, patient, and modest about their keen intelligence. Marissa described them as outwardly serious yet privately playful.

Gabriel was finally ready to begin the journey.

"Are you certain you have everything you need?" his mother asked for the third time.

He responded as he had twice before. "As far as I know."

Thousands of years of focus on following one's purpose had not diminished basic human curiosity, but Gabriel was better than most at accepting an unknown future. The Beacons communicated what one *needed* to know, not what one *wanted* to know. He had no idea why he needed to visit the High Temple and speak with the First Mother, but recognized that it was a great Necessity, and not just for him as an individual. He was part of something much larger, and although he had no idea what it was, he would follow this path, content to be what the world needed. Even if it was simply to be the one thousandth person waiting in a line somewhere to ensure that the one thousandth and first person didn't get to the front too early, he would do what the future called him to do, and do it to the best of his ability.

He turned to finally leave, and there was Sendra again.

"Don't make me come rescue you, little brother," she chided, and this made Gabriel smile. Suddenly she was embracing him with a strength of concern that his aloof older sister did not normally allow herself. She whispered in his ear. "Be careful, okay? All I can hear are the Winds of Change around you, and that's..."

"I know," he whispered back. "I know. I hear them too." He shrugged. "We'll just have to wait and find out what those changes hold."

Sendra backed up and took Gabriel's hands in her own for one last consideration. She was pressing something into his hand, and he gave her a questioning look. She nodded, released his hands, and he opened his fingers to see that she had given him a small disk of wood carved with a delicately etched web of interconnected curves. A thin length of silk was threaded through a hole in the center.

"A Winder's Knot?" His quiet voice conveyed amusement. The giving of a Winder's Knot was a tradition with thousands of years of history. Originally they were simply a special kind of knot tied in a loop of string or woven into some thatch, a manifestation of gifted good fortune—a way of saying, 'may some of the goodness that lays in my future find its way into yours instead'. As the centuries passed, the nature of the symbol evolved, originally into more complex knots and eventually to become little stone or wood carvings such as this. Regardless of whether one believed it was possible to pass one's own future good fortune to another, they were symbols of luck, devotion, and affection, and Gabriel was touched.

"I thought you didn't believe in such things," he said.

Sendra shrugged, then took the Knot from him and gently placed the silk cord around his neck. Once it was straight, she tucked the disk under his shirt so it could lay against his skin as was proper.

"There. Now wipe that stupid smile off your face and get moving. Daylight doesn't outlive the day, you know."

"Thank you," Gabriel replied. "I—"

"Go, you stupid toad."

He laughed. "I don't think you've called me that in fifteen years."

"You're my little brother. I can call you whatever I like."

"I'm twenty-five, Sen."

"Little brothers never stop being little brothers."

He nodded. "If you say so."

"I do." Sendra turned to leave, but then looked back to say, "And stay out of trouble for once."

He nodded again, slowly, as he regarded the sister who would never outwardly admit how deeply she cared for him. His smile broadened in appreciation of her concern. Then Sendra winked, turned to take her husband's hand, and led Kenth away without looking back again.

• • ● • •

Gabriel buried the remains of the rabbit the following morning. He placed no marker on the grave, but played a short, soft melody on his burnished travel flute as a tribute of appreciation. By the time the sun was casting green-tinted spotlights through the canopy onto the underbrush, he was already making his way towards Annaphora.

Even in the middle of summer the air held a chill this far north. Gabriel wore two layers now and built nightly campfires large enough to keep him warm until sunrise. Brushing frost off himself and his belongings had become an unwelcome morning ritual, and he regularly wondered what would possess anyone to settle down in this climate.

After three more days of hiking, now five dawns from the western shore, he came upon a broad, well-worn path running north and south. His nythlen called him to turn right, and so he did, although the road turned east within the hour. Travel became easier then; he covered more miles each day, and spent nights at village inns. There wasn't as much need for establishments like these in the forests of Jasseth where the Circle Massaea made their homes, but Annaphora was one of the largest cities on the planet and capital of the world. Between the city itself and the surrounding towns within a few days' ride, nearly half a million people lived in this chilly region, and it was said the population increased every year.

It certainly wasn't a bad place, but for a young man who had grown up in a quiet countryside where the people numbered in the hundreds rather than thousands, there was a certain ineffable *pressure* that Gabriel found uncomfortable. Long before reaching the city itself, where those numbers would grow to hundreds of thousands, Gabriel had soundly concluded that he would not care to live here.

• • • • •

The surrounding villages and small towns did not at all prepare Gabriel for his first sight of Annaphora. He had caught glimpses of the legendary spires of gray and white through the ancient trees, and those alone were impressive enough, but when he crested a rise in the road to find the full city shining upon the horizon, he stumbled to a halt.

Annaphora, a circular expanse of stone and glass, was over two miles across and built upon a wide, low hill at the center of a depression in the landscape that itself must have been nearly ten miles from side to side. The surrounding lowlands were covered in rich green grasses dotted with grazing sheep and apportioned by a seemingly haphazard maze of low stone walls. Nearly a dozen large manor houses—each with its own complement of cottages, barns, and stables—were scattered throughout the grasslands and connected by a network of cobbled roads that radiated out from the main city.

Even from miles away Gabriel could see that the city had its own complex structure. At the very center, where Annaphora rose to its highest, was the religious and cultural district. Upon the very apex of that was an immense hemispherical building that could be nothing other than the famed Syntrodome, the millennia-old complex from which the First Mother and the rest of the Chakrava saw to the order and stability of the entire planet. At the cardinal extremes of that dome were four tall towers with sacred temples at their tops. The north, west, and south towers were identical, but the eastern one rose a third again above the others and housed the High Temple, the holiest of spaces in all the world. It was there that the most sacred ceremonies were held. Even miles away, Gabriel shuddered at its sight. That tower was a piece of his future, and he could feel it calling to him.

The surrounding metropolis of Annaphora was divided into eight distinct districts by broad, shining avenues that ran like spokes to connect the Syntrodome to the grand park that encircled the entire city. From miles away Gabriel could not determine what was happening on that encompassing boulevard, but it was clearly busy with crowds of people.

"First time to the city, then?"

The voice shook Gabriel out of his awe. He had not even realized that he had stopped walking, much less that someone had come to stand beside him. It was a young woman, staring in her own appreciation of the city.

"It is," he replied quietly. "You too?"

"Oh, no," she responded warmly. "I've been here many times. But seeing it always has the same effect on me, and I like to . . . well, I like to do just what you're doing." They shared a smile. "I feel that if I ever get so busy, or so jaded, that I become used to its beauty, then I know I've lost my way."

Gabriel turned to look at the stranger more carefully, took in the shine of her blond hair and the misty look of appreciation in her eyes. Not too far away a group of half a dozen others were patiently waiting for her as she took these moments to appreciate the capitol. The moment hung still in the morning air, and then she finally turned her head and nodded to the group. They resumed their journey, and she joined their numbers as they began making their way to the city. The woman looked back at Gabriel and inclined her head. An invitation.

Gabriel nodded back, and fell into step.

• • • • •

It took over an hour to reach the edge of the Hespertaen, that broad paved park that defined the edge of the city proper. During that time they spoke of Annaphora. Apparently, the Hespertaen was a ring of celebration, and events were regularly scheduled at various points around the circumference. The grandest were mobile fêtes, circling around as the hours went by, and it was not uncommon to confer awards and recognition for participants that traversed the entire twenty-four-hour circle.

The group had also told him of the Eight Primaries, the wedge-shaped districts within the city. They would arrive where the Hespertaen intersected Brightwater Avenue, a wide thoroughfare that separated the District of Artisans from the District of Crafters. "Both are art," one of them had explained. "The difference is whether something is being made as a tool or a form of expression." Other districts, Gabriel learned, were focused on health, education, food and warehousing, finance, and various other essential drivers of society.

As they reached the Hespertaen, the blond woman asked, "So, Gabriel, what purpose brings *you* to the city?"

He explained that he did not know, only that he was being called to speak with the First Mother. She nodded thoughtfully, appreciatively, and then pointed toward the Syntrodome just visible at the far end of Brightwater.

"Simply walk straight up this avenue. Although, if you have a mind to explore, your wyrd has gifted you with an hour or two to discover some of the city. The

Chakrava are usually in council until at least two on most days, and it is only noon now. Brightwater will have you there in twenty minutes at most, fifteen if you hurry."

Then the woman and her companions wished him well and made their way clockwise along the park, leaving him on his own.

What immediately caught Gabriel's attention about Annaphora was the sharp delineations in styles. The Hespertaen was lavishly decorated with works of art—statues ranging in age from months to millennia, intricately carved trellises that lined the boulevard, and grand fountains with tiled mosaics amid plentiful gardens. In contrast, the streets and buildings within Annaphora's functional districts were strikingly stark. Walls were unadorned but for the occasional building designation engraved in small precise lettering, and the streets were completely free of obstacles. People appeared to have a slight preference for staying to the left and passing on the right, although that was far from a guarantee. More consistent were the rules for who had the right of way, which were clearly based on size and agility. Children gave way to adults, who themselves stepped aside for horses. Riders steered their mounts to give passage to carts and wagons, and on the larger streets the biggest wagons turned for no one at all.

What sparse signage Gabriel noticed was subtle and unassuming. Street names were most often carved on the sides of corner buildings or into the stones of the street itself when no structures were near an intersection. Stores relied on window displays to announce their wares. Gabriel noticed that some doorways bore small, tasteful plaques of brass or silver with what appeared to be family names, and that most entrances were slightly recessed from the street itself. It was uncommon to see anyone stopping to converse, but when they did, it invariably happened in these nooks. Perhaps from prescient awareness of the consequences, or possibly just as a courtesy ingrained in the culture after hundreds of generations, it was clear that one did not obstruct traffic in Annaphora.

During his explorations, Gabriel entered several shops and there he came upon another interesting facet of the city's nature. As if to compensate for the blandness of the streets, interiors were decorated with reckless abandon. Colors and other augmentations were profuse and vibrant, and any sliver of wall not vying to catch one's attention was clearly an insult to Annaphoran sensibilities. Paintings and masks were common, as were sculptures, both freestanding and mounted on walls. Where nothing else would fit, talismans—or even simple strands of beads—were hung about and between the larger objects.

When stepping inside, the behaviors of the people also changed. The 'keep moving' expectation of the outdoors clearly did not apply here. Shops were crowded with people milling about in conversation, far more focused on talking than transacting. Their preoccupation was so strong that hardly anyone even seemed to hear their own Beacons; more than once Gabriel had to push his wa past vivacious customers crowding the narrow aisles, an unexpected occurrence in a society attuned to the future.

What most surprised Gabriel as he explored was the character of the art. A trend had become apparent as he wandered the shops, but it didn't fully register until he entered an enormous outdoor market, easily two hundred feet across, where vendors had laid out their goods upon carpets and tables. Despite the vast differences in lifestyle between his own rural Circle and this big city thousands of miles away, the artwork followed surprisingly similar themes and designs. Statuettes, necklaces, carvings…paintings, stylized drinking vessels…hair clips, rings, illustrated scrolls…they all spoke of the same basic techniques used by the artisans in his own village. Some were better, some worse, and all had little variations that made them unique, but Gabriel realized that the cultural consistency he thought unique to his own Circle was far more pervasive. There was no explanation save that the entirety of Aerth shared a world-wide connection, a form of resonance. Inspirations in one corner of the globe seeded themselves in a species-scale subconsciousness to manifest…well, everywhere.

Gabriel suspected there was something important in that realization, but before he could consider it further, some internal sense demanded his attention. Standing at the front of a stall that offered the odd pairing of stonework jewelry and strips of chicken marinated in spices and fried in lard, Gabriel suddenly had the feeling that he was being watched. He spun about quickly, but the only people paying him any attention seemed merely to be responding to his sudden movement, and they quickly returned to their own affairs.

He quieted his mind and closed his eyes as focused on his nythlen. It whispered that his future lay in the Syntrodome. *Yes. I know that,* he thought to himself. *What should I do about this watcher?* He sent the question. Such questions rarely found answers from the Beacons, and this time was no exception. He heard only the call of the Syntrodome, the Chakrava, and the need to speak with the First Mother.

• • • • •

The figure at the edge of the market watched as Gabriel returned to Brightwater Avenue and set off toward the center of the City of Visions. It was clear that he had sensed something, and surprising that he had so easily—willingly—let it go. Few people were able to put aside their curiosity like that, even when the Beacons told them to.

Definitely a unique one, this Gabriel. It was a comforting realization. Aerth needed someone like that. In fact, both worlds did.

CHAPTER FOUR:

Champion Revealed

Just as the Hespertaen circumscribed Annaphora, so did the Raespertaen encircle the Syntrodome. This inner park was ornamented less densely than its broader, more expansive counterpart. The statues were fewer and smaller, and there were no fountains at all. The only gardens Gabriel could see were two manicured flower beds planted along either side of the tree-lined walkway used by visitors to approach the large south entrance of the Syntrodome.

A steady stream of humanity was passing into and out of the enormous structure and as he approached, Gabriel had to stay far to the left to avoid being caught up in that river of commerce. Drawing closer, Gabriel studied the intricate carvings that outlined the fourteen-foot-tall doors of the complex. Initially they seemed merely decorative, but once he was within a dozen paces he recognized letters worked into the relief. At a glance they appeared to be written in an entirely different alphabet, but he soon realized that they were merely stylized in a way he had not previously encountered. He shifted further to the left side of the walkway and stopped to read them, and was again overcome with the feeling of being scrutinized.

He pivoted quickly, scanning the surroundings, but it was hopeless. The Raespertaen coursed with the flow of humanity, people rushing about as if the world would cease turning should they not reach their destination in time. And then, with a careless step, he was caught up and the rushing crowd carried him into the Syntrodome.

Passing through the entrance corridor, the crowd quickly dissipated within an enormous entry chamber. Dozens of doors and passages lined the walls of the brightly lit space, and the few people who did not navigate their way into one of them instead approached the rows of tables filling the center of the room. Overhead, a crystal chandelier effused a bright, flameless light that Gabriel suspected was sunlight channeled through the black metal shaft by which the fixture was suspended from the ceiling.

He came to a halt, unsure where to go. There were so many options, so many official-looking women either standing stoically or engaged in lively conversation. He took a deep breath to collect his wits, calming his mind so that he could listen to the call of the Beacons. Even as he began, a tall, sapling-slender woman in her late forties broke away from a conversation with two colleagues and approached. Her stride was authoritative, although her eyes and smile sung of compassion. For no reason he understood, Gabriel's attention fixated upon a strand of hair that had escaped from a tight bun to wave rebelliously around her right ear.

"Can I help you?" she asked.

"My name is Gabriel, and I have been Called here to speak with the First Mother."

"I see," the woman responded with a hint of surprise. "Well, if you would be so kind as to come with me, you are welcome to meditate in one of the waiting chambers while your message is delivered."

She immediately began walking, and Gabriel had to trot to catch up with her.

"Miss?"

"Karelana," she introduced herself.

"Karelana. Yes. Hello. A pleasure to meet you." He put his nervousness aside. "How long does it usually take to arrange an audience with—"

"In most cases it requires only a week or two to find an opening in Her Holiness's schedule," Karelana responded. Then, seeing that Gabriel had clearly been hoping for a different answer, she added, "But sometimes it happens faster. Don't worry. Everything happens in its time, right?"

"There is some urgency to this. I . . . I have a feeling that today is the right day for us to meet."

The woman stopped unexpectedly, and Gabriel stumbled to avoid bumping into her. That he had not seen the pre-shadow of her halting made him realize just how nervous he truly was.

"I see," the woman said, and then studied him in silence for so long that Gabriel thought she was waiting for him to speak. Just as he opened his mouth, however, Karelana continued. "May I inquire as to the nature of the matter that has Called you here?"

"Honestly, I wish I knew, ma'am, but the Beacons only shared that I was to come and speak with her. Not why."

The woman's gaze grew slightly distant, as if she were looking through him, then she said, "Wait here a moment, please."

Karelana turned on her heel and strode back to the two women with whom she had been speaking when Gabriel arrived. They briefly conferred in hushed tones, and then they all looked over at him. Gabriel suddenly felt like a specimen under scrutiny in a school science class. Without another word, the trio marched over to him. They stared at him in silence for several more seconds before Karelana finally spoke.

"Gabriel, this is Ute and Linara. They are religious scholars."

"I see," he replied, somewhat baffled. Was this supposed to hold a particular significance to him? Why had Karelana made a point of mentioning it? Then remembering his manners, he added, "It is an honor to meet you."

The woman named Ute, who was surely in her sixties if not older, reached out and took Karelana's elbow in her hand. "I think you should bring his message to the Chakrava at once. Do not wait for a recess."

"Then you think—"

"Go, child. We will show the young man to a chamber."

Karelana paused, then nodded twice and rushed off into the maze of corridors.

Ute and Linara stepped to either side of Gabriel and, taking his arms in theirs, began leading him away. Linara was smiling kindly, although Gabriel sensed some discomfort in her. Ute made no attempt to disguise her discomfort and continued to stare at him intently even as she politely asked about his journey to Annaphora.

• • ● • •

The deliberation chamber of the Chakrava was a statement centuries in the making. Light, tasteful decorations balanced a foundation of ancient, serious furniture. The walls were of the darkest oak, with dozens of small shelves supporting ornate candles that illuminated the room. Beneath every shelf was some form of hanging, each a gift from prior First Mothers. In their own unique way, the hangings each told one chapter of an enduring story stretching back through the ages.

What most demanded one's attention, however, was the broad table crafted from a single piece of petrified wood, so polished that it practically shone on its own. It was so immense that the chamber's walls had been taken down temporarily to bring in the massive surface, and there was a popular rumor regarding its mass: that it was originally positioned slightly off-center, and the Chakrava of that era had elected to shift the north wall out by two feet rather than try to reposition the table.

Nine ornate chairs surrounded the semi-oval surface. At the peak of the table's curve was the official chair of the First Mother, slightly taller than the other eight that were distributed to either side. The flat end of the table was nearest the door, and it was from there that visitors would address the Chakrava. No seat was kept at that end, although from time to time one or more might be brought in when guests were expected to remain for a significantly long session.

In these nine chairs sat the Chakrava, the nine women who oversaw the functioning of the single civilization-culture of Aerth. The youngest of them, Edeiri, was only thirty-seven and already promoted to Seventh Mother. She had not been the youngest woman to ever become a member of the council, but she was the only one selected before the age of fifty for the last four hundred years. Most of the current council were considerably older, and oldest of them all was the First Mother.

No one knew Khalfani's exact age, although it was presumed that she had to be at least eighty-five. The First Mother herself claimed to not remember, but few actually believed that. Her intellect had only sharpened as the years passed and she was unexpectedly spry in her movements. And as was expected of any member of the Chakrava—but most importantly for the First Mother—her nythlen was as sensitive to the Beacons as anyone's, and far more than most. Thus, when she raised a hand for the council to be silent moments before a knock was heard upon the chamber door, it surprised no one.

"Come," Khalfani called in a firm voice.

The door opened silently and Karelana entered, head bowed in respect.

"Blessings to the Chakrava," she intoned.

The gathered Mothers responded with a single voice. "Blessings upon you, child."

Karelana raised her head, and the First Mother nodded for her to speak.

"Your Holiness, someone has arrived and requested an audience with you."

Soft murmurs erupted around the table.

The arrival of the Champion in this year had been foretold by the histories for millennia, and the Champion's absence had become an ever-increasing focus of the Mothers' deliberations for many months now. Some days it felt like they spoke of little else. Khalfani listened to the whispered commentary from around the table for a few moments, noting how the Chakrava's initial excitement quickly ebbed into cautious denial of the possibility, then finally settled into guarded curiosity. The whole process took perhaps four or five seconds.

The First Mother lightly rapped her knuckles on the table, and the room immediately fell silent.

"Has this visitor given a reason for the audience?" she asked.

"No, Your Holiness, but I believe—"

"You believe this may be the Champion."

"Yes, First Mother."

"Well," Khalfani began with a tired smile. "She certainly took her own sweet time appearing, didn't she?" This statement brought a round of relieved smiles from the rest of the women. "I will meet with her in my personal audience chamber once we have concluded our session."

Karelana held her voice for a moment, unsure whether the First Mother had finished. In the silence, the leader continued.

"Thank you for bringing us this news, Karelana. Please see to the comfort of the Champion until I can meet with her."

"Of course, Your Holiness. But..." she trailed off.

"Is something the matter, child?" asked Inthima, the Second Mother.

"It's just..." Karelana hesitated, suddenly wondering if perhaps she should simply withdraw and let the leaders discover this piece of information on their own. The First Mother, however, was now intently focused upon her with those bright, disarming eyes.

"Go on, Kara," urged Khalfani. "What is weighing upon you?"

"The Champion is..." Why was this so difficult to say? "The Champion is not what we were expecting."

The First Mother smiled at this. "No one knows what she will be like, or where her greatest strengths will lie. But fear not, for—"

"What I mean, Your Holiness, is that the Champion is not a woman."

A sudden tension gripped the room, broken only by the rustling of gowns and the minute sounds of idle fidgeting. Finally, the Third Mother spoke.

"A girl?" she asked. "Are you saying the Champion is a g—"

"Not a girl, Your Grace," replied Karelana. "This person...the one who requests the audience...is a *man*."

Now there were no sounds of rustled clothing or muted whispers. The entirety of the Chakrava was stunned into absolute stillness.

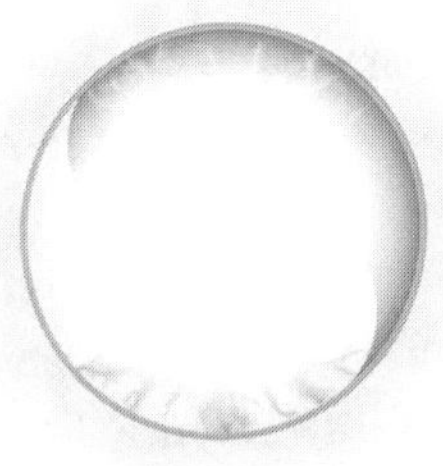

CHAPTER FIVE:

Champion Tested

Valerie threw her keys onto the kitchenette table of her tiny apartment. They slid off, landing on the floor somewhere near the refrigerator, and she made a mental note of the location. She would forget it within seconds, but Kelly would remember. She then gently placed her motorcycle helmet on the counter next to a plant that had somehow learned to survive on an alternating regimen of droughts and monsoons. Taking a stack of mail from under her arm, she flipped her way through it. "Junk. Junk. Later. Junk..." The envelopes followed deliberate if not accurate trajectories towards different corners of the kitchen.

When the 'sorting' was done Valerie grabbed a beer from the fridge, walked into the living room, and launched herself onto the couch in her usual style: feet pointed at the apartment door, back to the corner.

"Ow," she moaned. Something hard in her jacket pocket was pressing into her ribs. She shifted, reached in, withdrew the hemispherical crystal.

"Ah," she murmured. "I remember you."

She hadn't thought about the stone for over a day, a testament to the distracting nature of that slightly-Icelandic librarian and his intriguing accent. As well as...other features. She had not intended to stay so late at his place, but one thing led to several others and suddenly the sun was setting again. Val was vaguely aware that there was something she was supposed to be doing this evening, but it was clearly not that important or she would remember, right?

"Maybe," offered Kelly, "you were supposed to clean this place up so I'd have somewhere to sit." With no uncluttered surfaces in sight, Kelly settled herself on the floor near a steel-framed end table covered in small, exotic weapons. That stash was, without question, Valerie's favorite shrine. There was an ivory-handled butterfly knife given to her three years ago by Lea Moshe—her all-time Krav Maga heroine—after a competition in which they had both participated. Lea had technically won, but they both knew that it was just that: a technicality. Valerie was better, and this was Lea's way of saying it without saying it. At least, that was Valerie's interpretation, and she was perfectly content with it.

Next to the knife was a custom-made miniature flash-bang grenade, less than two inches long and an inch in diameter, given to her by the one and only Jason Parsons. She had met Jason while consulting for a French task force investigating how to improve the training provided for women joining FORFUSCO, France's Naval Special Forces, and the two had become immediate friends. She even remembered his real name, although Kelly insisted that was because the munitions genius was clearly and enthusiastically gay.

What was most dear to Valerie, however, was a piece of spy gadgetry. It looked like a lipstick canister, but was actually a tiny gun that fired 6 mm caliber bullets. She found the irony of the device thoroughly endearing. She could never take it anywhere, not so much for its illegality, but because anyone who knew her even a little would instantly realize that it must be a weapon. It was very well understood that Valerie would sooner dip uranium-laced chewing tobacco than wear makeup. Besides, she only had four bullets left from the original six after testing it at the range with…

"Amelia!" Val and Kelly exploded simultaneously. That's what she had forgotten.

As if on cue, her cell phone rang. She dug it out of her jeans pocket and didn't even bother to check who was calling before tapping to accept.

"Right. I know. I'm already on my way."

"No you aren't," Mel accused impatiently.

"Fine. I'm not. But I still have plenty of time."

"No you don't."

Valerie checked her watch and grimaced. She really didn't.

Mel continued. "If you don't ride slower than eighty, maybe you can get here only a few minutes late."

Valerie smiled at this. "Aw, Mel, since when do I ever ride slower than eighty?"

"Just get your butt here, Val. I get paid based on—"

"Yeah, yeah. See you soon!" She hung up, slipped the phone and the crystal back into a pocket, then made a bee-line for the door.

"Hey!" called Kelly from the floor.

Val turned to see her imaginary friend pointing at a pile of Lycra.

"Oh. Right."

She grabbed the workout clothes, stuffed them in a backpack, and headed for the door again.

"Hey!"

"What?!"

Kelly was standing in the kitchen now, pointing at the keys on the floor.

"Right. Thanks."

• • ● • •

Valerie came to a screeching halt in front of the studio where Amelia offered her yoga classes.

"Shit." There was almost never a free parking spot, but she could usually find some place to illegally squeeze her bike between vehicles. Not tonight. Everything was bumper to bumper. With a squeal of tires, she spun the bike around and returned to claim an almost-spot she had passed a block and a half back.

She had to dismount first and pull the cycle into place from in front of the handlebars.

"Plenty of space," observed Kelly from the curb.

Shut up. It fits.

"Uh huh. Right."

She tied her helmet to the back of the seat, and took off towards the studio at a jog. At the corner along the way she glanced down a narrow side street and came to a sudden stop.

About thirty or forty feet away, a gang of four men had cornered someone against the wall of an auto body shop. The situation was unmistakable: a mugging was underway. As she turned to face them, the man obstructing her view of the victim shifted, and Val saw a flash of soft purple fabric. Likely a woman, and so possibly not just a mugging.

Valerie instantly broke into a run, shouting, "Back off, assholes!"

The attacker furthest away grabbed the victim by the arms, holding her in place while the other three turned to face Valerie. At about ten feet from the nearest, she slowed to a walk.

"This ain't none of your business, bitch," the closest one snarled. He was heavy-set, with dark eyes, dark hair, and a pocked face.

"I'm making it my business," Val hissed. "Get lost before someone gets very, very hurt."

The second closest was bald, and covered in tattoos and attitude. "Too late for that, pussy—"

Back at the street corner, Kelly grimaced. There was a chance that man was going to say 'pussycat', but he never got the chance.

With blinding speed, Valerie launched forward, her arm shooting out like a viper. The heel of her palm connected with the bald man's nose, and his head snapped back as blood erupted into the sky. Faster than the other assailants could react, Valerie delivered a snap kick to the groin of the first man, followed by a knee thrust upwards into his descending face. Something crunched as the mugger slid to the ground.

By this time the third man had begun to react, reaching for something tucked into the back of his belt. Before he could get it, Valerie hooked her left heel out and back to pull the man's right knee forward. He fell onto it, his other leg now extended to the left. Suddenly Val was airborne, then landed with a crushing stomp on the outside of his left knee. The man screamed as it shattered and was unconscious before his head hit the pavement.

The entire fray took less than five seconds, and now Valerie stood only a few feet from the last assailant, who pulled the victim between them as a shield.

She met his eyes and bored into them. Fire behind ice.

The mugger knew he was in trouble. Valerie had seen the look a hundred times. She also knew that he wasn't thinking straight. The conflict between fear and ego flashed behind darting eyes. Or was it something else? The way the man kept glancing at his hostage, Val wondered if there was more going on in his thoughts than just fight or flight. Had he been pressured into the whole thing? Was that regret in his expression? Regardless, his nerves were building, and any second it would become too much to contain. He might simply turn and run, but many times when the adrenaline kicks in there's no stopping it. If he starts to swear at her, that would be the sign.

"You fucking bitch!" he screamed as his grip tightened on the blouse of his human shield.

And then Valerie was a blur. She seemed to leap to her right, and the man began pushing his hostage in that direction, but suddenly she had slid past him on the left. In a blink of an eye she was behind him, his right wrist in her right hand. A twist, a snap. Her left heel was kicking out his left knee. He fell sidewise, and tried to break his fall by reaching out with his left hand. She kicked it out of the way, and he landed hard on his back. His head struck the pavement, and everything was suddenly stillness and silence.

All four men lay unconscious in the street.

The intended victim had turned and was staring at her. To her great surprise, Valerie recognized the stylized yin/yang tattoo, the short-cropped hair with rainbow highlights. This was the person she had seen several days before at the diner.

"I know you. I saw you at Sally's." They blinked at her. *Probably in shock*, Val assessed. After an instant, they found their voice.

"What? I'm sorry, I don't..."

"At Sally's Café. You came in behind me. I held the door for you."

"I hope I said thank you."

Valerie laughed. "I don't remember."

“Well I certainly owe you a load of thanks now. I don’t know what I would have done if you hadn’t—”

“Forget it,” Val interrupted.

“I can’t imagine doing that.”

“Really,” continued Valerie. “It actually gives me a good excuse for being late for something, so in a way I should kind of be thanking you.” The androgynous person just stared at her, clearly at a loss for words. “You gonna be okay?”

“What? Uh, yeah. Yeah. I’m . . . I’m fine.” They looked at the men lying on the ground. “What . . . what should we do about . . .”

“You want my opinion? Just go home. They got what they deserved. It’s not your fault, and definitely not your obligation to do anything for them.”

The stranger nodded, but seemed unconvinced.

“Anyway,” continued Valerie, “I have to get going. You sure you’re going to be alright?”

They nodded. “Yeah. I’ll be fine. Thank you.”

Valerie gave them a last smile, then took off toward the studio.

When she reached the corner, Valerie stole a quick look back to see the stranger still standing amid the unconscious bodies, a clear expression of compassion, even concern, on their face. A twinge of pity briefly whispered through Val’s thoughts. Not for the men, certainly not, but for the stranger. *Some people just can’t accept that it’s okay not to be a victim.*

• • ● • •

The night’s yoga session was only modestly attended, Valerie noted as she emerged from the changing room and grabbed a mat from the pile near the door. About a dozen *yoggers*, as Val liked to call them, were in the middle of some kind of static stretch—maybe Reach-For-The-Cheese or Sidewise-Facing-Existential-Monkey or some such—as she strode toward the group centered on the hardwood exercise floor. Then she stopped. The woman leading the class was not Amelia.

I couldn’t be that late, Val thought with a quick glance at her watch. She wasn’t wearing it. *Right,* she thought, remembering that she had taken it off when she changed. She grabbed for her phone instead. It wasn’t in her pocket. She didn’t have any pockets. *Who the hell designs these workout clothes?*

“In your jacket,” Kelly reminded her. “In the locker.”

Just as she was turning to go back for it, Val noticed that one of the Sidewise-Existing Monkeys was shooting furtive, irritated glances at her from the back of the crowd. She changed plans and walked over, obtrusively flopping her mat down next to Amelia’s.

“What are you doing *here*?” asked Valerie. Then she laughed aloud, appreciating the play on words with her fictitious pose name. Sure, no one else understood it—and the whole class was now casting disparaging glances her way—but Valerie found it endlessly amusing. The yoggers soon returned to their somber Existential Monkeying.

Mel shook it off. "I *work* here, remember?" she whispered.

Valerie adopted some semblance of the stretch. "I meant, why aren't you teaching the class?"

"I'm hoping Natalie will fill in for me while we're in Iceland, so I'm seeing how she does."

The seconds sped past like eons.

"So this is it? Just this one pose for the rest of eternity?" asked Valerie.

Amelia's only response was a dirty look. Kelly didn't react at all, occupied as she was playing a rather inappropriate variant of 'duck duck goose' with the unwitting members of the yoga class. There were only two men in the group, yet somehow they were always the ones receiving the goose. Valerie snorted a laugh, then covered it with a fake sneeze.

Eventually Natalie had them shift into a new posture. "Now reach towards the Heavens with your right hand, and place your left palm flat on the floor. Spread your feet and your toes wide, and let Mother Earth fill your womb with Her energy."

Valerie looked over at Amelia, who was already staring back at her with threatening eyes. Val opened her mouth, eager to ask the two men if their wombs were full yet, but Amelia hissed at her. "Shut it, Val."

"I just—"

"Shut it."

Valerie made a 'zipping my lips' gesture with her right hand. Amelia's eyes grew wide.

"Why do you have blood on your hand?"

Valerie looked down at her fist. "Huh. Well, look at that."

"Why…" Amelia started to repeat.

"I'll be right back," interjected Valerie, and then she slipped back to the changing room.

When she returned, her hands were immaculate and the class was just finishing with a final Sun Salutation.

"I thought we were supposed to do these at the beginning," observed Valerie in a clinical voice.

"You're such an ass," Mel whispered back.

"Well," announced Natalie, "I hope you enjoyed today's class. We will be having…"

Valerie had already phased her voice out.

"Sorry about being late."

"Did you sign the sheet?"

"There was something going down on Monroe," Valerie continued. "I had to—"

"Go sign the sheet. I get paid—"

"Yeah, yeah. Paid by the dozen or whatever."

Valerie had apparently not been the only one to forget to sign in, and by the time she returned Amelia had just finished talking to Natalie. The new instructor gave Valerie a disingenuous smile before departing.

"For what it's worth, I am sorry for being late."

Amelia sighed. "I know. You can make it up to me with some coffee."

"Is that a flavor of beer?"

"Close enough. So what was with the blood?"

Valerie told her about the encounter.

"Right here? I can't believe it! This neighborhood has always been so safe."

"I keep telling you, Mel, there's no such thing as safe. That's why you need to learn to defend yourself." Valerie gave her thin smile. "And *that's* why I agreed to our little exchange of exercise. So if all that Sun Saluting and Downward-Flushing Dog has you warmed up..." She shifted into a fighting stance. "Let's see if you remember any of the blocks I showed you last week."

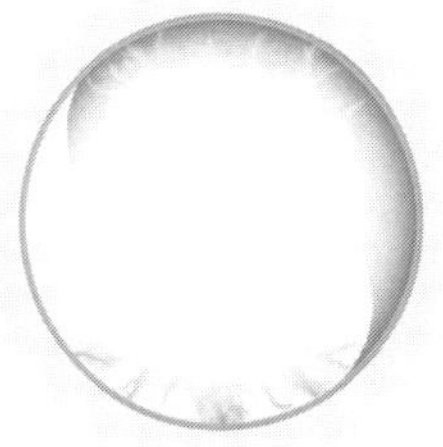

CHAPTER SIX:

Champion Prepared

Gabriel hit the mat, hard.

"What Aliesha just did is called Umsik Altur." Gabriel's trainer, Portalia, was the Docent for Military Training, and had a talent for making the painful sound academic. "It is best used when your opponent's balance is compromised. Like yours, when you stepped back. The pre-shadows are of no value when you cannot react to them." She twirled a finger in the air as she stepped back. "Again."

He stood and backed off the training square to let Aliesha know that he needed a moment to recover.

The heart of the training complex was deep within the center of the Syntrodome. It was an enormous, stone-walled gallery with a ceiling at least forty feet high. Its floor was sectioned into an array of twenty-by-twenty-foot squares, and each of those had a smaller, padded square mat set within it. The hall was always noisy and humid with people training day and night. Correction—women training. In the two weeks since he had begun, Gabriel only remembered seeing another man here once.

Portalia had told him one evening that people typically signed up months or even years in advance to receive instruction here. In Gabriel's case, however, the circumstances were obviously different. There was no greater priority in the world than his training, and the greatest teachers in Annaphora were all placed at his disposal. When she was in her prime, Portalia was considered the highest master in both the Av al Haidren and Misza Shar disciplines, two of the nearly twenty fighting styles taught to the Warriors of Syntra.

Gabriel knew a little of the Defense and Preservation Forces, those fierce women trained to serve and preserve the Circles of Aerth should violence arise, but it had always been a distant, academic topic. Sure, children fought, and most schools included some basic self-defense in their physical fitness curricula. Non-lethal versions of some of the more common fighting techniques had even evolved into a family of competitive sports. Rigorous training for the express purpose of inflicting pain or harm, on the other hand, ran counter to the way most people thought. Including Gabriel.

As he regained control over his breathing, Gabriel wiped a bit of sweat from his forehead with the corner of his brown, cotton gi. He took a small sip of water from a clay cup at the side of the mat, and then nodded to Aliesha as he returned to the inner padded square.

"You'll get this, Gab," she encouraged. "Just watch for the little flicker in the pre-shadow. It's subtle, but..."

He smiled. Aliesha was one of the six remaining candidates in the First Class, a group of women who were being prepared for...well, for his absence. Apparently the Chakrava had been anticipating the arrival of a Champion for a very long time, and as the years slipped past they began to feel that it would be prudent to prepare their own candidate. Just in case. The final six had risen to the top from an initial draft of over a thousand of the world's finest warriors.

"Hey!" Aliesha snapped her fingers in front of his face. "Wherever your thoughts are wandering, save them for another time. This is *combat*."

As she spoke the final word, Gabriel saw the pre-shadow of her fist swinging around towards the side of his head. It was a shadowy illusion of the moment soon to come, and he was lucky that his reactions were good, for the attack itself followed only a quarter second behind the warning. He barely ducked in time.

The pre-shadow of a kick followed, also a mere fraction of a second before the actual strike. Then another, and another. A twinge of panic came over him, and the delay between pre-shadow and event contracted even more. Aliesha saw his growing desperation and took a step back.

"What's going on with you? You're better than this."

Gabriel nodded, a silent apology.

"Are we going to do this, or what?"

He took a deep, calming breath, and turned his focus inward upon the awareness that emanated out of his nythlen. With that inner sense he 'saw' Aliesha step back, crouch into her ready stance, and nod at him. He waited until his eyes confirmed that she had actually done these things, then gave his own nod to let her know that he was ready.

Centered in his calmness, the pre-shadows grew, enabling him to observe Aliesha's intentions much sooner. His tranquility permitted him to flow out of their way with an easy, almost dance-like grace, planning his evasions before the strikes had even commenced. The interaction became less martial and more like a game of kinetic chess. He could see where she would strike, and once his subconscious committed to a defense, he even saw pre-shadows of his own body's movements. He knew that Aliesha was also watching those same pre-shadows and planning her own reactions. Prescient combat was not only about reflexes and strength; the best warriors were those with the intellect to quickly adapt and evolve their tactics.

Aliesha's attacks were now coming predominantly towards his left side, and he saw himself shift to the right in response. Suddenly a pre-shadow of her left leg was shooting out, and he realized that she had outmaneuvered him. Again. He could not avoid that kick without opening himself to even worse attacks, and then there was the pre-memory of pain where her foot would connect, that anticipation of the hit before it even happened. He winced. His mental control faltered, allowing an edge of panic to slip into his mind, and then the pre-shadows contracted again. The kick landed, and he grunted with the pain. Within moments the pre-shadows were all but gone and Aliesha's blows were coming out of nowhere. Before he knew what was happening, his legs were swept from under him. Gabriel fell to the mat, and his opponent came crashing down on top of him, seemingly possessed of a hundred jagged elbows.

She stopped an inch from his chest.

She smiled at him.

"Better." Aliesha nodded in appreciation as she rose to her feet.

"Was it?"

"Definitely."

He took an extended hand, and she pulled him to his feet. "It didn't feel like I did a particularly great job."

She gave him a light, good-natured slap on the shoulder. "I said it was better, not that it was good."

• • • • •

Khalfani, First Mother and Highest Priestess of the Circles of Aerth, tapped a nervous fingernail against the frame of the window as she looked out over the training floor below. Close by, two assistants awaited her needs in silence: Nanci, with her ever-present leather-bound journal, and Pranja, a young but promising woman only arrived in the capital two years prior from the continent of Fulsia.

Tap, tap. Tap, tap, tap.

The sound was like a hammer in the otherwise silent room, and Pranja shifted uncomfortably at every impact. Nanci glanced at her in amused silence, but also with a measure of respect for the young woman's sensitivity.

Tap. Tap, tap, tap.

But even Nanci had to admit that the First Mother was in a state unlike any she had ever witnessed. Her Holiness was normally a paragon of patience and seren-

judgement. Where a few idle taps would have signified nothing for the average woman, they were like the thunder of an approaching storm coming from her.

Without a word, the First Mother suddenly spun and strode out of the room. Nanci's back stiffened in surprise, and Pranja actually jumped the tiniest bit, and then they rushed to follow the head of state into the stairwell leading down to the training floor.

• • ● • •

The First Mother approached Portalia with a stately, purposeful stride. Every hint of her previous concern or impatience had been summarily banished and she smiled warmly at each instructor and student who turned to watch her progression. When she reached the Docent, Portalia bowed deeply before her.

"Peace be with you, Your Holiness."

Khalfani smiled an acknowledgement and gave her customary nod, a gesture that had become second nature after so many years, but her eyes immediately shifted to Gabriel. The question was clear.

"He is . . . progressing." The pause before that last word was slight but sufficient.

"How fast?" Khalfani could not leave this to chance.

Portalia lowered her eyes.

"I see. Thank you, child."

"I'm so sorry, Your Holiness. He is a quick learner without a doubt, and is making tremendous strides, but he came to us with very little experience. Even working night and day, there is only so much one can accelerate the training of reflexes, the—"

The First Mother laid her aged-spotted hand on Portalia's arm. "I understand. And no one holds you accountable. What you have been able to achieve in only a few short weeks is . . . most impressive."

"He is not without merit. When he is calm, we have seen evidence that his pre-shadows may be extending as much as two seconds."

Khalfani's eyes grew wide. That was nearly as long as some of the most revered warrior monks in—

There was a loud slap from the training area. Khalfani and the Docent looked over simultaneously to see that Aliesha had just pinned Gabriel to the mat.

"When he's calm," Portalia emphasized.

"Continue to work with him. If he is already nearing two seconds, who knows how far he may ultimately be able to extend."

Portalia nodded. "Perhaps if we paired him with another for the journey? Aliesha is an extremely gifted warrior. Personally I believe she is the most skilled of those who remain in the First Class. If . . ." She let the words trail off.

Khalfani was looking at her intently, weighing her words. "Has she indicated having heard such a Beacon?"

"No, Your Holiness."

"Well, then it appears that is not what the future has in store."

Portalia once again lowered her eyes. She made to step back then, but hesitated.

"Speak, daughter."

"Holy Mother, is there no hope for us? If he is the Champion, and . . . well . . ."

A kind smile came to the First Mother's face, a bright, warm expression that could have induced flowers to bloom in the middle of a snowstorm. "Do not despair, child. There is always hope. The Beacons know what they are doing."

"Yes, First Mother. And . . . thank you."

Khalfani patted the trainer's arm and said, "Have him come here. It is long past time for us to speak."

As Portalia moved to obey, the head of the Chakrava gave a curt gesture to her aides. This was to be a private conversation, and they were released to attend to what other duties called them. By the time Gabriel stood before the First Mother, Nanci and Pranja had already left the training floor.

"Your Holiness, it is an honor . . ." Gabriel bowed low.

The First Mother reached out and lifted his head. "Walk with me, my child."

She spun gracefully on her heel and led him away from the mats towards a long stone wall carved with the gentle curves of an extended logogram. From his first time visiting the training facilities Gabriel had felt drawn to the pattern, and spent a fair share of his recovery time appreciating its design. Aliesha had told him that it represented the transition of the novice into an artisan.

"How are your practice sessions progressing?" the First Mother asked.

"I would expect you to know the answer to that better than I would," he replied, surprised by the question nearly as much as she was by his response.

"Why do you say that?"

"I've seen you watching me."

"Oh?"

"Has that not been you behind the window? High up on the east wall?"

She smiled at that. The boy was so perceptive. That could be a very good sign, although it simultaneously made other things more challenging. She would need to be cautious indeed with the Champion.

"Yes, my child. It has." She reached out and ran a finger along one of the curves in the Mosaic of Transition. She found the slight depression, pressed inward and then gave a slight twist. A section of the wall slid back to reveal a paneled passage dimly lit by softly glowing vases affixed to the walls. Gabriel gave a quiet gasp and she chuckled. "Portalia says that you are learning very quickly," the First Mother said as she led him through. "She is . . . particularly impressed with your attunement."

"Thank you," Gabriel replied as she closed the secret portal behind them.

"And I am told that your test results are also very strong. Average pre-sight just under a second, with peaks almost twice that. It has been generations since anyone showed such promise, particularly after only a few weeks."

Gabriel didn't know how to respond. He grew uncomfortable under the harsh light of praise and tried to change the topic.

"Are there many passages like this? Hidden doors and such?"

"Oh yes. Many upon many. And undoubtedly ones of which even I am unaware. The First Mothers pass the secrets down, but I imagine that a portion of that knowledge must have become lost over the millennia." She paused to straighten a statuette of an owl, one of a set decorating a small table along the wall of the passage. "The Syntrodome will remain full of mysteries until the end of days, it is said."

"As will the First Mothers," Gabriel added.

Khalfani studied the young man's face. Was that appreciation? Respect? Accusation? The boy was very difficult to read. But his expression seemed genuine and kind, and she concluded that it was most likely a reflection of the awe that he felt for her and the Chakrava.

"We hope so," she replied, and then resumed walking. "A leader should always maintain at least a hint mystery about her, if only to remind her people that the universe is an uncertain place, and largely not understood."

"I appreciate you sharing the wisdom of your—"

The First Mother held up her hand. "Please. I can almost hear your mother's insistence that you show proper respect. Well and good. You passed. So now let us speak like normal people, shall we? We have a lot to discuss."

"Yes, Your Holiness."

"And perhaps we can start with putting aside our titles. In private, you may call me by my given name. Khalfani."

"Khalfani? But that's..."

"A man's name. Yes. My parents expected a son."

"They didn't know?" Gabriel could not imagine this.

"Ironic, isn't it. But that is the way of things. Anyone can mishear the Beacons, especially when their mind is clouded with expectation."

"I see."

"Take you, for example."

"Me?" Gabriel asked. "What about me?"

"Had we not been so convinced that the Champion would be a woman, perhaps we would have found you with more time to prepare." Khalfani motioned, and they turned into a hallway that branched to the left. "This way."

"Champion. You used that term when we first met, but said that it was not the time to discuss it. Now...?"

The question hung in the air for several seconds.

"Yes. Now is the time," the First Mother said quietly. "But let me first ask you this. Do you have any sense of what is to follow from here?"

"No. Not really," he replied. "I feel that something . . . important . . . portentous is on the horizon, that the future will call me elsewhere before too long. But where or for what, I have no idea."

"How long?"

"It's hard to say. Another couple of weeks, maybe? Certainly before the month is over."

Khalfani sighed. "So soon." Her voice sounded wistful, but then turned matter of fact. "Well, it is what it is."

"And what is it, then?"

"In a moment. I took the liberty of having a sitting room prepared for us."

She led him another twenty feet to a closed door, painted black and with silver trim around the edge. She removed a set of keys from a deep pocket in her gown, fished along the ring until she found the correct one, and used it.

Beyond was a small, cozy sitting room, warm from a fire burning in a marble hearth that was so clean that Gabriel wondered if this was the first time it had ever seen flame. In the center of the room were four delicate-looking chairs set around a low, round coffee table. The entire set was crafted of black locust stained to a deep red and polished until it shone. The chairs had cushions of black embroidered with silver thread. Gabriel noticed that they matched the door to the room. There wasn't a speck of dust anywhere.

A glass decanter of clear liquid and several crystal goblets had been positioned upon a cabinet against the wall across from the fireplace. Khalfani stepped over to it, poured two drinks, and returned. She handed one to Gabriel as she sat, motioned for him to sit as well. He took a sip and was surprised to discover that the liquid was simply water.

"Now then, let us speak of Champions." She took a drink from her goblet, placed it on the table, and made herself comfortable in the seat. For the first time since he arrived, Gabriel was struck by how old this woman was. She always seemed like a fountain of vitality, exuding a calm yet boundless energy that washed over everyone and everything around her, but at this moment she looked tired, worn thin.

"When I asked you shortly after you arrived," she began, "you said that you have never read any of the sacred texts. So we shall begin there.

"Roughly thirteen thousand years ago, according to the historical manuscripts, some manner of cataclysmic event occurred, and the world split. There is no record that describes the nature of that event, but the result was the cleaving of a single world into two, each diverging onto its own trajectory, its own . . . timelir of development. In other words, all of Aerth is but one of two Potentialities, as the records describe it, complemented by some other world that would be very much like ours, yet also very different."

"Different in what sense?" Gabriel asked.

Khalfani shrugged. "There is no way for us to know. Perhaps its sun rises in the west and sets in the east. Perhaps its people follow different traditions, or hear different Beacons. As no one from our world has ever been there, obviously, it is impossible to say with any definitiveness. And in fairness, this is all conjecture passed down for thousands of years. We cannot know for certain that it is factual at a concrete level. It could be more appropriately interpreted as allegory. It is possible that there is not a *literal* 'second world', but merely an underground society, or a latent awareness in our collective consciousness that is on the cusp of awakening. There is no way to test any such theories, however. And since the records speak as if it is a literal 'other world', it is our most sensible path to proceed under that assumption."

"Have you looked for an underground society?"

"We have, for many, many years... but have never found any evidence of such. Anyway," she took another sip, "let us continue. The records say that these two worlds are each following their own astral orbits, and that there will come a time when their paths will bring them together. This event, this... convergence.... has been called The Nexus."

At the mention of that word, the hair on the back of Gabriel's neck stood up. He knew in that moment, beyond any doubt, that this was the Purpose to which he was being Called. And he knew that it was indeed a true coming together of worlds, nothing metaphorical or allegorical. His nythlen felt electrified, giving off so many signals and sensations that his conscious mind could not accept them all, much less sort them in a sensible way. He was being both pulled and pushed towards this event by forces great beyond his comprehension of the meaning of greatness. And he knew with ultimate certainty that should those forces suddenly vanish, as impossible as that was, still this event would come to pass. It was as if he were falling down the center of an immense chasm with this Nexus awaiting him at the bottom.

Gabriel suddenly became aware that he had closed his eyes. He opened them to see the First Mother studying him intently. How much time had passed? A second? A minute? An hour?

She smiled at him, then gestured casually with her drink and resumed speaking.

"It is prophesied that when these two worlds come together, it will be a moment for a great decision. A Judgment. The Manuscripts of Purpose, four of our oldest and most sacred texts, tell us that each world will be represented by a Champion. Two Champions from the two worlds, brought together to determine which world will continue, and which world... will not."

Gabriel tried to wrap his head around that concept. "And what happens to that world, the world that doesn't?"

The First Mother shrugged. "I don't know. No one does." And then she added, "And I'd rather not find out, if it is all the same to you."

This made Gabriel smile. The leader of the Chakrava had a way of putting people at ease; he supposed that was why she was the leader. One of the reasons, anyway.

"Anyway," she continued, "you can see why we had hoped you would be better prepared. Literally our entire world is riding upon your shoulders, counting on you to emerge victorious from this ultimate battle."

"Perhaps the other world's Champion will be coming into this just as unprepared."

"Perhaps," she conceded. "But it would be foolishness to rely upon that, don't you think? No, we must assume that the other world's Champion will be their fiercest warrior, likely trained from childhood for this task."

"So," Gabriel said quietly, mostly to himself, "no pressure."

"Let us speak frankly, my son. You aren't ready, and it is not realistic for you to develop, in only the few remaining weeks, the martial skills we think you would require."

"That I *would* require," he repeated. "Does this mean you intend to send someone else then?"

"No," she responded immediately. "You *are* Aerth's Champion. You must do this, and you must do it alone. This is what is meant to be. It would be utter foolishness to attempt to circumvent the future. This is beyond my hands. Beyond any of our hands."

"So you believe we are already lost."

"Ahh, Gabriel, the world is bigger and more mysterious than people realize, and there are many paths to any victory." She paused then, letting the concept sink in.

After a time, she pulled a small stone from her pocket and held it out. It appeared to be a worry stone, a rock worn smooth by a stream or river over thousands of years. Some people carried them to run their fingers over, usually to distract the mind during stressful times. His sister, Sendra, often carried one, and suddenly he was keenly aware of the Winder's Knot that hung about his neck.

"I'm going to drop this, and I want you to catch it." The First Mother was watching him with an unusual intensity.

Gabriel was curious. This was a child's game, one of the earliest exercises in learning to hear one's nythlen. No child of Aerth beyond the age of two or three could fail to catch the stone unless they were completely distracted. Why was she playing with him like this?

He stared at the stone. Her pre-shadow released it, and his nythlen watched it fall. As premonition blended into the present moment, he reached forward and snatched the stone out of the air.

"Good," she smiled, and held out her hand. He returned the stone to her. "Now...again."

And again, Gabriel foresaw the stone's descent. He watched the pre-shadow, and reached out as the moment of release approached. Inexplicably, impossibly, the stone did not follow its destined path. Against the very laws of the universe, the First Mother tossed it to the left. It bounced once, coming to rest upon the plush pile of the thick brown carpet beneath their feet.

Gabriel blinked in confusion. "How...? That's impossible."

"It is called Dhokha di Maath. The Deceptive Heart."

"That...that's impossible," he repeated, insistent. "I heard the Beacon. I *heard* it."

"And now you are aware of something that very few people in the world know...that under some circumstances, it is possible for the Beacons to lie."

"To lie?" The concept defied the most foundational certainty he had come to accept in twenty-five years.

"Well," the First Mother conceded, "perhaps not *lie*. But...misinform. You see, the Beacons are not truly separate from us. Yes, they go beyond us, but they are part of us as well. They echo the delicate resonance between the world—what the universe has in mind, if you will—and ourselves, what we will do within the universe. The art of Dhokha di Maath is to bury one's true intention in a way that it emerges only in the instant of execution."

"No," Gabriel insisted. "If the intention is there, the Beacons will echo it."

"In Dhokha, a new intention, an alternate intention, is held out for the Beacons."

"You cannot lie to the Beacons. That's impossible!"

"True. It is impossible, but there are ways around the impossibility. As I said before, the world is more mysterious than most people realize."

Gabriel took a deep, calming breath. "How is it that I've never heard of such a practice?"

"Perhaps because it has been kept as a very closely held secret by the Ministry. It was originally developed as part of the Dho-Khadi, a martial discipline that emerged nearly fifteen hundred years ago. That style of conflict focused on misdirection and subterfuge. The art of Dhokha di Maath was considered its pinnacle. It was said that a master could walk unsuspected into the house of her most hated enemies, and they would welcome her with warmth and open arms."

The concept turned Gabriel's stomach. "It's a perversion of everything that is sacred."

"Yes," the First Mother agreed calmly. "Yes, it is. And for that reason, the teachings were outlawed, and its practitioners were..." She didn't want to offend the sensibilities of the innocent young man. "Cleansed."

"You mean they were killed."

"I wasn't there, so I cannot speak to what happened, but I do not believe anything inhumane transpired. But regardless of those specifics, the important thing is that all memory of the deceptive arts faded away."

"Clearly not *all* memory." His tone was accusatory, but Khalfani took no offense. She remembered very well her own reactions when she first learned of the techniques and the reasons they were preserved by the Ministry.

"My child, you are correct, and your feelings are not misguided. The few who know of Dhokha di Maath all feel exactly as you do. It is a blot against the purity with which we seek to guide our lives. But we retain the knowledge with very specific, and very rational, intentions."

She could see a measure of calm return to his face, although there was an undertone of chilly disapproval in his voice as he said, "Go on."

"The Ministry preserves the art through a very small number of women. Only the Chakrava know of its existence, and only the First and Second Mothers are trained in its ways. So you can see, this is a closely held secret indeed. As for why, the answer is twofold. First and foremost, we remember the form to ensure we are prepared should it ever surface again. After all, it was developed once, so we must recognize that its re-emergence is always a possibility."

"And the second reason?"

"Why, in case we need it, of course. It is, after all, a secret and very potent weapon. Ruling a world means recognizing that sometimes dire circumstances require dire measures." She reached out and took both his hands in hers. "Make no mistake, Gabriel. I fully realize that this goes against your nature. And believe me, I'm thankful for that. More thankful than I can possibly say. This is a dark art if ever there was one, and it would be deeply upsetting if our world's Champion felt comfortable with it. But if ever there was a dire need, we are facing one now. Our entire world is at stake in The Nexus, Gabriel. There is no measure that should not be taken to ensure its continuation, to ensure the survival of our culture and our Circles.

"You certainly cannot become a true master of Dhokha in a few weeks, but as quickly as you learn, I expect you will become a formidable practitioner indeed. And hopefully you'll gain enough skill to give you the advantage you will need to ensure our survival. I call that a worthy cause. Don't you?"

The First Mother's words sunk in, and Gabriel began to nod. It was unnatural, deceptive, dark. His moral compass spun in frantic, wild rebellion against the concept, but deep down, his heart told him that this was the path for which he was destined. And learning Dhokha di Maath was part of that path. Like it or not, he would proceed, and he would do his very best.

"We will speak more of this, Gabriel. And after supper tonight, perhaps you will want to have a look at the sacred texts."

He looked up at her in shock. It was said that no man had ever been admitted to the Inner Shrine where those ancient scrolls were kept. She seemed to read his thoughts.

"You are no ordinary man, Gabriel. As the Champion, no one on all of Aerth has more right, more *need*, to read those documents than you."

He nodded. "Yes. Thank you. I would like to see them."

"Of course. But now you should return to your training. We have little enough time for your preparations as it is. And tomorrow we will begin a new program, once I have rearranged my and the Second Mother's schedules. We will be at your disposal, my child."

As Gabriel returned to the practice floor, the import of her words sank in. The First and Second Mothers, the two most exalted leaders of the entire world, were at *his* disposal. Nothing up to that point had made him so aware of the incredible weight that the future was laying upon his shoulders. He suddenly felt very small, like the tiniest pebble tossed about in a maelstrom. *One step at a time,* he reminded himself. *Sometimes all it takes is the small rock to tip the balance.* The thought helped to keep the magnitude of the future at bay.

Once he had left the room, the door closed and her solitude secured, the First Mother allowed herself the luxury of fear. He was a gifted boy, and, frankly, a charming one. A boy that she would have been proud to have as a grandson. But her world didn't need a caregiver as a Champion, it needed a warrior—someone with a competitive edge, someone who knew how to use that edge to cut down her adversaries. Aerth needed someone who would do whatever it took, to win no matter the cost.

You are being unfair to the boy, she reflected. Gabriel would never give up. *But that doesn't mean that he has what it will take to defeat the other world's Champion.*

She replayed their conversation in her mind, felt a pang of guilt about her misrepresentations, about that one outright lie. But it was necessary. Gabriel was not prepared for that truth, and the last thing he needed right now was distraction. No, it was the right decision. If there came a time when he needed to know, she would tell him then. If he lived to be angry with her for it . . . correction, if *they all* lived for him to be angry with her, then it was worth it.

CHAPTER SEVEN:

The Path Revealed

There were three stars in the sky. On the left, beams of fiery red shot forth from a bright point of gold. They were like lasers, had Gabriel known what those were, flickering back and forth in seeming randomness, but his intuition assured him that a pattern was there even if he could not decipher it. On the right, that star glowed with a much softer hue, almost honey brown, with a surrounding aura that pulsed slowly, gently. And in the center, between the other two stars was... was... something. A third star, but he could not perceive it. And suddenly it went nova, a flash of all-consuming heat and white light to bring an end to...

Gabriel's eyes blinked open.

It was very dark in his dormitory room, only the thinnest of moonbeams drifting through the shuttered window. He could feel his heart racing with the memory of the dream. Slowly, he twisted about until he was sitting on the edge of his cot. Gabriel took the centering breaths and could feel the ensuing calm emanate out and over his body.

He had had that dream before, and more than once. He went deeper into the meditation, stilling his mind to focus upon his nythlen, the inner sense that listened to the song of the Beacons. A new harmony was there, soft and patient, but clear in its Calling. Gabriel felt his heart beat a little louder with anticipation of a revelation. He quieted it. Excitement obscured, distracted. Only in tranquility would the song ring out undistorted.

Gabriel reached out to where a small, square stack of sethrey paper lay upon the corner of his nightstand. He peeled off the top sheet, folded it in half, and then pressed the ends together more firmly. As the chemicals infused within the paper reacted, the sheet grew warm and began to emit a soft phosphorescent glow. He squeezed more of the sheet together between his thumb and forefinger until th light was bright enough for him to discern the shapes of his furniture.

Standing, Gabriel wrapped himself in chambray robe and left his room to navigate the passageways of the Syntrodome. Even in the middle of the night, the halls were not completely empty. Young women passed him, typically alone in their business but sometimes in pairs engaged in whispered conversations as they made their way. Without exception, they stepped aside in deferential respect to permit Gabriel to pass undisturbed. No, not for Gabriel; they stepped aside for the Champion. This had happened occasionally when he first arrived at the citadel but had become more common once he started taking personal instruction with the First Mother. It felt like everyone knew who he was. The truth was that it was only a very small minority, mostly women who worked around or for the Chakrava, but for a young man who had never been the center of attention, it was like waking into a different world. A few weeks was simply not long enough to adjust; he doubted any length of time would be.

The Library of Skies, as it was called, was on the upper levels. It was nearly fifty feet across and extended vertically through three levels. The main chamber was filled with large, cushioned chairs and oval study desks. Fireplaces were spaced regularly about the perimeter, each filled with the glow of coals that provided little light but an abundance of warmth. The women present when he entered were seated near those fires, each consumed so completely with their studies that they were, for all practical purposes, in their own private libraries. Gabriel noted with a touch of surprise that there was even another man here, a rare occurrence indeed. No one paid attention to Gabriel as he strode through, however, at least not beyond noting his presence as just another nightwalker.

As with any library, the primary and defining feature was the never-ending collection of books. Shelves upon shelves, lining the walls and piled upon carts. There was an organization to them that took even the sharpest librarians months to master. But Gabriel didn't need any assistance tonight. He knew what he wanted. He had combed through the pages of this particular book a dozen times already, never to any avail.

But tonight would be different.

Gabriel cradled the enormous atlas as he carried it from its home on the second shelf of reference books to a table at the north end of the library. Laying it gently onto a table, he stilled his thoughts and then, when he was finally ready, opened it with a motion that was almost a caress. His fingers drifted through the pages until he came to the right one, the fold-out map of the North Sea. On the continent of Therspia that bounded the sea to the west he noted the icon that designated Annaphora, but only for a moment. That was not what mattered. His gaze drifted east across the page until his sight fell upon a small island perhaps a hundred miles in diameter, maybe a little more. According to a small inset the island was home to a sparsely-distributed Circle of just under thirty-five thousand souls. This little oasis of green in the vast surrounding blue waters was labeled Havlanti, which in the old languages meant 'Land of Ices'.

• • • • •

The leader of the Chakrava sat behind her desk. While not tiny, it was a comparatively small surface for the ruler of an entire world but this was a necessity of its construction, for it had been crafted from a single growth of smoky quartz. It was beautiful, priceless, and almost completely covered with scrupulously organized stacks of paper that represented the First Mother's daily workload.

On the opposite side of the desk from Khalfani sat the Triad, the three women who oversaw the operations of the Aynslahti, the Chakrava's secret police. They were also, and not at all by coincidence, highly skilled assassins. Despite employing nearly a thousand women around the world, the Aynslahti appeared in no official record within the Syntrodome. Instead, its sizable expenses fell within the First Mother's discretionary budget under the heading 'organizational resources'. This room, around this priceless desk, was the only place these four women would ever convene, and they never entered via the office's only obvious door.

The group went silent a moment before a double knock came upon that door. After a brief pause, a third rap followed. Nanci and the other assistants employed a variety of knocking patterns to alert and inform the First Mother. This one meant someone had appeared early for a meeting. That would be Gabriel, as his training session with Khalfani was next on her schedule.

"Perhaps," she said quietly, "we should continue this discussion at a later time."

The First Mother opened a slender drawer in a small, decorative cabinet against the east wall and depressed a lever within. There was a soft click and a panel in the wall swung a few centimeters inward. The Triad put away the small, leather-bound volumes in which they kept their terse and encrypted notes, then silently filed out of the room into the unlit passageway beyond.

As the last woman was leaving, Khalfani put a hand on her shoulder. "Meraya," she whispered, "I have left a dossier for you to review."

"The usual drop?" asked the assassin.

"Yes, but not the usual mission."

"Is there ever such a thing?"

The First Mother smiled. "No. I suppose there isn't. But this task is . . . very sensitive, and cannot be trusted to anyone less than—"

"I'll see to it myself, Most Holy."

"That would be best."

Meraya was young, but then everyone was young in the eyes of the First Mother.

Of course, in its five-hundred-year history the oldest member of the Triad had been only thirty-nine. Most retired by thirty-five, and many by thirty. Meraya was thirty-two. Or had she recently turned thirty-three? Khalfani couldn't recall, and that bothered her. Yes, far more pressing matters were demanding her attention at the moment, but that was no excuse. She was the First Mother, and the First Mother did not forget the fine details. *I need time to meditate and center myself again,* she thought as she closed the secret panel. *Soon*, she promised herself.

Khalfani walked to the office's 'official' entrance, summoned her serenity, and opened the door.

Gabriel was waiting nearby, studying the gurgling stone fountain next to the door. It was a functional installation of art, the means to ensure no sound—and certainly no conversation—could be overhead through the thick door to the First Mother's office. She wondered why he was standing so close, then caught herself. She was letting the tensions of the job paint the worst of everything. It was a pleasant, soothing fountain. She had stood there in calm repose many times herself.

"Please, Gabriel, come in." He turned at the sound of her voice, and she could see from the change in his posture that he had been meditating. She noticed as well that with his concentration broken, an uncharacteristic excitement illuminated his face. Even before the door was fully closed behind him, she said, "Something has happened."

Gabriel could not contain his enthusiasm. "I know where the worlds will meet!"

Ah, she mused. *Do I tell him that we already know and pour cold water on this youthful enthusiasm, or do I feign ignorance and risk reducing his awe of our omniscience?* That it was not an easy decision told her something important about her own feelings regarding this boy.

The First Mother nodded, then replied. "The Isle of Havlanti."

"You knew? How—"

"We suspected. The ancients had predicted that it would be at the same location as the Shattering." She motioned for Gabriel to sit, then took her own chair as she continued. "In fact, this is the primary reason Annaphora was built here on Therspia, close enough for convenient access yet not so close as to obstruct what must ultimately come to pass. Of course, it was always conjecture. Only the Champion would know the location with absolute certainty."

"I see."

She noted the touch of disappointment in his eyes, and it saddened her. "Do you know when, my child?"

Gabriel shook his head. "No. Not precisely. But soon. I shouldn't delay. A day more or less won't matter, but..."

"Of course. We must follow as the Beacons call." Khalfani felt the concern stirring deep within her, and she was surprised to realize that a part of that concern was for Gabriel himself. Not that any individual could matter in comparison to the future of the world, of course, but he was a fine young man and...

With the practiced ease of an actor donning a role, Khalfani smiled warmly and supportively. He must never doubt that she had the utmost confidence in him. "Then let today's lesson be your capstone. And if the future permits, we'll offer you the blessing of the Chakrava at this evening's prayer."

"You honor me."

Khalfani stood again and walked around the desk to stand beside him. "Not many men receive that blessing, but if anyone deserves it, Gabriel, it's you."

He lowered his head in embarrassment, but she reached out and lifted it back up gently with a finger under his chin. "Our fates lay in your hands because that is how the future has spoken, but I want you to know this. I truly could not be happier with that choice. Your dedication has been unparalleled, and you are as quick a learner as ever I've seen. I have faith in you, my child. We all do."

Only a true master of Dhokha di Maath could have ensured that such a statement rang true to its very core while simultaneously concealing Khalfani's growing fear that Gabriel simply was not ready.

• • • • •

The 'evening prayer' was not a single gathering, even within the Syntrodome. Official prayers led by the most promising rising clergywomen were held for the public in the two largest temples on the ground floor of the unrestricted areas, and the demand was so high that to ensure everyone had an opportunity, the Chakrava had established that one could not attend on two subsequent evenings. Even still, hundreds of people would wait in line to participate in the ceremonies and there were always dozens, if not more, who were turned away for lack of space. It was said that attendance would bestow good fortune, but just as compelling was the deeply-valued social aspect of the gatherings. Each service was followed by guided meditation designed to help attendees attune their nythlen to whatever futures awaited them after that it was common for friends to gather for small group discussions over wine and other refreshments.

Far more exclusive were the invitation-only services held in the four tower temples. In the north, west, and south the services were tailored to particular themes or topics of interest, sometimes historical but more often in anticipation of future events. Most of the guests were emissaries and dignitaries from distant Circles, and it was customary for one of the Chakrava to lead these ceremonies.

The most exclusive service, almost always led by the First Mother, was held in the High Temple atop the east tower. In the last hundred years, there were perhaps only eight or ten times when a man was invited to attend this most holy of rituals, and so Gabriel's presence raised more than a few eyebrows. No one said anything aloud, but questioning glances were plentiful. From the women who did not know the Champion, the darting looks asked, 'who is this man, and what is he doing here?' From those who recognized him, the questions were even tenser, more demanding. 'Is it time? Has The Nexus arrived at last?'

When Gabriel first entered the temple through its main south doors, he was overwhelmed with its grandeur. It wasn't that the temple was exceptionally large, although it was certainly a generously-sized space, but rather that every aspect—down to the smallest fringe or table edging—was art of unparalleled craftswomanship.

The main altar was centered upon a raised dais in the eastern half of the inner sanctum. It was covered in a finely-woven cloth of azure blue edged in gold, and a delicate pattern representing the interconnectedness of Aerth's people had been subtly incorporated throughout the covering in the same glinting, gold thread. Spiraled candles in stylized holders flickered like amber-red stars at the altar's corners, and a faint floral incense infused the air as it wafted outward from engraved bowls.

Gabriel noticed how rays of colored light made the incense seem to dance, and his eyes followed the beams back to the windows of stained glass that encircled the temple's upper level. The windows on the western side were positioned high on the wall and crafted from smaller pieces of glass with more varied colors compared to the east, where a single expanse of shaded glass stretched from floor to ceiling. It was green at the bottom and transitioned into an azure blue near the top. In the early morning, he suspected, the temple would be infused by a gradient of color that welcomed the day.

The most notable feature of the temple's ceiling was a high dome centered above the altar. It was engraved and painted to give the impression that the Tree of Life suffused the very walls, or was perhaps growing out of them. From an array of fine, silver chains hung a myriad of crystals that gently swayed back and forth, turning as they did to refract colored rays of light onto the tree. Gabriel could see that one crystal—larger than the others and in the shape of a hemisphere with its curved side facing downward—was set in a silver ring and suspended directly above the center of the altar by four delicate silver chains attached to the dome's four pendentives.

The progression into the temple was a slow, reverent affair. Something about the overwhelming sobriety of the process struck Gabriel as humorous, as if the solemnity had been pushed over the edge to become a caricature of itself. He fought back the urge to smile in bemusement as he followed the woman in front of him. She turned into an aisle between two rows of benches near the back and he followed after her.

As he prepared to settle onto a soft, rose-colored cushion, a hand politely touched his shoulder from behind. It belonged to a young woman he had seen earlier, an acolyte assisting with the ceremony. In silence, she shook her head. He was not to sit here. With a smile she took his elbow in a firm but gentle grip and led him to an empty bench at the very front. He sat at her encouragement, but when he turned his head to express appreciation for her guidance, the woman had already vanished into the crowd of the shuffling congregation.

By the time everyone had settled themselves, only two others were seated in this first row. Both were older women, and both dressed in the same simple brown robes that Gabriel had been given. They too, he concluded, would receive blessings this evening, and that thought carried a second realization with it: everyone else here would not. He suddenly felt the weight of a hundred eyes staring at him.

Then they were all rising, and six members of the Chakrava filed into the temple with the First Mother leading the progression. The holy women took positions in a semicircle behind the altar, and the ceremony began.

Gabriel was first to be called up, and he was surprised at how nervous he felt. After all, he had nothing to do but simply walk forward. No speaking was required of him, Khalfani had explained when he had asked, and only a single action that would present itself at the appropriate time. As he came to a halt before the altar, Gabriel let his awareness drift. This made it challenging to focus on the specific words being intoned, but opened the channel for him to listen with his nythlen. When the moment came for him to look upwards and receive the blessing delivered through the Worldstone of Aerth, he did.

The Worldstone of Aerth...that hemispherical crystal suspended directly above the altar in a silver ring. It was perhaps ten feet above his head, and from this angle the temple's lighting caused it to shine and glitter with an almost otherworldly prismatic spray of colors. The effect made it difficult to focus on the details of the stone, and he suspected that this was no accident. In fact, he sensed that the entire sanctum had been designed around that primary purpose.

The realization made him all the more curious, and he squinted and shifted his head back and forth slightly to get a better look. Through the flashes and glitter, Gabriel was able to see that the Worldstone was not simply a hemisphere of clear crystal, but shot through with jagged veins of red, green, and blue, like lightning frozen in the sky. And in that moment an inexplicable insight came to him: they only *appeared* to be frozen. If he could observe the Worldstone over the passage of enough centuries, he would witness those veins shift and dance as Aerth itself developed through her lifetime.

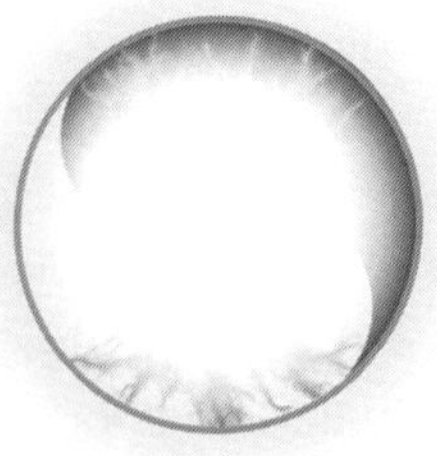

CHAPTER EIGHT:

Iceland's Treasures

The flight to Iceland was nearly thirteen hours of tedium, with a brief, non-disembarking layover somewhere near purgatory that lasted slightly longer than forever. Valerie and Amelia had an aisle and a window seat, respectively. At the time of booking there was no one between them, but two hours before departure some other flight was rerouted, or perhaps there was a coup in a sixth-world country somewhere, and every empty seat was immediately filled with enormous, salami-scented men.

At least that was how Kelly described it. She spent the entire flight strolling up and down the airplane's center aisle, returning to Valerie every ten or fifteen minutes to offhandedly complain how she was the only one without a seat. Valerie soon ran out of witty responses, then patience, and finally found other things to occupy her attention.

She had tried talking with Amelia, but that came to an abrupt halt. The old man between them, while neither large nor smelling of meat, clearly felt that any conversation that he could hear was a conversation he could join. Within moments Mel had pretended to fall asleep, and Valerie took a trip to the lavatory. When she returned, she was wearing her headphones with the music turned up loud enough to be heard in the cockpit, and that seemed to do the trick of buying some privacy.

In the end, she spent a fair portion of the trip staring at the mysterious crystal. Its veins of primary colors seemed completely random at first, but the longer she stared at them, the more she began to question that assumption. There was something ineffable about them, something that gave her the sense that these jagged strands were anything but arbitrary. She felt there must be some meaning behind them. Or in them.

After a while her eyes grew heavy and her mind began to drift, her awareness diffusing into that soft place between wakefulness and sleep. On the edge of that netherworld, she felt as if she could almost read the veins, almost hear some kind of song they were singing. As she listened, the music in her headphones faded to a distant background whisper and it eventually seemed like the crystal was singing directly to her. There was a story in those disjointed harmonies, a message that her subconscious mind seemed to latch on to, but that could not be articulated in words.

Then the plane jerked and they were landing at the Keflavik Airport in Reykjavik. Her eyes shot open, hands clenching the stone tightly to make certain it didn't bounce away...and the world was normal once more. Aerosmith was blasting in her ears, and she was suddenly aware that she had gone through her entire playlist. Twice.

Valerie and Amelia made their way through customs with no fuss and little conversation. Even Valerie—with her unquenchable desire for attention and the need to disturb the most irrelevant status quo—knew better than to behave like a smartass in an airport. People get detained that way.

Kelly, on the other hand, more than compensated for Valerie's good behavior. Bursting with energy from being confined to whatever nowhere she called home when Val refused to pay attention to her, the blond figment of Val's imagination wandered the queues, passed back and forth across every barrier labeled 'No Return Past This Point' in four languages, and stood behind officials as they reviewed passports. She issued a litany of creative warnings about each traveler, ranging from commentaries on their appearance to calling out illicit and morally-questionable belongings they were most assuredly attempting to smuggle into the fair kingdom of *Islandia.*

It was mid-morning on Wednesday by the time they had cleared customs. They purchased three espressos and a baguette at a small stand before approaching a bank of rental car agencies near the exit. Valerie had downed two of the espressos prior to being summoned to the counter by a woman with a severe bun of dark brown hair and a hint of eye shadow. The makeup was tasteful, perfectly matched with her crisply pleated uniform, and Valerie knew she must be tired because the clerk's attractiveness didn't bother her in the slightest.

"Góðan eftir—" she began, but Valerie immediately cut in with caffeine-fueled enthusiasm.

"Hi. We just arrived. From...well, I suppose you don't care where we came from, do you? I bet you get a lot of people telling you where they just came from, and you probably don't care at all." She grabbed the third espresso from Amelia's hand, took a big swallow, and handed it back. "I wouldn't. But I mean, it's your job to be pleasant, right, so you have to just listen anyway, don't you?"

The woman glanced over at Amelia, who just rolled her eyes, and then the attendant returned her attention to Valerie.

"Welcome to the Keflavíkurflugvöllur Thrifty. What can I—"

"Holy crap!" gasped Valerie. "Wait. Say that again."

"Keflavíkurflugvöllur."

"Kepler week ahh..."

The woman pronounced the airport's name syllable by syllable as Valerie followed along.

"Why are you doing this?" Kelly asked, materializing next to the woman behind the counter. "You aren't going to remember this in ten minutes."

"I'll remember it," she shot back.

"She didn't say you wouldn't, Val," Amelia interjected. Then she realized what was happening and tried to edge in front of her friend. "Maybe I can—"

"Shhh shhh shhh shhh," Valerie hissed, pushing her back. "I got this."

The clerk looked at Amelia with a patient smile. "Has your friend been drinking on the flight, perhaps?"

"No," Amelia sighed. "She actually handles alcohol just fine. A little too fine, honestly. Exhaustion mixed with caffeine, however, brings out this special person you're seeing at the moment."

"Will she be safe to drive?"

"Oh, yeah. Her reflexes seem to be wired to some part of her nervous system other than her brain."

"You are certain?"

"I'm right here, you know," Valerie said indignantly.

To demonstrate, Amelia reached out to flick Valerie's ear, and the martial artist's hand shot back like lightning to swat her away.

"Trust me," Amelia said to the clerk, "she's fine. Annoying, but fine."

Val spun to grimace at her friend. "Do you mind?" She turned back to the brown-haired woman. "Do you have any motorcycles?"

"Val..." Amelia grumbled.

"Oh. Right. What about a sports car?" The woman seemed surprised at the request, so Valerie added. "You know, something that corners well, and can get up to eighty in under five seconds."

"We actually do not rent any 'sports cars'. They do not do well on many of the roads here."

"Okay...What about something big and powerful. Like for off-roading."

"Yes, we do have several Toyota Land Cruisers in our fleet."

Valerie's eyes brightened. "I'll take it!"

The woman turned to her computer, but a moment later her expression transformed into a mask of polite disappointment. "Unfortunately, they are all in service at the moment. The first one that will be returned won't be until Monday."

"What?! Well, maybe I'll check with one of the other agencies."

"If you like, but we all draw from the same pool of cars."

Val grunted. "Nothing else?" The woman shrugged an apology back. "What about something with tinted windows?"

Amelia nudged her. "Val, I'm tired. Can we just—"

"Fine, fine." Valerie smiled at the woman. "I tell you what . . . can you put a hold on that Land Cruiser so we can trade up when it comes back?"

"If you like."

"I like. Until then, just give us the slickest car you have available in the pool at the moment."

"Of course."

With a deft clicking of keys and mouse buttons, a printer started spewing forth a library's worth of rental agreement paperwork.

• • ● • •

Valerie and Amelia stood in the car lot, staring at the vehicle in parking space number seventeen.

"You have *got* to be shitting me," exclaimed Val as she looked at what was surely the frumpiest car in the northern hemisphere.

"I think it's cute," chimed Amelia as she lightly ran her fingers over the rectangular pink chassis.

"It's a box. A tissue box. With wheels. Coated in Pepto-Bismol."

"It's pretty," Amelia replied. "A bit like a Christmas present."

"I'm surprised they didn't paint polka dots on it."

"Maybe they wore off." Amelia suddenly recognized that there was an opportunity here. "Say, Val. This is definitely not your kind of car. Why don't you let me drive?"

Valerie gave her a cold, hard stare, and then just when Mel was expecting a snort of refusal, Val tossed her the keys.

"Knock yourself out."

• • ● • •

"There."

"No."

They drove a little further. Another American chain restaurant came into view. Valerie pointed. "There."

"No."

"We're going to run out of options if we don't—"

"I didn't fly all the way to Iceland to eat the same greasy crap I can get in the States."

"I like greasy crap."

"I know," responded Amelia. "I don't."

"Yes you do."

"No, I don't."

"You eat it all the time."

"Because you always insist on going to greasy crap-au-rants. Try something new, Val."

Valerie turned to where Kelly was sitting in the back seat, angling for a vote of support. "You like grease, right?"

To her great surprise and disappointment, Kelly replied, "I'm with Mel. Try something new for a change."

"Seriously? You too? Fine," Valerie relinquished, and returned to scanning the buildings along the side of the road. "How about there?" She pointed to a small building with a long, unpronounceable name. There was a menu posted next to the door, so she was fairly certain it was a restaurant.

Amelia pulled into the parking lot.

• ● ● ● •

The three of them sat at a small, white table in the small, whitewashed restaurant, in a city of white-painted buildings. Any other person on Earth would deduce that they were in a country of conscientious, maybe even fastidious, people. Valerie kept looking for the catch.

"They're hiding something," she whispered to Mel.

"Just look at the menu," her friend replied.

"It's too clean. Nobody's this clean. And definitely not an entire city of clean people."

"Just look at the damn menu already!" Amelia and Kelly said in unison.

She did. A waiter soon approached the table, and an order was placed. The process involved a lot of pointing, some surprised looks, a few skeptical looks, and ultimately some placating smiles, but in the end they were fairly certain they had ordered both food and drink. The latter came almost immediately, and was tasty if not exactly what they were expecting. They took this as a promising sign.

"So," Amelia began, "I assume you have absolutely no plan whatsoever."

Val looked hurt. "Of course I have a plan." This elicited skeptical looks from both Amelia and Kelly.

"Okay, let's hear it," replied the one who wasn't imaginary.

"We drive east. Then . . . maybe north. You know, before we hit the water."

"I see. And that's it?"

"More or less." Valerie took a swallow of something that was beer. Or at least beer-ish. Or...

"And how do we know if it worked?"

"I have a feeling we'll know it when we see it."

"See what?"

"Whatever 'it' is."

Amelia shook her head. "And what if it isn't a 'thing'? What if it's a place. Or an event. Or a conversation, or—"

"Yeah, yeah, yeah," Val interrupted. "This is what I'm saying. Whatever *it* is, or whatever happens, I think we're going to recognize it." She turned to Kelly. "Right?" Kelly just shook her head in disappointment.

"I think," offered Amelia, "that our first stop should be the university."

"What? Have you lost it? I'm not wasting my time talking to some ivy-covered professor type. Not unless there's no other choice."

"Iceland's a big place, Val. We need to find out what's written on the map."

"Be serious. Iceland's slightly larger than a postage stamp. How long can it take to explore? We'll drive around for a few days, and if we don't find anything, then we'll—"

Kelly interrupted. "She's right, Val. We may not have a lot of time. What if—"

Valerie lowered her voice and replied to Kelly out loud. "What the hell are you talking about? We've got five days before I even get a real car. We've got time."

"Valerie," Kelly replied in a serious tone, "I really think we should go to the university first."

Valerie turned fully sidewise to stare into her green eyes.

"What is she saying?" asked Amelia.

"That she thinks we should go to the university." Valerie shook her head in disappointment. "Since when do *you* want to sit around doing research?"

"I've got a feeling about this," Kelly answered. "We need to learn what those runes mean, and we don't have a lot of time to spare."

"You've... You've got a *feeling*? What's next? Hug therapy?"

"Val," Amelia said as she put her hand on her friend's arm. "It's the sensible thing to do."

"Which is why," retorted Valerie, "I don't want to do it."

Her two friends stared her down. Seconds ticked by.

"Fine," Valerie finally relented. "So how do we go about finding someone to talk to at this university?"

Amelia smiled. "I already did. There's a center associated with it. It's called the Arni Magnússon Institute, and they specialize in ancient stuff. Like the map."

"And we can just walk in?"

"I made an appointment for tomorrow afternoon. One pm."

"Mel! You made an appointment without even checking with me first?!" Amelia just stared at Valerie, her eyebrows expressing a clear message: of course, because we both know you wouldn't. "Yeah, alright. You're right. I know." And then after a pause, "Thanks."

The food arrived then. It had an aroma that spoke of oceanic flavor palates and culinary adventures heretofore unimagined. Valerie didn't care. She was being forced to act rationally, and she was hungry. Nothing else mattered, so she dug in with gusto.

• • • • •

Khalfani sipped her morning haljra, wisps of steam from the dark, coffee-like liquid slowly drifting over the rim of the earthenware mug. Neither exquisite nor exceptionally functional, the vessel was a handmade gift from a young child many years ago, and her favored cup. Its stark contrast to the delicate china upon which her untouched breakfast had been served felt like a whispered promise of a more carefree life. Perhaps someday such a future would call to her.

Meraya watched the predawn shadows shift a lazy dance on the frame of the office window, her own breakfast similarly untouched on the opposite side of the gray quartz desk. The assassin was dressed in an outfit of dark leather under a brown, chiffon robe. The outer garment was simple and plain, crafted to permit her to move unnoticed in crowds yet easily removed and quickly rolled into a small bundle. The leather's pattern was designed to help her blend into shadows, and the material was so supple that it was completely silent in movement. Meraya's hair was a reddish brown today, dyed from the black it had been the day before, and pulled back into a short ponytail. It swished as her attention returned to the First Mother.

"Unless there is no choice but to act, it is imperative that you remain undetected," emphasized Khalfani. "If all goes well, this will be nothing more than an uneventful holiday to Havlanti for you."

"Yes, Your Holiness."

"Do not take chances. Gabriel is very sensitive." *Why am I repeating myself? Because I'm worried,* Khalfani realized, but continued despite the awareness. This was too important to allow for any uncertainty. "Only if it appears that he is going to fail—"

"I understand, Blessed Mother," Meraya interjected. The morning was slipping past with its usual celerity, and she would need time to leave the Syntrodome and get into position before the Champion was underway.

Khalfani took a deep breath. Few ever interrupted the First Mother, and the implications were not lost on her. But she also heard a compassion in the young woman's voice that balanced out the impatience, and...was that just the barest hint of amusement?

Meraya softened her tone further. "And don't worry, Your Holiness. I'll keep him safe."

The First Mother smiled at that. "I know. I know you will, my child."

• • • • •

Side by side, Gabriel and Khalfani entered the large, desk-lined entry foyer of the Syntrodome, an august entourage following at respectful distance. The rest of the Chakrava were there, escorting him directly from a private audience where they had given Gabriel an additional blessing in private just minutes earlier. Aliesha and Portalia, along with several other training partners, were further back. They had stolen him away after the prayer in the High Temple the previous evening for a different kind of blessing, one focused on good food, fine wine, and plenty of laughter. There were others in attendance as well, most he recognized but a few that he did not, such as the small figure with the tattoo on the side of their temple. It was not strange to see a few unknown faces, however. The work carried out within the Syntrodome required the efforts of so many, and Gabriel could not possibly remember them all. Nor was it surprising that people would want to be here for this moment. After all, the success of the Champion was of paramount interest to everyone.

As they approached the tall doors, Khalfani returned to expressing her concern. It had been the central topic all morning, and the First Mother was being uncharacteristically chatty. Gabriel recognized that as a sign of deep concern in the normally reserved, contemplative woman.

"You'll be careful," she said. "Are you certain you have everything you need?"

Marissa, his own mother, had said the very same words to him when he left Massaea, and the coincidence made him smile.

"What?" Khalfani asked at this unexpected reaction.

"Is this why you are called the First Mother?"

She stopped short, and then understood. The First Mother laughed lightly, and Gabriel felt a sincere, loving warmth carried in the sound. Then she took Gabriel's shoulders in her hands.

"Perhaps it is." She pulled him close into a long embrace and spoke softly for only his ears. "Oh, my son, you have been such a blessing to these eyes and these walls. Whenever I think I know what to expect from you, you surprise me." She pulled away again. "Perhaps that is why the future chose you. Return safely to us."

"I will, Your Holiness." Then quietly, only for her ears. "I will, Khalfani."

"Take time to rest on your journey to the coast. You are as safe as anyone could ever be here on Aerth, but once you reach Havlanti you must be on your guard at all times. Remember that the other world's Champion will be the best they have. Trained ruthlessly, with discipline and strength. She will be the ultimate warrior, with but one focus: to kill you."

• • ● • •

"Kill me," Valerie begged after another round of violent retching. She had practically wrapped herself around the delicate porcelain toilet to even fit in the stall. The tiny bathroom was clearly not designed with this in mind.

"Are you feeling better?" asked Amelia. "Can you speak now?"

"Kill me."

"Oh, poor hon. You don't mean that."

"Yes she does," piped Kelly, who stood behind Amelia with a cruel grin on her face.

"Shut up, Kell," moaned Valerie.

"Are you ready to come out now and—" Amelia's question was curtailed by another round of indelicate hurling. "Maybe not just yet."

After two more attempts to puke up her toes, Valerie leaned back, wiped her mouth with a fresh swath of toilet paper, and called out. "Did you look it up?"

"Are you talking to me?" asked Mel.

"Yes, you."

"What did you want me to look up?"

"Whatever the hell they just served me."

"What was it called again?"

"I don't remember," Val admitted.

Then suddenly Kelly was in the stall with her. "Hákarl," she provided with a little too much glee.

Valerie repeated it for Amelia, then began to spell it. "H...A...K..."

"Found it," Amelia called out as she scanned the search results, then selected a link. "Here we go. Kæstur hákarl, or just hákarl for short is..." Her face paled a little. "Oh. Oh my."

"What?"

"Nothing!"

"Mel," Val hissed threateningly. "Just read it."

"Oh, trust me hon. You don't want to know. Let's just get out of here and find a Burger Treat. Or maybe some other familiar—"

"I hate Burger Treat. What they call meat, and what they do to it, is a crime against nature."

"You may feel different about that if—" Amelia began

"Just tell me!"

She took a short, stoic breath and started reading again. "Kæstur hákarl, or just hákarl for short, is the Icelandic national dish of cured, rotten shark, whose putrid smell is said to—"

"Bullshit! You're making that up." Valerie stood and flushed the toilet.

"Wish I was, hon."

Valerie emerged from the stall and grabbed Amelia's phone. She started scrolling through the article, muttering to herself until she reached the pictures. Then she suddenly thrust the phone into Amelia's hands and rushed back and fiercely embraced the toilet once more.

After Val's heaves settled down once again, Amelia said, "You shouldn't have looked at the pictures."

Another flush, and Valerie returned. "What sick bastard would think to do that to a tourist?"

"Who would think to do it to a shark?" wondered Mel.

Kelly, checking herself out in the bathroom mirror, called back over her shoulder, "I really love Iceland. Don't *you* love Iceland? *I* love Iceland. This place is so much fun!"

Valerie shot her a dirty look. "If I imagine you eating putrid shark..."

"Doesn't work that way, girlfriend. You know that."

"Sometimes I really hate you, you know."

"Of course you do. I'm too much fun for people to not be at least a little jealous."

Amelia tapped Valerie on the shoulder to get her attention.

"Are you good enough to go back to the table now?"

"Yeah." Val checked her appearance in the mirror. "I'm definitely ready. Let's go."

They emerged from the bathroom and navigated to their table. As Amelia was pulling out her chair, Valerie picked up her leather jacket and turned towards the exit.

"What are you doing? We haven't paid yet."

"We also haven't sued yet. I think that makes us even."

Amelia shook her head in resignation, then quickly threw a few bills down on the table. "Wait, Val!" she called out, then rushed after her.

As Amelia left the restaurant, a figure wearing a hooded sweatshirt stood up and followed.

• • • • •

Outside, Valerie had reached the car and stood waiting, hands on her hips. "Keys," she called out as Amelia walking toward her at a leisurely pace. At the doo to the restaurant, a figure in a gray, hooded sweatshirt had just emerged. After a momentary glance at the two foreigners, the stranger turned right and walked toward the far side of the building.

"Keys," Val repeated.

"I gave them to you. At the table, remember? You said you wanted to drive after—"

"Oh, right."

As Valerie began patting down her pockets, Kelly knocked on the car window. She was sitting in the driver's seat. "You left them on the table, brainless."

"Shit," she muttered, then started back towards the restaurant.

Amelia took a few quick steps to catch up. "What...?"

"I left them on the..." Valerie stopped midsentence, distracted by a glimpse of gray just around the corner of the building. Something wasn't right.

"On what?" Amelia prompted.

Val shushed her and pointed at the corner of the building. As if on cue, a hooded head appeared around the corner to peek at them. Valerie instantly broke into a sprint, shouting at Amelia to circle the building the other way.

Valerie rounded the corner, but found nothing save an empty parking lot. She ran to the next corner and nearly collided with Amelia coming the other way.

"Did you see anyone?"

"No," Mel replied. "You?"

"Nothing."

"There was a back door by some trash bins," offered Amelia.

"Okay, go make sure nobody comes out of it!" shouted Valerie as she dashed back to the front of the restaurant.

No one was there, and no cars had moved. She peered into all the windows just to be certain no one was hiding in a vehicle, then went searching inside.

Waiting by the backdoor, Amelia soon heard some raised, angry voices, including Valerie's. Shortly thereafter, Val emerged, followed by a red-faced employee yelling something in Icelandic. Valerie ignored him.

"Whoever it was, they aren't in there."

The hooded stranger seemed to have disappeared into thin air.

With a glance over her shoulder at the man still shaking an angry fist and yelling something that contained far too few vowels for Valerie's liking, she urgently ushered Mel to their car. "We should probably get going."

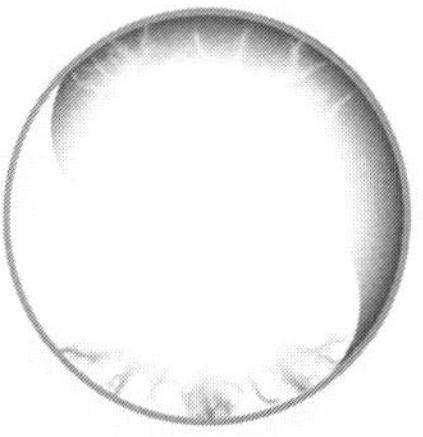

CHAPTER NINE:

Being Followed

That night they stayed in a small flat Amelia had reserved before they left. She assumed it would not occur to Valerie to think of things like lodgings, and had slept in the back of cars on too many occasions as a result of that. Her best friend had many wonderful qualities. She was intelligent, capable, fiercely loyal... Well, she had at least three wonderful qualities. Funny. Val's definitely funny. So that's four.

Not that she was really counting. They had been like sisters for as long as she could remember, and no ledger could capture what they meant to each other. *Besides,* she mused as she attempted to ignore the industrial-construction-machinery rumbling of Valerie's snores echoing out from the adjacent room, *it's not always clear just what's a positive or a negative with her.* For example, Amelia needed to know what tomorrow had in store, but Val had no concept of what it meant to plan ahead. Instead, she relied on an almost supernatural talent for rolling with whatever punches life threw her way. Was that a good thing? A bad thing? Or was it just... *a* thing. Amelia appreciated that Valerie's approach to life worked, and sometimes even led to some pretty amazing experiences she would never have had. For herself, however, improvising like that was simply not an option. She would come to a screeching halt until a plan could be pieced together.

Amelia suspected that was why she rarely dated. Val would catch a glimpse of a guy and after a ten second prowl she was hooking up with him. Men were mesmerized by her and did whatever she asked. Honestly, it was annoying as hell, particularly because Valerie never gave a damn about them. Not that they knew this, of course... at least not before it was too late.

Ironically, the situation had been exactly the opposite when they were younger. As the pair hit their teens, Amelia developed first. She wore perfume and sexy clothes; Valerie wore bruises and smelled of stale sweat. Martial arts was Val's life, and it came before everything else. Back then she rarely even brushed her hair, and had once literally laid someone flat for suggesting she put on some eye shadow for an awards ceremony.

It was funny to remember how she, Amelia, used to be the more outgoing of the two. That had definitely changed over the past decade. But some things had not. Amelia was still the stable one. Kelly may have been Val's immediate mechanism for coming to grips with the death of her parents back in the early years, but Amelia had always been the true rock to which she clung. Mel may not have had answers for everything, but she was flesh and blood, and sometimes there is no substitute for a real shoulder when the harshest tears are burning down your face.

Amelia's parents had welcomed Valerie into their family. Tried to, at least. Valerie could never bring herself to open up to them, which was not really a surprise. Val trusted essentially no one beyond Amelia and Kelly. Amelia suspected that her friend held a part of herself distant even from her own grandparents after that terrible tragedy, unwilling to feel dependent upon any adult lest that support get ripped away from her like her parents had been. Only Amelia could be trusted.

That trust became a cornerstone of Amelia's world. As the fourth of five siblings, she valued nothing more deeply than being that essential to someone. Valerie became her focus, her cause, and as they grew older their stark differences in interests and personalities somehow drew them closer together. Maybe it was because they both fought so hard to never let anything come between them. No, not *maybe.* That was definitely it. They had invested so deeply, so completely in each other that no difference would ever separate them. They were sisters more than any DNA analysis could assert. She would sacrifice anything for Valerie, and she knew beyond any doubt that the same was true in reverse.

They needed each other. If not for Valerie, Amelia would have no life. She would teach yoga, read, and sleep. She'd probably own a dozen cats by now. Valerie brought weird chaos into her life in the form of esoteric conferences, strange interactions with mysteriously-accented men in back alleys of foreign countries, and new and terrible forms of music at the concerts of musical groups no one had ever heard of—and if there was a benevolent deity in the universe, no one would ever hear of again.

And if not for Amelia, Valerie would eat nothing but cheeseburgers. She would sleep only in the back of rented vehicles or in the beds of objectified and misnamed men; she would accomplish basically nothing. It was Amelia who remembered to register her friend for Krav Maga competitions, who would remind her to pay her electric bill...seven times last year alone. If not for Amelia, Valerie would never learn what was written on the map, and they would wander around Iceland in hopeless circles until the world ended.

And that was precisely what she dreamt when, with her head buried beneath a pillow to drown out the snoring, she finally fell asleep.

The next morning the friends grabbed pastries and coffee from a small corner bakery and ate them while exploring the quaint, unpronounceable streets of historic Reykjavik. With irrational commitment both insisted they would not go anywhere near the Hallgrimskirkja, as any towering cathedral of that grandeur was clearly designed with nefarious intentions. So naturally, when the doors opened at eleven, the pair were at the front of the line. Their theories of evil, covert societies and next-generation Illuminati plotting to destroy civilization with genetically-engineered guinea pigs simply had to be confirmed.

By noon they were back in Miðborg, the central district, and sharing a sandwich of Cuban descent at a restaurant across the street from the Arni Magnússon Institute. They studied the people who came and went from the Institute like two spies building dossiers on potential threats. If anyone glanced their way, Valerie immediately took a picture of them with her phone while Amelia looked away in blushing embarrassment.

• • • • •

The ride to the seaside town of Praedon Vahl was awkward for Gabriel. In his Circle, carts were for carrying goods, not people, and it felt strange to simply sit there as the scenery rolled past. It felt impractical, as well. Even in summer the air in Therspia carried a chill that he and his thoroughly unnecessary honor retinue could have warded off by walking. Instead, they sat in silence, their cloaks pulled tight around them as the wagon rocked and swayed. He could have gotten here much earlier on foot, but the First Mother had been insistent. "There is a right way and a wrong way to do things, my son," she had said. "You are the Champion of an entire world. Be gracious, and let us show you our respect."

When he had turned his attention inwards to sense the proper choice, he had found only contradiction. The Beacons told him that time was growing very short, yet they also sang that the First Mother's wisdom must be heeded. The guidance was simultaneously 'make haste' and 'be patient and stately'. It made no sense.

• • • • •

Meraya arrived in Praedon Vahl by midmorning. She brought her golden mare to a small facility at the edge of town where they would either keep one's horse for a pre-specified—and pre-purchased—duration, or exchange the animal for a token that could be used to take a horse from a similar stable anywhere around the world. Not knowing how long this assignment would last, she took the token and hurried down to the waterfront.

The freighter christened *Sun Haze* was lashed to the pier, and a group of women stood in idle conversation at the foot of the gangplank. Meraya hailed them and explained that she needed to travel to Havlanti, idly mentioning her desire for a quiet, secluded voyage where she could work on her writing without disruption. Coins and handshakes were exchanged, and she was soon onboard and headed for the quarterdeck.

From atop a hill to the north, leaning against an old, abandoned barn, a cloaked and hooded figure watched the assassin disappear into the bowels of the ship.

• • • • •

The wagon deposited Gabriel a dozen paces from the pier where a light freighter was waiting. The captain, who had been standing behind the gunwale, came to meet him as he approached.

"You must be Gabriel," said the woman in a weathered voice. "It's an honor." Her face was like tanned hide and her short gray hair snapped back and forth in the wind like a thousand tiny pennants.

"Thank you, Captain," he replied. "The honor is mine."

Her laugh was the sound of breaking waves. "To have the Champion on the *Sun Haze*? The honor's all ours, I guarantee."

The captain escorted him up the plank, then turned Gabriel toward the fo'c'sle. "When Her Holiness sent word that you'd be sailing with us, I had the first mate clear her things down to the crew quarters for the journey."

"You shouldn't have," Gabriel replied, his embarrassment rising. "I just—"

"Pah! Wouldn't dream of it any other way." She gave him a wink and added, "I'd have given you my quarters, you understand, but then you'd have to captain us there."

He smiled. "Of course."

She pushed him toward a door that led to his room, then turned and shouted. "Well, what are you waiting for? We've got the Champion on board, ladies! Let's get him on his way!"

Atop the hill to the north, seated with their back against the barn, the cloaked figure watched Gabriel stumble into his cabin. Then they got to their feet and extended a hand to the wall of the decaying structure.

• • • • •

Valerie and Amelia entered the reception area of the Arni Magnússon Institute through a pair of glass doors that had been etched with a delicate, abstract design. Kelly practically pranced ahead of them, examining the decorative artwork with atypical focus, glancing back only occasionally to see if they were following.

At the far end of the sparsely-furnished space was a large, modern desk, behind which sat a woman wearing a simple yet stylish, black dress. An abundance of hair was captured in an elaborate braid on the top of her head, and she smiled as they approached. With a practiced assessment, she correctly deduced their native language.

"Good afternoon. How may I help you?" she asked with only a barely perceptible Icelandic accent.

"Hi. My name is Amelia. I called a few days ago and—"

"Yes, of course. You spoke with me." She pointed to a dark blue name tag camouflaged against her outfit. "Agda."

Amelia motioned to Valerie. "And this is Val."

"Ah, yes. Ms. Guerrero. It is a pleasure to meet you both. I hope your flight here was pleasant?"

"Well, I wouldn't go that—" began Valerie, but Amelia cut her off.

"It was very nice, thank you. At least as nice as any long flight can be."

"I understand." Agda stood, and they could see that she was at least six feet tall, perhaps even an inch or two more. "All I ever hope for is the flight to be over as quickly as possible." She motioned for them to follow her down a brightly lit hallway. "This way, please."

As they navigated the institute, the receptionist continued. "I have reserved time for you with Dr. Havasharatham. His primary research focus is ancient languages, but he has also studied geology for many years. I thought he would be the best resource for your graduate work."

Valerie gave Amelia a quizzical look and mouthed, "Graduate work?" Mel answered with an expression of amused indifference that spoke clearly to Valerie: *It seemed better than 'she found this map while not having sex.'*

"Nice," Val whispered in appreciative respect.

Agda glanced at Valerie as the three continued along the hallway. "Excuse me?"

"Nice," Val repeated. "It sounds like Dr. Hammershine will be perfect."

Agda smiled. "Havasharatham," she repeated slowly. "But don't worry. He always invites visitors to address him by his first name."

"I hope it's shorter."

"Much. Please, this way."

The receptionist pushed through a glass door that was clearly intended to cordon off a section of the Institute. Valerie assumed the purpose of that separation was specified by the thick black writing on the glass, although to her it was nothing more than an expansive jumble of Icelandic lettering.

Dr. Havasharatham's office was the third door on the right, and Agda knocked softly upon it. A muffled "yes" came from beyond.

"Your one o'clock appointment has arrived."

The door opened, and a short, Indian man—almost comical in comparison to the towering Agda—was smiling at them and motioning with both arms. He spoke enthusiastically, and with a thick accent.

"Yes, yes. Please come in. Have a seat." He directed them to a conference table opposite a large, cluttered desk. "Would you care for some water? I'm afraid it is all I have in here, but Agda could—"

"Oh, no, Dr. Havasharatham," responded Amelia sweetly. "We're fine."

Valerie gave Mel a look of appreciative surprise at her ability to pronounce the man's name.

"Please, call me Navi." He turned to the receptionist. "Thank you, Agda."

She smiled and closed the door, leaving them to speak in private.

Kelly explored the office, skimming titles in a vast collection of books crammed into two wide bookshelves, snooping about the papers on his desk, and examining the array of framed certificates hanging on the walls. She seemed appreciative that at least half of them were tilted slightly out of alignment.

"Agda says that you have a map of some kind," the researcher said as he slid an extensive assortment of volcanic rock samples to one side of the conference table to make space.

"Yes," Valerie replied. She unfolded the piece of parchment and passed it to him. She then picked up one of the rocks to examine it.

"Val!" Amelia hissed intensely, her glare demanding that she put the rock back immediately.

"Oh, no no. Feel free to look at them," Navi offered. "That is what they are here for. Sometimes students come by and..." The words trailed off as he became captivated by the map. It wasn't that the man seemed particularly surprised or shocked, only that the piece of paper was more interesting than his own words and he had lost interest in continuing the sentence.

Navi studied the map intensely for nearly a minute, silent except for the occasional 'hmmf'. Eventually he turned his attention to the material the map was drawn upon, turning it over in his hands and feeling its texture between thumb and forefinger. At last he asked, "Do you have the original?"

Valerie and Amelia exchanged a look; neither was expecting that question.

"That is the original," Valerie replied. "At least as far as I know."

"Well, well. The writing is very ancient. A language that faded from use thousands of years ago. The paper, however, is clearly contemporary." He tilted the page to catch the light at different angles. "The writing was done with ink, so not a photocopy. We will just have to hope it was copied accurately, although I think some parts were likely lost. Still, the contour of the island looks precise, so perhaps—"

"So can you read it?" Valerie interrupted him.

"Oh, yes. But the text is incomplete. Here." He pointed to one block of writing with a stubby brown finger. "This portion talks about two heights that conflict."

"What does that even mean?"

"Now you must understand that the translation is only an approximation. We don't fully understand how the language was used. This word, *hæðslérð*," he pointed again, "has roots shared with many other words. It could mean *plateau*, like some kind of flat place on top of a mountain. Or perhaps even a rough translation of 'world'."

"Could it maybe mean two conflicting worldviews?" asked Amelia.

"I do not think so," Navi replied. "It is not *conflict* in the sense of being different. More like coming together to battle, or perhaps joining forces in a battle."

"That's a pretty wide range of interpretation," noted Valerie.

"It is difficult to interpret correctly without more context. It is..." he rubbed his chin, then continued. "It is like the English word 'cleave'. Without seeing the context, it could mean to break apart or to forge together."

Amelia pointed to another block of text on the map. "What about this? Does it give any information that could help?"

Dr. Havasharatham shook his head. "No, no. That appears to be something completely separate. It states that a meeting is to occur in a place between two tables of Earth's bile."

"Two tables..." Amelia began to repeat.

"Twin tables, to be more exact," he added.

"Earth's bile," repeated Valerie. Her expression said she was losing confidence in the doctor's expertise, and Amelia knew that could quickly give way to no small litany of snarky commentary.

"What would that mean, Doctor?" Mel asked quickly.

"Please, please. Just Navi." He tilted his head as he considered. "It very likely refers to a pair of tuyas, eruptions of lava that have broken through an ice sheet. They form these flat-topped volcanos with very steep sides. Here." He rose from his chair and stepped over to one of the bookcases. Taking down a large, hardcover volume, he flipped to a page and put it on the table between Amelia and Valerie. "Like this." He pointed to a picture. "This one is Búrfell. It is perhaps seventy kilometers east of Reykjavik."

They studied the photograph for a moment, then Amelia asked, "Are there a lot of them around here?"

"Oh, yes. Quite a few. Though not many that are very large like this one. Let me think. Besides Búrfell, there are some others that are well known as tourist attractions. Hlöðufell is also nearby. Herðubreið and Esjufjöll are further away, in the northeast and southeast."

"Are they twins, by any chance?" asks Valerie.

"No, no. Not in any sense that I would say. They are very far apart."

Valerie noticed that Kelly had meandered over to the door and was suddenly very focused on it.

"Although..." Navi pondered. "To the southwest of Herðubreið is Öskjuvatn."

Her attention snapped back. "I'm sorry, what was that?"

"I said that Öskjuvatn is southwest of Herðubreið. It is a very pretty lake formed when the Askja volcano erupted in the late 1800's." He noticed Valerie's confused look. "Öskjuvatn is a lake. Near Herðubreið. Where did I lose you?"

Suddenly Kelly hissed, "Val!"

Valerie turned to see Kelly urgently motioning at the door.

Since when do you whisper anything? Valerie thought at her.

"Someone's there," she whispered again.

Navi had continued speaking. "Anyway, as I was saying, prior to that, there might have been—"

He stopped as Valerie stood and made her way slowly and quietly toward the office door. "Is everything alright?" he asked.

"Of course," she said as if her behavior was the most normal thing in the world. "Please. Go on."

"What the hell are you doing, Val?" Amelia demanded.

At that, Valerie charged to the door and flung it open. A dozen feet away, the hooded figure she had seen the night before was fleeing down the hallway. Valerie gave chase.

The stranger obviously knew the layout, twisting and turning with no hesitation. Valerie's feet pounded the floor as she sprinted after them at breakneck speed, slamming into walls rather than slowing down around turns.

"You're not getting away!" Valerie shouted.

The stranger just laughed and sped around another corner. Valerie followed, only a half dozen feet behind now. This new hallway had closed doors everywhere except midway down on the left. Her prey could only go there. Anywhere else and she would have her hands on them before they could turn the handle.

They turned left.

Valerie followed and found herself in a conference room. The hooded figure had taken several more steps and was against the far wall, still facing away from her.

"Nice little run," Valerie panted, "but you're done. Time to—"

She stopped short as they turned to face her. Valerie instantly recognized the stylized yin/yang tattoo on the side of the stranger's forehead and the traces of multicolored highlights beneath the gray hood of the sweatshirt. Val's eyes grew wide with recognition.

"You?" gasped Val, her voice a blend of shock and outrage. "How can you be...What the hell are you doing here?"

They just stared at her, a sly smile on their face as seconds ticked by.

"Look," said Valerie finally, her tone turned icy. "You might as well spill it. You're not going anywhere."

Praxis's smile broadened. "I wouldn't be so sure of that."

Then they stepped backward. As their back touched the wall behind them, a prismatic shower of sparks outlined their form, and in the blink of an eye they had stepped through the surface and were gone.

• • • • •

When Amelia and Dr. Havasharatham found her, Valerie was meticulously examining the far wall of the conference room, her fingers searching for any indentation or textural difference.

"What the hell are you doing?" asked Amelia.

"You wouldn't believe me if I told you," Valerie replied without turning around.

"Well, it looks like you're massaging a wall."

"Yeah. That's . . . yeah."

"So yes, you're massaging a wall. Ooookay."

"No, I'm *not* massaging a wall. Yes, that's what it *would* look like." Valerie turned to look at them. "Nammy, are there any secret doorways or passages in here?"

"It's Navi, actually," he corrected her politely.

"Whatever. Are there?"

"Secret . . ." he began. "No, no. Nothing like that in here. Or anywhere in the Institute as far as I know."

She quickly replayed the chase in her mind. It didn't help. "Did either of you see the person I was chasing?"

"Not really, no," Navi replied.

She looked at Amelia, who shook her head.

Could it have been . . . She looked over at Kelly, who was standing in the doorway. *Could the person have been a figment of my imagination?*

"I don't think so," Kelly answered. "They were real."

Something wasn't right about this. She, Valerie, had not heard anyone at the door, so how could Kelly have known the stranger was outside? Sometimes her imaginary friend did act on information tucked away in her own subconscious. Was it possible she had heard something but just didn't realize it because she was focused on the conversation with Mel and the doctor?

That didn't seem likely. She was rarely that focused on anything. Never, actually. But if no one saw the stranger except her and Kelly . . .

"Mel, do you remember that morning after I found the map, when I met you at Sally's?"

"Yeah. Of course," her friend replied, concern in her voice.

"Did you see the person who came in right after me?"

"I... I don't think so. What did they look like? Man? Woman? Tall? Short?"

"About medium height. I couldn't actually tell if it was a man or a woman. They had a tattoo on the side of their face though that was pretty memorable. Kind of a yin/yang thing. And short hair with rainbow highlights."

Amelia thought for a moment. "Honestly, no. But I don't think I was even facing that way."

"They sat at a table behind me, so you would have been facing them while we ate."

She shook her head. "Sorry, I don't remember anyone like that."

They all returned to Navi's office and tried to carry on from where the conversation had been interrupted. The doctor returned to explaining about the history of the language used on the map, and Valerie vaguely caught snippets of him describing Icelandic culture, but she found it impossible to focus on the conversation. Her mind was filled with questions, and not at all about maps or volcanos. Who was this tattooed stranger? Was it even a real person, or just a figment of her imagination? She thought back to the fight near Mel's yoga studio. Surely that was real. She had inflicted damage. Bones had broken. That *was* real, damn it.

But real people can't step into walls and vanish in a prism of light. And as far as she could tell nobody but her had actually seen this tattooed woman... man... whatever they were. Of course, the assailants had obviously seen the stranger, which meant that if *this* person was a figment, so were they.

This is not *good.*

Kelly's existence never worried Valerie. She had always understood at some level, even when she was eight, that Kelly was just an expression of some part of herself, an aspect of her subconscious that she needed to personify in order to reach... an icon to provide comfort, guidance... and escape. But there was never any actual, physical contact with Kelly. Not like with...

Although now that she thought about it, had she come into contact with the stranger? No, she hadn't. But she definitely came into physical contact with the assailants, and they had been in physical contact with the hooded stranger. *Definitely not a good sign.* Having more imaginary people appearing in her world was bad enough. Imagining actual, physical interactions... that smacked of psychosis.

Amelia continued to talk with Dr. Havasharatham for perhaps another hour. They eventually showed him the crystal, which immediately captured his attention. He told them that he suspected it to be finely crafted quartz. Specifically, he called it chiral beta quartz, a phrase that Valerie asked him to repeat three times before Amelia finally just had the doctor write it down.

He also suggested having the stone analyzed, an offer that led to a rather unexpected discovery. Valerie was initially against the idea, but when Navi explained that he could perform the test on a very tiny sample filed off from the rough bottom of the hemisphere where no one would be able to tell, she yielded. What didn't yield, however, was the stone. After ruining three diamond-coated files he concluded that whatever the substance was, it was not quartz, and that it would likely remain a mystery unless they wanted to dissolve the entire thing in acid.

In Valerie's 'cut to the chase' way of thinking, the whole afternoon resulted in more or less the exact same plan she had all along: drive around the island until they found something interesting.

"No," Amelia disagreed as they walked along the Skólavörðustígur. "We know that we need to look for a pair of tuyas. And what a tuya is."

"Sure."

Amelia gave her a penetrating look. "Sure?"

"What?"

"Alright. What gives?"

"What gives about what?" Valerie asked.

"I know you don't exactly excel at staying focused, but I think 'what gives about what?' is the longest, most coherent sentence you've uttered since you bolted out of Doctor Havasharatham's office. So what the hell is going on?"

Valerie explained her concern.

After she had finished they walked in silence for a time. Finally, Amelia stopped and turned to face her friend.

"You're not going crazy."

"Really? Because it kind of feels—"

"You're not. And I can prove it."

"You can?" she asked skeptically.

"Blood," Amelia stated flatly.

"Blood," Val repeated, not comprehending.

"You had blood on your hand when you came into the studio. Real blood. That you then went and washed off. And when you came back, you weren't bleeding or cut or—"

"Oh my god! You're right! I totally forgot about that!" Valerie suddenly gave her a fierce hug.

"Real blood, real attackers. Real attackers, real tattooed mystery woman. Man. Whatever."

"Okay, but hang on," Valerie mused. "I'm only actually halfway to not being crazy. What about the whole 'disappearing into the wall' thing?"

"Yeah, that's a little tougher to explain." Mel pondered this for a moment, then offered, "My theory is that it's an aftereffect hallucination from the whole hákarl debacle."

"*Debacle*?" Val asked, simultaneously incredulous and impressed by her friend's ability to pull the word out of nowhere.

"You'll probably see all kinds of things fade into and out of existence until you restore your cheeseburger imbalance."

"You know what? I like the explanation. I'm going with it."

"But seriously, Val. You're fine. There has to be an explanation, and I'm sure we'll find it eventually. And in the meantime, just remember: you're not crazy. Just weird."

"Thanks," she replied with heartfelt sincerity.

Amelia shrugged off the sentiment with a casual, "Of course." And then, as if the universe felt the need to gift her a little karmic token of appreciation, she suddenly spied a store across the street that made her jump for joy. "Oh my god! Look! The Handknitting Association of Iceland! We have to go!"

She was on the move before Valerie could say a word. Not that she would have anyway. That's the nature of sisterhood. Sometimes you just shut your mouth, shove your hands into your pockets, and resign yourself to hours of staring at knotted wool.

With a deep sigh she followed Amelia across the street.

• • • • •

The *Sun Haze* weighed anchor just as morning dawned over the tiny fishing village of Upthain. The freighter did not pull much of a draft, but the ocean floor sloped very little for nearly a hundred feet out to sea and only the very shallow flatboats dotting the shoreline would be able to traverse the final stretch. Even the captain's skiff only made it to within twenty-five feet. Gabriel had to remove his shoes and roll up his leggings to avoid saturating them with saltwater as he splashed the final steps to shore. The water wasn't especially cold, but he was glad to be out of it after only a minute or so.

Upthain was home to a Circle of perhaps two hundred souls, although fewer than a dozen were awake and about at this hour. Gabriel made his way through a seemingly random arrangement of wooden houses to the edge of town where he spied a stable with the three interlocked circles that announced it as a member of the Horsing Guild. It was tempting, and he had enough coin to spare, but in the end he opted for walking. He would make nearly as good time, and the last thing he needed was to worry over a horse.

The road out of town to the east went only a mile or so before forking. When he quieted his mind to focus on his nythlen, the Beacons rang clear. He turned left, and took off at a light jog.

Behind him, Upthain arose with yawns and barking dogs, and people slowly began the daily rituals of a fishing village. By midmorning the *Sun Haze* had taken on food and fresh water in return for a handful of coins, and was preparing to sail north. As the last skiff ferried its way back to the freighter, however, one woman remained ashore. She was dressed in dark-toned leathers beneath a brown robe, and headed inland as the ship departed.

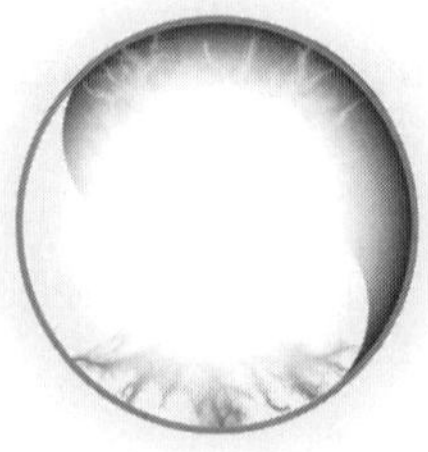

CHAPTER TEN:

Convergence

The frumpy, pink, box-shaped rental had no pickup. If one wanted to get from zero to sixty before lunchtime this was not the vehicle for it, and yet with the beautiful scenery and responsibility-free pause from her daily routines, Amelia was having the time of her life. Initially, at least.

The evening after speaking with Dr. Havasharatham, she and Val had assembled a list of tuyas to visit, prioritizing it by both size and location. More accurately, Amelia assembled and organized the list while Valerie expressed her enthusiastic support by consuming a plate of cheese fries, and then a second plate of cheese fries. And then a beer. Kelly, Mel later learned, had been less than helpful, spending the whole time calling out character names from action movies in a very heavy Icelandic accent. There were times when Amelia was very thankful that she could not hear Valerie's imaginary companion.

When they set out north from Reykjavik the following morning everyone was in a great mood. As the sun made its westwardly way they drove north through the countryside, pointing out one beautiful vista after another and more or less sticking to the travel plan. They hiked around four of the volcanic rises that day, and although nothing presented itself as being of particular significance to either the map or the stone, it was an unquestionably enjoyable day.

By the afternoon of the second day Amelia was still having a grand time, but it was clear that the fabric of Valerie's attention span was starting to fray. Mel grew suspicious when she noticed that they were driving down the exact same stretch of road they had traversed earlier that morning. It was soon confirmed.

"Which way do I turn?" Amelia asked as they came to an intersection.

"Left," Valerie responded without looking up.

"Are you sure? We turned left last time."

Valerie waved her phone back and forth. "Of course I'm sure. I've got the GPS."

As she spoke the words, however, the phone slipped from her hand and landed face up on Amelia's lap. Before Valerie could grab it, Mel looked down to see that Valerie was halfway through a game of Mahjong.

Things got quiet after that.

By the middle of the third day, Amelia wished for quiet. For her own part she said very little, content to focus on the scenery and keeping the car simultaneously on the road and off the sheep. Valerie, on the other hand, was getting increasingly irritable, and steadily losing patience with whatever diatribe Kelly was spouting. By noon, acidic barbs had devolved into an alternating and unpredictable pattern of tense silence and loud yelling. Although she could only hear Valerie's side of the exchanges, she was able to piece some things together. Kelly seemed uncharacteristically driven to discover the mystery of the map and crystal, and Valerie instinctively reacted by losing interest as if there was some kind of metaphysical law of conservation at work.

It was just before two in the afternoon, as they were driving past one of the smaller tuyas, that a particularly vicious string of insults landed them into an icy, uncomfortable silence. Amelia had learned long ago to stay out of things when Valerie and Kelly fought and being confined to a car was not the best way to make that happen. Without warning, she pulled over and parked on the side the road.

"What?" asked Valerie. "Why are you stopping?"

Amelia pointed to the steep-sided hill. "That's one of the places we planned to visit."

"Right, so again, why are you stopping the car?"

"This is as close as we can get without walking." Doubtful, Amelia admitted to herself, but not implausible, and Val was unlikely to question her.

Valerie thought about it for a moment. "Yeah. I guess. Okay," she said, then shrugged and unbuckled.

When they had walked about fifty feet Amelia innocently offered, "I'm thinking maybe you can go around to the right and I'll go left."

Valerie looked at her, clearly suspicious. "You want to split up?"

Amelia shrugged. "We can cover more ground that way."

"And you're not worried about getting separated? Lost? What if we can't find each other again?"

"We can keep tabs on each other with our phones," Amelia suggested. She opened an app and enabled Valerie to track her location. At her urging, Valerie did the same. "See? No problem."

"But you don't even know what you're looking for," Valerie pointed out.

"Neither do you."

"True, but I have the crystal. Maybe it has something to do with that."

"I'll take the chance," Mel replied.

Valerie suddenly understood. "So what you're saying is that you'd rather go stare at rocks alone in the middle of absolutely nowhere than spend another minute listening to me argue with Kelly."

"I never said that," responded Amelia as she started walking. When she was a few dozen paces away she added under her breath, "Not out loud, anyway."

• • • • •

For the first two days of his journey across Havlanti the Beacons guided Gabriel along dirt roads and through grassy fields with equal propensity. He interacted very little with the local Circles, only enough to purchase food and lodging with the money the First Mother had insisted he take. On the morning of the third day he was called to continue east into rockier terrain, and was sent on his way with a cured ham from the old innkeeper. It was a token of kindness from the gentlewoman who had explained that no one lived to the east, so he was unlikely to find any food in those regions.

By evening on the fourth day, the world started to feel…different. The Beacons still called out their directions to him, but an oddness, a sense of foreignness, came over the land. Or perhaps more accurately, Gabriel felt it well up from below. He settled in a field that evening after collecting armfuls of dead shrubbery and grasses for his fire, but just as he was drifting off a low rumble reached his ears. It was unlike anything he had ever heard, and in the darkness he was unable to discern the source. The sound initially came from the southeast and continued for almost a full minute before fading off in the southwest. It was too steady, too constant, to be an animal, and if it was truly beyond his range of vision it must have been moving impossibly fast.

He heard similar sounds every few hours after that, and they kept him from sleeping well. Groggy the following morning, Gabriel resumed his trek. About an hour after sunrise he came upon an extensive stretch of the most unusual rock he had ever seen. It was of unnaturally uniform width, perhaps fifteen or twenty feet across, and wove its way through the countryside as one continuous construct. Someone had painted a dashed yellow line down the center. It had the feeling of being a road, yet the Beacons warned him not to walk upon it. He discovered why not long after when a carriage came speeding toward him faster than any horse could run. It made the same rumbling sound from the night before.

The road was marked regularly with the symbol '848' on its surface, and a variety of unusual placards had been affixed to the top of metal posts spaced every few miles. As he followed the road east, more carriages sped past and the novelty diffused, although he remained baffled at their means of propulsion.

By the afternoon he began passing buildings of unusual design and construction, but he left them behind once he passed between two placid lakes. When the road turned north the Beacons called him southeast, and he was thankful to be back in the wilderness of low hills and scattered shrubs. The strangeness of the structures was a harsh reminder that he had entered a foreign world. That night the sunset was subtly different, as if the normal color palette had been slightly altered by some ingenious yet sadistic artist, and a tremendous sadness came over him. He shuddered with the acceptance that he had truly left his home, his entire world, behind. Gabriel wondered what his family was doing that evening, if they could sense his absence as strongly as he missed their company. It was with a feeling of profound emptiness that he cried himself to sleep that night.

• • • • •

By day five silence was the norm. Amelia had stopped commenting on the scenery and Valerie stared out the car window in silence. They were now driving through Iceland's northeast regions, and Amelia could see that her friend had left 'irritated' behind and was solidly entrenched in 'bored'. If she followed her usual pattern, Valerie would soon hit 'apathetic' and that would be the end of the trip. Once Valerie stopped caring about something, her interest almost never returned.

In the middle of that day they visited Öskjuvatn, then turned north to investigate the last and largest tuya in the area: Herðubreið. Like the others they had visited, Herðubreið had a shallow base with steep sides rising to a plateau, as if someone had taken a run-of-the-mill volcano, sheared the top off, then kicked a million tons of dirt around the bottom. The landscape between the Öskjuvatn and Herðubreið was flat and barren, fields of rock and shrub grasses broken only by the occasional short, scraggly bush. Amelia hummed quietly as she drove, mostly to keep herself awake, while Valerie continued her ceremonial Stare of Abject Boredom.

Kelly leaned forward from the backseat. "You still have the crystal, right?"

Valerie turned to look back. "What?"

Amelia glanced over, but saw that Val was not addressing her and returned her focus to the road.

"The crystal," Kelly repeated. "You still have it on you, right?"

"Of course I have it. What kind of stupid question is that?"

"Still have what?" Amelia asked.

"The crystal," she told Amelia, and then turned to look at Kelly again. "Why are you asking?"

"Just wanted to see it again."

"You…" Valerie wasn't sure what to say. It was not a request she would have expected from her imagination. "Sure," she said at last. "Whatever."

Valerie reached into her jacket pocket and withdrew the stone. She was about to throw it into the backseat when she remembered just who was asking. Instead, she held it up for Kelly to see.

"You can just put it on the dashboard. I can see it from here."

"Whatever," Val replied sullenly, and wedged the crystal between the dashboard and the windshield.

A few minutes later the road curved to the right, and something caught Valerie's eye. Seen against the darker blue of the eastern sky, she thought she saw...

She grabbed the stone and elbowed Amelia. "Stop the car!"

Amelia immediately pulled over while Valerie held the crystal close to her eyes with hands cupped around it to block out as much light as possible.

"What are you looking at?" Amelia asked.

"See for yourself." Valerie held out the stone, her cupped hands shielding it from the evening's light.

The veins in the crystal were glowing. The ruby streaks, now haloed by a soft pink aura, were easiest to see, but the greens and blues were also casting faint illumination.

They exchanged amazed, excited looks. All traces of Valerie's boredom vanished and she was practically bouncing in her seat.

Valerie motioned for Kelly to lean forward. "Look at this!"

From the back, Kelly yawned. "Fascinating. Very pretty. Can we head back now?"

Valerie turned on her. "What the hell is wrong with you?"

"Nothing," Kelly replied. "I saw it. Very nice. What else do you want me to say?"

"What do I want..." Valerie went silent. It was obvious that something was going on with her friend, but it was equally clear that Kelly was not prepared to talk about it yet. "Fine," shot Valerie. "Whatever."

• • ● • •

As the sun descended the crystal's glow became easier to see. At first they assumed it was just a consequence of the fading light, particularly once the road turned left and they were heading away from the sunset, but after night fell it was clear that there was more going on. The further south they went, the brighter the crystal glowed. By the time they were halfway back to Öskjuvatn, it was casting distracting reflections off the windshield.

And then it dimmed.

"Stop the car," directed Valerie. "Back up."

Amelia did and the stone glowed brighter.

"Could this be the place we're supposed to find?" Amelia asked.

They pulled off the road, got out, and looked around. It was difficult to see fine details in the moonlight, but there did not appear to be anything of interest there—just an ordinary stretch of road.

Kelly remained in the car and appeared only vaguely interested but called out, "Does it get any brighter if you walk away from the road?"

They tried it, and quickly discovered that there was an east/west variation as well.

It took about forty-five minutes of hiking west across the barren terrain to find the location where the stone glowed brightest. To their dismay, however, it was an unremarkable patch of ground, covered in the same dirt and shrubs as everywhere else. Some ancient glacier had concluded that it was a nice spot to drop a few large boulders, but that was about it.

Valerie got down on her hands and knees and picked through the grasses and soil by the light of her cell phone. "There's got to be something here," she demanded.

Amelia was scanning the horizon as she replied, "If there is, it's pretty well hidden."

Valerie sat back on her heels and looked around again. "Yeah. Pretty bleak. You know, Iceland isn't as pretty at night."

"They should put that in the guidebook."

Valerie laughed. It was the first time Amelia had heard that sound in days, and it felt like a weight was lifted. Her friend had returned.

"Maybe it's something buried," Valerie offered after a moment, and then returned her gaze to the ground. "Help me look," she said as she started digging.

Amelia joined her, but they soon realized that the soil was far too packed to make any progress without the proper tools. Mel finally sat back in frustration "Well, if there is something underground, we aren't going to find it without a shovel. And some decent light would be nice too."

Despite her newly-restored excitement, Valerie had to admit that her friend was right. They hiked back to the car to find Kelly asleep in the back seat.

Praxis was seated in an old rocking chair by the front window of Mr. and Mrs. Sigurðsson's house. The old couple had gone to bed over an hour before, and their home provided a perfect vantage point to monitor Möðrudalsleið Vegur, the narrow road lined with the majority of the businesses that comprised the sleepy village of Möðrudalur. Valerie and her friend had reserved a room in a rustic inn that was nestled perhaps a hundred feet down the only other road in Möðrudalur, and this house, situated at the intersection of those two roads, allowed Praxis to watch everything while rocking back and forth in the darkness. Quietly, of course. The elderly had a knack for answering nature's call unexpectedly, and at the least convenient of times. It had happened twice already.

As they waited, Praxis couldn't help but wonder if Möðrudalur would go down in history as the site where the two World Champions came together and completely fucked everything up once and for all. They hoped not, if only because nobody would be able to pronounce it. Of course, who would be left to try?

They had been waiting here since Valerie and Amelia had returned, parking that absurd, pink, boxy excuse for a motor vehicle outside of the inn. Praxis had considered moving closer, but their nythlen advised otherwise. This was the right vantage point, so they settled in and failed to relax and enjoy the solitude.

The minutes ticked by, and then there was a shift in the shadows to the north.

"So that's why this was the spot," they mused softly, finally understanding the Beacons' guidance as the unassuming silhouette of Gabriel resolved itself. Had they moved, they would have missed his appearance.

His appearance here, on this night, was . . . puzzling. It was too early. He should have been delayed by something. Praxis had no idea by what, but the estimations of generations of Keepers said The Nexus would not occur for another few days at least. Of course, maybe the other Keepers had gotten it wrong. Who could say just how precisely one can even chart astral motion. Or maybe something else was at play. Maybe the universe was just having a little laugh at them. Praxis was fairly certain that the cosmos was not above such things.

Gabriel paused in front of the Sigurðsson house and a wave of panic washed over Praxis as the young man started to turn their way. They immediately ducked below the window sill.

One breath. A second one. Then a third.

They lifted their head just high enough to peek out and saw that he had turned toward the little inn with the pink box parked outside. Unless a meteor came crashing down from the heavens, it seemed inevitable that the Champions were going to find each other tonight.

They glanced up at the night sky.

"I guess the Keepers got it wrong after all," Praxis whispered to themselves as they stood up and moved the rocking chair back to its original position. "I just hope that bitch hasn't screwed everything up." They walked over to the wall and added, "Both bitches, actually." Then they stepped through the surface and were gone.

• • • • •

As he approached Möðrudalur, Gabriel noted that the buildings here were of similar design as those he had seen earlier, and several of the self-propelled carriages sat quiescent along the streets. There was a single intersection in the town where the road he walked met a second that led off to his left for about a hundred feet before coming to an end. There were decorative lanterns on each corner of that junction, and they cast a strong and steady light—like feathery paper but much, much brighter.

Gabriel stopped to listen to the Beacons, and they Called him east toward one the buildings on the north side of the street. He wove his way through a set of carriages parked out front, including one boxy pink one that caught his attention more than the others for some reason. He paused briefly, but then continued; he knew his future awaited him inside.

• ● ● ● •

Amelia and Valerie sat at a table in the dining area of the small, rustic inn and tavern where they had checked in for the night. A generous salad sat in front of Amelia and she mixed some kind of sweet, pink dressing into it as her thoughts resolved into plans.

"So in the morning we hit the hardware store for some shovels."

"Uh huh," responded Val as she eyed the large fish staring back at her intensely from a textured plate. Yes, it was what she ordered, yet not exactly what she had expected. This was a creature that, even in death, effused attitude. No, not just attitude. Confidence. Defiance. It was daring her to even try to take a bite.

The seconds ticked by, and Val suddenly realized that Amelia was watching her, her head shaking in fascinated disapproval. "What?" Val asked.

"Hardware store. Shovels."

"Oh, right. Yeah. Sounds good."

"Val, just eat the damn thing or send it back. You aren't going to win this staring contest."

Kelly was sitting next to Val, elbows on the table, watching the faceoff between diner and dinee like it was an Olympic showdown. Finally, Valerie took a fork and jabbed. The fish had a wetness to it that neither looked nor sounded appetizing, but Val was damned if she was going to be defeated again. This time she could see the whole fish, knew with certainty that it was neither putrid nor shark, and so—as she saw it—she had the advantage.

She brought the fork to her face and sniffed.

"Not rancid," she observed.

"An interesting threshold of acceptability you've adopted there," observed Kelly.

Amelia watched the process, mystified.

Valerie touched her tongue to the meat, considered. "A little sour, but not bad," she concluded.

Amelia just shook her head and ate a bite of her non-defiant, unthreatening salad. As if that were a challenge, Valerie downed the bite on her fork, and immediately speared another piece and ate that too.

It started with a look of concern, a sense that something wasn't conforming to expectations along the digestive journey. Concern turned to worry, and Amelia and Kelly watched Val's face as her stomach entered into the initial skirmishes of what threatened to devolve into a civil war of gastronomic proportions. Val's expression turned stoic, then angry as she focused, willing herself to keep everything down. And it seemed to work. Valerie smiled finally, nodded, and forked a little more of the fish.

Then she burped.

It was a small burp, but it tipped the balance. The rebels had mounted a resurgence, and this time there was no defense.

"Excuse me," Val said calmly. She stood with dignity, and then tore away from the table in a panic, racing down the hall and crashing through a door marked with the international symbol for 'Vomit Within'.

Kelly shook her head in bemusement, and then vanished to join her friend in the bathroom. Amelia began turning back to her salad, but her attention never made it. The tavern door opened and she glanced up to see a strangely dressed young man enter; then she saw nothing else.

• • • • •

Gabriel pushed the door open and stepped inside.

It was clearly an inn, filled with all the expected fixtures like tables, decorative hangings on the walls, counters, and chairs, but the experience was disarmingly surreal. Everything had a 'too polished' feeling to it, as if the artisan had spoken the objects into existence rather than crafting them with her hands. As he looked around, Gabriel could not shake the sense that this building was somehow an illusion, or perhaps some idealized facsimile of what an inn should be like.

His mind struggled to find something, anything, that he could latch onto as a semblance of normality, and that is when he saw a woman staring at him. She was perhaps his age, with auburn hair pulled back into a ponytail, and soft brown eyes. It was hard to tell how tall she was, being seated at table with several plates of food upon it, but he could see that she was slender beneath a baggy sweater. Her blue denim pants were well-smudged with dirt.

She was smiling. He smiled back. Then she waved at him and he realized that at this moment a friendly face was what he needed more than anything else in the universe.

• • • • •

Amelia couldn't help but stare. The man was utterly captivating, the way his dark brown hair curled around the leather band that kept it in place. Mostly. And those soothing gray eyes, like the sky just before dawn. She could see that he was uncomfortable for some reason, yet even in that discomfort there was an aura of tranquility about him. No, not just about him. It seemed to emanate from his core and permeate the entire room.

He looked over, and Amelia realized that she was smiling like an idiot. She tried to stop, to look away, but couldn't. *I should definitely look away now or he'll think I'm some kind of crazy stalker babe.* He smiled and her heart started pounding. She wondered if she should wave, only to discover that she was already doing so.

Oh my god, he's coming over! He probably thinks I was trying to get his attention. Which I guess I was. And it worked. Oh my god, he's almost here. What am I going to say!?!

Gabriel solved that problem for her. "Hello. Do we know each other?"

His voice was like a velvet cushion, with an exotic accent that she couldn't place. Amelia wondered how many minutes she could last before saying something completely stupid. She bet it was less than one. *How would Valerie respond? She's so good at this.*

"No," Amelia heard herself reply. "But I think we should fix that, don't you?" *Was that me? Did I say that? Oh god, what if I'm being too forward or someth—*

Gabriel smiled and said, "That would be very nice indeed. My name is Gabriel."

"I'm Amelia. It's nice to meet you. Please, have a seat." She motioned to the chair where Kelly had been sitting, or at least so she assumed based on Valerie's behavior before sprinting off to relive her first and last bites of dinner.

• • • • •

Kelly stood outside the restroom stall, a smirk on her perfect lips as she listened to Valerie throwing up. "I want you to know that I'm really impressed."

"Shut up," came the reply from within.

"No, really," she continued. "A lot of people would have realized that they don't have the stomach for Icelandic seafood, but you really seem intent on making it work for you."

"Shut up and die."

"What are you thinking to try next? Maybe something's intestines stewed in—"

The sound of Valerie's renewed retching issued forth from behind the stall door. Kelly waited patiently for her to finish before continuing. "You probably shouldn't order stuff you can't pronounce."

"It was *your* damn suggestion!"

"Oh. Right."

• • • • •

"No, I have just arrived only now," Gabriel replied to Amelia's question. The woman was an intriguing combination of forward and reserved, as if two sides of her were in conflict, each struggling for dominance. Actually, no. It was exactly the opposite, like each side was trying to get the other to take over.

"So what brought you here?" Amelia asked.

"I..." He had not considered that someone from the other world might ask him this. In truth, he had not planned to speak with anyone from the other world at all. The Histories had been remarkably vague about what it meant to be the Champion, providing essentially no guidance whatsoever as to what the contest would be like, and from the way the First Mother described it, he would simply show up, fight, and leave. Having a conversation was... unexpected.

"You?" she prompted him to continue.

Gabriel realized that he had become lost in his thoughts, covered it with a smile. "I'm sorry. I'm a bit distracted." *Why did she blush at that?* "I came here to meet someone." *And why does she now suddenly look so sad?*

This was not the answer Amelia had been hoping to hear. "I see." She recovered quickly, however, and decided to at least make the best of a nice conversation. "So who are you meeting? Your wife?" Why in the world had she added that last part?

"No, no. I'm not married. I actually have never met the person. It is a Calling." Then he wondered if she would understand what the Beacons were and added, "If you know what I mean."

Amelia's eyes suddenly grew bright once more. "So you mean you had a sense that you'd meet someone here?"

"Exactly."

"Well, I'm someone. Maybe I'm who you came here to find."

Gabriel froze. Could that be the case? Had he been sitting here smiling at the woman he was meant to kill? "I suppose that's possible," he replied as casually as he could while he tried to focus on the Beacons.

It was as if his nythlen had gone out drinking. This was the place. This woman was a part of it. *Does that mean she is their Champion? Are we supposed to battle?* He simply wasn't sure. Nothing made sense.

Amelia smiled slyly. "Then perhaps we should try to find out. The sunsets here are really beautiful. Would you care to take a walk?"

"I think the sun set hours ago," he noted.

Okay, Amelia thought. *That was really dumb of me. Come on, brain, you can recover from this.* And suddenly she found herself saying, "I bet if we hurry we can find a few drops of dusk that haven't soaked into the shadows yet." *That was clever, right? Yeah. That was good. And he's smiling. That's a good sign. Now how would Valerie do this?* She stood up and reached out a hand. "Shall we?"

With a touch of hesitation that Amelia found utterly endearing, Gabriel took her hand. She gently pulled him out of the chair and led him outside to not watch the sunset.

• • • • •

Obscured in the shadows of a petrol station across from the inn, Praxis watched with an expression of abject confusion as Amelia and Gabriel emerged into the night and began walking down the street. Hand in hand they were leaning into each other as they spoke in quiet voices and pointing to the horizon where the sun had disappeared hours before.

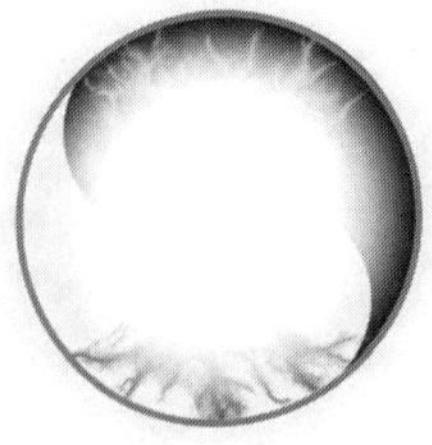

CHAPTER ELEVEN:

Conflict

Valerie sat back from the toilet and rested her head against the door of the bathroom stall. "I swear, this is the last time I'm listening to you."

Kelly smiled as she checked her appearance in a mirror mounted over the sink. "You always say that, but—"

"Well this time I mean it."

"Okay, okay. I promise not to . . ." Kelly trailed off, a look of concern suddenly coming across her face. "Hey, we need to go."

"Right."

"No, seriously. Come on. Enough puking for one night. Let's go back and order something else."

"In case you hadn't noticed, I'm kind of in the middle of something here." Val stared at the toilet, assessing if she was truly finished availing herself of its services.

"No, not in a minute. Now!" She was practically shouting. Kelly could be capricious, but this kind of insistence was definitely beyond the bounds of normal behavior for her.

"What the fuck has gotten into you lately? You've been acting really weird."

Kelly paused, and her tone returned to normal. "Sorry. I guess Iceland just has that effect on me or something. All the excitement and adventure."

Valerie emerged from the stall. "Riiight," she said suspiciously. "Because you're never one for adventure." Kelly just smiled at her. "So do you want to tell me—"

She interrupted before Valerie could finish the question. "Great. Finally. Let's go."

Valerie shook her head in annoyance. "Just hang on a sec. For Christ's sake, Kell, I want to wipe my face off."

She went to the sink and cleaned herself up. In the mirror she could see Kelly shifting nervously behind her, fingers impatiently curling a lock of blond hair. *She must be really wound up about something.*

Halfway through, Kelly impatiently blurted out, "You look great. Let's just go."

Valerie shot her a glare in the mirror, but did hurry up a little. When they finally exited the bathroom Kelly sprinted ahead, arriving at their unoccupied table in seconds and then motioning for Valerie to hurry up.

"That's weird," Val said. "Where the hell…"

She picked up her phone from where she had abandoned it in her haste and checked for a message from Amelia. There was one, and it read: 'Out for walk. Super cute. Back later. Hopefully much later. Don't wait up.'

"Well, good for her." Valerie smiled with pride. "It's about time."

She looked over at Kelly and saw that her friend was even more agitated than before.

"We need to go after her."

Val laughed. *Somehow I think that's the last thing she wants*, she thought in response.

"She's in danger," Kelly insisted. "I have a *really* bad feeling about this. We need to go after her."

Valerie sat back down and smiled up at Kelly. *I'm sure she's fine. That's definitely not a distress text.*

Kelly was suddenly right in Valerie's face, yelling. "No! Listen to me, damn it! I've got a really bad feeling about this! We need to go find her. Now!"

Valerie stared at her, assessing. This was like nothing she had ever seen in her imaginary friend, and it was unsettling. She couldn't imagine Amelia being in danger in this quiet Icelandic village, but the idea of her own subconscious getting this riled up had disturbing implications.

And Kelly's impatience was growing. "I mean it. We have to go now! Val, have I ever steered you wrong?" Valerie glanced down at the fish on her plate. "I'm serious. Have I ever steered you wrong when it matters? I have a really bad feeling about this."

Mel made it pretty clear that she didn't want to be disturbed, she thought back.

"Look. What's the worst that could happen? We find her, she's fine, you make a joke about her staying out past curfew, and we come back. And then you can give me shit for the next five years about how I was wrong."

Valerie finally relented. She called out to a nearby waiter that she would be right back and followed Kelly into the street.

• • ● • •

Amelia and Gabriel turned left down the Möðrudalsleið Vegur. Despite the star-filled, deepest blue-black reality, they bantered about how nice it was to watch the sun melt into the distant horizon as dusk's reds, pinks, and purples were sacrificed like hallowed offerings to the Divine Night. And they laughed at their own folly. Amelia continued to hold his hand, wondering if he could feel the pressure of her tentative hopes. Gabriel, on the other hand, found it difficult to concentrate on anything at all. While he had had relationships in the past, they weren't numerous, and frankly none of those women were anything at all like Amelia. But above and beyond the baffling emotional maze in which he found himself, Gabriel simply could not understand what to do with the conflicting messages the Beacons were sending.

One of those messages was a warning: all of this is about to change.

From behind them came the sound of running feet, and the pair turned to see Valerie rushing toward them. Val glanced to her left as if looking at something briefly, and Amelia realized that Kelly was there as well, running faster than her friend.

"What the..." Amelia muttered, confused as to why Valerie would come after her when she had been quite clear in her text that no company was required. It was her companion's reaction, however, that was beyond comprehension.

As Gabriel turned and saw Valerie running toward him, there was a shock of recognition. This was the other world's Champion. He knew it with the same conviction as he knew he was Aerth's Champion. This was the ultimate warrior about whom the First Mother had warned him, and she was charging at him full speed.

Weeks of training may not have forged Gabriel into a hardened fighter, but they had instilled certain instincts that kicked in of their own accord when a threat was imminent. He stepped back into a defensive posture, lowering his center of gravity and bringing his hands up in front of him, relaxed but ready to deflect any incoming strikes. His face went passive, devoid of expression to ensure he would give no hint as to his intentions, hints that might betray the misdirection he would emote through the techniques of Dhokha di Maath should it come to that. And most importantly, he calmed his inner self, letting his vision of the pre-shadows extend as far into the future as possible.

He was as ready as he could be.

• • • • •

Valerie saw the man drop into a fighting posture. If she had paused to think, she might have wondered if it was so strange for someone to take a defensive stance when a stranger was running down the street towards them. After all, she would have done the same. But in that instant, Kelly screamed with inhuman ferocity: "He's going to kill her!" This was a warning straight from her subconscious. From Kelly. From the piece of herself that had kept her alive ever since...

She broke into a sprint, covering the intervening ground like lightning and lashing out at the curly-haired man. Her fists and elbows struck like cobras, raining blow after blow at Gabriel. In almost ballet-like coordination, her feet and knees augmented the attacks from her arms. She knew her opponent would be on the ground in a matter of moments. She was as fast as they came. No one could evade her attacks. No one ever had.

But he did.

Again and again she watched the man shift and turn in precisely the correct way such that her strikes went awry. His reactions were even faster than her attacks. *Impossibly fast*, she realized. He began dodging and blocking literally the instant she began an attack, and a seed of fear took hold in the pit of her stomach.

He knows my fighting, my style. There was only one plausible explanation: he knew her. This man must have studied her, learned her fighting technique, and that in turn could mean only one thing. This was not a random encounter. Whoever this man was, he had come here prepared to fight her, and quite possibly with the intent to kill.

"You're going to have to kill him," Kelly said with forceful urgency. "It's the only way!"

Valerie doubled down on her offensive, shifting from Krav Maga into Judo. The man shifted with her. *Okay, how about Tai Jitsu.* And again, he adapted. She tried Dambe, the obscure Nigerian form she had studied for a summer after high school, but still he was prepared.

And then she realized something terrifying. *He isn't even making a serious effort to attack. He's...he's just toying with me.* The seed of fear began to bloom, and for the first time since she was a little girl, she began to wonder if she might be outmatched.

• • • • •

The other world's Champion was like a force of nature. The bombardment of her attacks was continuous and blindingly fast. Even with the warning of the pre-shadows, there were times when Gabriel only barely evaded, or was able to deflect her strikes enough to avoid a debilitating injury. She seemed almost unfettered by gravity, with kicks and sweeps coming from angles he would not have imagined possible. In those rare moments when he found an opportunity to strike, they were cautious blows. The pre-shadows warned that striking too hard would give her the opportunity to grapple him, and here was an interesting silver lining to the woman's preternatural speed—she moved so fast that even the brief window of his prescience was sufficient to foresee his own motionless body on the ground should he make a mistake. It was...motivating.

There were moments when his concentration threatened to crack. Amelia—now several dozen paces behind his opponent, for the onslaught had continued to push him back and south along the street—was waving frantically and screaming, although the sounds were muted by his own hyper-focus on the immediate needs of survival. At the periphery of his awareness he realized that townspeople were coming to windows and doors to see what all the commotion was about, but to pay them any heed would come at the cost of shortening his pre-sight, a choice that was simply no choice at all. He needed every advantage he could get.

The fight continued. Seconds stretched into minutes, and now there were brief pauses in the attacks as the combatants took short moments to catch their breath. Never very long, and certainly not enough to speak.

Up until this point Gabriel had not even considered using Dhokha di Maath. Despite all the training with the First Mother, in his heart the method remained an affront against nature, and he would not consider using it unless it was his only option. As the fight wore on, however, he was realizing that that moment was approaching. The woman was tiring, yes, but so was he, and if he had to guess who would wear out first, well...

He saw an opening. She had shifted to her left, and if the woman believed he was going to dodge to *his* left, she would turn to her right. He could then slip behind her and have a perfect opening for a series of strikes to her kidneys, knees, and head. Gabriel formed the false intention, and using the technique of the Deceptive Heart, projected it into the world.

There was no effect. It was as if the woman was not even paying attention to his pre-shadows, and that thought was truly terrifying. *If she's this fast naturally, what chance do I have?*

Despair started seeping into his heart and mind, taking its chilling hold. And as the fear rose from an ember into a flame, the pre-shadows began to shorten. He realized what was happening, knew he had to retreat and get himself under control again, but it was too late. In the instant between recognition and action, the woman had spotted a weakness in his form. His arm was extended just ever so slightly too far, and in the blink of an eye she had grabbed it.

The brown-haired tempest turned, twisted, and suddenly Gabriel's feet were off the ground. She slammed him into a storefront, half against the wall and half onto a window that shattered from the impact. The woman still held his arm, now in both of her hands, and he could see her intention to bring her knee up into his elbow. It would shatter the joint, and there was nothing he could do to stop it.

Then everything changed. She was no longer planning to attack. Her pre-shadow leapt back and away. Why? What demanded this new tactic? Then he saw it. Another pre-shadow: a tiny dart firing down from a rooftop across the street, and it was going to just barely miss striking her in the leg as she leapt back.

Before he could wrap his mind around how any of this could be, the Earth's Champion was releasing his arm and jumping away.

• • • • •

Meraya lay flat on the aluminum roof of a small bakery, her short blowgun extended in front of her. In the street below Gabriel and the otherworld Champion were fighting, and she couldn't help but be impressed. Both combatants were amazing in their own way. The woman was a superb fighter, clearly gifted with a natural talent that had been finely honed over many years. Gabriel's martial technique was less impressive—even strained—yet he held his own. She was convinced that he must have been seeing more than two seconds of pre-shadow. If she were to guess, and she had been making such assessments for a long time, it was probably more like three. Maybe even a little more. No one in a hundred years or more had...

Then she saw it. He was going to punch, but with his arm extended too far, and she saw the pre-shadow of the woman grabbing it, spinning Gabriel over her hip and into the nearby storefront. She didn't understand how he had not foreseen the error, but it didn't matter. The woman was about to kill her Champion, and that could not be permitted.

She brought the slender pipe to her lips. The dart inside was coated with a fast-acting toxin that would stun and disorient, more than enough advantage for Gabriel to finish the job. And the otherworld Champion had her back to Meraya. While it was possible for some people to detect pre-shadows without actually seeing them with their eyes, that gift was very rare. It was extremely unlikely the woman below would ever know what happened to her.

Meraya took aim. Gabriel's flawed attack came to be, and as she had foreseen, the other Champion seized his arm. Things were about to turn very bad for her world. She fired.

• • • • •

"Val! Get out of there!" screamed Kelly.

Valerie knew that tone, or rather her nervous system did, and she responded instantly, diving back and away. She spun around in time to see a shadowed silhouette withdraw from the edge of a rooftop across the street and heard the clatter of some kind of projectile striking a shard of glass from the shattered window behind her.

Time slowed to a crawl as the impossible conflicted in her mind. Kelly had warned her of dangers in the past, even during martial arts competitions, but it was always explainable. She was watching her opponents, and some part of her was processing motions that she could not logically categorize, intents only her subconscious could decode in those split-second moments. That was fine. Even that event in Dr. Hammershine's office, that was *possible.* Unlikely, maybe even suspicious, but theoretically *conceivable.* Maybe she had heard a sound from beyond the door. Maybe some subtle . . . whatever.

But this . . . this was different. This was impossible, truly impossible. She had been completely unaware of the figure on the roof, and the open street held too many variables. Random sounds, countless reflections, odors . . . there was no way any of that could have led to an awareness of the figure on the rooftop or the threat it represented. She simply couldn't have known. Even as the assassin had slipped back, the movement had been perfectly silent. It was *impossible.*

And then she realized that Kelly was still shouting at her, and time snapped back to its normal flow.

"He's not paying attention! Attack! Now!" Kelly was demanding.

She was right. The man had also turned his gaze to the shadowy figure on the roof. He was not paying any attention to her. She could finish this with a single kick to his throat.

"Do it!" demanded Kelly.

Before Valerie could act, a sparkling outline appeared in the wall behind the young man, and the mysterious, androgynous figure emerged. They had lost the sweatshirt from before and were now wearing a simple outfit of grays made from some type of soft, shimmering fabric the likes of which Valerie had never seen before. She could not make out the different colors that she remembered highlighting the stranger's hair, but the stylized tattoo seemed almost iridescent in the moonlight.

As Valerie stood there in shock, Praxis took two quick steps forward. They pulled their arm back, and then, against all rationality, smashed their fist into Kelly's face, knocking her backwards and onto her ass.

Kelly was stunned, although Val couldn't tell if it was from pain or surprise. Then, like an ocean wave assaulting the beach, the world came crashing back onto Valerie's awareness. Whatever manacles of disbelief had held her motionless were gone. Regardless of what was real or not, nobody was going to get away with attacking her friend like that. *And definitely not this asshole.* Valerie shot forward and grabbed the stranger in gray, one wrist in each of her hands.

As Valerie's palms came into contact with Praxis's skin, thousands upon thousands of images suddenly blazed into and through her brain. In just the barest fraction of a second, decades—or perhaps even centuries—of history rushed through Valerie's mind. Images of protest marches, gruesome memories of war, and scenes of uncontrolled destruction were littered through memories of joy, the birth of children, moments of tranquil serenity, and so many more that Valerie simply could not accept it all.

She staggered back, releasing Praxis. The flood of images vanished, and she was once again aware of her surroundings: the no-longer-quiet street in Möðrudalur, the alarmed faces of people staring out of windows and doorways, and the growing sounds of police sirens.

• • ● • •

Gabriel staggered to his feet. He could feel a wetness on the left side of his back where a piece of glass had sliced into him, although not badly. That was a problem to address after the immediates were resolved. Who was the figure on the rooftop, and why had they attacked the other Champion? What was that high-pitched wailing, and why was it growing louder and louder? Who was this figure in gray, where had they come from, and just what had they done? As far as Gabriel could tell, they seemed to appear out of nowhere and then punched... well, nothing. But their hand recoiled like they had struck someone, and in the moment of contact, just for the flash of an instant, Gabriel thought he had seen... what? Almost like the suggestion of gold and red, as high as the otherworld Champion was tall, but the vision disappeared so fast that he was certain it had to have been his imagination. Still, the way the other Champion reacted—how she stared at the ground, and then launched herself at the figure in gray—perhaps there really was *something* there beyond his ability to perceive.

And of course there was this last strangeness. The Champion had grabbed the stranger as if she was going to throw them to the ground, but then immediately let go and staggered back. Why? What had happened to make her do that? And now she appeared preoccupied, almost stunned.

It came to Gabriel that this was the opening he needed, the chance for a fatal strike, but his nythlen was crying out for caution. A great many things were happening, and none of them fit his expectations. The First Mother and the sacred texts had given him the sense that this would be simple. Not easy, but straightforward. Arrive. Fight. Win. Survive. It was to be a ritual combat between two Champions, and two Champions alone.

This... this was not that.

Yes, it was possible that he could strike out now and kill the woman while she was stunned. He could end it all right here. That would be an act of blind obedience towards an expectation that, more and more, appeared to be mismatched with the reality of the moment. No. That was not the right path. Gabriel realized that what he needed now more than victory, more than anything else, was time. Time to think, time to meditate, time to listen to the Beacons in the quiet of his inner self. He needed to understand what his future was Calling him to do, not what people had been telling him to do.

Gabriel looked up the street to Amelia. She appeared to be in a state of shock, as overwhelmed as he at these events. Although they had only known each other for a precious handful of minutes there was an undeniable connection between them. He wanted to explain things to her, to apologize for involving her in all of this.

But it would have to wait. He could see that beyond Amelia two of the otherworld carriages were racing to the fight, white vehicles with flashing blue lights. From the other direction, several individuals in dark clothing were approaching on a different type of conveyance. Sleek, two-wheeled, but with the same flashing lights.

He needed time to process all of this, and it was not going to happen here.

Gabriel began to run south.

The dark-clad figures dismounted and yelled at him to stop.

That didn't feel right, so he spun about and started sprinting the other way, only to find that similarly-dressed people had stepped out of their carriages. Each was pointing some kind of device at him.

He decided to turn right and flee into the darkness of the surrounding wilderness. In that instant he perceived the pre-shadow of a pair of darts flying towards him, wires stretching back to the device one of the men was holding. He began to run, then dove to the left just before the darts passed over his right shoulder. He rolled to his feet, perceived the pre-shadow of a second taser shot, and evaded that as well.

As he once again rose to his feet, he saw a swarm of pre-shadow darts flying at him from multiple directions. There was simply no direction to jump this time.

This isn't good, came the final thought, and then everything went black.

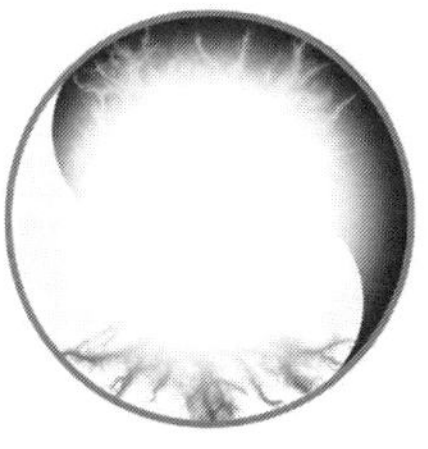

CHAPTER TWELVE:

Respite

Perhaps a ten-minute drive to the south of Möðrudalur, the town of Reykstaðir was nestled in a peaceful, glacier-carved vale of green hills. In the center of that quiet settlement was nestled the peaceful, non-glacier-carved police station and holding jail. And within that building, nestled in adjoining cells, were Valerie and Gabriel.

The jail itself was a testament to the Icelandic mindset. The holding cells were tastefully decorated with calming pictures of idyllic mountain landscapes; scented soaps were placed atop neatly-folded hand towels next to each personal sink. It made its point with aplomb: We advocate living in a civilized culture, and you should too. Start by taking an extra moment to attend to your personal hygiene.

Gabriel's unconscious form had been laid upon a colorful wool blanket stretched over his cell's sturdy cot. He was on his right side, facing away from Valerie's cell, and she could see that someone had bandaged a cut on his back. It had been done cleanly, professionally, and that too said volumes about the Icelandic mindset. They attended to details here.

She stared at his naked back. *Not bad,* she mused.

"Val, what are we going to do?" pleaded Amelia from the small sitting area in front of the cells. She had been practically in tears all night. Her question pulled Valerie out of her preoccupation.

"What?"

"What are we going to do?" Amelia repeated.

"About what?"

"About what?! About this! About everything!" Amelia pointed at her, then Gabriel, then just wildly about.

Valerie sighed. Mel was so excitable. "Nothing. They just put us here to cool off. Maybe we'll get fined for being disorderly or something, but it's no big deal."

"No big deal!?" Valerie could hear the hysterics straining to break free of Amelia's tenuous grip. "This may be just another day behind bars for you, but not for me!"

"Breathe, Mel."

"I've never been in jail before!" she cried.

Valerie shook her head in bemusement. "You're not in jail now. *I'm* in jail. *He's* in jail. You're *near* jail."

"This isn't a time for joking! I'm serious!"

"I'm serious too. And honestly, it seems like a pretty good time for joking. You need to lighten up."

This shut Amelia up for the moment, and Valerie returned to contemplating the man in the adjacent cell. Who was he? Why had he wanted to kill her? Or had he been trying to kill Amelia? Or perhaps neither. He had certainly waged a defensive fight.

"Why do you keep staring at him?" Amelia asked.

Valerie was silent for a moment before answering. "I just don't get it."

"Don't get what?"

"Him. I don't get him."

"Gabriel," Amelia supplied his name while simultaneously recognizing the futility. Valerie would never remember it.

"What was he after? What was he trying to do? Why was he toying with me like that?" The questions came rolling off her tongue.

"Toying with you? What are you talking about?"

Valerie sighed, then stood up from her own cot and walked to the clean, white-painted bars that separated her from Amelia. "Him. I've never seen anyone that fast. I mean, I'm fast. All modesty aside, I'm really fucking fast. It's one of the reasons I win competitions. But him..." She shook her head in amazement. "It's like he knew where I was going to attack before I did. His reactions were...inhuman."

"If you say so. Whenever I've seen you fight, it's always a blur."

"But the weird thing is...what I can't figure out is...if he was trying to fight back or not."

"What are you talking about? He—"

"I mean, he threw punches, he kicked. Not bad form. Not great, but not bad. He had obviously trained a bit, but...his attacks were pretty lame."

"Lame how?" asked Amelia.

"Compared to his defenses they were really slow. If someone can block so fast, why was his offense so shitty?"

"Maybe he wasn't trying to hurt you. I mean, you did charge at him after all. Maybe he was just defending himself."

"But if that's the case, why attack at all? It just made him vulnerable."

"I don't know, Val. I really have no idea. Maybe the whole thing was just a big misunderstanding."

"No. It couldn't have been. Whatever was going on, this guy knew about it. He knew there was going to be a fight, and he had prepared. I think he's studied me."

"Studied you?" Amelia asked incredulously.

"Studied my fighting technique. Techniques," she added, emphasizing the plural. "And what about whoever was on the roof? This guy didn't come alone."

Amelia gave her a puzzled look. This was clearly new information to her, so Valerie explained what she had seen.

And then Kelly was there, calm once again. "It was a setup," she said with her usual nonchalant confidence. "He was there to kill you. Both of you."

Amelia saw Valerie's attention shift, and realized that her friend was now addressing Kelly.

"And you. You have some explaining to do."

"What's to explain?" Kelly retorted. "He's trying to kill you, and you damn well better take him out before he gets another chance."

"No, stop!" Valerie's volume rose a notch. "No more bullshit! What the hell is going on? How did you know about the second attacker? How could you possibly warn me about something that I couldn't have perceived?"

Kelly shrugged it off. "You knew. You heard her intake of breath, and—"

"Her?!" Valerie pounced on the clue. "What do you mean, 'her'? How could you know it was a woman on that roof? I never saw—"

"You recognized the form from—"

"Stop!" she demanded again, a fury blazing in her eyes. "No! You need to come clean with me. I barely saw the figure at all, and there was nothing to suggest a gender. And I was totally focused on *him* before that. Hell, I didn't even hear the police sirens until after you intervened."

"And you're welcome," Kelly said dryly. "You know, for saving your life."

"Look," Valerie said, then took a calming breath. "Yes. You saved my life, and I appreciate that. Really."

"Like I have a hundred times before." Kelly walked through the bars to stand next to Valerie in the cell. "Why are you getting on my case? You're alive. That's supposed to be a good thing, you know."

"It's just... It's just that things aren't adding up." She started running through the list in her mind. "Why were you so intent that I had to follow Mel and that Gary guy?"

"Gabriel," corrected Amelia automatically.

"I told you," Kelly shot back. "I had a feeling that something bad was going to happen. *You* had a feeling. Since when do I have to explain myself like this?"

"Or what about earlier? Out of nowhere you start asking about the crystal, and then when it turns out to be glowing…fucking *glowing!*… suddenly all you want to do is take a nap?!"

Kelly just stared at her, defiant. Then with an angry shake of her head, she walked through the bars again and leaned against a wall in the waiting area.

"That's it? Nothing to say?" accused Valerie. "Do you want to know what I think?"

"I already know what—" Kelly began, but Valerie cut her off.

"I think you know something about this tattooed freak, this…this other figment of my imagination." Kelly just steamed silently as Valerie continued. "I think something's starting to crack inside me, and you're keeping it a secret. Who is this person? And why did they haul off and pummel you in the face?"

"Whoa, whoa. Wait," called Amelia, waving her hands in front of her. "Was this other person dressed in weird gray clothes?"

Valerie turned, clearly shocked.

"I'll take that look to mean *yes*," Amelia noted.

"Do you…" Val began. "Did you…"

"Yeah. I saw him. Or her. Or whatever. But I definitely saw them."

"So…so they're real," Valerie whispered, mostly to herself. She had been through this debate before, even with Amelia's help before, but the events of the previous night had shaken that resolve. *Only something imaginary could interact with her imaginary friend, right?* But clearly not. If Mel saw them, then the figure in gray was real. And there was no doubt that they had punched Kelly in the face. She had seen that, seen Kelly's ass land on the pavement. That was cause and effect in the most unambiguous sense possible.

She turned to look at Kelly. "How did—"

"He's waking up," Kelly interrupted indifferently, motioning over to Gabriel before becoming fascinated with a nonexistent hangnail.

Gabriel groaned softly and Amelia immediately rushed over to his cell. Valerie, however, remained focused on Kelly.

"Explain," she demanded.

"Believe me," replied Kelly without looking up. "If I could explain it, I would."

"You're my goddamn imagination, Kelly! How could—"

Gabriel groaned again, then shifted on his cot. Not fully conscious, but definitely on the edge. Valerie automatically shifted into projecting her thoughts at Kelly as she did when others could hear. *How could someone punch you? That's impossible!*

"I told you. If I could explain it, I would."

Gabriel began stirring more. His breathing quickened as consciousness returned and he shifted again, this time a little too far. With an unceremonious crash, he fell off the cot and onto the floor.

"Wh-where am I?" he stammered.

Valerie finally turned to look at him, her face a smiling mask of sarcasm. "You're in a downy fresh meadow, surrounded by bunnies and kittens."

"Shut up, Val," Amelia shot at her. Then her voice softened and she said to Gabriel, "You're in the Reykstu…the Reykstush…You're in a jail. The police put you here to cool off."

"In a jail…" he repeated.

"It's still the middle of the night. They'll be back in the morning," offered Amelia.

"Why am I in a jail?"

"Because," Valerie offered in a saccharine-sweet voice, "all the rooms at the Waldorf were booked, Sunshine."

Amelia waved her off. "Are you alright, Gabriel? I'm so sorry that Valerie came charging—"

"Valerie?" he asked.

Amelia pointed at her friend in the other cell.

"Your name is Valerie?"

"Guessing you've never been tased before, have you, Sunshine? Don't worry, the effects will wear off soon."

"You…" he began, then used the corner of the cot to leverage himself into a standing position. "You are magnificent."

There was a stunned pause, and Amelia's eyes went very wide. This was very much the last thing she wanted to hear Gabriel say about her friend. "What!?!"

The question was echoed a fraction of a second later by Valerie herself, but with a fair bit more bafflement and substantially less outrage.

"It is a shame that we are destined as we are," continued Gabriel. "But know that win or lose, it has been an honor. I wish things had been different."

Valerie blinked in complete confusion, and then Kelly rushed through the jail bars to stand beside Gabriel as he studied his otherworld counterpart.

"Don't listen to this bullshit, Val. This asshole tried to kill you, and he'll try again as soon as he has a chance. He's a snake, and he's just trying to lower your defenses."

Gabriel watched Valerie as she listened, and said, "You are hearing a Beacon, aren't you?"

"What?" Valerie replied.

"You are the first person I've seen do that since I arrived."

"What are you talking about?"

"Where I'm from, everyone listens to the Beacons, but you are the only one I've noticed doing that since I came to your world."

Kelly's anger was growing, as was the urgency in her voice. "Don't listen to him, Val. He's just trying to confuse you. Disorient you."

Valerie turned away as she tried to wrap her head around what the young man was saying. Meanwhile, Amelia was staring at him through the bars.

"Gabriel," Mel began, her voice demanding in its softness. "When you said 'your world', what exactly did you mean by that?"

"Just that," Gabriel answered. "We are from different worlds. Surely your friend has told you about this, has she not?"

Valerie spun back, irate. His words confused her, yet at the same time they struck a chord within her subconscious. It was infuriating. "What the fuck are you talking about?"

Kelly stormed through the bars and into her cell. "Enough! Stop listening to him! He's just messing with you!"

And then, as if some new cognitive floodlight had been switched on, Kelly looked very different to Valerie. She had seen Kelly in every conceivable mood, from carefree to menacing, but this . . . this paranoia, this insistence . . . was totally foreign. For the first time since Kelly had appeared in Valerie's life all those years ago, she felt disconnected from her in a deeply unsettling way. Kelly had shifted into a new kind of focus for her, no longer a psychological crutch or some complex facet of her subconscious mind. Valerie realized that her lifelong friend—the being that was both anchor and wind when she had been a sailboat lost at sea—had truly independent thoughts.

As she stared, trying to adjust to this disturbing new wrinkle in her world tapestry, a sparkle caught her attention from the periphery of her vision. Behind Kelly, a silhouette appeared on the cell wall, and Praxis stepped through. Kelly spun around to face them as Valerie looked into the other cell. It was clear that both Amelia and Gary could see the gray-robed stranger as well.

Kelly took a step back, and there was a twinge of fear in her voice. "You," she hissed. "You don't belong here."

Praxis smiled. "Sure I do." Then they opened a hand, revealing what appeared to be a fistful of dirt. "This, though, not so much." And they threw it at her.

The particles of soil splayed out as they flew forward, and passed directly through Kelly. Where they intersected her form, holes appeared. An instant later the holes began to arc to each other with a strange, almost electric light. The light connected the holes like fine filaments, then started to separate into gaps. Within moments, Kelly's form had lost cohesion completely and vanished.

"What have you done?!" Valerie blurted out in shock, and then rushed at Praxis. She was about to grab them, but at the very last moment remembered what happened before. She stopped herself.

"Nothing permanent," Praxis assured her.

"What was that?"

"Just dirt. But from his world." They pointing at Gabriel. "Don't worry. She'll pull herself back together in a few hours." Then their smile took on a bit of a vindictive edge. "Maybe a little longer."

"Who...who are you?" asked Valerie.

"Ahh, yes. I think the time has finally come for introductions. My name is Praxis." They extended a hand to shake. Valerie didn't move. Praxis waited, then flashed a roguish smile and winked like a kid caught playing a practical joke. "Good call."

• • • • •

"Okay, *Praxis.*" Valerie shifted nervously. "Can you give me even one reason why I shouldn't beat the shit out of you right now?"

"You mean aside from what happens to you when we come into physical contact? Okay, how about...because I'm trying to help you?" they replied.

"You're...You've got to be kidding me. I risked my life to help you in that alley, you..." Val struggled, unsure how to best swear at someone whose gender she couldn't nail down. "I risked my life for you, and you repay me by what? Following me? Spying on me?!"

"Well, I had to see what kind of person you are, didn't I?"

"Did you? And why, exactly?" Valerie demanded.

"Look, there's a lot to discuss, and I'm not sure this is the right starting point."

"And I'm not sure there's anything to discuss. The only things I know for sure are that you have been following me around, and you seem hell-bent on hurting someone who's an important part of me. That's your starting point, and it isn't a great one."

"Kelly isn't a part of you." Praxis stopped themselves and reflected. "Well, that's not entirely true. But she isn't what you think."

"And again, what reason do I have to trust you?"

"Well, none, I guess." Praxis admitted, then turned to look at Gabriel. "And what about you?"

"What *about* me?" he replied.

"Do you trust me?"

Gabriel closed his eyes for a moment of meditation, then opened them again. "No."

"The Beacons are telling you that I'm a threat."

"Yes, as a matter of fact, that's precisely what they're telling me."

"And they told you that you should kill Valerie."

Gabriel remained silent, staring at Praxis.

"But," Praxis continued, "at the same time, that doesn't feel right to you, does it?" He remained silent, and they continued. "There's another song underneath the

Beacons' alarms, isn't there? A whisper. A Calling so soft, so patient, that it can't be ignored. And for the first time in your life, you don't know what to listen to."

Gabriel finally asked, "What *are* you?"

Praxis ignored the question, a mischievous smile on their face. "Well, I should probably let you give it some thought. You aren't ready to believe anything I say right now." Then they turned, walked up to the cell wall, and vanished into it.

• • • • •

Rays of morning light were settling through a curtained window when Officer Strom returned to the police station carrying a cardboard holder with four cups of steaming coffee. His lined, leathery face contrasted a pair of bright, happy eyes, and he moved about the office with an ease that suggested decades of familiarity. Valerie suspected he could have navigated the desks and doors blindfolded without missing a step.

The policeman bade them good morning with a warm smile as he handed each prisoner a cup. Amelia had finally fallen asleep draped across a low bench, her calves and feet propped on a chair she had pulled over. Strom left her cup on a small table near her head, then returned to speak with the detainees.

He began with the simple questions he had not been able to ask of Gabriel the night before. Name, age, country of origin. Gabriel didn't even get through the first one without a struggle.

"Gabriel," he replied.

"Okay. Last name?" Strom prompted.

"Both first and last, as far as has been revealed to me. It's the only name I've had so far."

After some back and forth, they landed on 'Massaea', the name of his Circle, as his surname, but the friendly officer had become a notch less jovial during the exchange. Discussing his country of origin made it worse.

"And where exactly is Jasseth?" Strom responded when Gabriel told him where he was from.

Gabriel went silent, realizing that there was no way to explain this satisfactorily, which made the officer even more suspicious. When Strom repeated the question, it was clear that his patience was nearing its end, and for no reason she could understand, Valerie came to Gabriel's rescue.

"I think he is talking about Jasseth, South Dakota. In the States. Isn't that right, Gary?"

Confused, Gabriel looked between Valerie and the police officer. Finally he said, "Yes. Right."

"Didn't you say your name was Gabriel?" Strom asked with a glance at his clipboard.

"Yes."

"Then why…" Strom paused, deciding that he needed to understand this better. "Are you two traveling together?"

"No," Gabriel responded just as Valerie said, "Yes."

Strom took a deep sigh. It was going to be one of *those* days. He elected to wait them out, and eventually Valerie spoke.

"We technically didn't travel together. We came separately, but were coming here together. To meet here."

Strom turned to Gabriel. "Is that how you would describe the situation?"

"Uhh, yes."

"And why does she call you Gary if your name is Gabriel?"

Gabriel glanced at Valerie briefly and then replied, "She calls everyone 'Gary'."

Strom gave a little huff, but moved on.

"So what happened between the two of you?"

Gabriel and Valerie looked at each other, and an understanding passed between them. There was no answering this question honestly, at least not here and now. Gabriel inclined his head ever so slightly, and Val got it. *It's your world, you'll come up with a better explanation.*

"Well, it's a little embarrassing," she began. "Gary and I have been having something of a long-distance relationship, but when I finally caught up with him, he was hitting on my best friend."

"I see," the officer said dubiously.

"At least that's what I thought. And I got…upset."

"From the reports we received, it sounded like quite a lot more than a lovers' spat," noted Strom.

"Well, we're both really into martial arts, so…" She let the sentence hang unfinished.

"So?" the man prompted, unwilling to let it hang indefinitely.

"So," Val went on after a moment, "I imagine that it would look a lot worse to a bystander than it really was."

The old man studied them. "By all reports and appearances, you threw him through a storefront window."

"Yeah. That was an accident."

The officer obviously had his doubts, but decided to let that pass as well. "So then are you saying that neither of you wish to press charges?"

"No," Valerie responded immediately.

Gabriel was more hesitant, not understanding the question. "Charges?"

"You don't," Val inserted quickly. "Trust me."

"No. No charges."

Officer Strom nodded. "Very well. That only leaves the matter of the broken window. I will be speaking with the owner—"

"We will *definitely* pay for that," Valerie offered. "In cash. Right now. And the repairs too."

This seemed to satisfy Officer Strom.

"Anything else?" Valerie asked.

"No," the policeman replied. "I don't think so. I suppose we can get started on the release paperwork."

Valerie inwardly breathed a sigh of relief. The sooner they got out of here the better. At some point someone would discover a stray blowgun dart amongst the shards of glass, and that would be much harder to explain.

• • ● • •

Valerie and Amelia waited by the door to the jailhouse while Gabriel retrieved his personal effects.

"Do you trust him?" Amelia asked.

"Gary? Hard to say." She made a half-hearted and unsuccessful attempt to straighten her hair. "No. I don't think so. Kelly thinks he's a danger, and I trust her instincts. At least, I always have."

Amelia just stared at her. A comment like that required further explanation.

"It's just..." Val continued, "I've never seen her act like this before. She's been behaving so strangely. And then there's this Praxis person. It was almost comprehensible when I thought she...he...they...whatever, was a hallucination. You know, some new psychosis. That I could have handled. Well, maybe not handled, but at least understood. But this? A real person that you can see, and who can see Kelly? And can punch her in the face?"

"And who can disappear into walls, don't forget," added Amelia.

"It says something, doesn't it, when the guy who attacks you out of nowhere, for no reason, and claims to be from another world, doesn't even rank up on the list of weird shit going on."

"It wasn't for no reason, Val. You attacked him first."

"Yeah, I guess." The pair watched Gabriel in silence for a moment as he was finishing up. Then, "So what do you think?"

"I like him," said Amelia. "A lot."

"Do you trust him?"

She paused for a moment, assessing, then said, "Yeah. For some reason I can't quite put my finger on, I do." She knew what Valerie would ask next and beat her to it. "And no, not just because he's gorgeous."

"I wouldn't say gorgeous. Cute, maybe, but not gorgeous."

"Fine," Mel responded smugly. "The less you like him, the better."

"Really? It doesn't bother you that he claims he's from another world?"

"What were you saying again about people disappearing into walls?"

"I think *you* were saying that. I was just talking about how my imaginary friends seem to be in the process of becoming increasingly real."

"Ahh. Much better."

"Have you noticed, Mel, that all the people you really hit it off with turn out to be certifiable in one way or another?"

"Actually, I have noticed a bit of a trend."

They turned back to studying Gabriel. The women's knowing smiles made him uncomfortable as he joined them, but before he could say anything Valerie asked, "So what now?"

"Are you asking if we are going to resume our battle? If so, I would think we should go someplace more private." Then he added in a low whisper, "If we immediately begin again, the constable here might question the blatant lies you told him earlier. If he isn't already."

"That *I* told him?" Val replied. A modicum of respect for Gabriel deposited itself in her social ledger at his conversational jab.

"I certainly didn't suggest we were…how did you phrase it? In a relationship?" He noticed a sour look appear on Amelia's face at his comment. There was something going on, some kind of tension between the two women, but he sensed this was a subject to avoid at all costs.

Valerie also caught Amelia's reaction. She, in contrast, fully understood the source of Amelia's irritation and quickly changed the subject. "So is that what you want to do? Finish the fight?" She hoped the lump of fear rematerializing in the pit of her stomach was not coming through in her voice.

Gabriel studied Val in silence and that lump grew bigger. Then to her surprise he responded, "No. I don't want to. But I believe, as you do, that we are supposed to."

"Sorry?"

"Why else would you have rushed at me last night? You obviously sensed that our conflict was inevitable, and—"

"What? No. I…I thought…" Valerie wasn't sure how to explain what had happened, how her imaginary friend had insisted that Mel was in danger. And now, with all the strangeness surrounding Kelly, things were even more uncertain.

"Yes?" he prompted.

"I thought you were going to hurt Mel," she finally responded.

"Why would I do such a thing? Do you really think I would wish harm upon an innocent person? You're the Champion, not her. Surely you didn't think I would not be able to Hear the difference."

"What does that mean?" Val shot back in exasperation.

"What does what mean?" Gabriel replied in a soft voice.

"Why did you call me a Champion?"

"Do you really not understand?" he asked in disbelief.

"Do *you* really think you're going to get on my good side by making me repeat everything?" He stared at her, and Valerie saw the way he retreated. Not physically. It was more like the pressure of his presence was softening, and in the ensuing sense of peace she could recognize that he was not being belligerent, merely incredulous. Then to soften her own reaction, she added, "No. I really don't understand."

Gabriel was silent for a moment as he tried to work through the situation. Finally he said, "Something is very wrong here. This is not at all what I was led to expect." He studied the women for a moment, and then a thought came to him. "Amelia said that you are not from here, from Havlanti."

"Havlanti?" Val asked.

"Sorry. This place that you call Iceland. This is not your home."

"No, it's not."

"Then why are you here, if not to face me?"

Valerie narrowed her eyes as she considered him, then decided to share. "I found something that led me here. In my grandparents' house. In a hidden room. It was obviously important, and I wanted to see what it meant."

"So," Gabriel replied tentatively, "you were not following your Beacons?"

Val shook her head in frustration. "I don't even know what that means. I was following a map."

"A map," he repeated.

"Yes. A map. A literal map." She took out the parchment and showed it to him.

He examined it. "These are runes in the ancient writings. I saw ones like them in the Library of Skies."

"Do you know what they say?" Amelia asked.

"No, I'm sorry. I only saw runes like this on some scrolls, but I don't know how to read them. I'm sure the First Mother would, however. Perhaps we could bring this to her."

Valerie did not hear anything past 'I'm sorry', however, as Kelly had suddenly appeared behind her and began whispering in her ear.

"Val, I need you to trust me. I realize everything is a mess right now, and you don't know what to think, but you *must* believe me. That young man is not the innocent he's pretending to be. He was sent here to kill you, and he's going to do it the first chance he gets. I don't think he'll do anything here in the station, but as soon as you step outside…" She leaned in even closer, and her voice became icily intense. "You have to strike him down immediately. If you don't, Mel is going to die. And there's a good chance you will too."

Valerie turned slowly and studied Kelly in silence. It was *her* Kelly, her friend. The blond hair spilled over her shoulder onto the fiery red of her sundress, and there was an intense, worried look in her sky-blue eyes. The strange sense of foreignness from before had vanished, but even still Valerie was uncertain.

Kelly felt the hesitation. "You must do this, Val. There is literally nothing more important in the entire world. You have to trust me on this," she pleaded quietly.

Valerie gave a subtle nod and then turned back to Gabriel and Amelia. "Let's get out of here. Maybe find some breakfast."

Kelly reached out and put a hand on her shoulder. She could not feel the contact, but there was an emotional charge to the gesture. It was the first time in her life that Kelly had done anything like that. It was simultaneously endearing and unsettling. "Thank you, Val. You'll see that I'm right."

The entrance to the jailhouse of Reykstaðir was brightly lit by the morning sun. Amelia, Gabriel, and Valerie walked out the front doors and immediately squinted in the light. Kelly followed close behind Valerie but was seemingly immune to the brightness. As soon as the door had closed behind them, she leaned forward.

"Now," she whispered urgently. "Before he can attack!"

Why are you whispering? she thought back. *Since when is that something you do? It's not like anyone else can*...And then it occurred to Val that perhaps someone else actually *could* hear her. *What are you afraid of, Kelly?* she asked.

"You need to act fast, Val!" Kelly insisted.

Gabriel turned around, wondering why Valerie had stopped walking. His expression was unreadable, and Val wondered if he was about to attack just as Kelly had predicted. Her muscles relaxed into combat readiness out of pure reflex. Gabriel saw the change, recognized it, but remained passive.

"Do it!" Kelly hissed in her ear.

Gabriel waited. Something important was happening right now, and he knew, somehow, that actions in this moment had the potential for massive consequences. It was a *nexus*. Not *The* Nexus, but a moment where even the tiniest flinch of a muscle could steer the course of the universe. There was an intensely delicate balance at play, and Gabriel knew only enough to realize that he had no idea where the fulcrum lay. So he waited. And watched.

Valerie was staring at him, hovering on the edge of decision. As his nythlen overlaid its insights onto his vision he saw something he had never witnessed before. Flashes of pre-shadows appeared, but existing only for the briefest of instants. It was like Valerie's intentions were flashing back and forth between two extremes—one in which she lashed out with terrible fury, and another where she stood still, just watching him as he was watching her. In a flash of insight he realized that she was already fighting, but not with him. She was in a battle against her Beacons, torn between an instinct to follow their calling and a deeper intuition that denied the wisdom of their guidance.

He was certain of this, because it was exactly what he was experiencing. As he attuned himself to his own Beacons, he was overwhelmed by their discordance. Valerie was the other world's Champion; he was as certain of this as he was of his own role as Aerth's Champion. They had come together to join in an epic battle that would determine the fate of both their worlds on the other side of The Nexus. That was absolute *Truth.* And as he stood there, his Beacons were screaming at him. He should be fighting this woman. She was the enemy, and he had to do everything within his power to kill her before she destroyed him...and in destroying him, destroying his entire world.

And yet...

Deep, deep inside was that quiet, patient, but unrelenting song. His instincts told him that they had it wrong. He, this Valerie...the First Mother, the sacred texts...they were all mistaken. The previous night's conflict didn't feel right. How could violence be the answer to something so important? When had violence ever been the right answer to anything? No. They had it *wrong.*

And in that instant he realized. There was to be a battle, but not the one everyone expected. It was not a battle of one world against another, but of each world against itself.

• • • • •

Valerie saw a change come over Gabriel. She couldn't say what it was, for he hadn't moved a millimeter, and his gray eyes had remained fixed upon hers the entire time. But something was different. Then, breaking a stillness that might have lasted a second or a century, the man tilted his head to the side and said, "You are not my enemy."

She felt a wave of compassion wash over her. Kelly must have sensed it, for she was suddenly screaming in Valerie's ear.

"NOW! Do it NOW!!"

Valerie straightened, and her own head tilted to match Gabriel's. Then she pointed down the street and said, "I think I saw a little café down that way."

She started to walk past him, her back clearly and deliberately exposed.

• • • • •

Meraya had made herself as comfortable as she could on another rooftop, this one across from the Reykstaðir jailhouse. Her nythlen told her that this was the place to be, so she had climbed up and settled in to await the morning. The buildings here were easy to scale, and it was definitely safer to be where the local population could not easily see her.

She had dozed lightly through the remainder of the night but had begun an active vigil when the constable arrived slightly after dawn. Now, as the Champions and the auburn-haired friend emerged, she saw that the Beacons had steered her true. Not that she had had any doubt.

It was unclear at first just what was happening. There was obviously some kind of tension between Gabriel and the other Champion, and it seemed as if they were simply waiting for something. Perhaps the constable was watching, and they were biding their time until he left or went deeper into the building. Maybe they had agreed upon some kind of armistice until a designated time and place for the final battle.

But then Gabriel spoke, and Meraya's heart went cold. *You are not my enemy*, he had said, and his voice carried a resolve and sincerity that could not be mistaken. He meant it as deeply as one could possibly mean anything. It had been an oath, a devotion. It had been the purest commitment to a cause. Aerth's Champion had chosen not to defend his world.

'Only if it appears that he is going to fail,' the First Mother had instructed, and it was painfully clear to her that he had. Failed. Gabriel might still be alive, but if he refused to fight, then there was no choice.

The otherworld Champion would pass between her and Gabriel in just a moment, and neither was looking in her direction. It was possible they wouldn't even see a pre-shadow. She brought the tube to her lips, aimed, and…

• • • • •

Gabriel watched Valerie start walking down the street. Inside, his nythlen was screaming at him in that way it did when he was making a horrible mistake. Something was very wrong, but at the same time that inner voice was telling him that he had made the right decision. He took an instant to calm himself, and in that act he saw it—the pre-shadow of a dart shooting down from a rooftop across the street.

There was no time to shout a warning. As fast as Valerie was, even she could not react in time. There was only one choice.

With an artistry that would have made Portalia and Aliesha proud, Gabriel's foot shot out, kicking Valerie solidly in the middle of her back and sending her flying to the ground.

• ● ● ● •

"Damn you!" screamed Kelly as Valerie felt Gabriel's foot smash into her back. As she hit the ground, Kelly followed with, "I warned you!"

Before Val could respond, Gabriel had landed bodily on top of her. Her instant, instinctual thought was that he was pinning her down, but she quickly realized that was not right. His arms were *over* hers, not holding but covering. His legs were likewise shielding her own.

"Don't move," he whispered in her ear, but it was unnecessary. She already understood.

She heard the *clack* of a small dart striking the glass door of the jailhouse.

• ● ● ● •

Meraya crept back to the edge of the roof to see what happened. She had heard a body fall to the ground, but it had been too fast, too soon. Something was wrong.

She poked her head over just enough to look down. There was Gabriel, sprawled out, shielding the enemy…and staring right at her. Their eyes met.

He didn't look angry. Intense, yes, but not angry. Also not surprised. Was it possible that the First Mother had told him that she was being sent along? No, that was inconceivable. *What has happened to him?* Meraya could feel her anger seething, and Gabriel's placid, almost emotionless, stare was infuriating. *What turned our Champion into a traitor?* Her wrath was threatening to overwhelm her, but she knew her duty.

I must inform the Chakrava.

With a quick shuffle, she was at the back of the roof, and then on the ground and running.

• ● ● ● •

Valerie felt Gabriel shift. He rose to his feet and stepped forward, keeping himself between her and the roof. Valerie had heard the assailant fleeing, and wondered why he was standing there. Perhaps he was worried about a second assassin. *He's a cautious one*, she thought as she sprung into a crouch.

"His back is to you," whispered Kelly. "Do it! There'll never be a better chance!" Valerie stood and turned to face her. "One fist, Val. That's all it would take, just one—"

Valerie pointed her index finger at Kelly in warning. *Don't make me use the other finger*, she warned. It would have been funny in any other circumstance, but in the here and now it landed like a slap in the face. Kelly fell silent, but maintained a cold, steady stare.

A moment later, Praxis stepped out from the jailhouse wall and approached.

"Beat it, or you're getting another face-full of Aerth dirt," they threatened.

Kelly slowly turned to face Praxis. Valerie had never seen her apparently-not-so-imaginary friend look that furious. She could almost see a fire burning in Kelly's eyes, and when she spoke, it carried a quality of menace that was like a natural disaster raging to be unleashed.

"You dare threaten me, you insignificant speck?" Kelly growled.

"Just get lost," Praxis replied, holding out a hand filled with dirt.

Kelly was suddenly a dozen feet away.

"That's fine," Praxis called out. "Just stay away from Valerie and me." Then they nodded their head towards Gabriel and Amelia. "Them too."

"I will squash you like the insect you are," Kelly called out. "You know I can."

"Maybe. But I also know you won't. At least not right now."

Kelly glanced once at Valerie, then vanished.

"What the hell was that about?" asked Valerie.

"Later," Praxis murmured just as Gabriel took a step backwards toward them, still facing away to keep an eye on the building across the street.

"I think we have a problem," he stated.

"Oh, you have a lot more than just one problem, sweetheart," replied Praxis. "But I don't think we should talk about them here."

Praxis's casual tone stood in such stark contrast to the intensity of what had just happened that Valerie suddenly found herself laughing. It was an awkward sound, and at first Amelia and Gabriel just stared at her in disbelief. But she kept laughing, and in doing so felt the universe slowly thaw back toward normalcy. And then Amelia was laughing, and finally Gabriel as well. Only Praxis remained quiet, watching the others with the impatient patience of a kindergarten teacher who knows better than to insist their students stop laughing at the kid who just snorted milk out of their nose.

Finally the trio sobered, and Valerie said, "Okay, if we can't talk here, where do you suggest?"

"I'd recommend my place," Praxis replied. "But the trinket can't come."

Valerie shook her head in confusion, but it was Amelia who finally asked. "Trinket?"

Praxis pointed to Valerie's pocket. Val reached in and removed the veined crystal hemisphere. Gabriel's eyes went wide and he muttered, "How? How is that possible?"

Praxis smirked. "It's not what you think. That one's the Earth Worldstone. Aerth's Worldstone is still in your world."

"Worldstone? What the hell is that?" asked Valerie.

"That's *that*," Praxis replied, pointing at the crystal. "Earth's, that is. Anyway, it can't come with us."

Gabriel, Valerie, and Amelia looked at each other, then to Praxis, then back amongst themselves. Gabriel and Valerie finally both turned to face Amelia.

"Ah, shit," Mel muttered, and finally snatched the Worldstone out of Valerie's hand. "But you owe me." Then she leaned close and whispered in Valerie's ear. "And remember, I saw him first, so no hitting on him."

"Just stay safe, okay?" Val whispered back.

"I mean it. Hands off."

"Fine."

"Promise," Amelia demanded.

"I promise."

Amelia stood back, considered the stone, and then gave it a pat. "We'll be fine. I think I might take it for a walk or something. It looks hungry." She then turned and started off down the street as the others watched her go.

Praxis motioned for Valerie and Gabriel to approach the jailhouse wall. When they were all standing in a close circle, Praxis extended their hands and said, "Now remember. This is very important. Are you paying attention? If you puke on my rugs, you're cleaning it up."

Then without warning Praxis grabbed Gabriel's and Valerie's hands and pulled them through the wall and out of the universe.

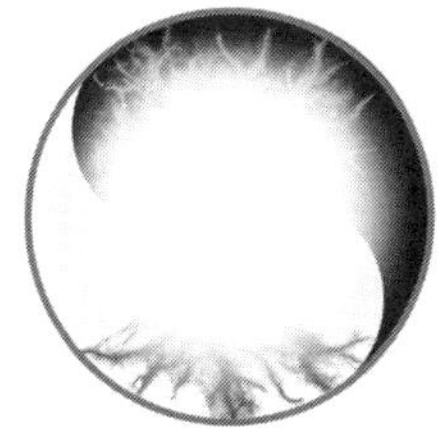

CHAPTER THIRTEEN:

The Interstice

As their hands touched, both Gabriel and Valerie experienced the mind-numbing flood of visions, moments throughout the history of both worlds intermingled at sanity-defying speeds. They could feel themselves spinning, with seemingly no ground beneath them and nothing but flashing images around them.

And then Praxis's hands were gone and the world came back into focus. Except it wasn't the world. Either one.

"Welcome to the Interstice," Praxis said as the Champions collapsed to a floor covered in plush rugs. "And remember what I said about vomiting. Especially you, Valerie. I've noticed you developing a bit of a habit lately."

Once they were finally able to lift their heads, the Champions saw that they were in a library. Sort of. It was a large, square chamber, easily forty feet on a side, and while there was no shortage of bookshelves, the most notable features were two giant, shimmering portals on opposing walls. Valerie and Gabriel had collapsed next to one of them and when they looked into it, scenes of Earth flashed past. The images appeared to be random: indoors, outdoors, day, night, rural, urban. They flickered past quickly, although nothing so intense as the onslaught that had caused the pair to grow nauseous and disoriented moments earlier.

"Yes," Praxis answered the unasked question. "That is a portal to Earth." They turned to point at the opposite wall. "Just as that is a portal to Aerth."

An open, uncluttered path between the two gateways divided the room into two distinct areas, each filled with shelves of books and scrolls, piles of papers, and various writing implements. There was also a liberal scattering of artwork, some on tables but most covering the walls. In the center of one of the walls without a portal—in a direction Valerie instantly and unjustifiably concluded was south—was a large fireplace. In front of it was a set of couches and large recliners. Wood was stacked high on either side of the hearth.

The 'north' side of the library gave the impression of also serving as a laboratory. Strange implements, some electronic and others that appeared thousands of years old, were laid out on tables, sometimes neatly organized but more often not. Centered on the far wall was a low table with two globes, each perhaps a foot and a half in diameter. The planets they mirrored had the same geologic structure, that is to say the same complement of continents, but there were subtle differences. The one on the left showed substantially more green on its landmasses, and Gabriel recognized it immediately as Aerth. The one on the right had more cloud cover, and Valerie thought she could see some areas emitting a soft glow from the surface.

"Is that Earth?" she asked.

"Later. For right now, sit." Praxis motioned to the sturdy furniture around the fireplace. "Let your stomachs settle," they said as they guided Val and Gabriel to the seats. They then went to an ornate sideboard upon which rested a decanter and matching glasses. Praxis poured a dark amber liquid into two of the glasses and handed one to each guest. "Here. Sip this. It helps." They then seated themselves in a deep recliner, threw a leg over one arm, and said, "So many questions. I know. And we are finally safe to speak freely, so ask away."

Gabriel began, his voice soft but intense. "Who are you?"

"As I said, my name is Praxis, like the Keeper before me, and the one before them, and so on for a great many centuries."

"A Keeper?" Valerie asked.

Praxis nodded. "The Keepers hold memories. I retain the memories of all those who served before me, and when my time is done the next one will inherit those memories along with my own. If there is a next one, that is. It's been a bit of a debate as to just what will happen to the Interstice after The Nexus has passed."

"A debate between who?" Valerie asked.

"Whom," Praxis corrected.

"What?"

"Never mind. A debate between Keepers. There have been different schools of thought about this over the years. Personally, I think this place will remain, that it has been here since the beginning of time and will remain until the end of the universe. My predecessor, on the other hand, was convinced that it came into being during the Shattering. There's no way of knowing, of course. At least not until The Nexus has passed."

"Right," Valerie said, although she was following essentially none of this. "And when is that?"

"Hard to say, actually. Soon. But as for an exact date, I don't know."

"So that's not your purpose, then?" asked Gabriel.

"What isn't?" they replied.

"To monitor The Nexus. I had thought perhaps..."

"Well, in a sense it is."

Valerie snorted. "So you're saying you're just not very good at it."

"Compared to what?" Praxis replied, a sly twinkle in their eye.

Valerie didn't have an answer for that.

"But you must have some idea," Gabriel prodded.

"It's a tough question to answer, Gabriel, because we talk about The Nexus like it's an instant in time, but it really isn't. That you were able to cross over into Earth means that, technically, The Nexus has already begun."

"So then when will it be completed?" Gabriel asked.

"Again, hard to say," Praxis said. "A week? Maybe two? Maybe tomorrow or the next day, although that would surprise me. I'd expect a lot more cataclysm if we were that far into it."

"What do you mean, cataclysm?" Valerie asked.

"No clue. We've never been through this before."

"You Keepers?"

"I meant our worlds. All of us." They smiled then. "A first time for everything, right?"

"Joy," Val muttered to herself.

"So are you from one of our worlds, then?" asked Gabriel.

"Yes and no," they answered. "I belong to this place now, although I was born on Aerth. Actually, not far from your home village."

"That doesn't seem possible," he replied. "I would have known you if you came from near my Circle. I would certainly remember your name, being so unusual."

"Ahh, but that was not my name when I was there. And besides, I left long before you were born."

"You look younger than me," he said. "I would have guessed only twenty-one or twenty-two."

"Thank you. But no. I was born over eighty years ago as time flows on Aerth," they explained. "You see, when one accepts the oath to become a Keeper, they become a part of this space, a part of the Interstice. I don't age as you do. The Keeper before me, for example, was over five hundred years old when they retired."

"Retired?" asked Valerie. "You mean they're still around somewhere?"

"Yes, in a manner of speaking," Praxis responded, and then pointed to their head. "In here."

"I have no idea what that means. Can we meet them? See them? Touch them?"

Praxis laughed. "No. When a Keeper retires, they are released from being constrained in a physical form."

"In other words, you kill them."

"No," they elaborated. "They simply decide to abandon having a body and become part of the Interstice in a more . . . intimate way."

"And why would they want to do that?" Gabriel asked.

"After centuries, it is something of a release. Being a Keeper is a very lonely life. You have the others, of course," they said, pointing to their head again, "but that's not quite the same as having relationships and interactions the way you do." They looked at Valerie pointedly and added, "Especially not like *you* do."

"You're a riot. So why not make some friends?" Val asked.

Praxis shrugged. "We sometimes find others to talk to from time to time, maybe play cards, chat about metaphysics, have a jam session or something. But in terms of making lasting connections, it doesn't really work out so well. Aside from the obvious issue of aging past everyone, there is a more fundamental reason the Keepers don't do relationships. Friends are there to complement each other, balance each other. Being a Keeper means being at the fulcrum of all axes."

Gabriel and Valerie looked at Praxis, then at each other, then back to Praxis.

"Think about the spectrums that make up your experiences," they went on. "For example, gender. Being a Keeper means being equal parts male and female, equal parts yin and yang. Where most people have some inclination, however slight, towards either intention or energy—direction or power, if you will—I do not. I am precisely balanced. Whatever imbalance I possessed before being called here, it was centered when I became part of the Interstice.

"This is necessary," they continued. "Here, we understand the nature and importance of complementarity, something that was lost in the Shattering. Take Earth, for example, with its focus on entropy and causality. The people of Earth are forever looking backwards, asking questions like 'what caused that?' and 'who is to blame?'. Now contrast that with *your* world," they said looking at Gabriel. "Aerth is focused on *purpose*, on syntropy. People do not explain things by looking for past causes, but by questing to understand the endpoint toward which their experiences direct them. On Earth, people guide themselves based on the past. On Aerth, they guide themselves based on the future.

"Now understand, neither of those is inherently better or worse. There is no right or wrong. These are simply complements. Here in the Interstice, we use both in equal measure—purpose *and* cause working in unison." They paused to assess how their guests were handling this. "Making sense?"

"Maybe," Valerie said.

"A bit," Gabriel offered.

"Well, it's a lot to absorb after a busy day." They stood. "Maybe get a little rest and we can continue later."

"Wait," Valerie said as she rose. "You mentioned something called the Shattering. What is that?"

"That's something that would be easier to show you than explain. Right now, let me give you a quick walkthrough of the place, and we can hit that topic once you're feeling a little more settled." Then they added, "Because seeing that will definitely unsettle you again."

• • • • •

Praxis led the Champions on a tour of What Lies Between the Worlds, an odd-yet-unexpectedly-comfortable combination of worldview influences. Valerie did find some things difficult to accept, however, such as Praxis's answer to the question of 'where does the hot and cold running water come from?'.

"It doesn't come from anywhere. It's just here."

There was a well-equipped and expansive kitchen sporting both an old-world fire pit with overhanging hooks for holding cooking pots, as well as a full complement of modern appliances.

"Why would you cook something over a fire when you can just throw it in the microwave?" Valerie had asked. Praxis just shook their head and smiled, then moved on to show them the pantry.

By the time they had reached a dormitory-like wing, Gabriel and Valerie found they were exhausted. They had only been in the Interstice for what felt like an hour or two, but Praxis explained that time was deceiving there.

"Don't worry," they said. "You'll adjust. But your bodies are right. You've been up for what they are feeling to be about thirty hours, so it's only natural. Take a nap and we'll talk more before dinner."

They showed Gabriel and Valerie into adjacent rooms, each arranged in the style of their respective worlds, and the two were asleep as soon as their heads hit their respective pillows.

• • • • •

Adjacent to the kitchen was an informal dining area with a rectangular table that had been stained a deep, chocolate brown. The edges sported a decorative leaf pattern, and there was an ornate circular relief carved into the middle of the surface. Valerie idly wondered if it was used for summoning culinary demons.

Praxis had prepared an aromatic stew from which a strong smell of rosemary filled the room, and there was a loaf of brown bread with a thick, hard crust. Gabriel dug into the meal with such zest that Val suspected it must be a staple from his homeland, a guess soon confirmed. It was called 'chevon', Praxis explained, and made with an array of herbs native to the middle latitudes of Jasseth. Valerie had no idea what kind of animal was responsible for providing chevon, but neither did she care. It was meat, and it was good. Although it did make her wonder where Praxis would have gotten it, as she had not seen any areas in the Interstice where one would keep livestock. For that matter, she wasn't sure there was even an outside to this place.

"There isn't," Praxis explained when Valerie asked. "I keep some stuff in the fridge, but just snacks really. For anything like this—meat, veggies, fruits—I just go out and grab it when I need it."

"Go out? Go out where?"

Praxis looked at her like Valerie had suddenly grown horns on her head. "I have two entire worlds at my disposal, and I can appear anywhere I like. Well, almost anywhere. Trust me, shopping is not an issue."

"When you say shopping," mused Val, "do you mean you go to stores and buy stuff? Where do you get the money?" That made Praxis laugh, and suddenly Valerie realized that they were not talking about shopping in the traditional sense. "You mean you steal stuff," she said in mock disapproval.

The insincerity of her attitude was not lost on Praxis, who smiled and replied, "If you want to call it that."

Gabriel's discomfort was more heartfelt. "You . . . you stole this?" he asked, motioning toward his bowl.

"No," Praxis replied. "I *made* that."

"But you stole the goat?"

"I took *some* of a goat. I hardly needed an entire creature for one pot of chevon."

"That's . . ." he began, but then fell silent. This seemed like a situation where it was perhaps wiser to keep his morals to himself, but Praxis clearly knew it was bothering him and continued.

"Gabriel, look at it this way. I'm one person serving the good of two worlds. My needs are so small in that context that it is hardly worth anyone's time to track it, and it's not as if I target one single person to take their stuff. If I were to waste my time with a job to earn money, we'd need two or three Keepers instead of one. Trust me, this is not hurting anyone."

"It's wrong," he insisted.

"Do you really think it's a life-changing problem for someone if one serving of food gets misplaced? There are billions of people in your worlds. The impact on any one of them is so small as to be truly non-existent." Gabriel was still shaking his head. "And it's not like I go take food from the hungry, or clothes from the poor. I take stuff where there's already excess."

"But—"

"No, it's not a reasonable means for supporting a population, but for one person living between worlds, it's very functional."

Valerie decided it was time for a new topic of conversation.

"So you can appear anywhere you want?" she asked.

"Almost. The portals in the library are on the walls. And since they're vertical, I need to have some type of vertical surface on the other side."

"So pretty much any wall?"

"A wall, a tree, a cliff, or even just a rock that's big enough for me to find a patch to slip through."

"And you just . . . what? How do you determine where you will appear?"

"As I said before," Praxis explained, "I'm part of this place. I can tune the portals to show me whatever I want. When I've locked in the right destination and can see that it's safe, I just step through."

"Whoa whoa whoa." Valerie's eyes went wide. "You mean you can use the portals to . . . watch . . ."

"Yes. And you can call it spying if you like. I won't be offended."

"So you're like the ultimate voyeur," Val observed.

"Oh, please. Like we could care less what you do with Mike in your grandparents' house." Then they added, "Or should I say 'Mitch'?"

Valerie's jaw dropped a little, and for the first time she could remember in all her life, a faint blush came to her cheeks. And that, more than anything else, infuriated her. Why should she care if Praxis watched her? She *didn't* care. In fact, she didn't even like Praxis. The bitch . . . bastard . . . whatever . . . was cocky, full of themselves, and... and . . . and if the truth were told, Valerie suddenly realized, Praxis was a lot like what she strived to be. Strong, independent, impervious, and—at least it seemed—totally in control. As much as she hated to admit it, she wanted Praxis to like her. No. Not 'like her'. She wanted Praxis to respect her. So naturally Val felt a growing need to show just how much she didn't care what they thought.

"I guess if a peep show is all you have to look forward to in life, that's your problem, not mine."

"Look, Val," Praxis responded in a tone of ultimate apathy, "try to understand. I'm not like you. I'm the present embodiment of a long line of Keepers. I assure you, after all the millennia of our line there is nothing you might do that we haven't seen a thousand times—no kink we haven't witnessed, no kindness or cruelty that we have even the slightest inclination to judge." They tore off another chunk from the loaf and took a bite. "More than you can imagine, I understand the past that has driven you to do the things you do, and I appreciate the purposes that call you to take the actions you take." They wiped up some stew with the remainder of the bread, and then added, "Simple fact is, I'm way too old to waste my time worrying about your insecurities." They popped the bread into their mouth, then had another thought and mumbled something incoherent.

"What?" Val asked.

They swallowed. "I said 'unless your insecurities get in the way of what you need to do.' Then I care."

This caught Gabriel's attention. "So you know what we are supposed to do?"

Praxis gave him a knowing smile out of the corner of their eye. "I know you two have better things to be doing than beating the crap out of one another."

"I have the sense that you know a great deal more than that," he said.

"Perhaps," they admitted, "but there is a difference between taking actions and following directions. The details of what you do are less important than the state of being that lies behind those acts." They smiled. "So no, I can't tell you what to do, or it wouldn't be *you* doing it. And it needs to be."

"That's a little frustrating," he observed.

"I know your Beacons are sending you all kinds of mixed signals right now. The only thing I can tell you is to perhaps stop listening to them quite so . . . devotedly."

"Surely you're not suggesting—" he began.

"You need to realize that Aerth is . . . a little confused at the moment, so you're going to have to be judicious in deciding what to listen to."

"My world . . . is confused?"

"Right. It's led itself astray over the millennia, poor thing. Don't judge it too harshly."

"Don't judge . . ." Gabriel had no idea how to respond to that.

"So anyway, it's not surprising that the Beacons would be thrashing you about. Just do what you think is right."

"That's not helpful. 'What I think is right' has always been what the Beacons Called me to do."

"Yeah," Praxis admitted with a sigh. "That's got to be frustrating." They patted his arm. "Just do your best."

"Right," he said.

"And don't screw up, or billions of people will die." They lightly slapped the table with their hands. "So, who's up for dessert?"

After they finished eating, the three returned to the library. Praxis led them to the table where the globes were slowly rotating and made a sweeping gesture.

"Well, there they are. Aerth and Earth."

"Not literally, right?" Val asked.

Praxis gave her a strange look as they tried to work out what she meant by the question.

"I mean," Valerie explained, "those aren't the actual, physical planets, right?"

"No," Praxis replied slowly, as if speaking to a child. A drunk child. "Those are *globes. Representations* of the planets. The actual planets are a lot bigger."

"Smart ass," quipped Val.

"You have seen a globe before, right?" Praxis continued.

"Enough already. I just meant…I don't know. I saw something that looked like the International Space Station moving around over the Earth globe and I just wondered…"

"Ah," nodded Praxis. "In that sense, yes. They are perfect representations of the worlds. I don't know what brought these artifacts into being, but it has been our understanding that if you could somehow focus down finely enough, these would be perfect reconstructions. Probably even down to the atomic level. We believe they reflect exactly how things are at any given instant. People, plants, everything."

"What do you use them for?" Val asked.

"Typically? Nothing. I imagine that if you wanted to get a sense of global-scale changes, it might be helpful to slide the globes back and forth through history, but I've never seen much value in that. There was a theory that they are somehow tied to the portals and everything else in the Interstice. Which makes sense if you—"

"Wait. You mean you can shift these in time? So can you see what is going to happen in the future?"

Praxis put a hand on the Earth globe, and it started to shimmer, dialing back through the years. "They only go as far forward as the present. You can go back as far as you want, though."

"This is amazing," murmured Gabriel as he reached out his hand.

Praxis watched him. He paused midway to look over, his eyes asking permission. They nodded. "Same rules apply, though. You puke it up, you clean it up."

As Gabriel's hand touched the Earth globe, his mind was filled with images. Within the briefest moment, they had grown to fill his sight as well.

"Focus." Praxis's voice came from nearby, although he couldn't see them. "Pick one thing and concentrate on it."

As he did, an image stabilized. At some level he could sense the other images were still there, but it was like discerning a single conversation in a crowd. As he concentrated on one, the others faded until they were merely background static. And the more he focused, the fainter that static became.

The scene before Gabriel took on a three-dimensional feel, and suddenly he was standing outside the jailhouse in Reykstaðir. He saw himself, Valerie, and Amelia standing in the morning sunlight, frozen in time. They had just walked outside; it was shortly before he had seen the pre-shadow of the assassin's dart.

But in this reconstruction there was something different. A fourth person was with them, a young woman with blond hair and wearing a red dress, standing very close behind Valerie. She appeared to be whispering in Valerie's ear.

"Who are you?" he said to himself softly.

Then Praxis's voice came to him again. "That's Kelly. She's…not normally visible to you."

"What is she doing there?" he asked.

"That's a whole conversation in itself." Then, as if eager to change the subject, they said, "You can shift the image in time if you like."

He tried this, and like a movie in slow motion, the moments slowly began to roll forward. The figures in the scene shifted, and then the dart's pre-shadow appeared. He froze the scene again.

"Can I move around?" he asked, but didn't wait for an answer. He tried taking a step and found that he could indeed walk around as if he were actually there. He navigated a cautious circle around the four figures, then made his way to the building where the assassin was concealed. He examined the structure, trying to find an easy way to the roof.

"You aren't really there, you know," Praxis's voice chimed.

"What?"

"In the scene. You're not really there." Then they corrected themselves. "Well, in this case you are, technically, but I meant the you that you're looking with right now. That's not a real body."

"I don't understand," said Gabriel.

Suddenly Praxis was standing next to him. "This." They prodded his shoulder. "This projection of meat stuff that you're thinking of as a body. It's not real. It's just your mind trying to make this interpretable. You aren't really here, so you don't need to move around like you are constrained by gravity or anything."

As they said this last part, Praxis began to float off the ground, and Gabriel understood. He willed himself to follow, and he too began to rise.

A moment later he was looking down at the rooftop and saw the leather-clad form of Meraya. She did not look familiar to him, but there was no mistaking the Aerth-style clothing, nor the blowgun in her hands. This woman had come from his world.

Praxis confirmed it. "Yes," they said. "She is from your world. The First Mother sent her as something of an insurance policy. Sorry, you wouldn't know that term. Khalfani sent her to help you in case things took a bad turn."

"But that's—"

Praxis cut him off with a wave of their hand. "Don't blather on about right and wrong to me. Those are just comfort words. She did what she did, what she believed was necessary, and that's all there is to say about it."

Gabriel nodded. There was wisdom in Praxis's words, and so instead he decided to focus on using this opportunity to learn. He willed the scene to roll forward, followed the assassin as she fled. After about a half mile, his vision started to turn hazy, as if a fog was deepening the further he went.

"What is that?" he asked.

"What's what?" Praxis replied.

"The wisps of... whatever that is. Why is everything growing cloudy?"

"What do you mean? I don't see anything like that."

And then Gabriel stopped short. The fog had become a solid, impenetrable wall. Praxis continued through it, then reappeared a moment later.

"That's interesting," they said in a clinical tone. "There must be some kind of limitation for you because you aren't part of the Interstice." They grunted in amusement. "It makes sense, though, I suppose. Your connection to the world is obviously tied to your presence in it. Learn something new every day, I suppose."

There was a pause, and then they said, "Go back to where you started. I want to try something with you and Valerie." And then Praxis's form vanished.

Gabriel started moving himself back toward the jailhouse, rewinding time as he went. He rewound faster, and a moment later he had returned, except now there were two Valeries, one frozen with the scene and the other moving around. Praxis was standing next to the latter.

"I'm going to steer us back a bit in time, if you don't mind. If my guess is correct, things will go blank for a little while, but just hang on. Nothing to worry about." There was a pause. "Unless you go insane. Or die. Then you should worry."

The scene started playing in reverse. The image of Kelly vanished, and the representations of Gabriel, Valerie, and Amelia walked backwards into the jailhouse. The changes accelerated, dawn receding into night. They watched two police officers walk backwards into the building, and a moment later their own past selves backed out of the building in the middle of the night, Valerie and Amelia on foot and Gabriel carried by the same two officers. And then everything went white.

"Did everything just black out for you?" Praxis's voice asked.

"It all went white," replied Valerie.

"Huh. White. Yeah, I guess that makes sense. Okay, just hold on for a moment."

"What makes sense?" Val asked, but there was no reply.

Seconds ticked by, and then the fog receded.

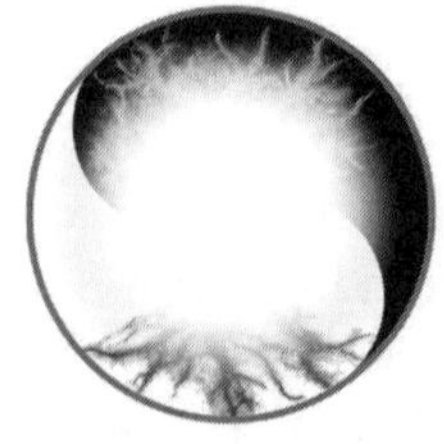

CHAPTER FOURTEEN:

The Shattering

Gabriel and Valerie, or at least their cognitive representations, stood with Praxis at the edge of a broad, manicured field. The sun shone directly overhead, and although they had no sense of temperature, it certainly looked like a beautiful day. Far in the distance, Valerie saw a feature rising over the horizon, and recognized it as Herðubreið, the last tuya that she and Amelia had explored. Scanning the rest of the horizon, she noticed that in the opposite direction from Herðubreið was another tuya of about the same size, one that had definitely not been there when she and Amelia were looking around.

And that was not the only difference. When she and Amelia had visited the day before, the land was barren, not the lush green she was seeing now. And it definitely did not have a shrine. The structure was situated in the exact center of the field, perhaps two hundred feet away from where they were standing. The details were hard to see from this distance, but there was a large crowd gathered around it for some kind of event.

"Can you see anything?" Praxis asked.

"Yes," replied Gabriel. "There is a crowd of people around some kind of—"

"I was pretty sure it would work."

"What are you talking about?" asked Val, starting to grow impatient with Praxis's enigmatic comments.

"Because you aren't part of the Interstice, you're not able to use it to access history as fully as I can. However, your presence in your world leaves an imprint. It makes a connection, in a sense. My theory was that it would not just be your presence, but also your ancestors'. And it looks like I was right."

"So one of my ancestors is in that crowd?" Gabriel asked.

"Not in the crowd, but nearby," Praxis replied cryptically. Then they nodded at Valerie and added, "And one of hers, too." It was clear they were hiding something that amused them. It was even clearer that they were aware that the vague comments were frustrating Gabriel and Valerie, and were rather pleased about it.

Valerie took another look around, but saw no one beyond the gathered crowd. She started to walk towards it, but Praxis reached out and put a hand on her shoulder to stop her.

"Trust me. I've played through this a hundred times. This is the best angle to watch from."

"I can't see anything from here." Valerie looked at Praxis's hand on her shoulder. "And how come—"

"We're not actually standing here, Valerie. I'm not actually touching you. We're just representations. But here, I can give you a better view."

Whatever Praxis did must have been purely mental, as their representation didn't move or change, but suddenly the center of Valerie's vision was expanded as if she were looking at the structure through a telescope. The construct was definitely ceremonial in nature, with every element a carefully-crafted work of art. The floor was a thick layer of glass, etched with patterns and writing and laid atop a matching mosaic of stones and crystals. There were no walls, but six dark wood pillars supported an elaborate web of wrought silver rods that in turn supported a hexagonal covering made from sections of a sheer, silk-like fabric. In the very center of the space was an ornate surface, a table or altar of some kind, carved with symbols. The sun and moon were prominent on each side and were encircled by representations of the fundamental elements.

Most of the crowd gathered inside and around the shrine were dressed in flowing robes, although the colors and styles varied widely. The ones in the center were dressed more consistently, and both Gabriel and Valerie had the impression that some kind of joining ceremony was in progress.

"Okay," Val said. "So what is this?"

"You asked about the Shattering. Well, here it is." They paused. "A few minutes before, actually."

"The Shattering is a ceremony?" asked Gabriel.

"No. The Shattering is an accident. What we're seeing now is a wedding ceremony. In theory." Praxis looked back and forth between Gabriel and Valerie, hoping for some kind of response or question, but neither spoke. Finally, they continued. "This place is called the Shrine of Unity. Personally I think the name is a little cliché, but it fits. They built it specifically for this ceremony, and it was designed with Feng Shui on steroids—ley line intersections, symbolism carved into every nook and cranny, the whole nine yards, as Valerie would say."

"I never use that phrase," she retorted.

"Whatever. It took them years to build, and they held off the wedding ceremony until it was finished."

"Wow," said Valerie. "Patient couple."

"Not really. They hated each other."

"Sorry?"

"Well, maybe 'hate' isn't the right word for it. What's a word that means 'even more hateful than hate'?"

"Why are they getting married?" asked Gabriel.

"Detest?" Praxis continued, paging through some kind of internal, mental thesaurus. "Despise? Abhor?" Then they realized Gabriel had asked a question. "What? Oh, right. Why. You see, these two individuals, the ones at the center on either side of that little altar, are Aidren and Ossessa. They're the leaders of the two most prominent civilizations in the world at this time."

"And when is this?" Valerie asked.

"About thirteen thousand years ago. Half the time for the Precession of the Equinoxes. Coincidence? I think not," they added with a knowing nod and a smile. Val and Gabriel just stared at them, clearly missing the significance. Praxis rolled their eyes. "You suck. Anyway, these two had a mutual friend named Berran. He's also in there, but he must be behind someone right now because you can't see him. Berran realized that humanity was in a unique position, and that if he could unite these two leaders, it would result in the unification of their respective civilizations. Consequently, the other tribes and factions around the world would have no choice but to unite with them as well, and the world would have a single civilization. People could stop focusing on conflict and get on with crazy things like love, helping one's neighbors, and so forth. Everyone agreed that it was a great idea. Even the bride and groom."

"But let me guess," said Valerie wryly. "Something went wrong."

"Did you grow up in a peace-loving world focused on balance, personal growth, and the minimization of trauma?" Praxis shot back.

"No."

"So there's your answer. Yeah. It all went to hell in a handbasket." Then, realizing that Gabriel would not know that phrase, they turned to him and said, "The Beacons all came crashing to the ground."

"The Shattering," Gabriel said.

"Right. And that's what we're here to watch." They glanced over at Valerie. "Sorry, no popcorn in this theater."

"I'll survive," she quipped back.

"Ha. Funny you should phrase it that way."

"What the hell is that supposed to mean?"

"Shhh. Just watch."

The scene started rolling forward. It was not a ceremony like either Gabriel or Valarie had ever seen, but the gist was clear enough: two souls coming together to join as one. It was also apparent that neither participant was excited by the prospect.

"Can you amp up the volume too?" Valerie asked.

"It wouldn't help. They're not speaking in a language you know."

A rotund, balding man stepped forward. His face was ruddy and kind, and he carried himself with a hint of awkwardness. This was someone who never felt comfortable with himself yet was possessed of an overwhelming empathy for others. His eyes were alight with joy and excitement as he held forth a crystal sphere, slightly larger than his palm and shot through with glowing veins of green, blue, and red.

"Recognize it?" Praxis asked.

"No," lied Valerie.

"It's the…" Praxis stopped themselves. "Well done. Score one for the Earth primate."

Valerie smiled. There it was again. As much as Praxis irritated her, Valerie could not deny feeling a sense of accomplishment and pride at gaining even a small measure of their respect. She again found herself wondering why she should care at all, but then Praxis was elbowing her.

"Focus," they chided. "It's coming up."

Something was indeed happening. The unhappy couple were talking over each other, irritation building towards ire. The rest of the ceremony had come to a halt, and the crowd of witnesses had become almost motionless in discomfort.

"What are they arguing about?" asked Gabriel.

"Titles. And name order. You see, the truth is that neither one of them was really prepared to rule as equals. Each expected the other to accede to their authority."

"I bet King Aaron started it," Val said. "He looks like a stubborn ass."

"It was Aidren. And yes, he is a stubborn ass," Praxis confirmed.

"I knew it. You can always tell the troublemakers. Something in the eyes."

"Couldn't agree more," they said. It sounded like a supportive comment, but Valerie had an inexplicable feeling that Praxis was laughing at her. She thought about probing the matter, but then decided she didn't want to know.

The argument in the pavilion had escalated from angry expressions into wild gestures. The altar was jostled, and the bride and groom were now screaming at each other.

Gabriel sighed. "This is terrible. Even for the sake of the entire world, they couldn't put their egos aside?"

Praxis shrugged. "Personally, I think they should have adopted a cat. Would've taught them a little humility."

The tension continued to build, and suddenly Ossessa grabbed the altar and threw it out of the way, clearing a space between her and the groom. In a flash, knives were drawn.

"Well that devolved quickly," Val muttered to Praxis. "Although you have to respect her strength. That altar looks pretty damn heavy." There was no reply. She glanced over and saw that Praxis had stepped back and closed their eyes. Their expression was one of terrible sadness, and Valerie suddenly saw that Praxis's earlier light-hearted quips were actually a defense mechanism, and, it seemed, an insufficient one. They were clearly finding this scene very upsetting.

Val looked back to see that Berran was now standing between the two rulers, separating them bodily. Aidren pushed him clear but at the cost of exposing his side. Ossessa seized the opportunity, slashing with her knife and leaving a long gash running from her groom's ribs to his waist. It wasn't deep enough to incapacitate the man, but blood was flowing freely, giving the scene an even more gruesome cast.

Aidren stepped back and out of Ossessa's reach, and they glared at each other as the congregation fled. In moments only the three remained. Aidren and Ossessa were crouched, looking for the right vantage for attack, while Berran recovered his balance.

Praxis, still with their eyes closed, groaned quietly in sympathetic anticipation, and then it happened.

Simultaneously, Aidren and Ossessa launched themselves at one another at precisely the same time that Berran leapt to insert himself between them. Ossessa thrust her blade forward and it slid between Berran's shoulders in the exact instant that the tip of Aidren's knife struck the Worldstone. There was a blinding flash of the whitest light and a thunderclap so loud that it deafened Valerie and Gabriel as it threw them backwards in the resulting shockwave.

• • • • •

"That's another reason why it's a good idea to watch from a distance," noted Praxis as the Champions stood up from the floor of the Great Library. "There's no explanation for why it should have any physical effect on someone watching from the Interstice, but it always does. In all of history, that one moment is so energetic, so charged, that it generally knocks people onto their asses in the real world."

"I'm amazed I'm not deaf and blind from it," observed Valerie.

"You have to remember that you aren't really there. You're kind of remembering it. There is no actual light to blind your eyes, or sound to burst your eardrums."

"So all those people who were there," Gabriel mused. "Or who had started to run..."

"Oh, them? Totally vaporized. Not even ashes remained. And you remember that spot, Valerie, where the Earth Worldstone glowed the brightest. Out in the plains southwest of Herðubreið? That whole plain has remained barren ever since. I think the explosion did something to the land. Compressed the soil or something, so now very little can grow there."

"Wait," said Valerie. Something had just registered. "You said this Shattering always has that effect?"

"Right."

"So we're not the first people to come here?" Valerie found the idea that other people had seen this place a bit of a let-down for some reason.

"Of course not," Praxis replied. "Keepers get bored too, you know."

"Anyone I would have heard of?" she asked.

Praxis thought for a moment. "You've heard of Leonardo Da Vinci, right? He used to hang out here for weeks at a time. Actually stayed in the same room where you're staying."

Her eyes grew wide. "That's pretty fucking awesome. Wait until I tell Mel that I shared a bed with Da Vinci!"

"We changed the bed out for a new one about a century ago."

"Not when I tell the story, you didn't," grinned Valerie.

"I find myself wondering something," Gabriel mused. "Given the severity of the explosion, it seems like it would have extended for miles or more."

"That's right," Praxis confirmed.

"But you said that our ancestors were there."

They smiled, seeing where his thoughts were headed.

"That's also correct."

Gabriel furrowed his brow. "But how is that possible? Everyone there would have died."

"They did."

"So how—"

"The only possibility is that your progenitors were born prior to the Shattering," Praxis explained.

"No," Valerie suddenly muttered to herself.

Praxis took a moment to assess her expression, and recognized that Valerie had finally reasoned it out. "Sorry, Val."

"What are you talking about?" Gabriel asked, now feeling like a runner standing at the starting gate, unaware that the race had already begun.

"Valerie just figured out the identity of her ancestor."

"Who?" asked Gabriel.

"It was Ossessa," she replied. "I'm right, aren't I?"

"Actually…"

"Oh, no. Not…" Valerie shook her head. "Please don't say I'm descended from—"

"The stubborn ass. Yep. I'm surprised you didn't see it right away." They were smiling broadly, enjoying Valerie's discomfort with the notion.

"So does that mean that I'm a descendent of Ossessa?" Gabriel asked.

Praxis nodded. "Anyway, there you have it. It was that moment, that instant when your mother stabbed a dear friend in the back, and Valerie's father cracked the Worldstone into two, that the universe fractured, two parts flying off to follow their own trajectories until whatever fundamental attraction pulls them back together in The Nexus."

"And then what?" Valerie asked.

"The Chakrava believe that only one world can survive, that only one can pass through The Nexus," Gabriel said.

"It's a sensible theory," Praxis observed. "You can see how they came up with it. Basic symmetry. Everything started with a single world, so it stands to reason that it is going to have to end that way too."

"So Valerie and I are going to have to battle," Gabriel concluded. "To determine which will pass through. Just as the First Mother said."

Praxis just stared at him in silence.

Valerie waved a hand in dismissal. "Maybe—and I can't believe I'm the one saying this—but maybe this isn't about fighting. Maybe what you and I need to do is *decide* which world should continue."

The Champions looked at Praxis, who remained expressionless as they stared back.

"Or," Gabriel offered tentatively, "perhaps Praxis should be the one to decide. If they are at the center of all things, who better to make that kind of decision?"

"But," Val responded, "the Keepers come from your world, so that would make it unbalanced."

"Actually," Praxis interrupted, "that's not true. I was born on Aerth, but the Keeper before me was from Earth. It switches back and forth with each new Keeper."

"How did you become a Keeper?" Val asked. "Did you walk into some metaphysical recruiter's office and…"

"It's a Calling. This is a sensible, even trivial, concept for Gabriel, or any inhabitant of Aerth. For the people of Earth, it is not as easy to accept. Think of it as simply *knowing*, beyond any shadow of a doubt, that you were born for a single, specific purpose. For those born with this particular purpose, to become a Keeper, they eventually discover within themselves how to travel here to the Interstice."

"So it's like these Beacons that Gary keeps talking about."

"Yes," agreed Praxis. "That's a reasonable way to think about it."

"Then how would anyone from Earth ever come here? We don't have Beacons."

"Don't you?" they asked with a sly look.

Valerie considered this. She remembered how Gabriel had thought she was listening to a Beacon when…

"Is that what Kelly is?" she asked. "Is she a Beacon?"

"Yes," Praxis replied, and Valerie felt a measure of pride for having figured this out, but the feeling was short-lived as they added, "and no."

"What the hell does that mean?"

"Okay, if we are going to get into this, I'm getting a drink and sitting down."

The three of them walked to the other side of the library. They all poured themselves some wine from an unmarked bottle and settled in. Valerie took a sip.

"This is good. What year is it?"

"I have no idea. It was bottled before they came up with the idea of using labels. But to get back to your question, there isn't just one type of Beacon. Every level of awareness gives rise to its own Beacon. From basic cellular needs up through the collective consciousness on a global scale, all awareness exists in a bidirectional flow of energy and information. Past into future, and future into past.

"Gabriel is struggling with conflicting signals because the Beacons arising from a societal-level awareness—actually more, from a *global,* whole-planet consciousness—are convinced that the 'proper' future is one in which he kills you, Aerth passes through The Nexus, and Earth ceases to exist. You see, Aerth's people have kept records over the millennia. They were anticipating The Nexus, planning for it. In fact, their entire civilization is built around ensuring that Aerth survives The Nexus."

"And what about my world?" Valerie asked. "Seeing as how I've never heard of any of this, I'm guessing we've pretty well fucked the whole thing up like we do with everything else."

"Again, yes and no. It's true that the people of your world have no clue about any of this, but the world itself, the planet-level consciousness... *it* is very well aware of what's going on. Both worlds are. The Dynamic of Earth and the Persistence of Aerth, they both know. And they're both scared. Both want to survive. What world wouldn't? It's very sensible, if you think about it.

"Just like Aidren and Ossessa couldn't accept the thought of not being primary, the Yin and the Yang embodied by your worlds' consciousnesses can only imagine a future in which they are the central principle. On Aerth, this world-level Beacon has worked for thousands of years to convince all the Mothers throughout history to believe that when The Nexus arrives their Champion will have to be victorious against Earth's, and thereby win Aerth's continued existence in the future. Likewise, Valerie, even though Earth didn't bother with influencing the planet's whole population, you have been guided to a similar goal."

Valerie shook her head. "That's not true. I wasn't guided, at least not by anything more than a map. And a crystal. Beyond that, nothing."

"Be serious. Your family managed to pass down the Earth Worldstone, and that map to show you where it had to be delivered, for over ten thousand years. Do you really think that level of continuity could happen without some kind of protective element, some form of guidance?"

"I...I don't know. But *I* certainly never received any kind of guidance."

"Really?" Praxis asked, an amused look on their face. "You don't think that your friend Kelly ever tried to influence you in any of this?"

Valerie thought back, and a hundred little things clicked into place. She remembered Kelly asking her to see the stone when they were close to Herðubreið, her odd behavior when Amelia left with Gary, the way she...

"I know you have always thought of Kelly as your imaginary friend, but you couldn't be more mistaken. She is not imaginary, and she is definitely not your friend. She is an embodiment of the Earth's—"

"No!" Valerie shouted. The reaction was unexpectedly vehement, and Gabriel and Praxis stared at her until she got herself back under control. "No. I'm sorry. This is all too...too crazy. The fact is that I don't really have any reason to trust you any more than Kelly. In fact, less. Way less. Kelly has been with me for most of my life. She's been there for me through the worst. She's saved my life more times than I can remember. And now you tell me she isn't my friend? No. Just no."

"Valerie," Praxis pleaded in a soft, comforting voice. "Try to understand. Kelly has been there for you because she needs you to be her Champion. She's a personification of the dynamic spirit of your world, and she...but I really should be saying *it*...believes that *it* is destined to be the primary principle of the universe. Kelly is manipulating you. She's been doing it since you were seven. Whose idea was it for you to take up martial arts? Who has pushed you constantly to hone those skills until—"

"Maybe she was the one who suggested Krav Maga. And maybe she has encouraged me to become the best. But that's not manipulation. That's being there for me. Helping me. Helping me become strong, capable. Making sure I never become a victim like my parents were. And I'm not going to throw away twenty years of everything that friendship has been to me, has given to me, just because some stranger says so. A stranger, might I add, who has followed me and could very well be manipulating me right now. I owe my sanity to Kelly. And if she really is something more than my imagination, that doesn't change the fact that I owe her more than I could ever repay."

The fire crackled in the trailing silence. Praxis regarded Valerie with an expressionless face, which finally softened into a kind smile. "You know what? You're right." Valerie was taken aback. "You're right," they repeated. "You have no reason to trust me, and all of this has come at you very fast."

Valerie didn't know how to respond.

"Take some time," they continued. "Think about it. *Feel* about it. Decide what seems right, and do it without my interference. I'm going to get some rest, but feel free to come and get me if you want to talk. Or use the globes if you need to reflect upon the past. And of course, help yourself to anything in the kitchen."

And with that, they drained the last of their drink, put the glass back next to the decanter on the sideboard, and strolled off toward the dormitory wing.

• • • • •

Praxis closed the door to their personal chamber, a pyramidal room with three sides and just the barest slope at the peak. It was a shape that seemed to upset most people who stayed in it for too long, but Praxis found it deeply relaxing. The prior Keeper had positioned a high, wide bed in the corner to the right, but when Praxis became Keeper they replaced it with a simple, thick mat; they preferred the feeling of sleeping on the floor. They had also removed a pair of nightstands. After all, the entire floor was really just an extensive 'bedside table' to hold all the things one might want in the middle of the night. Closest to the mat were a variety of drinks ranging from water to whiskey, a pad of sethrey paper, a tall stack of books, and a notepad and pen guarded by a fierce, feather-wielding plush bunny clad in a tiny leather jerkin.

The left corner of the room was crowded with a variety of musical instruments, most resting in custom-made stands and arranged by age and origin. Praxis had a predilection for a silvered trumpet they had obtained in New Orleans, and also for a dwair, an Aerthan instrument vaguely resembling an esraj with its long, stringed neck, but this instrument also had a small drumming surface over the resonant cavity. Those two rested on the floor beside a worn, cushioned chair, upon which sat a Gibson Custom 1959 Les Paul autographed by Eric Clapton. There was an amplifier against the wall, but Praxis never bothered to plug it in. Far too much effort, particularly when there was no one else around to listen.

The center of their chamber was dedicated to meditation and was delineated by a circle engraved into the floor. The basic pattern of the relief was a combination of the traditional yin/yang symbol like their tattoo, but overlaid with a spiral representing the archetype of the labyrinth. Around the outer edges were recessed holes for candles, but those took even more effort to set up than the amplifier and had not been used in decades.

Praxis seated themselves in the center of the circle and slowed their breathing. They had known this task would fall to them, known that it would not be easy. The Champions were bound to be stubborn. Just look at their ancestors, after all. But so what? Failure was not an option. History would not look back and think, 'well, at least Praxis gave it a solid effort.' There was no *good enough* here. Not in this. If Valerie and Gabriel could not find the right path on their own, more direct measures would be required.

They shuddered. *Please don't let it come to that.*

Their meditation was not off to a good start. Another set of deep breaths. Let the thoughts melt away. Release the boundaries that define you as yourself, feel the connectedness to the universe.

It's just that it was all happening so damn fast. That was the problem. The stupid pair had both waited until the last possible minute to do anything, and now The Nexus was barreling down on them like one of those mag-lev trains. Damn it. If only the Champions had started sooner, there would be more time for gradual adjustments. But there was no leeway for gradual now, only sudden, jarring shifts.

Don't borrow trouble, Praxis. Things might be just fine. They realized they were thinking again.

Breathe, Praxis. Breathe.

Well, none of it really mattered anyway. There was nothing more they could do at the moment. They had laid the bait, and now had to step back and give the Champions the space and time to take it. Alas, time was the one commodity they did not have in abundance.

"Fuck this," Praxis muttered. Meditation was clearly a lost cause tonight. They stood up, walked over to where a bottle of Glenfiddich 30-year was winking at them, and pulled out the cork.

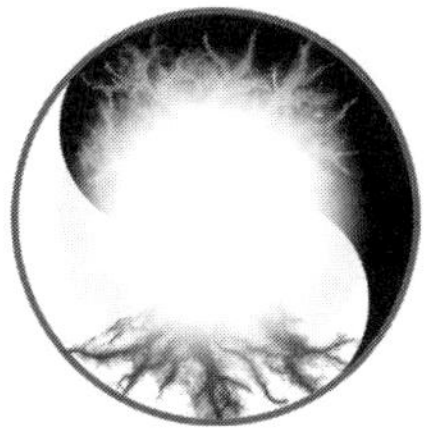

CHAPTER FIFTEEN:

The Past

"Do you believe them?" asked Valerie once Praxis had left.

Gabriel thought about it. "I don't know what to believe," he finally concluded. "I've lived my whole life listening to the Beacons, and they've never steered me wrong. But something has certainly changed. Maybe it's what Praxis said. I mean, it seems possible. It's an explanation that fits."

"It could also be a lie."

"Yes. I suppose it could be. But when I touched the globe . . . I . . . saw things. They were exactly as I remembered them. Well, almost."

"What do you mean, almost?" Valerie asked.

"I saw us outside the constable's station. In almost every respect it was exactly as I remembered it, but there was someone else there. A woman."

That piqued Valerie's interest. "What did she look like?"

"She had blond hair, and was wearing—"

"A red dress?" Val finished.

"Yes."

"That was Kelly. You saw *Kelly*." Valerie took a drink. "I don't know what's happening, but there is one thing I do know for certain."

"What's that?"

"That I *really* don't know what's happening."

The comment made Gabriel smile. "Do you think we can trust these visions to be true? The Shattering Praxis showed us, could it have been a fabrication?"

"There's one way to find out, I guess."

Valerie hopped up and returned to the Earth globe. Without hesitation, she slapped a hand on it.

The barrage of images returned, and Valerie focused her attention on the moment outside the jailhouse. This time it took only the span of a breath before she was there, seeing the frozen forms of herself, Amelia, Gabriel, and Kelly. She advanced time until Gabriel was kicking out, then rewound a half-second. She saw him focused on the top of the roof across the street, and turned her own attention to examine where he was looking. There was nothing there. Absolutely nothing. Whatever he was reacting to, it was not visible.

She nudged time forward slowly, instant by instant. His foot lifted off the ground. Still nothing on the roof. His leg was striking forward. Still nothing. Then the moment of impact, and there it was. The barest break in the line of the roof resulted from the top of someone's head, and as Valerie focused on it, she could just make out the narrow tube of a blowgun. Even staring at the rooftop as she was now, it was incredibly difficult to discern.

How could Gabriel have known? It was impossible. There was no question that he had reacted to the threat before it was perceptible.

And now there was something else she had to know.

Time sped backward until her awareness was in the middle of Möðrudalsleið Vegur. Her past self was frozen mid-stride as she was sprinting to reach Amelia, Kelly a few paces ahead and to her left. Gary had just stepped back and away from Amelia, and was lowering himself into a defensive stance.

What made me think he would attack Mel? He just distanced himself, not approached. He was ensuring a perimeter of free action.

She brushed the thoughts aside for the moment and advanced the scene in slow motion. She charged and struck with a right-handed attack. He blocked it easily, brushing it to his right while shifting to his left. She froze time, then nudged it back a fraction of a second to the instant just before her strike started.

There it was. His left foot had already come off the ground. He had begun his defense an instant before she had brought her striking hand up. He *knew. He* knew, *damn it!*

She continued to skim through the fight. A part of her—conditioned from years of studying videos of her own fighting—couldn't help but take mental notes of little imperfections in her own technique that she would have to work on later, but what most caught her interest was *him.* The evidence was here, and it was undeniable. The man really was reacting to her actions before she had even started them. Repeatedly. There was no way this could be coincidence. Gary was seeing the future.

God help me if this really comes to a battle, she thought. *How do you defeat someone who can see your attacks before they've even started?*

An answer came to her. *Attack him while he's asleep.* It could almost have been Kelly's suggestion, and she instinctively looked around for her. There was actually an image of Kelly in the scene, shifting her attention between the fight and a building down the street. It was the building from where the dart would shortly be fired. Kelly knew someone was up there, and was keeping an eye on them.

Valerie walked over to the image of Kelly. "What are you?" she whispered, but the memory did not respond.

She tried to summon her friend as she had so many times in the past. She listened for the voice, and thought she could almost hear Kelly saying, "Now what do you want?" But it was different. This was her, Valerie, projecting the *idea* of a conversation. She was imagining what Kelly would say, and pretending that she could hear the words. There was no question. This was what imagining would have been like.

How could she not have realized? How could she have not noticed the difference between figments of her own imagination and the experiences she had of her friend? Surely she had imagined other things, pretended other illusions. Surely.

Or had she? Was there a time when she had reason or need to imagine something or someone else?

Valerie began to search her past for such a moment, the memories materializing before her eyes. She was in a grocery store, and her seventeen-year-old self was standing in the checkout line. In front of her, a mother and daughter were chatting. She didn't know them, and was surprised that she could recall the moment in such exquisite detail. She had felt a pang of jealousy directed at the girl, and it returned now, a dissociated emotional echo from the past. Why should *that* girl have a mother to buy her potato chips when…

This *was* her life. She was really seeing moments from her own past, and in perfect clarity. And if Praxis had been telling the truth, she would be able to see things that were not just in her direct line of sight, but a fair distance away. She had at her disposal the means to find answers to…

Valerie was outside the diner in Reykjavik. She had just turned back for her keys, and there was the glimpse of the hooded figure she had seen. She played time forward. The image of Valerie was running now, and the figure had ducked around the corner. She froze time, and trotted over. She saw Praxis reaching out a hand to touch the wall of the restaurant. Time resumed its flow, and Praxis slipped into the wall with a halo of rainbow sparks to vanish a moment before Valerie's own likeness rounded the corner.

"Fuck," Val muttered. Then, "I wonder…"

There was a blur of images, and she was standing on the street corner near Amelia's yoga studio. About fifty feet down the main road she could make out the form of herself parking her bike illegally, but what she really wanted to see was down the side street. Praxis was standing in front of the four men who had been about to mug them, but something was very different from the scene she would be encountering in a few moments.

Valerie walked down the street to them, and allowed time to flow again.

The image of Praxis was smiling softly at the men, who were standing casually, and then they spoke. "She's coming."

The men adopted menacing postures, and this was the scene she had witnessed as she came upon them.

"That fucking..." Val growled. "They set me up!" An intense hatred for Praxis was beginning to take root in her gut. Who the hell was this asshole to screw with her like this? And then Valerie remembered what she had done to the attackers, and that hatred grew. She had maimed those men, men who were obviously recruited as actors in a fake assault. *How could the bitch... bastard...* It was difficult to swear about someone when you couldn't put a gender to them. *Asshole. That applies to everyone.*

On a whim, she rewound time to the first time she had seen Praxis. Not surprisingly, there was nothing accidental about that 'chance' encounter either. Praxis had been waiting around a corner, timing their approach to Sally's so they'd arrive an instant after she, Valerie, had opened the door.

"What the hell are you playing at?" she wondered aloud. Then an even more disturbing thought struck her. *And for how long?*

She began to flip through moments in her life, wondering if Praxis had been there at other times, earlier times. And they were. Not often, but in situations where a person could easily hide, Valerie was able to catch glimpses of their tattooed face. Nights out crawling the bars, martial arts competitions, lecture halls... Praxis had been keeping tabs.

As Valerie scrolled backward through her life, the appearances of Kelly became more persistent. It was interesting to note how Kelly's visual appearance had paced her own growth, and she found herself reminiscing about moments of her youth. She would not have described herself as having a happy childhood, yet was surprised to see how often she and Amelia were laughing. She and Kelly laughed as well, and at times even all three of them would share a joke in that strange dynamic they had. Sometimes Mel would speak to Kelly, and Valerie would convey her responses.

Wait a minute, Val thought. A pattern had suddenly struck her, and she flipped through the sightings of Praxis during her teenage years to confirm it. She was right. Prior to last week, Praxis never appeared when Kelly was around. Not once. That couldn't be coincidence. Knowing this, she should be able to scan back for appearances of the Keeper without trying to examine every single memory. This would narrow down the possibilities tremendously, especially when Valerie was very young, since Kelly was there more often than not.

Blur... Valerie's grandfather is picking her up from school in that big green truck that she loved. Her heart was suddenly heavy as she gazed at the old man. Valerie was far from a sentimental woman, but seeing him again like this brought a rush of feelings, and she had to fight back tears. When she finally pushed down the emotions, she looked around to see Praxis watching from a second-story school window.

Blur... Valerie is having a birthday party. It was in her grandparent's house, and the array of candles on the cake announced that she had just turned nine. Val hated the way she looked when she was nine. So awkward. And her hair looked stupid. How had she never realized that? Not that it mattered, but come on. Have some dignity.

The memory of birthdays had captured her thoughts, and without deliberately shifting, she was now seeing her eighth. Her parents had died only a few months before, and one could hardly call this quiet gathering a celebration. It was more of a salute, a somber acknowledgement that her youth had been abruptly curtailed. Her grandparents were there, as was Kelly, but that was it. She had not met Amelia yet.

Seeing Kelly, Valerie realized that she had lost track of what she was doing. This was supposed to be research, not a walk along memory lane. She wanted to know how long Praxis had been watching her. She steeled herself, then…

Blur…It was her seventh birthday, and she was standing in her childhood home. The white drapes of the living room…she immediately remembered that the one on the right would have a dirty brown smudge where she had wiped chocolatey hands on it, then tucked it out of sight behind the couch. That brought a smile to her face, and she was instantly lost in the moment again.

The bright, cheery room was filled with nearly a dozen children playing party games, and…and there she was. Young Valerie, dressed in pink and flowers, her worn, plushy Frombit tucked under one arm as it always had been in those days. She considered her young self, and was struck by how much she had changed since then. So little of that child remained. Years had transformed innocence into apathy, and if there was anything left of the carefree spirit, it now expressed itself as a predilection towards reckless abandon.

She had worked very hard for those changes, been proud of them, but now as she stared at that little girl running toward the kitchen, she began to wonder if perhaps she had lost something that...

No. Stop this indulgent crap.

She let time flow.

Seven-year-old Valerie turned the corner. She watched herself jump at her father as he came through the doorway that opened into the kitchen. He staggered backwards in surprise as she had laughed and laughed, grabbing him about the legs until they were both in a tumble on the floor. Her mother came over to make sure they were okay, and…

Valerie became aware that tears were streaming down her face. There they were…her parents…the image more perfect than any memory could ever be, and she was overwhelmed. Joy was suffused with the most intense sorrow she had experienced since their deaths, and she started to lose herself. She felt disconnected, distant. Some irritating, clinical corner of her mind was whispering, *you are in shock, stupid*, but the thought held no significance for her. She was turning seven again. The world was safe and happy and perfect, and nothing else mattered. In fact, it would get even better soon.

Blur. It was the evening after the party, and she was sitting on the couch between her parents. The television was on, but the old Valerie didn't even spare it a glance. She was mesmerized by the image of her young self falling asleep in the arms of her mother and father. And as those innocent eyes grew heavier and finally shut, her racing pulse slowed and her adult eyes closed with them. For a sweet moment she experienced the peace of falling asleep in the safety of her childhood home.

Valerie's eyes shot open. Her childhood home. Safety. Her mind knew that these two thoughts could never go together. This childhood home could never be a haven.

Blur.

Valerie stood in her childhood bedroom. Her younger self was sleeping softly, nestled in her comforter. Suddenly the little girl was jolted awake by the sound of shattering glass. A door downstairs was opened, followed shortly by the muffled sounds of her parents scrambling out of bed.

The representation of today's Valerie stood glued in place as her younger self sat up and grabbed the pink and yellow Frombit that had migrated to the foot of the bed. As she pulled it toward her, the door opened and her mother appeared, fear painted across her face.

"Get under the bed, sweetheart!" her mother whispered fiercely. "Now!"

Young Valerie scrambled out from beneath the covers, and a moment later was hiding between boxes in the cave beneath her bed. Valerie watched her mother quickly rearrange the blankets so no one entering the room would be able to see underneath. Then she bent down, lifted a part, and put her face close.

"Now stay there and don't make a sound," she whispered. "Not a sound, you understand?"

Valerie remembered hiding under that bed. She remembered nodding in mute confirmation, remembered the fear and confusion as her mother disappeared.

The memory of her mother was closing the door now, and she knew what was to follow. A debilitating fear seized her, and Valerie suddenly noticed that she was shaking in terror.

And then rage exploded, shattering the self-imposed cage. She was not a seven-year-old victim. Not now. She was an adult and she was lethal, as lethal as any human could be. And it was time for answers.

With a flash, she was in the hallway outside her bedroom, watching her mother racing down the stairs. Valerie started to follow, but then remembered that she was not bound by space and time here.

Blur. She was in the kitchen. Her father, dressed in pajamas, stood in the hallway that led to the stairs. A red light was blinking on the house alarm panel near him, and she saw him glance at it momentarily. Then he was yelling.

"Get the hell out of my house!"

A gun fired behind her, and her father's hands clutched his chest. Blood spurted out from between his fingers, and she heard her mother scream in the hallway behind him. He collapsed to the ground, and Valerie spun around to face the intruders.

Ever since the day her parents had been murdered, Valerie had believed that if, by some strange miracle, she ever saw the men who killed her parents, she would recognize them. She would see them, and the seeming randomness that had robbed her of her safety and her childhood would melt away to reveal some underlying pattern. She'd understand what had happened, and maybe even find an avenue for justice, for revenge. She knew the fury would remain forever, but at least she would understand.

But she didn't.

These men were strangers—two unknown, nameless strangers. One had a scruffy beard, the other clean-shaven but for a day's growth. The first was taller and fatter, the other looked like he was made from coat hangers and broomsticks. Both had dark hair, and neither face carried any meaning for her at all. She finally saw the killers...and yet the randomness, the helplessness, remained.

As she stared, the shorter man pulled a gun from beneath a brown, threadbare jacket and fired.

The bullet passed through Valerie's representation. Behind her, her mother screamed again and Valerie heard her body fall to the hardwood floor.

A blind rage overtook Valerie, and she charged the men. With a flurry of fists and feet, she lashed out at the killers. She watched her hands pass through the intruders' forms, but she couldn't stop herself until the sound of distant sirens restored her senses. Finally recognizing the futility of her rage, she screamed in frustration and froze the image.

It took her several breaths to regain some measure of control, but she finally managed it. As her heart rate slowed she realized that the men had been saying something, and she rewound history to hear it.

"You said they don't got no alarm!" the scarecrow accused his partner.

"That's what she told me!" the other spit back.

"God damn it!"

Valerie stopped the scene again as they turned to flee.

"That's what she told me," Valerie repeated quietly. "What the fuck..."

These men were not in her house by chance. Someone had directed them here, and Valerie was going to find out who. She let time roll, and followed the pair out the back door. They jumped the low fence in her backyard and fled down a paved walkway that ran alongside the neighbor's house. When they reached the street beyond, they paused.

"We gotta get the car!" the fat man demanded.

"No fucking way! It's near the house and the cops'll be here any second."

And then they ran.

Valerie followed them through the neighborhood and then down a country highway. After about five minutes they hotwired a car parked in front of an auto-body shop and took off in a squeal of burning rubber. She followed, but soon everything grew cloudy, and moments later she hit the barrier.

The killers had escaped.

After a rant both extensive and useless, Valerie returned to the time and place of the murder. There had to be some clue. She examined the killers' clothing, their guns. She watched the minutiae of every gesture, listened to the inflections of their accents. Anything that could help her identify who these men were.

"You said they don't got no alarm!"

"That's what she told me!"

"God damn it!"

Valerie stared at the frozen figures. "Who?!" she demanded. "Who told you that, you fucking bastards!?" If only she could get a wallet or…

Wait a minute. They may have escaped in the future, but what about the past?

Valerie started to roll the scene backwards. The killers backed out of the kitchen, and the broken glass in the back door reassembled itself. She followed them around the house to the front, watching their backward gait as they retreated along the driveway to stand near the mailbox. They spoke there, and Valerie played the scene forward to listen.

"This is the place," the tall one said.

"Don't look rich."

"Oh, them's rich."

Valerie was baffled. They hadn't been rich. Not poor, certainly, but far from wealthy.

"How do you know?"

"Trust me. I got a source, and she ain't never wrong."

A source? Who the hell could it have been?

The shorter man pointed to a security placard near the front door. "Look. It's got an alarm."

"Nah. It's fake. She told me they put the sign out when they go away. To scare people off, you know."

"You're sure?"

"Absolutely."

They started walking toward the house, and Valerie froze time. *It doesn't make any sense,* she thought, but underneath she realized that it did. They were petty burglars, and someone gave them the wrong address. Or this mysterious informant was just making shit up. Either way, the purpose she had expected, yearned for...it didn't exist. It was all just bad luck. These men didn't know her parents. They didn't know anything. It was all just some stupid, pointless accident.

Valerie wondered if she should simply let the whole thing go, but she just couldn't. It felt like surrender. This was the closest she had ever come to some measure of closure on the event that had so painfully, so drastically rewritten her life. No, she needed to explore it as far as possible, if only to know that she had done everything she possibly could.

Time flowed backwards again.

The burglars had walked down her street like two casual friends out for a stroll, although now in reverse. They turned the corner, and she continued to watch as they retreated to a brown sedan parked awkwardly on the side of the street, one tire up on the curb. They backed themselves into the vehicle, and she saw them debating something. It only made sense to rewind to the beginning of the conversation, but she never made it that far.

Suddenly, appearing out of nowhere as time flowed unnaturally backwards, there was a figure in the back seat. How could that be? That meant someone had been there, and then vanished into thin air in the middle of the conversation. The only...

Valerie's stomach twisted into an icy pit of bile as she approached the car. *Please, no,* she begged of no one, of everyone, as she lowered herself to look in the window.

There in the backseat, blond hair cascading over slender shoulders and onto the red dress Valerie could never fail to recognize, was Kelly.

Valerie's knees buckled and she let out a blood-curdling scream of anguish. Then she collapsed, her entire universe ripped apart.

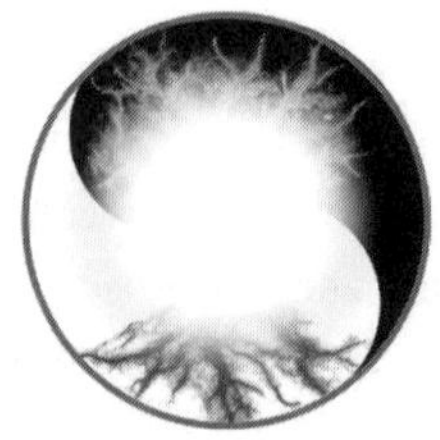

CHAPTER SIXTEEN:

Moving Forward

Gabriel rushed forward, reaching Valerie barely in time to catch her head before it struck the floor. Although she had released the Earth globe, Valerie's body was quivering uncontrollably; her eyes were wide and they darted around, although she did not appear to be reacting to anything around her. Gabriel wondered if Valerie's mind was still somehow trapped in the past she was viewing.

He called her name, but there was no response.

After lying crumpled on the floor for perhaps half a minute, Valerie began curling into a fetal position. She was now rocking back and forth, and although her lips were moving, no sound emerged. Gabriel cautiously extended a hand towards her. A pre-shadow warned that she was going to strike out in response and he pulled his arm back, although just barely in time. He thought she had been fast before, but this took it to a new level. He would have sworn she wasn't even watching him.

He waited patiently for whatever would follow, but apparently that one strike was all she intended. He took a cautious step towards her but she remained curled, rocking, and seemingly oblivious to everything. Gabriel looked into Valerie's eyes and recoiled from the horror and rage within.

Suddenly Valerie uncoiled like a wound spring and was on her feet. She charged in a mad, mindless sprint toward the exit leading to the dormitory wing. Gabriel wondered if she perhaps had closed her eyes as she ran because rather than passing through into the hallway, the left half of Valerie's body smashed into a bookshelf next to the doorway. Books toppled onto her from the shelves as she collapsed to the floor again, and he could see a trickle of blood running down the side of her face.

She immediately curled into a ball again where she landed, and now Gabriel could hear her whispering "no, no, no, no, no . . ." as tears poured down and mixed with the blood.

The minutes ticked past, each one adding pressure to Gabriel's sense that he should be *doing* something. But what? She was clearly still alert, and he had no doubt she would lash out again if he were to try to touch her.

In the end he concluded that the only sensible course of action was finding Praxis, and as if the thought was the missing component of some arcane summoning spell, the Keeper appeared an instant later. When they walked into the room, it was obvious that they were already well aware of the situation. There was no surprise in their expression, only sadness.

At Praxis's suggestion, they waited. After another half hour, Valerie finally fell silent and was asleep soon after that. Gabriel then picked her up and Praxis guided him to her sleeping chamber. Once she was deposited in bed, they returned to the library.

"I don't know what she saw, but it was obviously traumatic," Gabriel said.

"Very."

"So then you know what it was?"

Praxis shrugged. "Not with certainty. But I know what her life has been like, and I have a decent sense of what kind of person she is . . . where her breaking points are. There aren't many things that would evoke that reaction."

"Will she be alright?" he asked.

Praxis studied Gabriel, impressed with the intensity of concern he obviously felt for someone he thought he might have to kill.

"Yeah. She'll be okay."

Gabriel stared at them, and Praxis could see that he recognized the lie.

They offered a half-hearted smile in their defense. "I don't know," Praxis finally continued. "Maybe. If what she saw was just concerning me, she'll definitely be fine. *I* may not be, but she will."

Gabriel wanted to ask what Praxis had done that could have upset Valerie so badly, but it wasn't his business and his intuition told him that they were still deflecting. "But you don't think that was it," he said flatly.

Praxis sighed. "No. It's unlikely. If what she witnessed just had to do with me, she'd be angry, but not shattered. There's really only one thing I can imagine that would have had that effect."

And again Gabriel wanted to ask, but decided against it. If Valerie decided to share the experience, he'd find out. If not . . .

"Did you . . . ?" Praxis motioned with their head toward the globes.

Gabriel's gaze followed. "No."

Praxis was not surprised. For Gabriel, as was the case for most people of Aerth, the past was not all that compelling. It made for interesting conversation but was not terribly impactful. The future was what mattered.

"So what now?" they asked.

"What do you mean?"

"What I mean," Praxis went on, "is that it seems pretty clear that you don't intend to fight her."

"I will if I have to," he responded cautiously.

"Let me rephrase. It isn't your first choice."

"No. It isn't. Whatever happens, I don't like the idea of ushering in a new era with an act of violence. I can't believe that's how the universe would want things. And if what you showed us was truthful, it certainly didn't do anyone any good the last time."

"Sound reasoning," Praxis observed.

"I think that if the worlds split when the Worldstone was broken, it's more likely that our goal is to reunite the two halves than to throw one of them away."

Praxis's heart was suddenly racing with hope, but they forced themselves to remain calm, impassive. At least outwardly. "I see," Praxis said in tone that hinted at boredom.

"You're a strange one," Gabriel observed.

"Of that there is no doubt. Wouldn't have it any other way."

Gabriel wondered if there was some kind of subtle message in their response, but if so, it had passed him by. He changed the subject.

"Are you willing to help us?"

"What have you got in mind?"

"In the High Temple in Annaphora, the Aerth's Worldstone is hanging above the altar. Can you get it?"

Praxis considered the question briefly before answering. "No."

"I see," Gabriel replied, clearly disappointed.

"It isn't that I'm unwilling, Gabriel. When I say that I can't get it, it's because I literally have no *means* of getting it. At least not any that aren't also at your own disposal. But even if I could, I don't think I would."

"Why not?" he asked.

"The risk is too high."

"Because you'd be taking sides."

"No. I've already taken sides."

"When you punched Kelly."

Praxis smiled at the memory. "Certainly then, but honestly, a long time before that. No, the truth is that I'm not sure what would happen if I were to touch one of the Worldstones."

"What do you mean?" Gabriel asked.

"When I became a Keeper, I ceased to be part of Aerth. I'm part of this place now." They gestured about them to indicate the Interstice. "I know the stones cannot leave their respective worlds, and so there's some justification for believing that bad things would happen if I came into contact with one."

"Bad things?" he repeated. "How bad?"

"There's no way to be certain. Personally, I don't think anything would happen. My reasoning says that if I can go into the worlds and safely touch stuff there, why would I not be able to touch the stones?"

"Makes sense," he agreed.

"But other Keepers have different thoughts on the matter. Some believe that the stones have a consciousness, and they'd react like people react."

"Which is . . . how?"

"Do you remember the flood of images you receive when we touch? That's because I serve as a kind of gateway for you. Like touching the globes, but much more intense. Anyway, if the stones are conscious, what would a flood of memories like that do to them? I don't know. Or, and this is a bit more disturbing, because those stones are the rawest, most concentrated *essence* of your worlds, the flow might go the other way. And it might be much more intense."

"It was already intense," he noted.

"Right. And the last thing I need is to get my brain fried like a mozzarella stick."

"Like a what?"

"Doesn't matter. Anyway, you can see why I'm not exactly in a rush to go experimenting. And some of the past Keepers who spent a lot of time chomping through the metaphysics have even scarier theories. Like I might not go insane, but I'd cease to be a Keeper. Or that I could be obliterated, which—between you and me—sounds like absolutely no fun at all."

"Oh."

"And still other Keepers have hypothesized that it could go the other way, where the entirety of Aerth, or Earth, would get sucked into the Interstice and be obliterated."

"Oh."

"So, you know, not good either way."

"Okay," Gabriel mused, "what if I got the Worldstone, and then you helped me escape with it."

"No can do. I already told you, the Worldstones can't come into the Interstice."

Gabriel nodded, and made a 'boom' explosion gesture.

Praxis shrugged and said, "Maybe, if you found some clever way to get it here, but I was being much more literal. A few thousand years ago one of the Keepers tried having someone bring one of the stones in. It simply could not pass through the portal."

"So how do I get it to Earth?" he asked.

"You can't. The Aerth Worldstone is part of Aerth. It can't leave. Just as Earth's

Worldstone can't leave Earth. They're intrinsic to the existence of—"

"Then this is impossible! If there's no way to get the two stones together, then they can never be recombined. So what's left?"

"It's not impossible, Gabriel. You would just need to bring them together somewhere that Aerth and Earth both exist."

Understanding dawned. "In The Nexus."

Praxis smiled and echoed him. "In The Nexus."

• • • • •

Valerie jolted awake and was immediately aware that she was not in her own bed. That was neither unusual nor inherently alarming. She was also immediately aware that she had absolutely no recollection of who she had slept with the night before. That *was* unusual, and slightly alarming. She may not bother with names, but she was always careful to assess how clingy a guy was likely to be. She also made a point of knowing where the doors and windows were, and this place...

It all came rushing back as she took in her surroundings.

The overwhelming panic was staring her in the face again. This time, however, she reacted by picking up an emotional bat and beating the metaphorical shit out of it.

Fuck everyone, the thought flashed through her mind. Kelly had always told her that she shouldn't trust anyone. She just hadn't realized that that applied to Kelly as well. *That bitch.*

So that left Amelia. And that was fine. Amelia was enough.

Valerie sat up, swung her legs over the edge of the bed, and realized that she was ravenous. She stole a quick glance in a small mirror on the night table. Wrinkled, tear-streaked, hair like the Rats' Nest of the Apocalypse. Good enough.

She navigated her way to the kitchen to find Gabriel and Praxis in the middle of a quiet breakfast. Someone had made pancakes, and Gabriel had a fork raised halfway to his mouth when she entered. It froze there as he turned to look at her, carefully assessing as she approached the table.

"How are you feeling?" he asked once she had stopped in front of him.

Rather than answering, she took the fork from his hand and ate the piece of pancake on it. Acceptably edible. Valerie slid his plate in front of an empty chair and began to sit down. She made it halfway before a thought stopped her. She leaned over and pulled Praxis's plate to her as well, and then Gabriel's half-full glass of orange juice.

Only then did she sit and begin eating.

"Why, no, not at all," Praxis said softly. "Go right ahead."

"Shut up. We're not on speaking terms."

Praxis considered this. "And may I ask why?"

"You lied to me," she answered between bites. Gabriel's plate was empty now, and she started on Praxis's.

"Did I? Interesting. When was that, exactly?"

"When you..." she began, but stopped. Had Praxis lied? They actually hadn't. "Alright, not lied. You spied on me."

"I studied you."

"My entire life! You manipulated me!"

"Manipulated you? I never even came near you until a few days ago. Hardly your whole life, and I didn't manipulate you. I simply needed to understand you. I have a job to do, and you're—"

"Bullshit! You set me up! You orchestrated a mugging, and I fucked up four innocent men because of you, you heartless asshole! You don't think that's manipulation? What do you call it?"

Praxis stared at her, the epitome of serenity, until Valerie fell silent.

"I call it a mistake. I make those occasionally. Just like you do."

"A mistake," she repeated sullenly, and returned to eating Praxis's breakfast.

"Yes. A mistake. And I feel terrible about what happened to them. I had no idea how ruthless you would be in defending me." Valerie just glared at them as she chewed. Praxis continued. "I thought you would drive them off, not..." There was no point in describing what Valerie knew full well.

Valerie cleared the plate and looked up. Praxis pointed to the counter where several more pancakes were stacked on a cutting board. Valerie rose and retrieved them.

"I never manipulated—"

"Syrup."

"Valerie, think back. I never—"

"Syrup," she repeated more insistently.

"In the fridge."

Val went to get it as Praxis began again.

"Valerie, I'm serious. I never manipulated you. I've watched you, yes, but that's my job. I needed to understand who and what you were. I watched Gabriel too. I needed—"

"You did?" he asked in surprise. And then added, "Of course you did."

"But," they continued, "I never manipulated you. Hell, I never even interacted with you. I remained out of sight." They paused, assessed, and then took a calculated risk. "Which is more than you can say about Kelly."

Praxis saw Valerie stiffen. There could be no question about it. Valerie had discovered who arranged the death of her parents. Not that they had doubted it; it was really the only explanation, and it was all but inconceivable that Valerie would not have used the globe to investigate that night.

Valerie sat down hard in her chair and opened the bottle of syrup. She then inverted it over the pancakes and let it pour out as she glared at Praxis.

"Uh, Valerie," Gabriel offered tentatively as the brown liquid began to overflow the plate and pour onto the table.

Valerie just kept staring. When the bottle was empty, she tossed it aside, returned her eyes to the pancakes.

The problem—the real problem, Valerie realized—was that Praxis was right. They had not actually done all that much to her. Voyeurism. That was the bulk of it, and Valerie was not a particularly private person anyway. Hell, there was this one time when she had hooked up with a guy at a ski resort and they…well, that didn't matter right now.

Kelly had been the real betrayal. But Kelly wasn't here. Praxis had brought her to a place where Kelly could not come, and then showed her…

She looked up at the Keeper, momentarily mesmerized by the yin/yang tattoo on the side of their forehead. She forced herself to focus again, and said, "How do I know any of this is true?"

"Any of what?" asked Praxis.

"The visions, the things I saw."

"Do they feel like lies to you? Did you see things that were not as you remembered them?"

"Well . . ." she paused. "No. But I saw things that were new. New to me…unknown. How do I know that those were real? How can I be sure that Kelly really had my parents murdered?" She heard Gabriel gasp and turned in time to see the stricken look in his eyes before he looked away.

"What do your instincts tell you?" Praxis said.

"Fuck my instincts! Use logic! It doesn't make any sense. There's no reason why she would do that!" She quaffed down the remainder of the juice from Gabriel's glass, and then reached for a pitcher in the middle of the table. Praxis, informed by a pre-shadow, grabbed it first and poured some into a glass. They slid it across the table to Valerie, and then—with a pointed look at the empty syrup bottle—placed the pitcher far out of Valerie's reach.

"There is a reason, Val. A very good reason, if you understand what Kelly is."

"Go on."

Praxis paused, considering the best way to explain it. "Kelly is a manifestation of Earth's awareness. She represents the Earth and is driven by the needs of that world, a world that has known for a very long time that The Nexus is coming. And she knows that it's here. After thousands of years, you are that descendent of Aidren who will champion Earth.

"Earth represents Yang, the dynamic, and like Aidren in the Shattering, it has no interest in compromise. Kelly feels that the only way for Earth to survive through

The Nexus is for Aerth to be destroyed. That is why she kept insisting that you kill Gabriel."

"But Gabriel wasn't there when my parents died. How could that possibly—"

"You need to expand your thinking, Valerie. Kelly knew you were to be the Champion. And she needed you to be the most exquisite fighting machine that Earth could forge. Look back on your life, and you will see a pattern. Every single thing Kelly has ever said or done was designed to make you as aggressive and lethal as humanly possible.

"Who knows what kind of person you would have become had your parents not been killed? No one can be sure, of course, but think about it. Why did you go into martial arts in the first place?"

Valerie knew the answer to that all too well. It was to make absolutely certain that no one could ever hurt her or her loved ones again. It was true. The loss of her parents had turned her into a fighter, a protector. And as she thought through the moments of her life, those ultimately impactful interactions with Kelly, the pieces clicked into place. Praxis was right. Kelly had been forging a weapon.

"How could I have not seen it?" she whispered to herself. "All those times..." She put the glass of orange juice back on the table, gently, and looked up at Praxis. "I honestly thought she cared about me. I've been so blind."

"No," Praxis disagreed. "Not blind. You couldn't see it because there was no way you could have appreciated the bigger picture. Kelly wasn't lying to you. She really was protecting you. In her own way. And even from herself, at times. You are a child of Earth, and Kelly *is* that Earth. She wants you to be victorious, and in that sense she does care about you. The problem is, Kelly's idea of victory is as twisted as Aidren's was."

There was a long silence as Valerie let the words sink in. It made sense. It was awful, and touching, and oh so disturbed. It was ultimately unfair. But it made sense. Despite Kelly's genuine desire to help and protect her, she was the enemy.

And she was the Earth.

Holy shit. How the hell do you overcome an entire planet?

"Well?" she asked finally.

"Well what?" replied Gabriel.

"You two have had all morning. I assumed you've come up with a plan by now."

Gabriel and Praxis shared a look, and then he said, "Well, actually..."

• • • • •

It wasn't a plan. It was barely an outline. And there was only one thing about which Valerie was absolutely certain.

"It sucks," she said.

"What does that mean?" asked Gabriel.

"It means... never mind what it means. You can't just walk up to your favorite momma—"

"First Mother..."

"—and say, 'Can I please borrow the holy artifact to help me defy your expectations?' She'll laugh in your face."

"She would not laugh in my face."

Valerie turned to Praxis for confirmation.

"She wouldn't laugh," said the Keeper.

"See?" Gabriel said proudly.

"She'd throw him in a dungeon," they finished.

Gabriel took a calming breath. "We need the Worldstone."

"I agree," replied Valerie. "And that means we're going to have to steal it."

"No."

"It's the only way," Val insisted. "Do you really think she's going to hand it over?"

"What I think," said Gabriel, "is that resorting to theft before even taking a step down an honorable path is *unacceptable*."

Val turned to Praxis. "He's infuriating!"

"He's Gabriel," they replied.

"Gabriel the Infuriating," she muttered.

And so the afternoon wore on.

In time they found a compromise. Gabriel could attempt to request the Worldstone, but if—or as Valerie insisted, when—the First Mother refused, they would be prepared to react instantly and steal it. What made this difficult was that the Worldstone was kept in the High Temple, and the entire east tower was not merely populated with people running the government, but guarded. The presence of anyone without legitimate business would fire off Beacons left and right. Gabriel was confident that using Dhokha di Maath he could navigate the tower without being detected, at least on the way in. If the Worldtone were stolen, nothing would keep the Chakrava from sensing that.

This meant that they needed a diversion, something to hold the attention of the Chakrava until it was too late to stop Gabriel from escaping.

After deep consideration, Gabriel offered, "I think we need to ask my Circle. If I can explain to them just what is at stake, and why I am not really abandoning the needs of Aerth, I honestly believe they'll help."

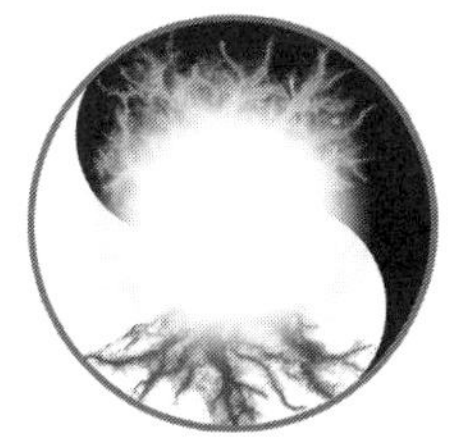

CHAPTER SEVENTEEN:

Forging a Plan

The Aerthen forests of southern Jasseth were deep and rich, filled with kapok and bloodwood trees. Smaller, more colorful flora were clustered in isolated pockets, and insects flitted everywhere. Praxis had placed the three of them close to Gabriel's home while no one was there who could possibly sense a sudden change, and now it was merely a matter of passing the time until his family returned.

"So you have no computers?" asked Valerie incredulously.

"I have no idea what that means."

"No guns?"

"The devices that your constables carry? No."

"No television."

"No—"

"No radio, no microwaves, no buses, no trains? No cars?"

"Those are the speeding carriages, right?"

"Yes."

"Then no. None of those."

"So how do you get from one place to another?"

"We walk. Or ride horses."

"What if you need to get someplace far away?"

"We leave earlier." Valerie's dubious look made Gabriel laugh, and he continued. "You have to understand, when you live with a focus on what the future is holding for you, you make decisions with the intent of getting where you are supposed to be when you need to be there. We're not as distracted by trying to pack as many activities as possible into our lives." He looked at her and added, "Or finding revenge for things that happened in the past."

Valerie's expression darkened. Was he criticizing her? The memory of her parents' death, so freshly relived, came unbidden into her thoughts. "Sometimes the past is important."

He nodded. "True, but is it really as important as the future? Or even the present, for that matter? I mean, in all your rushing around at top speed, don't you ever miss taking a little time to enjoy the journey?"

Valerie locked her memories away again, and her tone took on a sparring edge. "I enjoy going fast."

"Well, that's something, I guess."

She looked around. "It's beautiful here. I'll give you that. Most people in my world would describe this as pure heaven. Of course, then some asshole would buy it and turn it into an amusement park." Valerie took a deep sigh. "An entire civilization with the common sense not to destroy the land for a few bucks...must be nice."

"It is," he agreed. "In many ways. But Earth has its own positives to offer."

"Like highways where you can do a hundred and five on the straightaways."

Gabriel rolled his eyes. "Like...in your world, everything is so...varied. The buildings are so different, and from what I saw in the shop windows, the artwork has a tremendous feeling of inspiration."

"Well, it is artwork," Valerie noted. "It's supposed to be inspired."

"What I mean is, here we learn to do things just like people have done them before. We make little improvements, but you never really see a totally new type of art springing up. At least not quickly. Perhaps it's a result of the underlying connectedness. Our inspirations spring from a common source. Honestly, if someone came up with something that was truly radical, I suspect people would treat it with disdain. On Earth, though, you come up with new things just for the sake of creating something different. That's...nice. At times. In moderation, I guess."

She didn't know how to respond to that. Should she tell him that radical ideas met plenty of resistance on Earth too, or just let him hold on to the illusion? The silence stretched out. Gabriel seemed perfectly comfortable with it, and Praxis had closed their eyes in meditation. Valerie, however, found the intense quiet overbearing.

"I can't believe you don't have cell phones. How do you communicate with each other?"

"Hmm? What?" Gabriel responded.

"How do you communicate?"

He looked at her like she was an absolute idiot and said, "Talking? Writing?"

"But you must have conflict, right?"

"Of course."

"Are you telling me that if there's a war, the generals send orders around on pieces of paper delivered on horseback?"

"First of all, people generally know what they're supposed to be doing. We don't need someone to send orders. And we promote the people most in tune with the Beacons, so if some young soldier doesn't know what she should do, or mishears the Beacons, her immediate commander will help her."

"Her..." Valerie repeated, imagining what it would be like to live in a world where women like herself were the norm.

"Most soldiers are women, of course. They're better prepared for fighting. But not all. There are some men. Just as it is in your world."

Valerie laughed. "In my world, it's the men who fight."

"But...you fight. You're the Champion."

"I'm the exception."

Gabriel took this in, trying to reconcile its strangeness. He finally thought he understood. "So it's more like a colony of ants, where the queen directs things and the males..." He saw Valerie shaking her head at him. "No?"

"In my world, nearly everything is run by men. Government, businesses...everything. When you see a woman fighting, it's usually for equality."

"Strange."

"Almost as strange as not having telephones."

"Telephones?"

Valerie pulled out her cell phone and showed it to him. "These. Devices we use to talk over long distances. Or send other information, like text or images."

"Well, we have something like that. Not for pictures, but for critical information we have a network of stations that are within sight of one another. Messages can be passed by encoding them as a series of gestures that can be seen from a great distance. We use devices we call 'telescopes' when the stations are very far away from each other."

"We have those too."

"Using that network, a message can reach out across an entire continent within hours."

Valerie laughed. "In my world, we can send messages literally around the world in seconds."

"You're joking," Gabriel accused. "Seconds?"

"If that. Usually it is less than a second."

"Interesting." Gabriel considered this, and then asked, "And do you find that this rapid communication leads people to be happier and more fulfilled? Or to understand one another better?"

Valerie opened her mouth to respond, paused, then closed it again. A moment later she pointed to a group of four people, one older couple and one younger, walking towards Gabriel's house. "Is that them?"

He smiled. "I'll take that as a 'no'."

• • • • •

"Why are we still waiting?" Valerie asked.

"When the moment is right for us to approach the house, I'll know."

They continued to wait. The sky began to darken as the sun drifted into the horizon.

"Gary? What the hell are we waiting for?"

He considered correcting her but decided to let it pass. "I'm waiting," he explained, "for the Beacons to tell me when it is time to approach."

"And what if the Beacons never tell you to approach?" she asked.

"Then I won't. But they will. I have put forward my intention, and we simply need to be patient. You know what that word means, don't you?"

"Is it anything like 'dork'?" she shot back.

The minutes ticked by. The sky turned a deep blue as the sun completed its descent, and eventually the trailing pink and crimson wisps gave way to the evening. Still they waited. In the soft light of a waxing moon, Valerie saw the younger couple leave and make their way to another nearby house.

"Who's that?" she asked.

"That's my sister, Sendra, and her husband, Kenth."

"Maybe we can go talk to them instead."

"Will you just be patient?" Gabriel said.

Under her breath, Val muttered, "Dork."

Another hour passed, and the last of Valerie's patience passed with it.

"Gary, this is getting stupid. Maybe your Beacons are broken or something."

"Beacons don't break," he explained.

"Well, can you test them somehow? Because whatever they may be telling you, my common sense is saying that we're sailing past any optimal time to go talk to anyone."

There was no harm in considering the question, and Gabriel quieted his mind. He focused on his nythlen, and...something *was* different. His expression grew worried.

"What's wrong?" Val asked.

"I...I don't know." He turned to where Praxis was sitting, their back against a tree and as deep in meditation as when they had all first arrived. "Praxis?"

There was no reply. He called again, but they didn't stir.

Valerie went over and nudged them with her foot. They snorted, and their eyes shot open. "Sorry. I must have drifted off." They looked around. "Oh, look. It's dark."

Gabriel approached them and crouched down. "Something seems strange here, but I can't tell what."

Praxis looked around, then tuned in to their own nythlen and listened. "I'm not sensing anything unusual. Can you describe what you're feeling?"

"It's as if the Beacons have been muted. I can still sense things, but it has a . . . a tinny feeling to it."

Praxis nodded slowly. "Ahh. It feels like the sensations are harder to detect?"

"Yes, exactly," he replied. "Do you know what's going on?"

They nodded. "I have a good guess."

"Which is?" he asked anxiously.

"I think you've been cut off."

"What?! What does that mean?" The tone of his voice conveyed a desperation Valerie found unnerving. Even while battling for his life, or discovering that Praxis had been watching him since birth, he had remained reasonably calm. In comparison to such events, what could possibly make him so upset now?

"It means," Praxis explained, "that you might not be receiving any kind of sensation or information at the longer wavelengths. Like from the planet, the civilizations, the cultures . . ."

"Are you saying he's been disowned by his planet?" Valerie asked incredulously.

"Actually, that's a great description. It's what happened when I transitioned to being the Keeper. Once I ceased to be a part of the Aerth ecosystem, the timbre of the Beacons changed." They could see the anxiety on Gabriel's face. "Relax. You'll still hear the local things. The immediate actions, the pre-shadows, and all that. You just won't get any guidance on the bigger stuff."

Gabriel, however, was edging closer to uncontrolled panic. "You say that like it's nothing to worry about! For me, that sounds like being sentenced to desolation!"

Praxis shook their head. "You kids. Always so excitable. Look, in its own way this is kind of a blessing. You couldn't really trust those larger Beacons anyway, could you? You knew you were in disagreement with what Aerth thinks is the 'right' future. So honestly, what are you worried about missing? Now you can enjoy a little more peace and quiet." They punctuated the last sentence with a light-hearted smile that Gabriel found to be anything but comforting.

"So what do I do now?" he asked.

"What do you *think* you should do?" they replied.

"I don't know!" Gabriel was practically shouting in fear, and the forest responded by going silent. The change caught his attention, and then—as if the stillness was a suggestion from nature itself—he closed his eyes and went silent too. The seconds flowed past, and Valerie watched as his breathing steadied and his face slowly returned to its normal mien of placid serenity.

When he finally opened his eyes, they were tranquil gray mirrors of the sea after a storm. "We should talk to my sister," he said, and began walking.

• ● ● ● •

The three of them crept slowly around the outskirts of the village. Sendra's house was not very far from Gabriel's and was soon visible among the trees. A flickering light leaked through the windows. If a fire was burning in the hearth, Gabriel's sister would still be awake.

"Wait here," he said.

"Uh, not a chance," Valerie replied.

"I'll return with my sister, and we can all talk, but I don't want to alert Kenth. He's rather timid and very much about following rules. Right now, that's a risk we don't want to introduce."

"You think I can't sneak up on a house?" said Valerie with an air of casual conceit.

"Not here, you can't."

Praxis leaned over and whispered to Valerie. "People have a sense of things here that goes beyond what you're used to. You're not a natural part of this region. Even if you were perfectly silent, they'd know something was out of the ordinary if you get close."

Valerie pointed at Gabriel. "But not him?"

"No," he said. "Not me."

"Because he's from here? Hasn't he recently had his world membership card revoked? I think he'd be even more out of place than I would."

"Normally you would be right," conceded Praxis. "But Gabriel has... other tools at his disposal."

Gabriel spun about as if he'd been struck. *How did they know?* He looked hard at Praxis, who simply grinned, then gave a casual shrug.

"I know things," they said. "Remember, I have the best DVR system in the universe."

"What is DVR?" he said.

"Never mind. Just go."

Gabriel took several steps towards his sister's house, then began projecting.

He was supposed to be here. He was expected, yet ignorable. He required no attention.

When Gabriel reached the window of his sister's dining room he discovered that Fate was smiling upon him. Sendra was seated at the table, facing him, and across from her husband. After a few moments, she looked up to see her brother's face and her eyes went wide. Gabriel quickly put his finger to his lips, but Kenth was obviously asking her what was wrong. He saw the pre-shadow of her husband turning around, and quickly ducked below the sill.

Someone came to the window and cracked it open.

"There." It was Sendra's voice. "I think a bit of breeze will help." Suddenly the window opened wider, and she stuck her head out. "It's nice," she called back as she looked down at him. He motioned toward the back of the house, and her eyes narrowed. She mouthed 'How?', clearly at a loss to understand his lack of discernable intentions.

He motioned again, and crept away.

Sendra emerged through the back door a few minutes later. She was dressed in a pale yellow shift that Gabriel remembered being one of her favorites when she was still living in their parents' house.

"Gabby?" she whispered

"Surprise." He kept his voice similarly low.

"What are you doing here? And how come—"

Gabriel held up his hand. "I know you must have a thousand questions, and I'll be glad to answer them all, but not here. Can you come with me for a few minutes?"

"No," she said with an odd impatience. "Are you crazy, coming here?"

"What do you mean?"

"Don't play stupid with me." She sounded angry. Or was she hurt? It was hard to tell, but the insistence in her voice was unmistakable. "You need to leave. Now."

"What? Why? What's going on, Sen?"

"Don't act like you don't know." She turned around, making certain that Kenth had not followed before continuing. "I don't know what kind of trouble you're causing, but the Beacons have been resonating with warnings about you for days. And not just here in the Circle. Planet-wide, Gab. Planet wide!"

So it's true, he realized. *I have been cut off.*

"Do you know why?" he asked.

"No. But the intention is very clear, and it's coming from the First Mother herself. You are to be captured and sent to Annaphora. Whatever the reason, it's definitely not positive. No one's looking to award you any honors, Gabby." Sendra shook her head and said, "What have you gotten yourself into?"

"I..." How could he explain? If he had an hour, he might barely get the basics across, but there was no way she could disappear for that long without raising Kenth's suspicions. There just wasn't time. "I'm sorry, sis. I can't explain. Not right now. Just believe me, I haven't done anything wrong, even though the First Mother may think otherwise. It's just...It's just that I discovered something that the Chakrava doesn't know, and...and it's changed things."

"What in all the skies are you talking about?"

"Please believe me. I may not be doing what they expect or want, but I'm doing what's right."

She nodded. "I do believe you. I trust you. I don't know why. Maybe because you're my baby brother. Maybe because I'm a fool." She put her hand on his shoulder, and there was a deep, unquestioning love in the gesture.

Sendra saw a section of silk thread visible at the neck of his tunic and smiled. She tugged on it, lifting the Winder's Knot free from where it lay beneath. "It looks like this hasn't brought you terribly much luck."

Gabriel laughed softly. "I don't know. I'm still alive, right?"

Her expression softened. "Please be careful, you idiot." He nodded. "I haven't got another brother. Don't break this one, okay?"

"I'll do my best."

And then Kenth was calling out from inside their house, asking where she had gone. She gave Gabriel a gentle push, and he vanished back into the trees.

• • ● • •

"Where's your sister?" Praxis asked when Gabriel returned.

"There's a change of plan," he replied.

"Just what the hell does that mean?" Valerie demanded.

"It means we aren't getting any help here. Nor from anywhere else on Aerth."

"Great," Valerie muttered. "I hope you have some good news to balance that off."

"That *was* the good news."

"Does that mean there's also bad news?"

"I suppose I should mention that the entire planet appears to be looking for me, with orders to bring me to the First Mother. That feels like bad news."

Praxis started walking toward one of the wider trees. "I think there are better places to continue this conversation."

"You want to know what I think?" asked Valerie. They looked over their shoulder at her. "I think you just like making us sick to our stomachs."

"Guilty as charged," they replied with a grin. "Now let's get going."

• • ● • •

"You're absolutely positive we need to get his Worldstone?" Valerie asked after they had recovered from the portal and settled down in front of the fire. "We couldn't just 3D print a replica or something?"

Praxis chuckled. "That should work. The really important mystical artifacts are all coming pre-fab these days."

"I have no idea what half of that means," said Gabriel, "but the question remains. What do we do from here? Aerth may have given up on me, but I haven't given up on it."

"Do you still think your First Mommy is going to just hand the Worldstone over, or have we progressed to what I said in the first place: that we have no choice but to steal it?" Valerie asked.

Gabriel nodded. "Agreed. Although you were still wrong," he added.

"I was right and wrong at the same time?" she retorted. "Are you channeling Mel or something?"

Gabriel ignored the quip, although Valerie noticed that his expression flickered at the mention of Amelia's name and it made her wonder just how close they had gotten in the short time they were together. She briefly considered asking but by then he had resumed.

"There was no reason to think it wasn't an option at the time, so jumping right to 'let's steal it' was wrong. But don't worry. It just takes some people longer to become an adult."

Valerie narrowed her eyes at him. Was he trying to be playful or insulting? He stared back at her, his unflinching expression giving nothing away. She decided it was probably both. "Some people don't feel the need for rushing into things," she replied.

Simultaneously, each gave a nod of respect to the other, gestures of appreciation for a move well played.

"So you need a diversion," Praxis offered, attempting to get them back on topic.

"Do you have any suggestions?" Val asked.

"Yes. I suggest you don't ask me to solve your problems. I'm a Keeper, not a Champion."

"But you just suggested a diversion. Isn't that you helping to solve our problems?"

"No. That was just me stating the absurdly obvious, the obvious that you already knew damn well because we already talked about. I was just trying to get you back on topic."

"Can you at least give us a hint?" Valerie asked.

"No," they replied, a twinge of exasperation edging into their voice. "No, because I've never been in a situation like this, and if I had, I still wouldn't ruin the future by undermining what you're destined to do." Then they added, "For better or worse, like every single person in both worlds, I have to just put my faith on the line and hope you two don't fuck things up too badly."

"Fine." Valerie turned to Gabriel. "Okay, Gary, just how big of a distraction do we need?"

"Why do you keep calling me—"

"Are we talking people with signs walking down the street, or large explosions taking out half a city block?"

"What we need is something that will capture the attention of the people of the city, and most especially the Chakrava."

"So something bright and flashy. Ideally in the sky so everyone can see it."

Gabriel shook his head and glanced at Praxis for sympathy. They shrugged with an expression that spoke volumes. What can you expect from someone who doesn't have any Beacons?

"No," he explained. "It doesn't have to be visible to everyone. It has to be…how can I describe this…It has to be significant. The Chakrava are very sensitive, as are the city guards. They will sense anything that is happening, and if it gets the attention of the people in the city, their added focus will amplify the impact."

"Okay, so yes on the flashy, but no need for it to be visible. And how long does this need to last?"

"Long enough for me to get to the top of the east tower, into the High Temple, and grab the Worldstone. I would guess perhaps ten minutes. Maybe a little less."

"Why waste your time going up the tower?" She turned to Praxis. "Can't you just portal him into the temple?"

"Interesting thought," Gabriel mused. "Can you send me in without going yourself?"

"No," Praxis replied. "I'm part of the system, as it were. I can take you with me, but at least part of me will need to enter the world."

"Then that won't work," Gabriel said, turning back to Valerie. "The High Temple is the holiest of places in the Syntrodome. In the world. If someone were to enter it without a valid need, the Chakrava would instantly know. As would the temple guards."

"Think of it like a security system that can't be shut down," Praxis added.

"Our only hope is to keep people so focused on something else that they don't realize what's happening until it's too late." He looked over at Praxis. "I think we could start a few floors up in the east tower, though, don't you?"

"Stop asking me to help plan."

"But you just—" Valerie began, but Praxis immediately cut her off.

"Look, I'm happy to be a resource, but you two have to be the masterminds of this journey. You make the plans. I'll just bring the snacks and drive you around, okay?" They glanced back to Gabriel. "Er, handle the reins."

He rolled his eyes. "I got it. I may be cut off from my planet, but I can still use context."

"Oooh, someone's developing a bit of a snarky bite," Valerie teased.

"Anyway," Gabriel continued with a sigh. "The first two levels are open to the general populace. I think we can safely start there. So if we can just…" He saw a smile growing on Valerie's face. "What? Do you have an idea?"

"Can you give me a sense of how things are arranged?"

"Arranged? What do you mean? In the temple? In the Syntrodome?"

"Not inside. Unless it is unlike any building I've ever been in."

"Well, it's unique, but—"

"There's no way I can run around for ten minutes inside a building without getting caught. Especially not by people who know which way I'm going to turn before I do it. I meant the city."

Gabriel motioned to the globes. "Can we just show her?"

Praxis shook their head. "She wouldn't be able to see anything in Aerth beyond what she saw earlier today."

"I don't suppose you have a map?"

"The country, yes, but not of Annaphora."

"I'd like to at least get a sense of what the area surrounding this temple is like."

"The temple is in a tower, and the tower is part of the Syntrodome. And *that* is in the center of Annaphora," Gabriel explained.

"Can you show me what the city is like?" she asked.

"If you just want to get the flavor, we can use the portal." Praxis got up and walked over to the wall where shimmering images of Aerth flashed by faster than the eye could focus. Gabriel and Valerie followed.

"Here is the Syntrodome."

Praxis concentrated for a moment, and the portal stabilized on a view of the large, domed, stone structure that housed the primary functions of Aerth's government. It was cast in gray shadows from the moonlight. The perspective was from the outer edge of the Raespertaen, the broad ring that encircled the city's center, and although there were lamps set at regular intervals it was difficult to discern any details about the building.

"Can you show me a daytime view?"

"The portals are not like the globes. We are looking at how things are right now, not in the past. We could wait until morning."

"No, it's fine. I mostly just want to get a sense of city, not figure out how to scale a wall or anything."

Praxis shifted the view. "This is Skyline, one of the eight main spokes that connect the Raespertaen to the Hespertaen. To the left is the district where most of the financial organizations have headquarters. To the right..."

Over the next fifteen minutes they led Valerie on a shadowy, moonlit tour of Aerth's capital.

"Okay," Valerie said finally. "This could work."

"What could?" Gabriel replied.

"I've got an idea for how to create the diversion we need." A broad, wicked grin grew on her face. "But I need to make a stop at my apartment first."

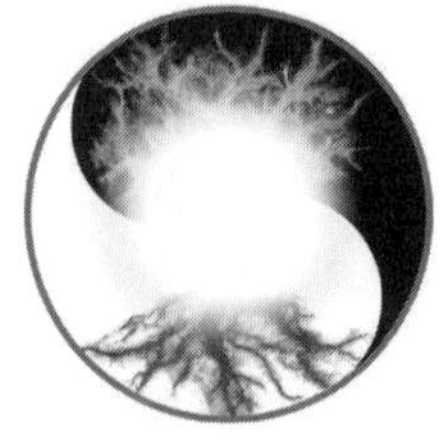

CHAPTER EIGHTEEN:

Executing the Plan

It was mid-morning in Annaphora. Wisps of clouds drifted lazily overhead and a soft, easterly summer breeze carried the aroma of freshly baked pastries into the financial district. People went about serious business through austere streets. On the corner of a building a bird was singing its heart out to accountants and tax planners far too engrossed in their ledgers to notice. It was a day like any other.

The bird stopped, its attention rapt on a section of wall, perhaps three feet above the street, that had suddenly begun to shimmer with a rainbow of sparks. Like the sensible, skittish creature it was, it didn't wait for what was to follow before taking flight for safer havens.

Suddenly a sleek, black Yamaha YZF-R1 motorcycle came flying out of the wall. It landed on the cobbles and screeched to a halt. The passenger in back—an androgynous figure dressed in soft grays and topped with hair shining like a rainbow after a storm—dismounted and stepped over to a white, stone wall. The rider in front flipped up the visor on her helmet long enough to wink at them, and then Praxis reached out, touched the wall, and was gone.

Valerie turned her bike's speakers to full blast, and the drum solo intro to *Walk This Way* began vibrating the nearby windows. When the bass guitar kicked in, she let out a wild scream of exhilaration, gunned the engine, and roared off down the Avenue of Tranquility as the music of Aerosmith cried out into the city.

• • • • •

In an empty hallway on the second floor of the east tower, Praxis and Gabriel stepped into existence. He wrapped himself in false intentions, nodded at Praxis, and started towards the stairs with the air of someone on a vital, uninteresting, and—most importantly—totally legitimate errand for the Chakrava.

• • • • •

Valerie sped down the streets of Annaphora. The roughness of the cobbles forced her to go slower than the glory she had envisioned, yet avoiding people was not the challenge she expected. The thunderous roar of the motorcycle caught their attention, and their touch of prescience ensured they were out of the way long before she was anywhere close, sometimes even before she had turned down a street. Regardless, people were noticing. Lots of people. Quite possibly everyone. Which was the point. If this wasn't a distraction, nothing would be.

And the rock music definitely helped.

She had been cruising for nearly five minutes before the local constables appeared and attempted to stop her. It happened on the Street of Dreams, although not being fluent in their writing, Valerie had no way of knowing that. As she turned a corner, an authoritative woman was standing about thirty feet ahead in the middle of the street. She was dressed in a body-hugging uniform, supple leather dyed a stylish combination of teal and brown, with a short sword scabbarded at her hip. Valerie was a little jealous. *If I ever go into law enforcement, it's definitely going to be here.*

The officer had her hand out, palm forward.

"Stop!"

The woman's voice was clear, strong, commanding. It was the voice of a woman used to being respected. It was the voice of authority, and no one would dare to disobey. Valerie flew by, the wind of her passing tossed the woman's hair into a cyclone of curly brown tresses. *That would have made a fantastic shampoo commercial*, she mused.

"Stop!" the officer repeated as she spun around in surprise.

"In your dreams!" the Champion called back as she sped down the Street of Dreams.

• • • • •

There was nobody at all on the stairs to the third floor of the tower, and only a pair of messengers on the rise to the fourth. They were women headed downwards and preoccupied with their own business; they didn't give Gabriel a second glance.

The fifth level was where things would become riskier. The curved stairway that hugged the lower levels ended here and one had to traverse a long, straight hallway through the center of the tower to reach the base of the next staircase. Offices lined that hall and people were regularly moving about, but the real challenge was at the end. Gabriel remembered that guards were stationed at the base of the upper stairway, and they would be actively focused on anyone attempting to pass. It was their job to ensure each person had a valid reason for ascending to the upper levels.

This would be the first true test of his skills in Dhokha di Maath.

He traversed the hallway with a stride purposeful but deferential. He was, after all, a man, and that made him conspicuous. Several women even stopped to watch him pass by, although no one said anything.

And then he was at the checkpoint.

There were four guards in attendance, and they all turned to study him as he approached.

I'm on an errand for the Chakrava, he projected. *It's important. And boring.*

Without hesitation, he approached the stairs. They watched, but there was no tension. He was doing what was right and reasonable. One of them nodded at him, but he saw that her eyes were twinkling with a hint of... non-professional interest. He smiled back demurely but didn't pause. His fictitious business was urgent, his intentions lied.

And then he was around the curve of the wall and climbing towards the seventh floor.

Back at the checkpoint, a woman—deliberately seated to be out of sight to anyone heading up the tower—rose and began to follow him.

• • • • •

Walk This Way ended, and *Crazy* kicked in. Fitting in its own way, but too slow for a high-speed rampage through the city. She advanced the track. *Dream On.*

Oh, I love this one, she thought. But still not the right mood. She tapped the button again. *Rag Doll.* She listened to the beat for a few measures before concluding that it would do the trick.

Valerie reached a broad, straight boulevard with smoother paving stones, and braked to a halt. To her left, perhaps a quarter of a mile away, she saw a large, domed structure that she recognized as the Syntrodome from the previous evening's 'city portal tour'. To the right was a longer stretch that would take her to the outskirts of the city. She turned right and gunned the engine. With a squeal, her tires left skid marks on stones that would likely never again feel the touch of rubber, and she shot off down Brightwater Avenue.

She had gone perhaps a mile when she saw an entire troop of police lining the sides of the street. She estimated at least two dozen, probably closer to three. *So here the resistance begins for real,* she mused, and found she was oddly, perhaps even morbidly, excited to see what they had planned for her. She liked a challenge. What clever technique would the police of this world use to stop something as foreign as a motorcycle? Had they laid down spikes to puncture her tires? A rope they would pull taut once she was too close to stop? But she couldn't see anything in the road. Valerie glanced over her shoulder; another large crowd of officers had emerged and spanned out across the road behind her.

She slowed.

Now she noticed that to either side, more policewomen were standing in each of the smaller streets. They had her surrounded. There must have been over a hundred of them.

Valerie continued to cruise forward, slowing further to a mere twenty miles per hour as she tried to guess what they had in mind. There were no caltrops or spikes, but upon second thought that was perhaps not surprising. The police in this world dealt with wagons; they would have no reason to believe that tires could be punctured.

As she progressed the policewomen started pouring into the street. *They plan to literally just grab me,* she realized. *Well, let's see how that goes for them.* She popped the clutch, and the bike shot back up to fifty. She wished her radio hadn't already been maxed out. This would have been a perfect time to turn it up.

"Yes, I'm movin'" Valerie belted out the lyrics as she raced towards women now sprinting to make a line in front of her. "Get ready for the big time!"

She let Steve Tyler go it alone as he rang out, 'Tap dancing on a land mine'. Her concentration was entirely focused on steering and stability. She wondered if they were truly willing to take a motorcycle to the chest, hoped it wouldn't come to that. She leaned forward and aimed right between two of the blockaders. They had their arms linked with one another and Valerie felt bad for what was now inevitable. She lowered her head. The windscreen was low on her bike, too low to fully protect her, but this would be a glancing blow off her helmet. And at this speed…

She smashed through the line. Valerie felt the impact of a woman's forearm against her helmet and heard the snapping of bones. She grimaced in sympathy as she sped down the road. These people were just doing their job, but she couldn't afford to be caught. Worlds were at stake here, and that outweighed a few broken ulnas. *Ulnas? Is that right? Ulni? Ulnae? Wait, no. Isn't the ulna in the leg? Oh, screw it. How much longer do I need to keep this up?*

Valerie stole a glance at the little clock on her dash. Seven minutes so far. Not long enough.

A moment later she reached the outskirts of Annaphora and skidded left onto the Hespertaen.

• • • • •

Gabriel topped the stairs on the eighth floor, just one level below the High Temple.

The upper floors of the east tower were unlike the lower levels, which were entirely about functionality. As one ascended, the hallways and chambers reached back into antiquity, almost like the tower had been built from the top downwards over thousands of years. Where the first few floors were well lit and adorned with decorations that carried the freshness of recently woven tapestries and modern motifs, here the stonework exuded a sense of tremendous age and consisted of deeply carved reliefs of the most primordial archetypes. As he made his way towards the center of the tower, Gabriel noticed that the carvings were intertwined, a flowing story from Aerth's rich mythology.

This penultimate floor, he recalled from when he attended the service just before he departed for Havlanti, was configured like a starburst. A large central room served as a gathering chamber, with seven passages extending outwards in a radial pattern. Once he reached that room, the hallway to the south would take him to a U-shaped stairway that would open into the antechamber of the High Temple.

Gabriel had only proceeded a dozen feet towards the center when he heard a footstep behind him. He felt a chill, and then a familiar voice called out.

"Gabriel."

He knew the voice. It was Aliesha, his trainer, and the woman the Chakrava would have sent in his place had he not appeared to claim the role of Champion.

Adrenaline rushed through him, but he turned around slowly to give himself a moment to calm his now-racing pulse. By the time he was facing her, his expression was kind and welcoming, a match for softly spoken words.

"Hello, Leigh." He smiled and redoubled his projection of false intentions. "It's so nice to see you again."

"What are you doing here, Gab?"

"I'm on an errand for the First Mother. She asked me to retrieve something for her from the High Temple."

Aliesha took a single step towards him, and he could see that she was struggling with the uncertainty of an impossible contradiction.

"You're lying. I know for a fact she didn't send you." Her brow furrowed. "So how can it possibly be that you think she did?"

Gabriel took a step backwards, prepared to run.

"Don't," she said. "You know you can't."

She was right. They both knew she was faster. He relaxed, stood up straight to face her. "Aliesha . . ." he began.

"What are you really doing here?" she asked again.

"The First Mother sent you to watch for me," Gabriel said as he pieced it together. "It's the only explanation. So what did she tell you? Did she not give you a reason?"

"Don't make me ask again, Gabriel."

"You know why I'm here. There's only one reason Khalfani would have sent you to watch for me."

"Yes. She wanted someone here who would recognize you, even if you . . . looked different. And someone who could stop you, bring you back to her. But no, she didn't tell me why... only that she feared that the Beacons would not alert us if you came." She paused. "And apparently she was right, although I can't imagine how it can possibly be." She shook her head in disappointment. "What happened to you?"

Gabriel sensed that she was more than simply disappointed. She was hurt. She feared he was betraying her, betraying everyone. He saw that this was not just a woman following the orders of First Mother. This was very personal to Aliesha.

"Things are not what they seem, Leigh. What the Chakrava believe, it's . . . it's wrong."

"The Chakrava are wrong? You think they—"

"They've been misled. Not in some kind of nefarious plot, but by Mother Aerth herself. Our world can only envision one possible—"

"Stop!" she demanded, and the ensuing silence was overpowering. The seconds crept past, and finally Aliesha continued. "You can't seriously expect me to believe that you, a boy who had never laid eyes upon the sacred texts until a month ago, had not even been to the Syntrodome for that matter, could possibly—"

"I know there's no reason to believe me," he interrupted, and then his voice turned steely. "But I was there! In the moment. I was face to face with the Champion from the other world, and I'm telling you that what everyone expects, this 'fight to the death' prophesy, is not the right answer!" He studied her, looking for a sign that she could see the futility, the *wrongness*, of that way of thinking. "The Nexus is the beginning of a new age for our world. Does aggression really sound like the right way to usher it in?"

"I don't know, Gabriel," she answered at last. "What you say makes sense, but this really isn't for me to decide. The First Mother gave me very specific instructions. You were to be subdued and brought to her. Maybe we can skip the subduing part, but I need you to come with me." Aliesha paused, and her expression grew worried. "I don't understand why you aren't casting any pre-shadows, and that's very... eerie. So come on. Let's just go talk it out with the First Mother, okay?"

"My heart tells me that is not a good idea. The First Mother is listening to the Beacons of our world, and those—"

"That's what she's *supposed* to do! For the love of light, Gabby, that's what *you're* supposed to be doing!"

"But the world is wrong! It is only one half of the whole, only sees one half of the picture."

"And you know better." Her voice was filled with skepticism.

"I've seen things, Leigh. I saw how the two worlds were split apart!"

"Can you even hear yourself? Can't you... Don't you realize how crazy you sound?"

Gabriel took a deep breath, then stepped to her and took her arms in his hands. He wanted to release the false intentions of the Deceptive Heart and truly let her inside, but he didn't dare. It would be noticed instantly, and the guards would come rushing. Instead, he tried to show her in the only immediate way he could.

"Look at me, Leigh. Look in my eyes. Listen to my voice. Do I look like I've lost my mind? Do I sound insincere, or in doubt of what I'm saying?"

She shook her head. "You lied to me two minutes ago, Gabby. How can I trust the way things feel now?"

"I can't answer that. For the good of our society, I can't say why your nythlen isn't showing you what you expect. The First Mother can, and maybe she'll give you an explanation that will help. All I can tell you is that there is more happening than anyone here realizes. If you come with me to the High Temple, I can introduce you to someone... someone who can help you see, with your own eyes, the things that I've seen."

He could sense that she wanted to believe him, that her Beacons were becoming as conflicted as his own had been.

"Please, Aliesha. I *can* save this world, but I can't do it following the path the Chakrava want me to walk."

"I don't know."

"Look, just... just come with me to the High Temple. After I have the Worldstone, you'll see that I'm telling the truth. And if you still don't believe me, then you can bring me to the First Mother. And I'll go. I promise."

She stared at him long and hard, then muttered, "I must be out of my mind."

He hugged her fiercely, and they started towards the High Temple together.

• ● ● ● •

When *Love In An Elevator* came on, Valerie banked left to swerve around a long, narrow wading pool. She had been on the Hespertaen for nearly two miles, and was starting to feel as though staying on the thoroughfare would be overly predictable. And for at least the next five or ten minutes, she absolutely needed to stay one step ahead of the authorities.

She was confident that every single citizen in Annaphora knew about her by now. The streets were completely empty, but nearly every window sported at least one head watching her ride past. Many had two heads; a few had three. In one particularly wide window she had seen four.

Valerie turned left, heading back toward the center of the city along a winding road. After about a hundred yards it came to a tee intersection, and to her left she saw a large troop of officers watching her from the next street over. Even at full speed it was unlikely she could crash through that crowd, and a lot of women would get injured in such an attempt. Undoubtedly including her. She turned right.

The street ran straight at first, but soon gave way to a series of zig-zag turns. Rounding the last of them, she saw that the entire road had been blocked off with a pile of crates stacked at least fifteen feet high.

"Nope. Not that way," she muttered to herself as she spun her bike around. She heard the sound of something crashing from the direction she had come, and a sense of imminent, impending awfulness took hold. "This isn't good."

As Valerie made her way back, slower out of a growing caution, her fears were confirmed. A large stack of crates had been dumped into the street from the rooftops on either side. Dozens of women watched her from atop the buildings, police she surmised based their leather outfits.

"That really is a fantastic look," she said to herself as she brought the bike to a stop. Checking her clock, she saw that she had been riding around for just over eight minutes. "Hope that's enough time, Gary, because I'm pretty sure things are about to turn very, very ugly here."

Valerie heard more people approaching from behind and turned to see at least two dozen officers emerging from building doorways.

"Praxis," she whispered. "Praxis?" She looked around. "*Now* would be good."

There was no reply.

She dismounted her bike and held her hands up. "It's okay," she called out. "I just got lost." The police were approaching cautiously, their expressions unmistakably . . . well, not happy. Very not happy. She pulled her helmet off. "I don't suppose you want to see my license and registration?"

Why weren't any of them saying anything?

She backed up against the wall of a tall building labeled with indecipherable symbols. There was a door next to her, and she gave the handle a try. Locked.

"Praxis!" she hissed and slid over a couple of feet to free up lots of wall space on either side of her. Even as she was doing it, she realized it was a pointless move. Praxis could create a portal on the door as easily as on the stone of the wall.

The policewomen were only a dozen feet away now, and continuing their cautious approach. She pressed on the surface behind her. Very solid.

Then the troop stopped advancing, and a single woman stepped forward. She had a pair of iron manacles in one hand, the other resting on the hilt of the sword on her belt. "On your knees. Hands behind your back."

Valerie glanced around once last time, but still saw no sign of the Keeper. *How the hell am I going to get out of this?* She could maybe take on four or five of them at a time . . . maybe . . . but not this many, and certainly not if they could predict her attacks like Gary did. She had to stall.

The woman with the iron shackles took another step forward. Valerie smiled sweetly and said, "Oh, I really look terrible in wrought iron. I don't suppose you have something in silver? I can wait."

"On your knees. Hands behind—"

Valerie's autonomic defiance instantly flared in response. "Make me, bitch!"

The woman held up an arm, elbow bent, and a moment later Valerie felt two stinging bites, one in her shoulder and the other in her thigh. Her head lolled forward involuntarily and she saw a dart protruding from her leg, and then she saw nothing at all.

• • • • •

Gabriel stood in the doorway, hesitant. The High Temple was arranged as he remembered, the major elements in their respective places: the altar in the eastern section of the inner sanctum where the Tree of Life grew around it, the benches lined up before it. What differed were the little things. Everything that was not absurdly heavy had been put away. He remembered seeing a set of candles and some polished bowls, and even a series of braziers by the walls. They were all gone. Even the altar cloth had been stowed. His nythlen told him that something was wrong here, that something important was eluding his thinking, but the seconds were rushing past and each one urgently whispered 'time is running out' as it went by.

"What's wrong?" Aliesha asked.

"I don't know," he replied. "I just... Nothing." He wanted to explore that nagging feeling, but the urgency of his task was overwhelming. The conversation with Leigh had taken too many precious minutes, and he strongly suspected that Valerie had already been stopped. Or worse, captured. And if that were the case, the Chakrava would be returning their attention to other matters, like sensing the presence of strangers in their holiest of temples. They may have already sent people to investigate. Perhaps that was the source of this overpowering sense of... wrongness.

"Come on," he said, and walked over to the altar. It had been covered when he had last been here, but now he saw that the altar was formed from a single block of the blackest onyx. It was perfectly smooth, and perhaps three times as wide as it was deep. If ever there was a gemstone crafted for protective energies, this was it.

"Everything about this feels wrong," Aliesha whispered from immediately behind him.

"Yeah. I know. But it isn't."

The Worldstone was suspended high above, and climbing atop the altar felt tremendously like desecration. *You're stealing from the High Temple, Gabriel. You already crossed that line*, he reminded himself. Then he gave a hollow laugh. *Not just crossed it. Charged over it like a starved jaguarondi.*

He hefted himself onto the stone surface and reached up. Even on his toes, the Worldstone was at least three feet beyond his reach. He jumped, and heard Aliesha gasp in shock at his irreverence. The crystal was too high. He tried again, but it was clearly out of reach.

"I need you to come up here and give me a boost," he said.

"You can't be serious."

"Leigh, this has to happen. We can pray for forgiveness later, but we're really running out of time."

"You may be running out of time. Not me, and I'm very much not at all comfortable with desecrating the altar. Or the temple. Or..."

He looked down at her, his gray eyes pleading.

• • • • •

Meraya remained in a crouch. Her hiding spot was ideal, but it was imperative that she free herself from any intent to act unless it became absolutely necessary; she remembered all too well how sensitive the Champion was. And since at this moment, at least, it was not clear that she needed to take any action, there was only one choice: just watch.

• • • • •

"I really don't want to have to start throwing my shoes at it," Gabriel pleaded.

"Gabby," Aliesha pleaded back. "Let's just go. We can—" She stopped. The look in his eyes was clear. If she didn't help him, she would have to stop him.

"Once I have the Worldstone, you're going to understand."

She shook her head, a gesture of disbelief at her own insanity. She was actually going to do this. "You'd better be right."

"I am. I guarantee it."

She kicked off her shoes and climbed onto the altar with Gabriel.

"Thank you," he said.

"Just shut up," she replied, and laced her fingers together.

Gabriel lifted a foot, stepped into her hands, and prepared to leap. He fixed his eyes on the Worldstone, focusing on his trajectory.

Leigh counted them down. "Three, two..."

He saw himself tumbling. How was that possible? He cried out, "Wait!" just as Leigh shouted 'one', but it was too late.

• • • • •

The traitor was going to try it, and that meant she no longer had a choice. Meraya put the tube to her lips and blew. Pre-shadow or not, he'd have no way to avoid the dart once he was already in the air.

• • ● • •

Aliesha heaved Gabriel upward, launching him towards the Worldstone just as the dart's pre-shadow appeared to her. She did not see the projectile itself, but its tranquilizing effect was instantaneous and obvious. Aliesha shifted, reached out, and broke Gabriel's fall, pulling him back towards herself as she landed hard on the top of the altar.

She turned her head at the sound of a footstep, saw Meraya approaching. The woman stopped and tilted her head, considering what to do next. The stranger lifted a blowgun to her lips. With Gabriel on top of her as he was, there was no possibility of avoiding the shot.

Everything went black.

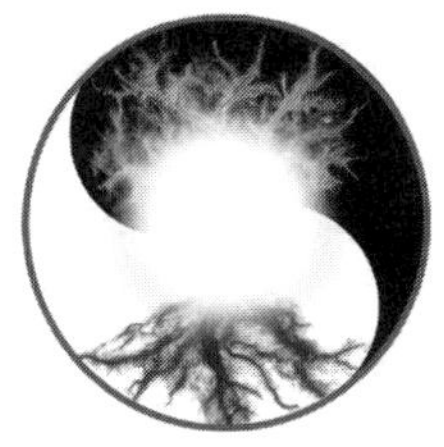

CHAPTER NINETEEN:

Executing the Champion

Gabriel sat cross-legged on the floor of the gray, stone-walled holding cell in the lower levels of the Syntrodome. It was not for the lack of a chair or cot in the space, as there was one of each, although the cot was occupied with the sleeping and manacled form of Valerie. He was simply more comfortable using the seat of the chair as an armrest.

For the past twenty minutes he had been looking furtively about the cell, hoping Praxis would appear through one of the walls now that he and Valerie were together, but the Keeper was apparently keeping their distance for some reason. What could they possibly be waiting for? Or perhaps what kept them away was the presence of the pair of guards.

The two women stood motionless on either side of the cell door. They were dressed in black leather like the assassin had worn, and possessed a calm confidence that Gabriel found simultaneously admirable and intimidating. The guards had been standing there since he awoke from his drug-induced blackout and neither had spoken. He had asked them what was happening, but they refused to even acknowledge the question.

Gabriel had to assume that he was here because the First Mother wanted to speak with him, and that was probably the cause for this waiting. She was always busy. No, that was not it. There would be no higher priority in the world than what was happening here. She was delaying for some other reason. To make him nervous? Doubtful. She knew him well enough to realize that he would use the time to settle his nerves, not lose them.

Valerie stirred. *Ah,* he thought. *She's waiting until we're both awake.*

Valerie groaned and shifted.

Gabriel couldn't help but find the situation somewhat ironic. For the brief time that they had known each other, a disproportionately large fraction of it had been spent in some type of jail cell. Although, when one thinks about it, isn't life itself a form of cell where—

Valerie rolled off the cot and landed on the floor. Her eyes shot open, and she struggled against the manacles as if she had not realized they were there. Then she saw him.

"Seriously?" she asked, more than a hint of exasperation in her voice. "Seriously? You just sat there and watched me fall off a bed?"

The juxtaposition was amusing, and he smiled despite his better judgment.

"This is funny?" Valerie said.

"It's a bit ironic at the least, don't you think?"

"How so?"

"It wasn't that long ago when I was the one falling onto the floor while you just watched."

"We were in different cells, you idiot. I couldn't have helped if I wanted to."

He considered this. "Would you have helped if you could?"

"No," she admitted.

"Well, there we have it. Irony."

"What you call irony, I call Gary being a jackass," she retorted.

"You do know my name's Gabriel, don't you?"

"Whatever."

Gabriel rocked forward and rose to his feet. He helped Valerie up and they both took a seat on the cot. The guards watched them, passive yet alert.

"And who are the ladies?" Val asked.

He shrugged. "They haven't introduced themselves."

"Has anyone else made an appearance?"

He knew what she meant. "No. Not that I've noticed, anyway."

She nodded. "So . . . any luck?"

Gabriel gave a sardonic chuckle. "If you include bad luck, then yes. Plenty."

"Anything you'd care to share?"

He looked up at the guards, saw their attentiveness. "No, not really."

Valerie nodded, and then suddenly thought of something. She stood, and her hands patted the back pocket of her jeans. "Fuck," she muttered.

"What's wrong?" he asked. "Aside from the obvious, that is."

"The bitches took my knife. I mean, I get it, prisoners and all, but still." She took a step towards the guards. "Can I get my knife back when we leave?"

There was no response.

"It was a butterfly knife. Ivory handle. It has a lot of sentimental value."

Still no response.

"I realize that it's only natural to disarm people in jail," Valerie continued, "but I mean when all this is finished, can I get it back?" The guards remained silent. She walked back to the cot and sat down. "Talkative gals, huh?"

Gabriel heard footsteps and saw the pre-shadow of the cell door opening. When it opened a moment later, Khalfani entered. She wore a long, black robe that just touched the floor, and walked with such steady grace that she almost appeared to be floating above the ground. Gabriel wondered if the garment had been designed with that effect in mind. Beyond he spotted two additional guards who took up positions outside the cell. *Do they really think I would so demean myself as to attack the First Mother?*

The head of the Chakrava stopped two paces into the cell and considered him with sad eyes.

"Peace be with you, Your Holiness," he greeted her.

"And with you, my son," she replied. Then she looked at Valerie. "And who is this?"

"I'm Betty," Valerie replied immediately. "Betty Smith, barista and motorcycle enthusiast."

The First Mother considered her, her face a mask of impassivity.

"This is Valerie," Gabriel said. "She is the Champion from the other world."

"You're an idiot," Valerie said with a roll of her eyes. "You know that, right?"

"You cannot lie to the First Mother," he explained.

"I can lie to whoever I want."

"No, I mean—"

Khalfani waved him to silence and said, "Peace be with you as well, child."

Valerie snorted and rattled her manacles. "You're shitting me, right?"

The First Mother studied Valerie for a time, a smile coming to her lips that wandered back and forth between amused and appreciative. Then she retrieved the chair from the far wall, adjusted it to face the cot, and sat.

"Child, please understand. I hold no ill will against you. To the contrary, I have a profound respect for you, and for the demands that The Nexus has placed upon you. I understand that you are simply following your Beacons, as are we all."

"Actually, I make my own decisions, thank you," Valerie shot back. "You know, thinking for myself and all that."

"You have a lot of anger for a warrior," Khalfani observed.

"They typically go hand in hand," Valerie replied.

"Do they? I find that anger *typically* stands in the way of perfection."

The First Mother's enunciation of 'typically' told Valerie volumes. It was exquisitely pronounced to carry just enough contempt to be mocking, yet not enough to legitimize offense. It unnerved her, and the best response Valerie could muster was, "I guess you've never tried being perfectly angry."

The First Mother cocked her head as if she was listening to something, and then turned to study Gabriel. Valerie felt dismissed, and it infuriated her. But what could she do? She was manacled, and the bitch had let her have the last word. A crappy last word. Damn, this old woman was good.

Khalfani's tone took on a firm, almost judicial, tone as she addressed Gabriel. "I am told that you refused to kill this woman even when the opportunity presented itself."

"Yes, Your Holiness," he replied.

"I was further told that you protected her life with your own." Gabriel nodded. "May I ask why?"

"I do not believe that killing her is the right thing to do."

"I see," Khalfani replied in a curt, matter-of-fact tone. "Do you have doubts as to whether she is the otherworld Champion?"

"No."

"Do you have doubts as to whether you are our Champion?"

"No, Your Holiness."

"Is it possible that you have developed an attachment to this woman?"

Gabriel just looked at the First Mother in silence. Finally he said, "Any attachment, or lack thereof, is not a factor in this."

"Please help me understand, my son. The future of our entire world lies at stake, and yet you appear ready to sacrifice it for... what? Surely you do not feel this is an unreasonable question for us to ask."

"I do not believe that our future lies in killing Valerie."

"You believe that it is more appropriate to allow her world to survive at the cost of our own?"

"I think there are more possibilities than this 'either-or' that you and the Chakrava envision."

"My son," Khalfani started. Most people would have missed the irritation that was beginning to surface in her tone, but not he, not someone who had studied Dhokha di Maath under her tutelage. "Gabriel. These Necessities have been understood and documented for thousands upon thousands of years. The wisdom of countless generations of Chakrava have been recorded. The call of the Beacons over—"

"The Beacons are wrong."

The statement clearly shocked the First Mother, and she was silent for several seconds before continuing. "Wrong? The Beacons have been successfully, and faithfully, guiding us towards our Purposes for millennia."

"And yet, most holy First Mother, they're wrong."

"How could that possibly be?"

"They see only a portion of the truth. But there is a greater balance than what they can perceive."

"Fascinating. You are claiming that the Beacons are... short-sighted..." mused Khalfani. She shook her head as she considered the hypothesis, and Gabriel could see that she was unconvinced. In a sudden flash of insight he realized with overwhelming certainty that *this* was the true battle Aerth's Champion had to face, had to win. And just as certainly, he realized that he was losing it.

"You must believe me," he pleaded. "Try to understand that—"

"And now you seek to teach *me*?" she cut him off. Her tone was soft and unassuming, but he knew that that modesty was a trap, a thin veneer over a deep anger. It was an act, an illusion for the other women standing witness, so that the First Mother would retain the aura of a leader poised and in perfect control of the situation.

Gabriel took a calming breath and attempted to explain again. "We cannot heal past trauma with renewed aggression."

"Fine words, my son, but you are asking me to disregard the insights of thousands of generations of the wisest people our world has ever known, and all on the word of one *man*."

Hearing her inflection in that final word, he realized that he had lost. Perhaps he'd never stood a chance. Convincing the First Mother to disregard the Histories would have been difficult for anyone, but for such seditious counsel to be delivered by a man...

"No," Khalfani continued. "I believe it is you who are mistaken."

"Khalfani, please—"

"How dare you?" The First Mother shot back with a sudden, terrifying intensity. All traces of sympathy had vanished. "Very well. If you will not fulfill your destiny willingly, then we will assist you with it."

The First Mother stood. As she floated out of the cell the guards motioned for Valerie and Gabriel to follow.

• • • • •

The passage they traversed was dimly lit with evenly-spaced patches of phosphorescence. There were no windows in these lower levels, but the light was more than sufficient for Gabriel to see that they were in trouble.

He and Valerie were surrounded by four guards. The leather-clad women who had been inside the cell walked behind. In front, and maintaining a precise two-pace separation from the First Mother, were the other two guards. They wore the green and teal of Annaphora police, but the uniform was different in style. These were no ordinary enforcers of the law. Gabriel guessed them to be in their early thirties, and had the strong impression that they trained continuously. He had no doubt they were extremely capable warriors. Unless Praxis appeared, there would be no escape. Gabriel kept his eyes on the walls as they walked, hoping to catch a glimpse of the tattooed Keeper or their shimmering portal, but all he saw was gray stone and dark shadows.

Gabriel couldn't help but recall the last time he had walked the halls of the Syntrodome with the First Mother. She and the rest of the Chakrava had escorted him like an honor guard as he set forth to face the otherworld Champion. This was similar, wasn't it? There were guards, and the entire situation was a consequence of his dedication to acting honorably. And the otherworld Champion was still the crux of the issue. The manacles were a new element, of course, and it was hard to get past the icy tension that was threatening to destroy . . . well, everything. Literally.

Gabriel chuckled lightly, a sound that won him a confused look from Valerie. He certainly had not imagined back then that he would be bringing her to the Syntrodome to meet the First Mother. He wondered what would have happened had he approached the leader alone. Would she have been more willing to listen in a private setting? Would he have even been permitted to speak with her Holiness in private? Probably not. Once the assassin had reported that he had protected Valerie, everything changed.

Gabriel watched the First Mother as she marched along the corridor. He knew she was furious, and yet she carried herself with that same stately grace she always did, like the surface of a lake on a windless day, a surface that would brook no ripple. She neither rushed nor hesitated as she piloted them all towards Valerie's death.

And possibly his.

After a few minutes, Valerie inclined her head towards him and asked, "Where are we going?"

"A room has been prepared," the First Mother responded immediately. "In that place, Gabriel will kill you, even if it means we must force his hand to do so."

"You attempt to push the present toward a future you wish to see," said Gabriel. His voice carried a clear undertone of disappointment, and just for the barest moment he thought he saw the First Mother stiffen slightly at the rebuke. He had struck a nerve, but she kept walking without response.

"A wise friend once warned me about what can happen when one's mind is clouded with expectation. I cannot help but wonder what the Chakrava of old would say to how you defy the Beacons now," he said, hoping to goad her into a discussion that might halt their progress.

Khalfani's pace did not falter. She did not even turn around as she replied, "It is *you* who has strayed from the path, Gabriel. It is *you* who ignore the Beacons. I am merely trying to set us back on our destined path, a path from which we have strayed as a result of your misguided choices. This is a correction that must be made, for your own sake as well as everyone else's."

They turned a corner, and Valerie lost her footing. She stumbled into Gabriel, her face pressed against the side of his. In the barest whisper she said, "Next time, reach into my bra."

The statement threw him completely. He must have misheard. But what else could she have possibly said that would sound even close? And if he had heard correctly, what could she be thinking? Surely this was not her idea of a romantic gesture. Valerie was certainly inclined towards unpredictability, and behaved as far outside any social norm as one could possibly imagine, but this was not the time for...

She was glaring at him. Valerie obviously recognized his confusion and was not pleased. She glanced down at her own chest and then back at him, her gaze hard, unrelenting. Whatever else she was, she was serious.

At the next corner, she stumbled again. This time she crashed into him and they both tumbled to the ground. As she had demanded, he feigned trying to protect himself by putting his hands up to where her breasts were falling towards him. As they tumbled, one hand slipped into her cleavage to find a strange canister, small enough to easily fit in his palm. It was perhaps two inches long, and there was a tiny ring affixed to one end. He closed his fist around it as the guards pulled them to their feet.

Valerie immediately began screaming at him.

"What the hell do you think you're doing?! As soon as my hands are chained you think you can just feel me up?!"

Val charged and body-checked him into a wall. In a tangle of limbs they fell to the floor again. "You bastard!" she shouted, and then tried to bite his ear. Her teeth missed, and an instant later she was whispering, "Close your eyes when it goes off!" Then the guards had them both again, and they were pulled to their feet.

Val glared at Gabriel, and said, "Just what kind of crap are you trying to *pull*?"

"What are you talking about?" he responded in complete bafflement. "I didn't do anything. You—"

"I said, what are you trying to *pull*?"

"You fell into *me*. I didn't do anything."

"Move!" ordered one of the guards in black leather, and pushed them forward.

Valerie was shaking her head in frustration, and then tried again. "You think you can *pull* some kind of *ring* on me?"

Gabriel simply stared at her, utterly confused.

She finally gave up on subtlety. In a low voice she said, "Pull out the damn ring and throw it in the air, you moron."

It took one more brief moment, but understanding finally dawned. Gabriel did as she ordered, squeezing his eyes closed.

As the cylinder sailed into the air, Valerie cried out, "That's mine! Give it back!"

The mystery of that statement had exactly the desired effect. The guards in front, as well as the First Mother, turned around to see what Valerie was talking about. What they witnessed was the miniature flashbang grenade tracing a gentle arc through the air, and then disintegrating in a blinding light as an explosive roar echoed off the stone walls.

Without hesitation, Valerie jumped high into the air and swung her manacled hands under her feet so they would at least be in front of her. She screamed at Gabriel, who could barely hear her for the ringing in his ears, “Which way is out?”

He pointed and began to run. They reached an intersection, and Gabriel turned to the right. Valerie grabbed his tunic and dragged him the opposite way. He understood. It was an attempt at misdirection, or at least what passed for it on Earth. It wouldn’t fool anyone here, but they had a head start as the guards tried to recover, and hopefully that would be enough.

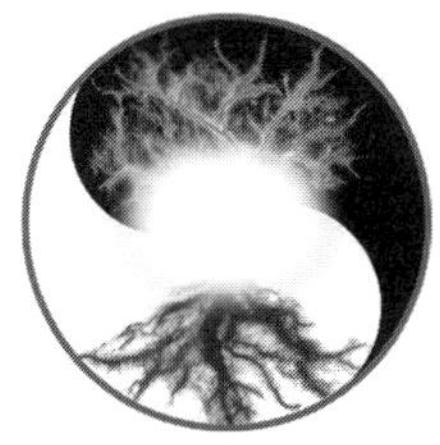

CHAPTER TWENTY:

Executing the Executioner

"Where the hell is Praxis?" demanded Valerie as they ran.

Gabriel didn't respond. Valerie's own hearing had recovered after a minute or two, but she wondered if perhaps his had not.

"Can you hear me?" she panted.

He nodded. "I need to focus. I'm trying to throw them off our trail."

This made no sense to Valerie, but there wasn't a lot about Gary that did.

"You *are* taking us to the temple, right?" she asked. His only response was an offended look. "Just making sure."

They continued to run. Gabriel was selecting the less-traveled passages. It was a little longer, but seemed worth the extra seconds. Even a single confrontation would delay them far more than they could afford. There were still people around them, but not many and the few they did encounter were focused on their own matters and quickly cleared out of their way.

Once they reached the base of the east tower, they raced up the stairs two or three at a time. There was still no sound of pursuit as they crested the top of the first staircase. Valerie expected there to be more guards, but was beginning to realize that a lot of what she thought of as common sense did not apply in this world. Gabriel took off immediately down the long hallway in front of them, and she put on a burst of speed to catch up.

The Champions charged into the checkpoint room together at full throttle. The guards there had obviously heard them running down the hall and were spread out in the middle of the room, swords drawn and at the ready. There was no question that these were women trained to fight, but Valerie also saw telltale traces of hesitance. There was something about this encounter that was leaving them more ill-at-ease than a guard would normally be, and Valerie wondered if Gary was perhaps doing something that she could not perceive.

The Champions split apart, her veering right and him to the left. She couldn't help but be impressed with the way she and Gary were in sync, how they instinctively adapted to what the other was thinking. Or was that a consequence of his seeing a second or two into her future?

She dove forward, placing the farthest guard between her and the next nearest; with a quick glance she saw that Gary had done the same. *Is he copying my technique?* she wondered.

The woman nearest to Valerie rushed at her, sword pointed forward like a spear. *These four are clearly not the Syntrodome's A-team*, she mused.

Valerie didn't care for swords. She found that when she used one she became preoccupied with the weapon and thought less about other forms of attack. This guard apparently suffered from the same inclination. As the woman charged, Valerie swung the chain of her manacles upwards. It looked like an attack on the sword, which the guard flicked up and out of the way. The woman failed to appreciate that her face was also in line with the motion of the chain, at least until it broke her nose. Val used her preoccupation with that injury to slam her heel down on an exposed ankle. As the guard fell, Valerie relieved her of the sword and jumped backward. *One down.*

Meanwhile, Gary had been less successful in lining up his adversaries, and two of the guards were closing in on him. It was not looking promising, and Valerie wondered what would happen if the stupid boy died before The Nexus arrived. But as she watched, the strangest thing happened. Both guards jumped to their left for no comprehensible reason. It was if they were convinced he was going to make a break for it in that direction. Instead, Gary ducked to their right and was instantly inside one of the guard's defenses. He had her on the ground with a leg sweep, and then kicked. The strike was not aimed for the woman's head, yet she stupidly shifted her face directly into the path of his foot. There was impact, and the guard went limp. It was fascinating to watch, and Valerie wanted to ask him what was going on, but there were more immediate demands upon her attention.

The woman facing her held her weapon in a defensive stance, and Val decided to press the attack. As their blades came together, Valerie's left hand shot forward and grabbed the woman's sword-arm wrist. Her opponent tried to leap back, but Valerie was too fast. With the woman's wrist now firmly in her grasp, she twisted, lifted, and twisted the other way. The guard's sword clattered to the ground, and a moment later the rest of her followed. Val smashed the hilt of her stolen weapon into the back of the guard's head, and she too went still.

When Valerie looked up, she saw that Gary had already neutralized his second opponent and was standing at the base of the steps.

"Are you finished now?" he asked with a hint of boredom, but she could see a playful twinkle in his eyes.

• • • • •

Gabriel stopped just outside the entrance to the High Temple.

"What's wrong?" asked Val.

He put a finger to his lips, then examined the room beyond. He had the same feeling of unease as before, but he could not determine whether it was a message from his Beacons or simply a matter of caution born of experience.

"I know you're in there," he called out.

Valerie looked at him quizzically, and he responded to the expression with a shrug that said 'I have no idea if anyone's in there'. It almost made her laugh, but she could not ignore the foolishness of alerting anyone inside to their presence. Instead, she whispered, "You really don't understand the element of surprise, do you?"

He motioned for her to back away from the door and then brought his lips next to her ear, "This is my world, Valerie. Things work differently here. Including surprise."

"Fine, whatever. But we don't have much time."

"If someone *is* inside then right now they're probably putting a poison dart into a blowgun. At least, that's what she's doing if it's who I think might be there."

"Do you really think your Holy Mama would still have someone positioned here given that we had already been caught?"

He shrugged. "There's absolutely no reason to, but for that reason alone I think she might. The First Mother is neither stupid nor careless."

"Nobody actually says 'nor', Gary."

"What?"

"Never mind. So how do we do this, Mister This-Is-My-World-So-I-Call-The-Shots?"

"I'll go in first and head for the altar. If the assassin is in there, she'll try to subdue me again, and that will give away where she's hiding. You need to keep an eye out for blowgun darts."

"What if she hits you?" asked Valerie.

"That's not likely."

"Someone's getting cocky."

"I'm sorry. I wasn't trying to—"

"Don't apologize, for Christ's sake. That was a compliment." She could see that she had left him slightly baffled yet again.

"I'm really starting to wish you came with a book of instructions," Gabriel muttered. "Or at least some form of interpretation guide."

"I get that more than you'd think."

"Actually, I expect you hear it less than I'd think."

Valerie winked at him. "Be careful in there, okay?"

He nodded and was about to enter when she whispered to him again.

"Hey, Gary." He stopped and looked back at her. "Why did you protect me before? You know, back at the jailhouse. When the assassin tried to kill me."

"Do you really want to know?" he asked.

"Yeah."

"Enough to start getting my name right?"

She let out a heavy sigh. "Fine, *Gabriel.* Why?"

He smiled. "Make sure we both get out of here alive and I'll tell you." With that he charged into the room.

"Pain in the ass," Valerie mumbled as she crept forward, the manacle chain held taut to prevent it from rattling.

Gabriel cut right towards the altar, and the pre-shadow of the dart was passing through his chest before he had taken half a dozen steps. He dove to the left and rolled as the dart passed over him. He continued running and could hear Valerie's footsteps behind him as she rushed into the temple. As he jumped onto the altar he caught a glimpse of her.

Valerie had found the assassin behind a folding screen, the kind used for creating sections in the temple when the need arose. It was only three feet high and had been carefully arranged to appear like there would be essentially no space behind it. As Val charged, Meraya leapt out and over to face her. Gabriel saw Valerie trying to kick the blowgun out of her hands, but the assassin was obviously skilled and had the advantage of pre-shadows.

"She's about a second ahead of you," Gabriel called out to Valerie.

"Not for long," she shouted back.

Gabriel was tempted to go help her, but he had his own purpose, and time was short. The Worldstone hung about ten feet over his head, suspended in a silver ring that was held in place by four silver chains stretching up to the domed ceiling above. He doubted he could reach it now any better than before, but jumped anyway on the off chance that the desperation of this moment might somehow gave him more lift than the last time. No. The very tips of his fingers fell almost a foot short.

Without the objects that had been in the room during the ceremony, the only way to free the stone would be throwing something he'd brought with him. His shoes were his best chance. He pulled one off, took careful aim, and threw. It hit the crystal, but only caused the fixture to sway for a moment before gravity restored it to its center.

He glanced to where the shoe had landed and in doing so could see that Meraya had pushed Valerie back. The Earth Champion's attacks were still lightning fast, but the assassin clearly had the advantage. If Valerie fell, he realized, everything would be lost. He jumped down and called, "I'm coming to help!"

"Don't you *fucking* dare!" she spat back at him. "This bitch is mine! Get the stone!"

How could she not see the logic of defeating the assassin first? Even he could see that Valerie was slowing down. The woman in black must have struck Valerie's left arm, as she was noticeably slower in defending that side. But there had been iron determination in her voice, and he obeyed.

Back upon the altar, Gabriel pulled off his other shoe and took careful aim. He hurled it, and the toughened leather of the sole struck directly on the bottom of the stone. And bounced off with no effect.

That isn't possible, he thought in frustration. *It should have knocked the stone right out of the ring.*

He squinted at it, trying to understand, and saw something that made his heart sink. There was a fine silver mesh cupping the Worldstone from beneath—too fine to be easily noticed but rigid enough that he would need far more than a shoe to knock it free. It was designed so that the Worldstone could only be lifted out from the top.

Gabriel heard shouting in the distance. Reinforcements were coming; he estimated they had less than a minute before the room was overrun with guards. Glancing over to where Valerie was fighting, he saw that she had fallen back towards a recess in the wall, a kind of tall piscina where one might expect a statue or other sculpture to be placed so as to be visible yet out of the way. Did Valerie think it would provide her some form of protection?

Valerie saw him watching her, and screamed, "Get the fucking rock, you moron!"

The shout cost her another step toward the wall but it shook him out of his morbid distraction. He suddenly remembered that there was one other thing that he had with him, and it was something that could possibly do the trick. His hand went to his collar, took hold of the silk cord, and he pulled off the Winder's Knot from around his neck. It might just be long enough.

He would need more height, and the only way he'd get that would be to take a step or two along the altar before leaping. It meant he would probably leap right off the edge, but he saw no other way.

With the wooden disk of the Knot in his right hand, he backed up to the edge of the onyx surface, eyes fixed on the Worldstone. With two quick steps, he leapt. As Gabriel reached the apex of his arc he swung his arm and the loop of silk stretched out, falling over the flat half of the crystal. As he began falling, he pulled as hard as he could.

The smooth material of the cord slid against the Worldstone, launching it up and out of the holder. The empty holder swung back and forth as Gabriel crashed down, his back scraping hard against the edge of the altar. Pain ripped through his shoulder, but he dared not take his eyes off the Worldstone, even as he felt blood seeping out from where the storefront glass had sliced him.

The Worldstone fell straight down, landed on the edge of the silver ring . . . then tipped over the side and dropped onto the altar with a cracking sound. Gabriel scrambled up from the floor and grabbed the crystal. It was unharmed.

He turned to look where Valerie and Meraya were fighting, and saw that the assassin had pushed her even closer to the alcove.

"I've got it!" he shouted to her.

"About fucking time," she shot back, and then suddenly, like a switch had been flipped, everything changed.

Valerie's attacks had been fast before, but now they were blinding. Two jabs to either side of Meraya's head forced her to jerk back and forth quickly, and in the resulting instant of disorientation Valerie was on the ground sweeping at her legs. The assassin jumped into the air to avoid that attack, and Valerie rolled under her, coming to a crouch on the other side. As Meraya landed, Valerie's foot shot out in a powerful roundhouse kick, and the assassin had only two choices: stand and have her ribs crushed or jump backwards to avoid the strike.

Meraya jumped . . . directly into the alcove.

Valerie stepped forward into a fighting stance, a cold smile on her face as she entrapped her opponent. "Good luck now, bitch."

And then the onslaught truly began, a continuous flurry of attacks. Meraya tried to defend herself, but there was simply no room to maneuver. Blow after blow landed, glancing at first and then more damaging as Meraya's concentration dissolved. Within moments Gabriel heard bones snapping.

He also heard the stomping of running feet in a not-distant-enough hallway, and realized that even with the assassin defeated, he and Valerie were still trapped. There was only one door out.

Where in all the skies was Praxis?

• • • • •

Valerie landed a palm strike to the assassin's forehead, sending her head crashing back into the wall of the alcove. As it recoiled back, Val grabbed the woman's ears and pulled down while simultaneously bring her own knee up. There was a crunch, and the woman in black went limp. Val let her find her own way to the ground.

Spinning around she saw Gabriel standing near the blood-stained altar, desperately casting about for some avenue of escape. The concept of going through a window was obviously not in his arsenal of alternatives, but she had no qualms about a little vandalism when the situation called for it. And this situation definitely called for it. Loudly.

She grabbed one of the benches in front of the altar as Gabriel looked on in confusion. "Holy shit this is heavy! Gabby, grab the other end!" He looked baffled. "Now! Don't think, just do it!"

He lifted and she started trying to maneuver it around to the other side of the altar. Gabriel, however, was clearly not getting the plan. "Through the window!" she yelled.

He was shocked at the suggestion. "We can't—"

"We really can. You just stole a priceless artifact. This isn't the time to get sanctimonious!"

Together they began to pick up speed, and seeing how upset he looked she added, "You can feel terrible about this later, okay?"

When they were only a few feet away from the window she cried, "Heave!" and they did. The bench smashed through the blue-green stained glass window, shattering it out into the sky beyond.

They stepped up to the opening and peered out. All that remained was to grab on to something, make their way outside, and climb down. What Valerie hadn't counted on, however, was that there was nothing to grab. No handhold of any kind. Just a smooth stone face and a drop of at least a hundred feet to a very squishy death.

Valerie turned around as a dozen armed women charged into the room. She glanced over at Gabriel, but he stood transfixed by the sight of the bench crashing into the ground below.

• • • • •

The First Mother stepped into the High Temple and came to a halt as the first set of guards rushed in around her. Khalfani had intended to walk straight to the altar and say something wise about how the Beacons may have infinite patience, but The Nexus would not be delayed. Now, however, as she looked at what had transpired in this holiest of shrines...seeing the shattered window, the blood, the body of Meraya...here in this place that had until today known only peace and purposeful spirituality for ten thousand years, she was at a loss for words. She needed a moment to compose herself.

There's blood on the altar, her thoughts flared. *On the* altar *of all places*. She noted that Gabriel was barefoot. *At least he had some tiny shred of sense*. Then, as she focused on the onyx surface, she saw a blemish and her anger flared again. *Is that...could he...did that foolish boy actually chip the altar??*

He and the woman were standing where Dawn's Blessing had been shattered. *And how had they managed that?* Khalfani scanned about, saw that one of the benches was missing. *What possible purpose did he think* that *would serve?*

A second, larger contingent of guards was only moments behind, and she had to regain a measure of calm before speaking in front of her people. The dignity of the entire line of First Mothers was her responsibility. Khalfani took several deep, cleansing breaths. *Well, we are where we are,* she told herself. *This is what happens when you give an important task to a boy.*

The First Mother studied the Champions, Gabriel gazing down at the ground far below and the woman, Valerie, staring defiantly back at her. She couldn't help but think that if this Valerie had been Aerth's Champion they would be comfortably transitioning through The Nexus by now. The woman possessed an aura of confidence that was impressive. She was resourceful and clever, and had a remarkably strong will for one so young. She would have made a fine addition to the Chakrava.

"Well, what do you know," Valerie snarled as their eyes met. "It's the Big Mama."

Forget all that. There was no place for this woman in her world.

"And just what did you hope to accomplish through these acts of desecration?" she asked. "Is this some form of rebellion? Did the woman turn your inner eye to the past, instilling some pointless taste for revenge?"

Gabriel didn't turn. He seemed mesmerized by the mortal descent that was but one step away.

The second group of women came rushing into the room behind the First Mother. She glanced back and noted that it was larger than expected. There were guards from the tertiary station near the main entrance to the Syntrodome, women who had clearly sprinted at great speed to defend their holiest of shrines. It bothered Khalfani that the High Temple should be in such a state of desecration when so many people were seeing it for the first time.

"There is no place to run, my son," she called to Gabriel. "You cannot escape your Purpose. You know that."

He turned to face her. His eyes were so sad. It pained her to see him like this, so lost. And the way he looked at her. She wondered if he was able to sense how much self-control it was taking for her to remain calm in the middle of this maelstrom of chaos he had rained down upon them. Could any of these people see how difficult it was for her to keep the anger and frustration under her skin? She could only hope they couldn't.

"What will you do to Aliesha?" Gabriel asked.

The question surprised her. "You need to focus on—"

"What will happen to her?" he insisted.

"Nothing, Gabriel. Nothing will happen to her. She fell victim to your influence, to your cleverness. You and I both understand how such things can come to pass."

Gabriel gave the barest of nods. "Then no harm will befall her?"

Why is he so concerned? But then Khalfani remembered. *This is the man he is. Compassion and honor. He would never want someone to suffer for his own failings.*

"Only that harm which her own Beacons deem necessary. But no, the Chakrava hold no malice or ill will towards Aliesha. And she is a fine warrior. I'm confident her future will be a bright one." Gabriel relaxed a little, and his gaze drifted upwards as she continued. "If..."

He tensed suddenly.

He thinks I am going to threaten him. How naïve this boy is. But then, he is so young. Then she recognized that she had misjudged his reaction. *No. He's staring at something*, she realized. *What is he looking at?* She started to turn, but he spoke suddenly, pulling her attention back to him.

"If what?" he asked.

"If...there is even a world left, a world for her to have a future within. Come. It is time for you to fulfill your Purpose, to do what you must do. Stop turning your eyes away from your path." A quote from scripture came to her mind, and she said, "She who walks backward into the future knows only the fears of her past."

Gabriel was silent, and again she saw concern in his eyes. *The poor boy.* He turned, looked out the window and down to the ground far below, and then back to her. Suddenly his intentions hazed into a blur.

He is using Dhokha di Maath. Surely he does not think he can escape from here. What is he planning?

"You really believe that the only path forward is for me to kill this woman?" he asked.

"We both know that is the only way," she responded.

The look in his eyes changed. It was no longer sadness, but... *Is that pity?* It was. The foolish boy truly believed he knew better.

"Fine," he said with a determination soft yet infinitely firm. He took Valerie's hand, and without another word stepped backwards out the window, pulling the otherworld Champion along with him as they both plummeted to their deaths.

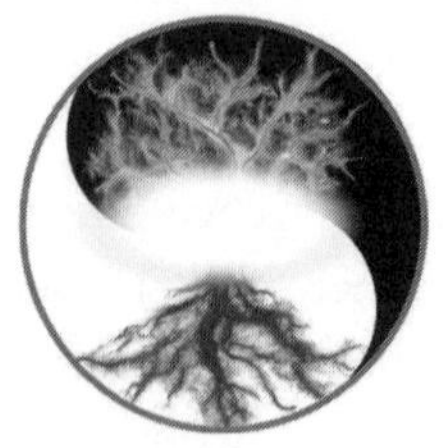

CHAPTER TWENTY ONE:

Escape

A portal sparkled on the wall of the east tower, barely two feet below the remains of what had once been a beautiful stained-glass window. The upper half of a rainbow-haired stranger in gray robes was leaning out of it, and as Gabriel and Valerie began to fall, Praxis grabbed a leg and an arm and pulled the pair into the Interstice.

Far below, the Aerth Worldstone landed with a thud in a flowering garden, surrounded by shards of colored glass and the remains of a large bench that had splintered into thousands of pieces of ancient wood.

• • • • •

"Where the *hell* have you been?" Valerie demanded.

Praxis shrugged. "What? I was tired, so I took a nap."

"You *what*?!?"

They rolled their eyes. "I'm joking. Wow. Lighten up."

"We almost died in there!"

"The Syntrodome's a big place, Valerie, and I can only look through the portal in one spot at a time. Tracking someone isn't as easy as you think. Especially not two people. And even worse when they keep moving around all over the place, disappearing around corners—"

Gabriel waved a hand, but neither Valerie nor Praxis noticed in the heat of their argument.

"And what gives with the 'jump out the window' brilliance?" Valerie demanded.

"Val, calm down," Praxis replied, but that only made her more agitated.

"You could have just popped out of the wall next to us and pulled us back through!"

"Excuse me," Gabriel tried to interject again.

"And risk getting shot by one of them?" Praxis spat back at Valerie. "I'm as susceptible to tranq darts as you, Miss Mensa. If they'd knocked me out, then what?"

"Well..." Val started, but found she had no comeback.

Gabriel coughed. "Excuse me."

They both turned to look at him, and then Praxis said, "And just what the hell do you think *you're* doing?"

"What am I—" he began. "What?"

"What did I say about bleeding on my rugs?"

Gabriel thought for a moment and then replied, "Nothing."

"I made it very clear. No blood—"

"Actually," Val piped in, "you only said we can't throw up on them."

"Well then let me be more explicit." They started ticking rules off on their fingers. "No vomit, no blood. No spilling wine, no—"

"Do we really want to leave the Worldstone just lying there in the garden?" Gabriel asked.

Praxis took a breath to say something, but then changed their mind and released it. "Fine. But just stay put for two seconds." They rushed into the galley, returning a moment later holding a first aid kit that they were in the process of ripping open. "Turn around," Praxis commanded. When Gabriel did, they slapped a large adhesive bandage over his seeping cut.

"Thank you," he said with a grimace.

"Oh, crap," they muttered.

"What?"

"I should have put on an antiseptic."

"What is—OWW!" Gabriel screamed as Praxis ripped off the bandage. He screamed louder when they doused the wound with a splash of some clear liquid from a brown bottle.

"There," Praxis said, and applied a second bandage. Then they gave it a solid pat, which elicited a look far nastier than Valerie had imagined Gabriel's face could manage.

Praxis nodded. "Now let's go. You can clean up the blood stains when you get back." They turned to the portal, concentrated, and moments later they were all looking out from the base of the Syntrodome's east tower. Praxis and Gabriel walked out, leaving Valerie to appraise the vehicle on a trailer parked in the middle of the Great Library.

Valerie patted white fiberglass with a greedy look in her eyes. "Always wanted to get behind the wheel of one of these babies."

• • • • •

Praxis had already returned to the Interstice by the time Gabriel located the Worldstone amongst the flowers and debris. The Keeper and Valerie had other things to do if this was going to work, and there wasn't a lot of time to spare.

Gabriel projected false intentions of heading north and began running east as soon as he was out of direct sight from the Syntrodome. The logical direction for him to go was south along the road to the coast, and he hoped this would throw the Chakrava off his trail until it was too late. His instincts warned him that he would be followed, but finding someone in Annaphora was not easy under the best conditions. Tracking someone who could mask his intentions would be nearly impossible. And once he reached the road to the east of the city, his lead would become insurmountable. That is, of course, if Praxis and Valerie were successful in their part of the plan.

He continued to jog for another half hour, then slowed to a walk to conserve his strength. The fields surrounding Annaphora were full of crops, and for some reason they instilled within him a feeling of pensive sadness. This was his world. In many ways he was like these crops: born from this soil and nurtured by the sun and wind and waters. For his entire life this world had whispered its Beacons to him, and now all that was gone. He was an outcast. He was like a stalk of wheat that had been pulled from the ground and thrown into the sea. Gabriel was certain beyond any doubt that he was doing the right thing, but the sadness remained.

It was still another hour before he reached the woods encircling the plains of Annaphora. They were thicker here than in the south, and he trudged through gorse and clinging branches for still another hour before reaching an old dirt road. He quieted his thoughts and focused on his nythlen.

There was no reason to change their plan. He turned south and continued walking.

About twenty minutes later he heard a rumbling. It was low and now familiar. Well, at least not unfamiliar. When the motorcycle appeared through the trees ahead of him, he was surprised to see that it was metallic blue instead of Valerie's black.

Valerie skidded to a halt, pulled off her matching metallic blue helmet, and called, "Need a lift?"

"This doesn't look like your vehicle," he observed as he swung his leg over the back of the bike.

"We couldn't find it. Your stupid First Mommy must have had them stash it someplace out of the way." She patted the handlebar of the motorcycle. "So we borrowed this baby from a dealer outside of Manchester." She revved the engine. "I like it."

"Someone let you borrow this?" he asked.

"I may have used the word 'borrow' a little loosely. It's night in England right now, so we—"

Gabriel held up his hand. "I don't want to know." Then, as Valerie put her helmet back on, he asked, "Where's mine?"

"You wanted your own bike? How would I have—"

"Helmet. Where's my—"

"There was only one. You just need to make sure you don't fall off."

"Wonderful," he muttered, but not even the local wildlife heard him, for just then Valerie popped the clutch, spun the bike, released the brake, and they roared back the way she had come.

• • • • •

While the road took them mainly south, it steadily drifted east as well and soon they could smell the ocean's salt in the air. Valerie slowed to a slightly more moderate speed, and fifteen minutes later she brought the motorcycle to a stop. Through the trees they could make out slivers of blue water and the occasional whitecap.

"I'm pretty sure this is the spot," she said as she cut the engine and pried Gabriel's arms from around her waist. "Fun, right?"

"Not the word I would have chosen," he responded as she removed her helmet.

"Exhilarating?"

"Not that either. Maybe death-defying...or emotionally scarring..." he offered.

"I'll take it."

They dismounted and abandoned the bike on the road, pushing their way through the narrow stretch of trees until they reached a thin beach of caramel sands. About thirty feet out from the shore, Praxis was at the helm of a sleek white speedboat. Valerie immediately called out, "There she is!"

Gabriel cocked his head. "I hadn't realized Praxis was female."

"Fuck Praxis. I'm talking about the boat, baby!"

"Are you drooling?" he asked, but Valerie just barreled on.

"If you thought the bike was fast, just wait until we get this girl up to speed!"

"Oh, good. Just...great," Gabriel said as he gave the craft an appraising look. "I suppose the flames painted on the side make it go faster."

"I'm pretty sure they do," she called over her shoulder as she waded through the surf.

Once they were all on board, Valerie asked, "So we're pretty sure this beaut is never going home, right?"

"Very unlikely," Praxis answered. "Why?"

A gleam came into Valerie's eyes. "Oh, no reason." She shooed Praxis out of the captain's seat and put her hands on the wheel. "No reason at all."

• • • • •

There was no practical way to hold a conversation as they sped across the ocean. The roar of the speedboat engines was deafening, and Gabriel and Praxis realized almost instantly that they had to choose between being strapped in or thrown overboard. As the hours slipped by, all they could do was watch endless waves race from one horizon to the other.

Valerie slowed the craft to less ludicrous speeds once the shores of Havlanti rose out of the waters to the east. They approached cautiously and turned south to cruise around the coast. Valerie smiled and waved at the women in old wooden fishing boats who gawked at the sight and sound of their vessel, but she kept her distance and everyone seemed happier for it.

The shoreline curved east, and a few miles later they saw a modern Earth sign that read Golfklúbbur – Seltjarnarnes in reasonably familiar characters. "Ahh, home," Val sighed, surprised at how nice it was to be back in familiar territory, even if that territory used a funny looking alphabet and served seafood that made her want to die. Repeatedly.

To be certain she had truly made it back to Earth, however, there was one critical test.

Yes. Her cell phone had two bars.

And one hundred and fourteen missed texts from Amelia.

She dialed. The phone had barely begun to ring before Amelia's voice erupted out of the speaker.

"Where the fuck have you been!?!"

"Hi, Mel."

"Don't 'Hi Mel' me! Where did you vanish off to? Do you have any idea what's been going on around here?"

"No, I don't. I've been offworld."

"Funny."

"Truth, actually. Oh, and some place that isn't in any world, but—"

"The shit's starting to hit the fan around here. We're getting earthquakes, Val. Fucking earthquakes! And not just one. Lots! And people are saying that Iceland never gets—"

"Mel!" Val shouted into the phone. "Just relax a minute."

"Oh, right!" her friend shouted back. Valerie held the phone away from her ear, but Amelia's voice could still be heard clearly. "While you were off having a nice little nap or whatever the hell you were doing, I've been watching buildings collapse! Do you know what happens when earthquakes keep . . ." she struggled for the word, "quaking?"

"You don't have to mix your own drinks?" Valerie offered, but she was looking over at Praxis.

They shook their head and quietly said, "Not a good sign."

Val put her hand over the phone as Amelia continued to rant and asked the Keeper, "How long do we have?"

"Until what?"

"What the hell do you think I'm asking about? The Nexus, you idiot!"

"Oh. Well, based on what your friend was describing, I'd say it's here already. So the real question now is how long we have before the worlds are destroyed."

"What?!" Valerie and Gabriel gasped.

"Do you know how they say that two things can't exist in the same place at the same time?" Praxis asked. "If I had to guess, it sounds like Aerth and Earth are trying to disprove that. Personally, I think the theory has a lot of merit, so if I were you I'd get your asses back to Amelia and put the Worldstones together before the worlds find out they're wrong."

"How long do you think we have?"

"I wouldn't stop for sightseeing."

Valerie took her hand off the phone and brought it to her ear.

"Val!" Mel was shouting. "Don't you dare ignore me, Val!"

"Sorry, Mel. There was a...a...whale. I had to steer around it."

"Don't pull this crap with me right now! Not right now! I am so furious—"

"Hey, we're going to meet up with you soon, okay? How soon can you get to that place where the crystal started glowing?"

"What?"

"You know, near Hard-to-Break!"

"What the hell are you talking about?" Amelia demanded.

"Harta...You know, the mountain. The tuya. The one where the crystal glowed!"

"Herðubreið?"

"Right! How soon can you get there?"

"I don't...I guess...Maybe forty-five minutes?" Mel estimated.

"Great. Make it thirty. Oh, and here's Gabriel." She tossed the phone to him, and turned to Praxis. "How quickly can we grab a car and portal back to the other side of the island?"

"You really struggle with this, don't you?" Praxis responded.

"What?"

Praxis looked Valerie in the eye and spoke very slowly. "You...can't...take...a Worldstone...into—"

"Right," Valerie interrupted. "Right right right." She grabbed the phone back from Gabriel. "Mel, it's me again. Change of plans. Meet us there in like three hours."

"Put Gabriel back on the phone," Mel replied.

"Three hours, okay? So you can get breakfast or whatever."

"It's one in the afternoon."

"I said 'or whatever'."

"Put Gabriel—"

"Three hours!"

"Fine. Three hours. Now put—"

Valerie didn't hear the rest because she had already thrown the phone back to Gabriel.

• • ● • •

Valerie wanted a Lamborghini. She had always wanted a Lamborghini.

"But I suppose it isn't practical," she sighed dejectedly. "We need something that seats three, and as low as it is to the ground, it just wouldn't work, would it?"

"You know Lamborghini makes an off-road vehicle now, right?" Praxis replied.

Valerie's face went practically neon. "They... Oh my god, Praxis. You are my new favorite person in the whole... wherever the hell we are!"

• • ● • •

Praxis and Valerie stepped out of the wall at a dealership in Los Angeles, where it was still the middle of the night. Right there in the showroom was a four-seater with heated leather seats and a bright green exterior. Valerie was practically hyperventilating.

Finding the keys took nearly twenty minutes, and by the time they actually had their hands on them, no fewer than seven independent alarm systems were excitedly sending alerts to the local police, the dealership owners, and who knew where else.

It didn't matter. The sports SUV had vanished without a trace long before the first responder arrived.

• • ● • •

Once they had returned with the car, Gabriel slid into the back seat and Valerie took off like a bat out of hell. The GPS insisted it would take seven hours to get to their destination, but that was an estimate grounded on assumptions Valerie fully intended to ignore, such as driving at anything close to the speed limit or even constraining one's self to the roads. It took a little longer than three to reach the site where the Shattering had cleaved the world so many millennia ago.

During the transit the ground shuddered with the occasional tremor, and as they approached their destination the earthquakes were growing both more frequent and more severe. They saw that other travelers had pulled their cars over to the side of the road, but that didn't make any difference to Valerie, who had been ignoring the roads altogether for the past half hour anyway.

They soon pulled to a stop in what appeared to be the middle of nowhere.

"Do either of you see her?" Valerie asked. "Or an ugly pink tissue box of a car?"

No one did.

"I could have sworn this was the place."

"It is," Praxis confirmed. "Gabriel, can we look at the Worldstone?"

He withdrew it and they could all easily see that its colored veins were glowing brightly.

"Where the hell could she be?" demanded Valerie in frustration. "Oh, wait." She grabbed her cell phone from the cubby in the dashboard and pulled up an app. A flashing diamond showed that Amelia was over a mile away.

"What the fuck, Mel!?" Valerie started the engine again. "She must have gotten the place wrong. I swear, I could kill her."

Valerie placed a call. "Pick up pick up pick up...Answer the fucking phone, Mel!"

She didn't.

Valerie slammed the car into gear and began racing across the barren landscape. A couple of minutes later Praxis's hand shot forward from the back seat.

"There!"

On the horizon, where the land rose slightly, Valerie could discern the outlines of two figures. She pressed even harder on the accelerator, but just then another quake shook the ground and jolted the car so badly that she almost lost control.

Ahead, one of the figures had been thrown to the ground while the other seemed completely unaffected.

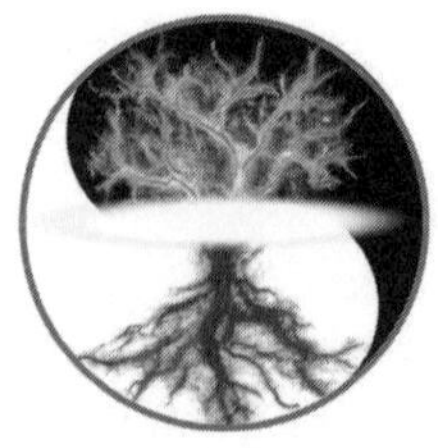

CHAPTER TWENTY TWO:

The Nexus

Amelia stood on an island of rock. It was perhaps eighty feet across and isolated from the rest of the world by a wide ring of lava. Across that fiery moat stood Kelly, arms crossed and foot tapping impatiently next to where Amelia's cell phone lay on the ground. The blond-haired manifestation was staring off to the northeast where Herðubreið poked its crown over the horizon.

After trying to check out from the inn—a futile effort as everyone was far more concerned with the tremors than conducting business—Amelia had hopped into their pink rental and taken off to meet Valerie. Her GPS showed that the closest she could get to the meeting place by car was to curve around to the south, and that's where she saw the woman in red lying on the ground.

Over the years, Amelia had often wondered what Valerie's friend looked like. She had a vague idea based on the features Val had described: blond hair, angular cheekbones, and a slender form, lithe and animated. Yet somehow, seeing the woman collapsed and weakly trying to wave her down, Amelia hadn't made the connection. After all, Kelly wasn't real. She couldn't be seen by anyone but Valerie. Why would she even think that the stranger could be her.

Amelia had stopped the car and rushed over. The woman was clearly injured, with blood and dirt smeared across her face, and she was whispering something. Mel had leaned closer to and heard her moan, "call . . . help . . . please!" She rushed back to the car, grabbed her phone, and punched in 9-1-1 as she returned. There was no answer, and then she remembered that the emergency number in Iceland was 1-1-2.

This time the phone rang, and an operator asked for the nature of her emergency. She explained the situation, and agreed to be put on hold due to the extreme number of calls they were currently receiving.

The next tremor struck moments later, and it was a bad one. It knocked Amelia to the ground and the phone flew out of her hand. Once the quake subsided, she stood and discovered that the woman in red had crawled away. She was on her knees about thirty feet away, one hand on the ground to steady herself and the other clutched to a gash in her side where blood was flowing out and forming a puddle beneath her. The woman was wailing in agony, and Mel rushed over.

The instant she reached the stranger there was another quake, even more severe than the previous. There was a thunderous cracking sound as the rocks around her began to split apart, and she was once again thrown to the ground. When she finally managed to get onto her hands and knees Amelia discovered that the woman in red had vanished. The ground subsided its shaking, and she leveraged herself into a standing position to look around.

Around her, Mel could see that she was now alone and surrounded by a channel of steaming, molten lava. She closed her eyes and blinked them open again, convinced she must have been hallucinating.

She wasn't. The lava was there, and on the far side of it stood the woman in red, now completely unharmed and casually running a hand through her blond hair. It was a carefree gesture, as if she were standing on the balcony in a commercial for some luxury hotel.

"Hello, Amelia," Kelly had said in a tone that was simultaneous warm and icy. "It's nice to finally meet you."

"What's happening? Who are you?" she had replied in confusion.

Kelly had ignored her. "I mean, I've seen you quite a lot over the years, but this is the first time you're seeing me."

And that's when Amelia made the connection. "Kelly?"

"Look, Mel, I want you to understand that I mean you no harm. Honestly, I never really thought it was a good idea for Val to bring you along in the first place. I could hardly make a case for it, though. Not without raising suspicion, you know what I mean?"

"What's happening?"

If Kelly heard her, she gave no indication. "I can see where you might feel that this is in some way personal," she continued, "but I want to assure you that it isn't. Not at all. The stakes are simply too high not to use every possible tool at my disposal. You understand, right?"

"No!" Amelia had yelled. "I don't understand at all!"

"Well, you will when they get here." Kelly went silent then and began gazing out to the northeast.

Now a cloud of dust rose in the distance, and suddenly the ground rocked again. It knocked Amelia back to her knees.

"Here they come, Mel," Kelly said as if nothing unusual was happening. "Everything will be over soon enough."

"What the fuck are you talking about?"

"And I want you to know that if...you know, if things don't go smoothly...you'll die for the most important cause that ever existed."

Amelia's jaw dropped in stunned amazement as a green sports SUV skidded to a stop about fifty feet away.

• • ● • •

Valerie jumped out of the Lamborghini the instant it stopped. She was halfway to Kelly before Gabriel had figured out how to unbuckle his seatbelt.

"You fucking bitch!" she screamed as she charged.

"Val, wait!" Kelly shouted back. "I did what had to be done. That's all."

By then Valerie had reached her, possessed with a rage like nothing she had ever experienced. She shot a fist directly at Kelly's nose, but it passed harmlessly through her.

"You lied to me!" she spat as she threw another punch. It too passed through Kelly's form without effect.

"I told you what you needed to hear."

"You killed my parents!" Valerie launched an all-out attack, but with no more consequence than before. Kelly watched passively until she stopped, exhausted.

"I had to prepare you, Valerie. You had to be the best our world could create. Don't you understand?"

"You...killed...my parents," Valerie panted. "What else? What else did you do? How else did you fuck up my life? What shit do I not even know about?"

"Nothing, Val," Kelly replied quietly. "I swear."

"You lying bitch!"

"No. I've been your friend—"

"You have no idea what that even means!" Valerie screamed. The mention of the word 'friend' calmed the fury enough for her to remember that Amelia was there.

She ran to the edge of the lava. The band of molten rock was at least ten feet wide, perhaps even fifteen.

"Don't worry, Mel! We're going to get you out of there!"

Praxis and Gabriel caught up to her. Gabriel was casting about, trying to find anything that would help bridge the gap. Valerie faced Praxis.

"Is there any way...?" she began, but Valerie already knew the answer as Praxis shook their head. There was nothing on that island upon which they could open a portal.

And then Kelly was standing next to her. "You want her out?" she offered. "I can do that. All you need to do is kill Gabriel."

"Fuck you!"

"Kill him and I'll make a bridge. It's that simple."

But Valerie was no longer listening. She looked over her shoulder at the car, and then back to the lava. If she were to drive the car into the gap, it might work as a stepping stone that Amelia could jump onto and escape.

"Hang on!" she cried, and made a dash for the SUV.

Kelly appeared between her and the car door. "Don't do it, Val."

Valerie ran right through her, opened the door, and jumped in.

Suddenly there was a deep rumble and the ground shook again. A burst of steam rose from the ground where Amelia stood. Val jumped back out of the car and stared. Amelia was scrambling backwards as more of the rocky ground crumbled. In mere moments, the moat around the island had expanded to a width of at least thirty feet, far too wide for her plan to work. She ran back to the edge.

"Val!" Amelia screamed.

"Mel! We're gonna get you out of there!" Valerie screamed back, and then the Earth shook once more. Another few feet of lava consumed the ground near Amelia's feet, shrinking the island even further. Valerie turned to shout accusations at Kelly, but she was standing right there.

"I didn't do that one, Val. The Nexus is here! Right now! It's crushing the world to pieces. Both worlds!" She pointed at Gabriel and said, "The same thing is happening in his. The worlds are literally colliding, and if you don't act now, if you don't kill him *right now*—"

"No."

"—we are all going to die. Mel, you, *me*. Gabriel. All of us!"

"NO!!" Valerie screamed. "You're lying!"

And suddenly all pretense of being Valerie's friend disappeared from Kelly's voice. "Don't you get it, you stupid bitch!? Even if you don't kill him, he's still going to die! At least make his death worth something!" Valerie just glared at her. "Look around you! Everything is being destroyed. Only one world can pass through the conjunction, so why shouldn't it be ours?"

Valerie turned to Praxis and said, "Get her out of here."

Praxis reached into a pocket, and suddenly Kelly vanished. Gabriel yelled out a moment later, pointing across the lava. "There!"

Kelly had appeared next to Amelia. There was another rumble.

"That one wasn't me either, Val," Kelly called out. "Can't you feel it? The world's growing more unstable. If you don't act now, Mel's going to die."

Val took a deep breath and then called back, "Alright! I'll do it, but on one condition. Give me the crystal, Kelly. Give me the crystal, and I'll kill Gabriel!"

Kelly laughed. "You always were a crappy liar."

But it was the missing clue that Amelia needed. She reached into her purse and took out the Earth Worldstone. Kelly instantly turned on her. Amelia saw fire in her eyes, and she wasn't completely certain it was a reflection from the lava.

"Don't do it, Amelia. That stone is the only thing keeping this little island intact. If it leaves..." Kelly's gaze momentarily dropped to the lava, the implication perfectly clear.

Amelia steeled herself, and Kelly saw the resolve in her posture. An instant later the edge of her island started to crumble, forcing Mel to step back.

"Put it back, Mel," warned Kelly. "Don't make me do this."

The ground continued to erode, and finally Amelia thrust the Worldstone back into her purse.

"Wise choice," Kelly whispered, and the ground became stable again.

Amelia looked out across the chasm at her lifelong friend. They made eye contact, and she called out, "Val?"

"What?" Valerie called back.

"I'm sorry."

There was only one thing she could have meant. *Don't you dare, Mel, don't you...*

In the blink of an eye, Amelia brought her hand back out of her purse and hurled the Worldstone across the chasm of lava.

As Earth's Champion caught the stone, Kelly let out a scream so filled with rage that it sounded more bestial than human. She vanished from the island, which instantly began to disintegrate, and within moments Amelia was thrown from her feet and fell into the lava below.

Valerie went numb. She wanted to scream, or cry, or rage, but her mind refused to process anything she was seeing. Kelly was suddenly in her face, yelling something at her, but the words were muted gibberish.

And then Gabriel was there. His gray eyes filled her vision, and they overflowed with a compassion deeper than she had ever seen before. He tilted his head to the side, and she saw a tear run down his cheek. Suddenly the world returned.

"This is your fault!" Kelly was screaming at her. "You could have saved her, and you let her die! Just like your parents! How many more people are you going to let die because you're too weak to do what has to be done?"

Valerie ignored her. She looked over at Praxis, nodded, and they understood. Two steps closed the distance, but Kelly vanished before Praxis could banish her.

Gabriel held up the Aerth Worldstone, and he and Valerie nodded to each other. This was the moment. This was what the Champions were meant to do. It was never about one world or the other. The Nexus was their chance to heal the division that hubris had created thirteen thousand years ago. This was the moment to restore both worlds into balance.

She reached out with her left hand and took his, and they each held their own worlds' symbols out. Their eyes locked as they brought the flat sides of the crystals together.

• • • • •

Nothing happened.

They did it again. Nothing.

The ground trembled with another quake, and they were thrown to the ground. Gabriel held on to his stone, but Valerie's escaped her grasp and rolled toward the lava. She dove after it, catching it just in time. For a moment she thought it was vibrating again, but it was just the ground beneath her. She stared at the stone, saw the faintly glowing veins, and remembered.

"Not here!" she cried out. "We're in the wrong place!"

Valerie, Gabriel, and Praxis piled into the Lamborghini and the engine roared. Spinning tires kicked up a cloud of dust and pebbles as they raced across the barren valley towards the site of the Shattering.

• • • • •

Another earthquake shook them violently, and a section of rock split directly below the car. The passenger side dropped several inches, and the grating squeal of scraping metal filled the vehicle. Valerie threw the wheel to the right, and with a shower of sparks they were on four tires again.

Unlike before, this quake didn't stop. Around them, huge chunks of earth were heaved into the air as the ground shifted and ripped. Valerie swerved left and right to avoid being crushed as enormous boulders embedded themselves into the ground. A fist-size rock smashed into the windshield, blossoming into a spider web of fracture lines.

The crystals were glowing more intensely, but not brightly enough.

Valerie shifted into fifth gear.

"You're not going to make it in time."

Valerie glanced at the rearview mirror and saw that Kelly was in the back seat with Praxis.

"I think we are," Val replied.

"Don't be a fool!" Kelly shouted, and then, as if she suddenly decided that volume was unnecessary, she reverted to a calm, steady voice that Valerie found far more unnerving. "You can see what's happening. The worlds are colliding. Right now. All around you."

Kelly shot both hands out in front of herself, and about five hundred yards ahead a huge section of ground sheared away, creating a vast chasm, miles deep and easily a hundred feet or more across. The stone slab on which the car was traveling began to lift and tilt precariously to the left.

"Time's up, Val. What'll it be? Him . . . or everything?"

Valerie and Gabriel shared a look, and simultaneously each gave a barely perceptible nod.

Valerie shifted into sixth gear and floored it.

• • • • •

Blue sky filled the windshield as the Lamborghini sailed off the edge of the cliff. The car tilted forward and the azure was replaced by the blacks and grays of craggy rocks as gravity pulled them downwards. Valerie freed the Earth Worldstone from her jacket pocket as they fell, brought it towards the Aerth Worldstone that Gabriel was holding out. Both were glowing brightly now, slivers of red, blue, and green radiant against the darkness of the surrounding rift.

The stones touched, and there was a soft click—more felt than heard—as the two fused into one.

• • • • •

The bright green sports car crashed into the bottom of the chasm and burst into flames. From the middle of the burning wreckage, a single spherical Worldstone began to vibrate. Had any living person been there to perceive it, they would have heard a soft, throbbing hum that grew stronger and stronger until perhaps a dozen seconds later when it gave off a flash of light like a nuclear explosion—the brightest, whitest light one could ever imagine—followed almost immediately by a roar like a thousand thunderclaps erupting into the sky.

Then everything was still.

CHAPTER TWENTY THREE:

Unification

In the Great Library of the Interstice, the two globes—one representing Aerth and the other Earth—drew closer, closer...and then touched. On the scale of a planet, it was the barest grazing of two surfaces, happening at a place one world called Havlanti and the other Iceland. And not even the whole of that tiny island. Just on the eastern part, centered between the tuya Herðubreið and Lake Askja which is sometimes called Öskjuvatn. And where the worlds came together, the tremendous masses deformed. On the scale of a planet, it was the barest of deformations, almost like the kiss of two dear friends reunited after a separation far too long in duration for a human's limited mind to comprehend.

And then, as if that kiss was the manifestation of permission, the two globes began to pass into one another. In that moment, the opposing portals on the walls emitted a flash...and vanished. Simultaneously, a new, shimmering portal appeared on the wall behind the globes, and three figures tumbled out of it.

Praxis was the first to regain their feet. They stared around in confusion for a moment, then back at the new portal behind them. With a disgruntled sigh they said, "Well, I guess that makes sense, but now I'm going to have to redecorate the whole damn place."

• • • • •

Praxis considered getting started immediately with moving the bookshelves around, but changed their mind before lifting anything. They were tired, and not just a little. They deserved a break. Sure, they were not directly responsible for bringing the two worlds back together. They realized that. It was all Valerie and Gabriel, but...well...it wasn't *all* them, was it? *I mean, I played a part in it, right?*

Look at this one, one of the older Keeper's memories thought at another of the Keepers in Praxis's mind. *I told you they'd get all full of themselves.*

They're young, the other Keeper's memory replied. *Let them enjoy the moment.*

Praxis smiled. The Ancients were always full of opinions, and it was rare to have one actually stick up for the present Praxis. Usually everyone thought they could have done it better, whatever the *it* might have been. Armchair Keepers, that's how Praxis thought of them, although that was a private thought not to be shared in whatever passed for 'out loud' when everything was happening in the confines of your own mind.

You go ahead, honey. Enjoy the moment. Have a cookie. You did good.

That made Praxis smile again. It *felt* good. There would be a lot of uncertainty in the years to come as these two worlds struggled to integrate with each other, but that wasn't their problem.

It's not, right? Praxis asked of the others.

There was no response. They understood. No one knew the answer to that question. Whenever no one knew, everyone went silent.

Over by the fire they saw that Gabriel and Valerie had settled themselves on opposite sides of the hearth. The Champions had helped themselves to some strahlla, the dry amber liqueur that was like honey whiskey with all its sweetness distilled away, and were sipping it as they conversed in quiet voices. A little conversation with someone not inside their head suddenly sounded like a much better plan than rearranging furniture.

Gabriel and Valerie turned to look at them as Praxis walked over.

"Did we succeed?" Gabriel asked.

"What do you think?" Praxis asked in response.

"I think," Valerie said, "that just once, it wouldn't kill you to answer a question without an accompanying truckload of attitude." Valerie's tone carried a hint of irritability, but Praxis realized that it was a defense mechanism. Not a conscious one, but a habit to which she had conditioned herself over the decades.

Praxis also suspected that it wouldn't be long before the aperture of Valerie's thoughts widened to the bigger picture, and that gave them more than just a pang of concern. When Valerie stopped thinking about escaping death at the bottom of a pit she'd remember what happened shortly before, and that was going to be really rough. Praxis wondered if it might be kinder to just piss her off and let the anger keep her distracted for a while longer.

"Why are you staring at me like that?" Val asked.

"Yes, you succeeded," they said with a soft smile, then twisted to point over their shoulder at the globes. "Look."

"They're touching," Gabriel observed.

"So what does that mean?" asked Valerie.

Praxis turned back to face them. "They are beginning to merge. Unification. It will take a while, probably years, maybe longer, but they are in the process of becoming one again. I suspect in the ways that matter most, they already have."

Gabriel asked, "What do you mean? What is the way that matters?"

"The essence of the two worlds have been reunited. You two did that when you restored the Worldstone to a single whole. No longer are there two distinct consciousnesses embodied by Yin and Yang, or whatever spectrum you like to think across. Now there is only a single spirit in which both reside." To emphasize the point, Praxis tapped the tattoo on their temple.

Gabriel and Valerie stared at it, and Praxis asked, "What?"

"It's..." Valerie started.

"It's shimmering," Gabriel finished. "What does that mean?"

"Oh. That. Nothing. It does that from time to time. I'm surprised you hadn't noticed it before."

The Champions simultaneously mouthed 'oh' and turned away.

I'm going to have to check that out, Praxis thought with a touch of concern.

It's fine, one of the others reassured them.

It's never done it before, Praxis thought back. *Am I about to explode or something?*

There was no reply.

Great. Just great, Praxis thought. But so what if they were? They'd done what was needed. Beyond that, what did it matter if they joined the other Keepers as a memory in the halls of the Interstice?

Praxis put the thought out of their mind and studied Valerie and Gabriel. What would happen to them? Would they want to return to their own worlds? Correction, to *the* world. Would the world want them back? They were fairly certain the pair would be welcome, but one could never know until you heard it with your own nythlen. They contemplated asking Gabriel if he was hearing the songs of the Greater Beacons, but this wasn't the time.

"So," Valerie said, and then paused. She took a deep breath and continued. "So that all really just happened, then?"

Oh, shit. Here it comes. Praxis considered grabbing Valerie in a big hug in hopes that the resulting flood of images might just knock her out cold. They looked over at Gabriel, and could see that he was starting to think beyond the explosion, but so far it all looked very analytical.

"Where is the Worldstone now?" he asked.

"I can't be positive, but if I had to guess..." Praxis trailed off as they considered.

"What?" he prompted.

"I'd assume it is lying comfortably in the smashed remains of a green Lamborghini." They looked over at Valerie, saw the pre-shadow of her shaking. *Fuck fuck fuck.* This was going to happen, and Praxis couldn't think of anything that would stop it. And frankly, selfishly, they really didn't want to be around for it.

"So we could possibly go get it," Gabriel mused.

He's adapting more slowly, but once she…

Valerie started to tremble. It was barely perceptible, but it was going to get worse.

Praxis moved to sit on the edge of the table that separated Gabriel from Valerie, positioning themselves to block his view of her. "I doubt it. When the Worldstone split in the Shattering, it released a tremendous amount of energy. I would guess that when it was made whole, the same thing probably happened. Or maybe it would absorb energy. But either way, I expect that it is now sealed up miles beneath the surface of Havlanti."

"Oh," he replied.

"Assuming there still is a Havlanti. I don't know just how big an explosion we'd be talking about. If you're curious, you can go use the globes and see for yourself." *Please go. Please, please go.* They could feel Valerie getting worse behind them—like an electric current creeping up their spine—and it would be so much easier if…

"Are you okay?" Gabriel leaned to the side to get a clearer view of Valerie.

And then it all came pouring out. The memory of Amelia's sacrifice had returned full force, and Valerie was sobbing amid gasps of air. Gabriel began moving around the table to get to her, but halfway there his questing mind had pieced it together. Praxis watched helplessly as concern gave way to loss and his own torrent of emotions erupted.

Gabriel collapsed on the chair beside Valerie, and they both sobbed uncontrollably.

Praxis found themselves thinking that there was a certain irony here, how in the wake of the greatest conceivable reunification, these two poor kids were now suffering through their own Shattering. It was the first time in a great many decades that Praxis found themselves wishing that they could offer one of them—both of them—a comforting hug, or at least a shoulder to cry upon. But that was impossible. Well, perhaps not impossible, but certainly not a kindness. No, all they could do was sit nearby, a silent companion holding the space as heart-wrenching pain and loss released itself in a flood of anguished tears that was, in its own way, as devastating as the explosion that reset the surface of Havlanti thirteen thousand years before.

• • ● • •

The Chakrava had cloistered themselves within their oak-walled deliberation chamber once Aerth's Beacons began crying out. This Calling was like nothing they had ever experienced, nor even read about in the Histories. It was a pervasive fear that suffused every fiber of the world. The assembled Mothers could sense the alarm—the low-grade concern—that was steadily building across the Great Circle. The world was afraid, and when that happens it is only natural that the individual lives that comprise it have reason to worry.

Please just let it not fester into panic, the First Mother prayed.

When the quakes began ripping into the island of Havlanti, the Beacons' cry became a jarring screech. The Chakrava did not know specifics of what was happening on the island, but there was no mistaking the severity of the crisis. Their discussion, already subdued to a quiet staccato of unanswerable questions, had halted completely as they waited for the Beacons' wail to subside.

It didn't.

"He's failed!" the Third Mother whispered at last, and many of the other women around the table nodded in agreement.

"Then we all failed," replied Khalfani. *Why did I say that?* she reprimanded herself. *That is not what we need right now.*

The others had turned to stare at her, and the First Mother could feel the pressure of their deepening anxiety. It was like a chasm opening up, threatening to swallow them whole into the bowels of the Aerth. They needed her, now more than ever before. There was terror here, and the Chakrava had no salve to ease the raging fear. No salve but her.

"But, my friends... my Sisters... let us not succumb to hysterics. There is reason for hope." It took all of the First Mother's will not to glance over at Inthima, the Second Mother and the only woman in the room who might detect her use of Dhokha di Maath. Of course there was no hope. What, save the impending destruction of their world, could call the Beacons to cry out like this? But she'd be damned if the leadership of the Great Circle would face the end of days like a gaggle of panicked schoolgirls.

No. We will meet this fate with dignity. With optimism. With pride.

"Yes, there is reason for hope," she repeated. The faces of the Chakrava were all poised, staring at her, waiting for the reasoning upon which to draw such a conclusion. They felt her conviction, but they needed more.

The First Mother smiled. "We are still here, are we not?"

Eyes shifted. It was something, but Khalfani could sense that it wasn't enough.

She continued. "Nobody could predict what The Nexus would mean. In the Shattering, our world was shaken. That's what the Histories tell us, is it not? The world shook, and split, and Aerth survived."

She looked around. She could see that the edge of panic had receded slightly. Only Inthima looked the same, and Khalfani was fairly certain that the Second Mother knew what she was doing. Or at least suspected. And then the Second Mother spoke.

"We were never promised that passing through The Nexus would be a comfortable journey."

Oh, bless her! Khalfani thought. *Bless her thrice, and thrice again.*

"No, that's right, Inthima. And for such a passing, it is only reasonable to expect a . . . a bumpy ride."

That did it. The First Mother could see the little half-smiles on the faces of the council. It wasn't a laugh; nothing could bring humor while the Beacons wailed this way. But it was an explanation . . . a reason. A reason upon which a woman could hang her belief. A reason why everything might not be lost.

"So what do we do, then?" asked Shresta-Lin. She was the Fifth Mother, though Khalfani imagined that she would be First one day after Inthima. She was a solid soul, and impressively down-to-Aerth. Khalfani was not surprised that she would be first to turn to the practicalities.

"Let us take our next breaths in meditation. Although the Beacons cry out, I believe that if we quiet our minds, we may yet detect an undertone of guidance within them."

As one, all nine women bowed their heads, each calming her mind and reaching inwards, connecting with her nythlen and attempting to discern some quiet Truth that was hidden beneath the wails.

And then it stopped. Everything. In the shock of Aerth's silence, even the little Beacons fell completely still.

Are we dead? the First Mother wondered. Was this, the utter silence, the void beyond everything? Before she could even begin to formulate a test for such a hypothesis, however, there was a sound. A click, like something falling into place, snapping . . . home. But it wasn't a *sound* in the usual sense. It was more like the *essence* of a sound, the feeling of a click. And the music returned. It was quiet music, the music of personal Beacons, and as Khalfani looked around she could see that the same was happening for the rest of the Chakrava.

And more than that, she could see that the tension was gone.

He did it, the thought came unbidden to her. *In the last moment, Gabriel came through for us.* She was about to say something, but the Fourth Mother voiced Khalfani's private thoughts.

"He did it," the woman breathed like a whispered prayer. And then louder, "The Champion has succeeded. I know it. I can feel it."

"I believe you are right," agreed the First Mother. "I think we have survived through—"

Then the Greater Beacons returned. It was like a crescendo, an opening to a great symphony, but . . .

"Something's different," whispered Inthima.

The First Mother heard it too. Something had changed within the Beacons. Something massive, something foreign, something…

Oh, what has that stupid boy done?

• • • • •

Valerie, Gabriel, and Praxis held a ceremony for Amelia. There were no speeches, no stories, no fancy decorations. But there were also no tears. Each of them simply took their own time standing before a small shrine that Praxis had placed next to the twin globes. Each of them stood and reflected on the sacrifice that Amelia had made, considering how that act of ultimate selflessness had shifted the course of both worlds—a shift that had allowed Valerie and Gabriel to undo the damage their ancestors inflicted millennia ago, and meant the difference between destruction and survival for billions of people today.

As Valerie stared at the shrine, she remembered the trip she and Praxis had taken a few days earlier to Amelia's apartment to retrieve a simple, silver ring. It was something that Valerie had given her when they were little girls. There was nothing written on it, no engraving or other kind of pattern—just a simple circlet of white metal. It had adorned Amelia's finger constantly up until the age of twelve when a growth spurt made that impossible. For a time after she had worn it on a chain, but that eventually raised too many questions with the boys and so the ring found a place on Amelia's dresser, and there it had remained for over a decade.

When Valerie held it up for Praxis to see, something changed in their eyes. A kind of mistiness came over them.

"That's it," Praxis had said, and turned to go.

"Wait, I think there might be other things…"

But they shook their head. "No. That's it. That's what we need. Let's go."

The ring wasn't the entirety of the shrine, but it was the centerpiece. Praxis had somehow crafted a base of crystal in the shape of a four-sided pyramid, and the ring was affixed, on its edge, to the very top. Transfused within the pyramid was a dusting of…something. Valerie couldn't tell if they were flecks of other crystals, or perhaps just microfractures that refracted the light, but they glinted across the entire spectrum of colors.

As Valerie stared at it, she felt a presence by her side and glanced over to see that Praxis was standing next to her.

"Pretty perfect, huh?"

Val gave just the barest hint of a smile. "Which? The shrine or Amelia?"

"Both, I guess."

Valerie nodded. It really was a beautiful memorial. Minimal, tasteful. Amelia would have liked it.

"I particularly like the symbolism," noted Praxis.

"Which symbolism is that?"

They pointed to the ring. "The perfect circle. That's the nature of things. Cycles. No beginning, no end. Just a continuation. And if you lean down and look through it..." They did this to demonstrate. "You can see the scenes through the portal. It's like it has become its own gateway in a sense. And then, of course, there's the planets."

"What?" Valerie had not thought of the globes as being part of shrine, but now she realized that Praxis's placement had not been accidental.

"The two globes," Praxis continued. "Touching at the one spot. Doesn't that remind you of anything?"

"A pool hall?"

"You really are hopeless, Val. No, not a pool hall. Infinity. See? Look at the outline. It's an infinity symbol."

Val saw it then. Praxis was right. Next to the ring was this almost-magical planetary representation of forever. No, not almost magical. It *was* magical. Valerie felt tears threatening to well up, but she fought them down. She had made a promise to the memory of her friend that there wouldn't be any more tears. That's not what Amelia would have wanted.

"Forever, huh?" Valerie asked.

"Well, forever-ish."

"What do you mean?"

Praxis shrugged. "The globes will eventually combine into a single planet. Then it will be just the two circles—the ring and a single globe, side by side. But there will be a special kind of beauty to that, too."

"How long will that take? For the globes to merge, I mean."

They shrugged again. "Don't know. A couple of years? A couple of decades? A century maybe. I really have no idea. It's hard to wrap one's head around scales like planetary orbits and solar systems and that kind of crap. But honestly, who cares? There's no rush."

Then, gently growing in volume, they heard the sound of a flute and turned to see Gabriel sitting by the fire, the small, shiny instrument at his lips. The music was soft, but the notes carried through the library on a breathy whisper. It was a slow, simple tune, although Valerie would not have necessarily called it a sad song, at least not until she saw that Gabriel's eyes were moist.

She and Praxis joined him by the fire and watched the flames flicker a dance to Gabriel's dirge until evening drifted into night and they all eventually drifted to sleep along with it.

• ● ⬤ ● •

Valerie and Gabriel remained in the Interstice for several more days, or at least what felt like several days. Praxis had warned them that time flowed differently there and when asked, they said they were fairly certain that wouldn't change just because Aerth and Earth had begun to recombine.

"So what do we call it now?" Valerie asked one afternoon.

"What are you talking about?" replied Gabriel.

"If it's one planet now, do we call it Earth? Aerth? Eaerth?"

Gabriel remained silent for some time, so long in fact that Valerie assumed he had decided to simply ignore the question. When she finally sat back in her own chair, however, he quietly replied:

"Home."

She realized that it was more than the answer to her question. Valerie had no family left, no one to return to, but that was not true for him. Gabriel had a Circle.

"You should go," she said. "Home. To your sister. Your parents."

"I'm not sure the world will welcome me back."

"I don't know about the world, but I'm pretty sure your family will."

"Oh, I suspect my family will be happy to see me, but I fear not Aerth. The Beacons would have begun singing again if my planet wanted me to return."

"Nah," Val said, kicking him lightly in the shin. "They're probably just planning a surprise party for you."

"A surprise party," he said flatly.

"Mm hmm. I hope there's cake."

"Oh, you do?"

"I like cake."

Gabriel tilted his head and stared at her.

"Yes," she replied to his questioning look. "Of course I'm going."

"Why?"

"Never been there. Well, not really. I mean, I saw a few trees and got bit by some nasty flying bugs, but... you know."

"What?"

"I never got cake."

"Oh," was all he said.

They left the next day.

• • ● • •

As he stepped onto the soil of his Circle, Gabriel fell to his knees. It had nothing to do with homesickness or some kind of ceremony of appreciation. It was nothing of the sort.

It was the Music.

The song of the Beacons washed over him, and he felt like his soul had slipped into a hot bath after a cold winter's day. Warmth was flowing into his existential core. What staggered him more than anything else, however, was the instant recognition that the Beacons had changed.

Gabriel had grown up infused with the song of Aerth playing through his nythlen and into his heart. It was a part of him. As he listened now, however, he perceived a depth to it that had never been there before. That infinite Call of Aerth had become . . . somehow . . . impossibly . . . more infinite. It was like he had only ever heard the music being played by gentle strings, and suddenly he was witnessing a performance in which there were horns and drums . . . and an array of instruments of which Gabriel had never before conceived, all adding their own delicate and intricate harmonies. The Beacons had a richness to them that was beyond description, and now that he had heard it, the Song of old would always seem incomplete in comparison.

Praxis had come over to him.

"You okay there, Gabby boy?"

"Yeah," he managed to whisper in reply. "I'm . . . okay. I'm good."

"Beacons come back?" They didn't wait for a reply. "Looks like they have."

"You can hear them then?" he asked.

"Nope. Like I said, I'm not of this world anymore. No Aerth Beacons for the Keepers."

"Even now? Even after . . ."

Praxis shook their head.

"I'm sorry," Gabriel said. "You deserve to hear this."

"I heard it. Before I became a Keeper."

"Not like this, you haven't."

Praxis's eyes went distant as they considered his words, and then they nodded. "There's more to the song, huh? I guess that makes sense." Then they turned away, but not fast enough to keep Gabriel from noticing a tear in their eye.

Valerie came up next to him and asked, "What did you say to Praxis?"

"It's hard to explain."

"I think they're crying."

"Yeah. I think it's because they won't get to hear the full song of the Beacons. After everything they did, it must be pretty upsetting. Pretty unfair, honestly, and I imagine perhaps even a little devastating."

"I don't know," Valerie disagreed. "They didn't look sad. Just . . . tearful. They could even have been tears of joy as far as I could tell."

"Trust me, it's sorrow."

Valerie turned around and called out to Praxis. "Hey!" When they turned around, she continued. "Are those tears from being happy or sad?"

Praxis gave an odd little laugh and replied, "Same thing."

"What?" replied Valerie.

"Happiness... sadness... they come together again on the other end of the spectrum."

"That makes absolutely no sense," Valerie called back.

Praxis studied her, then said, "It will once you get there." With that, they turned back around and walked off into the woods.

Valerie watched Praxis go, then looked down to where Gabriel was still kneeling on the ground. She lightly elbowed him in the back of the head. "Are we going to do this or what?"

Gabriel stood, rolled his eyes at her impatience. "You really do like to go fast, don't you?" he asked, but then turned and led the way to his parents' house without waiting for an answer.

He went around to the front this time—as that was what the future had in mind—and was not at all surprised to see his family gathered there, waiting for him with broad smiles on their faces. They watched as he approached, but then his father's patience faltered and Reimas raced over to grab him in a great bear hug. A moment later everyone joined them.

Gabriel's family deluged him with questions about where he had gone, what he had done, and what was in his future. They only gave him a moment's pause when he promised to tell them everything.

"Will you be staying?" his father probed, hopeful. "For a while at least?"

"Let the boy's future sort itself out, Reimas," replied Marissa. "There are more immediate matters, you might remember."

"Like what?" his father asked. And then he clearly did remember. "Oh, yes. Of course."

"What matters are these?" Gabriel inquired.

"Gabriel," Sendra said as she tapped him on the shoulder. He turned to look at her, and his sister motioned with her head towards Valerie, who had been hanging back several paces. "Who is that?"

"Ah. This," he began while motioning for Valerie to join them, "is Valerie. She is the Champion from the other world."

"What does that mean?" his father whispered in his ear as Valerie came forward.

"Hey," Valerie greeted them all with a curt wave.

"Valerie..." repeated Sendra as if she were testing the name, and then she looked at Gabriel and raised an eyebrow. It was not the time to answer the dozens of questions he heard in her tone, so Gabriel merely shrugged in response. That made Sendra laugh and she said, "You're always just full of surprises, aren't you?"

"What is the future but a chance to be surprised?" he replied.

"Well, if you ask me, I think someone's Beacons have been having a little joke with him."

"And what is that supposed to mean?"

"It means," Sendra said teasingly, "that my sensitive little brother has clearly stopped listening—"

"Gabriel."

Everyone fell to silence at the sound of that voice. It was the voice of wisdom and strength, foresight and compassion. Gabriel turned to watch as the First Mother walked toward them from the front door, her gait measured and stately.

"Welcome home, my child."

"Blessings to you, Holy Mother," Gabriel replied. No one could have missed the caution in his voice.

A month ago, Gabriel would have allowed his mind to relax into the aura of love and acceptance that the First Mother effused. But now, a journeyman of Dhokha di Maath himself, he realized that anything could be hidden beneath her apparent intentions. Was she truly here to welcome him back? Had she come to imprison him? Question him? *Surely she'll want to question me,* he thought. *She must be beyond curious.*

As if she could read his concern, the First Mother said, "Relax, my son. There are no deceptive hearts waiting for you here in Massaea. Only friends and family who are glad to see you returned."

"Thank you, Holy Mother."

Khalfani looked at Valerie, then. "Welcome back to Aerth, my child. Seeing you again is…a pleasant surprise." And then she added, "Which is itself a pleasant surprise."

Valerie opened her mouth to speak and Gabriel saw the acerbic comment in her eyes. Val glanced at him for the barest of moments and caught his pleading look. *Please don't.*

"It's a pleasure to be back," she replied instead, and Gabriel breathed a sigh of relief. They all knew it was not what she had intended to say, but actions speak louder than intentions.

The First Mother smiled kindly to her and was just about to turn back to Gabriel when Valerie went on.

"Of course, it's not really Aerth anymore, is it?"

Why? Gabriel wanted to shout. *Why why why would you say something like that right now?* And then, *Because it's Valerie. Of course she'd say something like that.*

Khalfani tilted her head in a curious sort of way, particularly for the First Mother, and without even a hint of surprise or annoyance said, "I wouldn't say that. It may be more than Aerth, but it is certainly not less." Then her tone became very casual. "Gabriel, might we have a word?"

As if that were some kind of prearranged sign, Gabriel's family suddenly became enamored with showing Valerie their home. As they led her along the paved walkway that sloped upwards through the middle of a modest, tiered garden, Sendra hung back. She leaned into Gabriel, patted him on the chest where the Winder's Knot rested beneath his tunic, and whispered, "Good luck." Then she kissed him on the forehead and scurried off to catch up with the rest of her family.

And then Gabriel and Khalfani were alone.

"I..." Gabriel began, but paused. Khalfani waited. "I was not expecting to see you here, Holy Mother."

"No," she replied. "I imagine not."

"Then why—"

"I came because there are some things I needed to... share with you. And the Beacons told me that if that's what I wanted, then it was my turn to come to you."

Gabriel remained silent, and the First Mother continued.

"First, and certainly most importantly, I want to... No. I *need* to say thank you. Thank you for saving our world, of course, but not just that. Thank you for not listening to me, when that would have been the easiest thing under the skies. And..."

She paused, and Gabriel could see that she was holding back a well of emotion. When she had regained control, she continued. "And thank you for shining a light into a place of darkness within me. While it is rarely appreciated in the moment, it is truly the greatest gift a person can offer. And if you are willing, I would be honored..." She paused again to take a deep, calming breath. "I would be honored to consider you not just as my child, but as my friend."

Gabriel was stunned. Thinking back, he realized that in all the weeks he had spent with the First Mother, he had never heard her speak of friends. Surely she must have some, he felt, but as he considered it now, he wondered if that were really true. A woman in her position wouldn't have much space in her thoughts or schedules for personal relationships, and in a sudden insight he realized what a rare invitation she had just extended.

"It is I who would be honored, Holy Mother," he responded. His voice only shook a little, and he was proud of that.

She smiled, broad and warm, and said, "Good." Then she embraced him tightly. When she released him she added, "And to my thanks I would add an apology. For snapping at you when you used my name in the cell. From now on you may call me Khalfani whenever and wherever you please."

"Thank you, Holy Mother," he said with a smile.

Khalfani laughed. It was bright, sincere expression of happiness, and immediately contagious. Then she tussled his hair, put an arm around his shoulder, and began walking towards the house. They only made it a few steps, however, before she stopped.

With a snap of her fingers she said, "I almost forgot."

Khalfani reached into a pocket and withdrew a stone, held between her thumb and forefinger. It was really more of a chip, barely a centimeter across and a tenth of that thick, and perfectly black. She held it out to him.

"What is this?" he asked as he took it from her.

"This," she explained, "is a little piece of the altar in the High Temple. It chipped when some oaf dropped the Worldstone on it."

Gabriel's eyes grew wide. "I'm so sorry—"

She patted his hand. "No. It wouldn't have happened had I listened, so the fault is mine. We considered having it repaired, but the Beacons told me that there was a better path." She closed his hand around the stone and then continued. "You probably were not aware of this, but that altar was crafted nearly eight thousand years ago with the intention of providing a protective spirit across the world. This chip may be small, but it should be more than enough to keep you safe, I think." She winked at him. "At least I hope."

"Thank you, First… Khalfani."

"Now come," she said in a matter-of-fact tone. "I don't know how long your father will be able to hold out before hearing your story. And I'll admit to some modest curiosity myself." She motioned towards the house. "Shall we?"

"Yes. And it's probably not a great idea to leave Valerie alone with my family for too long. She has a way of saying things that…"

Khalfani nodded knowingly. At that moment, they heard Sendra's voice. The words were indistinct, but the tone was challenging.

"That line may have already been crossed," she observed.

They hurried inside.

• • • • •

The Champions related the story in sparse detail. At least, they tried to. Valerie wasn't big on specifics and wanted to summarize the entire experience as 'this dude attacked me, and then we saved the world after I got behind the wheel of a speedboat and a Lamborghini in the same damn day.' This was not hyperbole. It was precisely how she first described the events when Gabriel's family asked. Gabriel was inclined to relate things in slightly finer resolution, but his modesty often led him to gloss over certain aspects. His family knew him all too well, however, and was adept at identifying those points where a little prying was warranted.

What fascinated Valerie was the variation in their interests. Gabriel's father asked questions ceaselessly. How did such and such make Gabriel feel? What were the Beacons telling him? When Gabriel described the moment he first saw Amelia in the inn, the man literally shifted to sit on the edge of his seat.

Marissa was almost exactly the opposite. She interrupted rarely, and when she did it was to explore aspects that Valerie considered to be the core of what transpired. They were the kinds of questions that Valerie herself would have asked, and through the evening she found herself developing a profound respect for the woman. Gabriel's mother was straightforward, direct, decisive.

It was hard to know what to make of Gabriel's sister and her timid husband. Kenth said nothing the entire night, and whenever Valerie looked over at him, his eyes were on Sendra. Valerie found this amusingly ironic, since whenever she looked at Sendra she found the sister looking at *her*. There was nothing overtly hostile in the woman's constant... attention. *No. Not exactly* attention. *Monitoring*. But Valerie felt a distinct tension there. Almost a challenge. Those looks made a clear declaration: if Valerie wanted Sendra's approval, she would have to earn it. And Val found herself wondering if Sendra could sense just how deeply she didn't give a damn. Except for perhaps once or twice, when for no reason—with no sensible explanation—she found herself wondering if some part of her maybe did.

No, Val concluded. *I really don't.*

Unquestionably most unexpected behavior of all was that of the First Mother. The woman asked almost nothing of Gabriel, but seemed acutely interested in Valerie's perspectives. She asked a little about Amelia, a fair bit regarding technology and life on Earth, and rather a lot about Praxis. There was no mistaking, however, that the woman's greatest fascination was Kelly. Her interest was puzzling to Valerie, and also rather unsettling. Fortunately, Khalfani was both sensitive and polite, and quickly recognized that the topic made Valerie uncomfortable. She continued to slip questions into the conversation, but they were artfully crafted to minimize that discomfort. There was no denying that Aerth's leader was a brilliant, insightful woman worthy of respect. Sure, their first interaction had centered on the bitch trying to kill her, but you can't hold that against someone forever, right?

It was long past midnight when everyone finally retired. Valerie slept on the floor in the central room and was awakened just after dawn by the sound of the First Mother entering.

"You're up early," Valerie quietly observed.

"No more than usual," Khalfani replied. "You're a light sleeper."

"A lot more than usual." Val sat up in time to see a faint expression of good-humored amusement flicker across the woman's face.

"I suppose recent events would force anyone to change their habits."

"I suppose so," agreed Valerie. Then, "If I asked you a question, would you give me an honest answer?"

"Of course..." Khalfani had been about to add 'my child', but stopped herself. The adjustment was not lost on Valerie.

"Why did you come here? Really. Was it just to learn what had happened?"

"That was part of it."

"How did you even know we would be here?"

"I didn't. Not with certainty. The Beacons directed me, and there wouldn't be too many other reasons I would be called to travel all this way to a tiny Circle in the middle of Jasseth."

The way the First Mother spoke was so strange. *I would be called... directed me...* Gabriel spoke that way too, but when it was only a single person it was easier to dismiss as an idiosyncrasy. When an entire people thought like this... *No, not just* thought. *Lived like this.*

"How long did it take you to get here?" Valerie asked.

"Only a few weeks. I came by ship most of the way, and made no stops for other business. I'll be longer returning to Annaphora."

"If you like, I could ask Praxis to take you back through the Interstice. Assuming I could find them, that is. Although knowing Praxis, they're probably watching us right now."

Khalfani smiled. "That's very thoughtful, Valerie, but there is no need. Other business is seeking my attention during my return, and I'll be back at the Syntrodome in plenty of time for whatever will be waiting. In my position, I do not receive the luxury of travel very often, so I enjoy the opportunities whenever they arise."

The First Mother turned around, slowly taking in the small, welcoming house with appreciative eyes. Valerie noticed that the woman had a satchel on her back, and blinked at the strangeness of it. Here was the leader of an entire world, and she carried her own clothes on a journey of weeks or longer. Things were so, so different here.

"But there's more," Khalfani said as she finished looking around.

"More?"

"More reasons than to learn what happened. I came to deliver a message to Gabriel."

"What message?" The question tumbled out before Valerie had a chance to think about it. Once the words were spoken it was too late, but she immediately wondered what had made her ask, and especially like that.

"A defining characteristic of it being a message for Gabriel," the First Mother explained patiently, "is that it was *not* a message for you. But," she added quickly to ease the sting of her words, "I have now come to understand that I have one for you as well. If you would hear it."

Valerie gestured for her to continue.

"You and I did not have the most comfortable of beginnings. I want you to know that there was nothing personal in what transpired. I truly believed that the only way to save my world was through your death. And whether you can find it in yourself to believe me or not, I want you to know that I am very glad to have been wrong. You are strong-spirited woman and a warrior of tremendous potential. I do not know what your future holds, but should it take you back to Annaphora, or anywhere in these lands, I want you to know that our people will welcome you with open arms. As will I. You have the respect, and deepest appreciation, of our entire world."

The First Mother's tone was kind, but with a hint of formality as though she truly was speaking with the consent and backing of an entire civilization. Valerie wasn't sure how to respond. Was she apologizing? Offering her a job? Was the sincerity a ruse, and she was simply trying to throw Valerie off balance? As she tried to make sense of it, the First Mother adjusted her satchel and stepped to the front door. She looked over her shoulder, and the woman's voice resumed a more casual tone—still commanding and utterly in control, but somehow more human.

"And Valerie?"

"Yeah?"

"Would you be so kind as to extend my appreciation to Marissa and her family for their warmth and hospitality? I wouldn't want to wake them for such a thing."

"Won't they already..." Val made a waving motion, wiggling her fingers. "You know, sense it or whatever."

"Perhaps, but why not extend the gift of certainty when one can, hmm?"

With that, Khalfani opened the door. Sunlight streamed in, nearly horizontal, and illuminated particles of dust in the room. They seemed to sparkle in that light, and then the woman closed the door and the effect was gone. Valerie was struck by a similarity to the prismatic sparks that announced Praxis's portals, and it made her wonder just how many such similarities had passed her by unnoticed over the years.

• • • • •

Valerie remained with Gabriel's family for several weeks after the First Mother departed. She explored the lands around Circle Massaea, and took in enough of the culture of Aerth to appreciate just how foreign it truly was. On the surface, though, one also found similarities. People ate, laughed, and cried, and each strove to fill the days with things enjoyable, educational, or preferably both. Those similarities reminded her that whatever the differences, at the core they were all human, and all fundamentally connected.

One afternoon as she and Gabriel were returning home from a visit to Yemnalyn Falls, the memory of a past conversation unexpectedly surfaced into her thoughts.

"Gabriel?"

"Yes?"

"You never answered my question."

"You haven't said anything since we left the Falls."

"No. Before that."

Gabriel gave Valerie a sidelong look. "How much before that?"

"When we were outside the High Temple."

Gabriel went silent. She couldn't tell if he was trying to remember the question, thinking of an answer, or simply ignoring her. She decided it might be the first and added, "When I asked you why you protected me from the assassin."

"I remember."

"And you said that you'd tell me if we both made it out alive."

"I remember that too."

"Well? Here we are. We made it out, and I'm pretty sure we're both alive."

"Indeed we are."

Gabriel had continued walking, and his eyes were fixed forward on the road.

"So . . . why'd you do it?"

"I lied."

"What?"

"I lied," he repeated.

"I heard what you said. I just didn't understand it."

"What part did you not understand?" Gabriel could feel her getting ever so slightly irritated, and forced himself to keep a straight face.

"We're here, we're alive, so tell me why the hell you protected me."

"Hmmm. I don't think so."

"I'm gonna kill you."

He pondered that for a moment as well and then repeated, "I don't think so."

"You are such a pain in the—" She grabbed for his arm mid-sentence, but he had already started running. "God damn pre-shadow bullshit!" she shouted as she took off after him.

When they arrived back at Gabriel's house later that evening Praxis was sitting on the ground near the front gardens, waiting for them.

"What happened to you two?" they asked.

Gabriel and Valerie looked at themselves, then at each other. They were covered in dirt and grass stains.

"We had a disagreement," Gabriel said.

"You have a bruise on your cheek," Praxis observed.

He shrugged. "She's really fast."

"And you," Praxis nodded their head at Valerie. "Why are you wearing only one shoe?"

"Because," Valerie started, her voice carrying an odd mixture of annoyance and respect, "Gabriel's a sneaky little bastard, and some trees are very hard to climb."

Praxis stared at them a moment longer, then stood. "You know what I think?" The Champions shook their heads. "I think this is not my problem. And moreover, you two have a bigger problem to deal with. A much bigger problem, and one that cannot be put off any longer."

Valerie and Gabriel looked like a couple of children who had just been told that they would have to attend summer school. The air of play was gone, immediately replaced with a cautious concern.

"Let's go," Praxis said as they walked over to the wall of Gabriel's house. "Now."

The passage through the shimmering portal was as unpleasant as ever, but familiarity with the experience was helping to mitigate the aftereffects. Stepping into the Great Library, they immediately saw that the place was in complete disarray.

"What happened here?" Gabriel asked.

"It looks like the place has been ransacked," Valerie noted. "Who did this?"

"I did," Praxis replied.

Valerie shook her head in confusion. "Why?"

"Because I needed to rearrange everything. I told you I was going to do that, remember? But, when I got over to that wall, do you know what I found?" The Champions just stared at Praxis. "Come look."

Praxis led the two over, then pointed down at the rug. Squatting, Valerie could see a crimson stain on the plush fibers. Gabriel joined her to examine it, then both rose to find Praxis holding out a bucket of soapy water in one hand and a scrub brush in the other.

"One rule," Praxis said as they shoved the bucket into Gabriel's hand and the brush into Valerie's. "I told you. One rule. You make a mess, you clean it up." They strolled over to the fire where a glass of strahlla was waiting for them on the table. Turning back, Praxis saw the Champions just staring in bewilderment. "Go on. It isn't going to scrub itself. And make sure you get the whole stain out or you're going to be weaving me a new rug."

Gabriel and Valerie blinked. Then blinked again. Then, with resigned smiles, they got to work.

Epilogue

It was precisely one year to the day since Valerie and Gabriel had plunged into an abyss and, in the wake of Amelia's sacrifice, forged two halves of the Worldstone into a unified whole. On a small island—east of Therspia and west of Norway—the worlds of Aerth and Earth had begun to merge and the appearance of other-worldly settlements was doing wonders for the local tourism trade. It was levying a more significant burden on the quaint fishing villages of Havlanti than upon the larger towns of Iceland, but the Circles were quick to recognize the benefits. Many said that it was the balancing of karma for the substantial damage incurred when a large section of the eastern landscape had been torn asunder the prior year, a topic that continued to spark lively debate. Inhabitants of the tiny Aerth settlements on the west coast insisted that the explosion and the inexplicable appearances of otherworldly towns were inherently connected. The citizens of Reykjavik and other modern towns were conversely impassioned that such a connection was nothing more than their imagination. But however enthusiastic the debaters became, they all remained civilized. It was Iceland after all, and there were statutes mandating that any serious disagreement had to be discussed over drinks, preferably with a cheeseboard close at hand.

Valerie pulled over to the side of the road and parked. She had wanted to find another boxy, pink embarrassment of a car in honor of Amelia's death, but as far as she was able to tell from several hours of internet research, there had only been one like that in existence and it was now vaporized from the Unification. Or buried beneath miles of jagged volcanic rock. Whatever its fate, Valerie was forced to settle for an Audi. It was silver-gray when she and Praxis 'borrowed' it, but now a wide, fresh stripe of pink ran down the center of the hood, up the windshield, and across the roof. She had run out of paint before reaching the trunk, but it didn't matter. It was the thought that counted.

She had left Gabriel and Praxis asleep in a small motel in the town of Egilsstaðir and snuck out to the car just before dawn. The plan had been for all three of them to go, but when the moment arrived Valerie was overcome with a sense that she had to do this alone. *Maybe this is what Gabriel means when he talks about Beacons.* And then she found herself wondering if he and Praxis had known all along that she'd go off without them. If so, why did they agree to get a room on the island instead of just portaling in that morning? Did they know that her desire to drive to the spot—to, in some semblance, recreate the path that they had followed that fateful day—was really about giving her the opportunity to sneak away? For that matter, had she been planning this subconsciously? Was she somehow aware that…

She stopped thinking about it entirely. This was precisely the kind of paradox that threatened to melt her brain whenever she and Gab started talking metaphysics. It didn't matter. She made her choices, and that was that.

When she got to the car, however, she found Gabriel waiting in the passenger seat. He wore a smug expression, the meaning of which was abundantly clear: you didn't really think I wouldn't know, did you?

"Uh huh," she nodded. "Should have guessed. What, no Praxis?"

Gabriel gestured with his thumb towards the back seat where Praxis had stretched out, apparently fast asleep. Their yin/yang tattoo shone in the moonlight, and Valerie was suddenly glad that they were here after all.

"Alright, let's go," she said.

"I took the liberty of making a playlist," he said.

"You...you...made a playlist? On what?"

Gabriel took out a portable player and gave it a little wave. "Praxis helped."

It took close to an hour before the road came to an end. Around the epicenter of The Nexus, there was a new feature in the landscape. A wide ring—easily a dozen miles across if not more—was filled with enormous boulders and slabs of volcanic rock that had been ejected by the explosion that resulted from the reunification of the Worldstone. Overhead imagery had revealed that at the center of the broken countryside there was a wide, smooth disk of stone that geologists were calling the Central Plateau. The scientific community was hypothesizing that there must have been some kind of energetic accumulation deep underground that had burst forth with such intensity that the rocks directly above had become fused into this mirror-like feature.

When Praxis had read about this theory in one of the local Icelandic papers, their only response had been, "Sure. Something like that, I guess. If you don't want to think about what a big platform like that might be for. But whatever." They then, with a grunt of mild disgust, immediately flipped to the back of the paper and started picking at a Sudoku.

And now here they all were, as close as a road could take them to the epicenter of The Nexus. It was time for some hiking. Climbing, actually, as they soon realized. While the enormous monuments of volcanic rock were relatively sparse out where the road ended, they quickly became a continuum of crags and towering spires. Valerie insisted on taking the lead, but found the landscape to be an infuriating maze. She would climb to the top of an outcrop only to realize that there was no way forward. The second time this occurred she returned to see Gabriel and Praxis just sitting on the ground sharing some quiet conversation.

They looked up as she approached.

"You knew," she accused. The pair shrugged. "You knew that it was a dead end. And you didn't say anything."

"You were having so much fun leading," Praxis said in a tone of complete innocence.

"I hate you both."

They made better time after that, although sometimes even the best path was still challenging. Once they reached the edge of the Central Plateau they were all covered in scrapes and bruises. The group had considered traveling here directly via the Interstice, but somehow the little injuries felt like an important piece of the pilgrimage, and the trio were oddly thankful for them.

The enormous disk had a glassy appearance, and the late afternoon sun reflected off it so brightly that it was difficult to look straight west. The stone was warm to the touch, easily a good twenty degrees hotter than the surrounding rock. There was only one explanation: the enormous disk was still cooling.

The setting sun watched as they made their way towards the center. There was a pervasive feeling of calm here, accompanied by a steady breeze from behind. Val found herself wondering if the wind was headed west…or inward. She suspected it was the latter. Although the sky above was overflowing with birds, there were no animals of any kind on the Central Plateau, and they traveled in a silence broken only by the rhythm of their footstep. They all instinctively knew that this last leg of the journey was intended for introspection. The stillness wasn't eerie, just solemn, private. Almost sacred.

When they finally neared the exact center, that solemnity was interrupted. Ahead, a lone figure was shadowed against the setting wine-red sun. The orb had a halo of amber gold, and the mysterious stranger was positioned in just such a way that it formed a hemispherical arc around them. Even with their eyes adjusted to the dimness of the surrounding sunset's swaths of pinks, ambers, and violets, it was impossible to discern any details, yet there was no doubt in any of their minds that the stranger was waiting for them.

They drew closer, but Valerie suddenly became aware that Gabriel and Praxis had stopped walking. She turned to cast a questioning look their way.

"You coming?"

Gabriel responded in a whisper. "You should go first."

"Why?" Val asked suspiciously.

"In case it's radioactive or the guy has a gun or something," Praxis replied. "No point in all of us dying, is there?"

Gabriel gave Praxis a bemused look, then turned back. "We don't know. But you're supposed to approach alone."

With a slightly annoyed shake of her head, Valerie resumed walking. As she drew closer she was able to determine that the stranger was a man, perhaps an inch or two shy of six feet tall and dressed in some kind of flowing gown. With the evening sky casting everything in muted hues it was difficult to discern colors, but for some unknown reason Valerie was certain his gown was a rich magenta, and the way his hair reflected the colors of the sunset, she guessed it to be blond, or perhaps white.

"Hello, Valerie." The voice was *not* that of a man. It wasn't quite female either, but had a timbre that placed it precisely in between.

Is this a Keeper?

Valerie spun around, but saw that Praxis had hung back and was sitting on the ground with Gabriel. She turned back, then took a few more cautious steps forward. Now only a few paces away, she could see that the stranger's hair was indeed blond, and longer than she had originally thought. There was something intensely familiar about their face, but she couldn't place it.

"You look familiar, but..." She trailed off. The end of this journey already had a rather surreal feeling, and suddenly that sensation had magnified tenfold.

The stranger approached. As they moved their form became infused with a myriad of superimposed appearances, as if some hidden projector was casting images upon the person like they were a screen. When they took their initial step Valerie thought she had glimpsed a red dress, but it vanished in an instant to be replaced by a simple brown robe. The image of the dress, however, had fired a recognition that sent a jolt of adrenaline through her.

"Kelly?"

The figure smiled, and it was almost like a physical connection. It was warm and comforting, yet simultaneously encouraging. It was challenge and acceptance, full of promises and explanations.

"Somewhat."

"What the hell does that mean?"

"Just what I said. Somewhat. I am both Earth and Aerth, Kelly and the totality of the Beacons."

"So you *are* Kelly," she said, making no attempt to disguise the rage that was surfacing.

"A part of me *was* Kelly."

"I'd like to have a word with that part."

Inexplicably, Valerie found herself calming down, and that irritated her. *No, I have a right to this anger.* She thought about the death of her parents and Amelia, fanning her rage back into bright flames.

"That is not possible. The consciousness you knew as Kelly can no longer be realized any more than one can separate the water and tannins in a cup of tea."

"I don't drink tea," she replied, her voice steeped in surliness.

"Way to avoid the point, Val. It was a metaphor."

The tone, the phrasing...the spirit of Kelly was riding beneath those words. But it was the Kelly of her teenage years. Teasing, yes, but completely devoted. It was the friend, the anchor. The drive. Valerie's anger dissolved again, and again she flamed it back to life with memories of loss.

"No, don't you dare."

"I can't undo the past," they replied. "But if I could, I still wouldn't unravel the future for the sake of you . . . or anyone else. Or even *every*one else. But I do want you to know that it brings me great sadness that you experienced the pain that you did."

Valerie felt the bitterness slipping. What was it about this person that made it so difficult to stay angry? She grabbed for the hurt again, and said with an icy, jaded tone, "Let me guess. You regret it all, but there was simply no other way, right?"

The figure shook their head. "No. And that's perhaps the saddest part of all. There was another way. A very simple way. But divided as I was, neither half was able to comprehend it."

She was not expecting that response.

"You see," they continued, "both facets of myself understood that there was conflict, but they thought the conflict was with each other. They could not appreciate that the true conflict was with themselves. Rather than fighting to become dominant, they had to tame themselves in order to recognize the value of being part of something greater than themselves. Had they, the two halves, focused on unification rather than the illusion of victory, there would have been no need for Kelly to do the things she did."

They breathed a tremendous sigh and then continued. "I told you a year ago how much I appreciate the sacrifices you have made, Valerie—"

"Wait. What?"

"Well, not directly. I had the First Mother pass the message along. My children of Earth are, unfortunately, still too distracted to listen properly just yet."

"So . . ." Valerie held up a finger. "So when she said that stuff about being welcome and everything, that was *you* speaking?"

"No. That was Khalfani speaking. I told her that you were welcome, and then she graciously agreed to pass along the sentiment. Make no mistake, child, your choices are your own. Always have been, always will be." And then they added, "As annoying and inconvenient as that can be from time to time.

"But now here we are, face to face. I wanted this moment in hope that I would be able to help you find a way to forgive Kelly."

Valerie opened her mouth to respond, but the stranger continued without pause.

"Not for Kelly's sake. There is no Kelly now to receive forgiveness. For *your* sake. That you might find a way to let the wounds begin to heal."

"So kind of like a big emotional lobotomy, huh?"

"No, child. Not even remotely. If you really wanted it, it is within my abilities to wipe those memories from you. I could even give you new ones, I suppose. But

I don't think you would want that. Pain has made you who and what you are, and that person is..."

"A pain in the ass?"

They smiled. "Yes, although that wasn't what I was going to say." They fell silent.

"So what *were* you going to say?"

"Sorry, too late. The moment's passed."

"No. No no no no no. You're like god or something. You can't do that."

"I really can."

Valerie blinked in amazement. "You're seriously going to leave me hanging like this?"

"Yep." Then they added. "But it was complimentary. That's all you truly need to know."

"Forget me. *You're* the pain in the ass."

"I know. Where do you think you get it from?"

The implications of the comment left Valerie stunned.

"Now," the figure continued. "If you aren't in a rush, there is one other matter I'd like to discuss."

"Oookay," Val replied with growing trepidation.

The figure waited for a moment as Gabriel and Praxis joined her. She didn't know how they knew to approach, but... *Yes, I do. I am really going to need to learn how to do that,* she mused.

"Children," the Totality began. "I'm very proud of you all. You know that. But there is one last thing that I'd like the three of you to do for me. If you don't mind."

"How long is this going to take?" Valerie asked, glancing at her watch with a playful smile upon her lips. "I was hoping to grab some dinner soon, and..."

"Not long."

"Well, okay then. I guess I can help," quipped Valerie.

Gabriel leaned over to her and whispered, "Val, you're talking to a planet. I'm not sure you appreciate the nature of what 'not long' might mean to them."

Before Valerie could respond, the stranger held out a hand. Upon their palm rested the Worldstone.

"Keep an eye on this for me, alright?"

Acknowledgements

No work of literature comes to its final form absent the aid and guidance of others, and Nexus is no exception. In truth, writing this section is actually a bit scary, for fear of accidentally omitting even a single name. Such is the nature of aging, I suppose. But I'll take a chronological approach, and hope that this helps with remembering all the generous contributions so many have made along this publishing journey.

At the very start, long before this story formed into characters and plot, was the impetus from Ulisse Di Corpo, co-author of "Syntropy: The Spirit of Love". During a conversation on how to best raise general awareness of the concept of syntropy, I suggested that he write a novel that incorporated it in some fun way. Gauntlet thrown. He then said something to the effect of, "Actually, that's not really my thing. Why don't you do it?" Gauntlet picked up and thrown back. Okay, fair enough.

The story of *Nexus* was originally crafted as a radio play, an ill-fitting medium for this story. Later, in conversations with Black Carpet Productions about creating a feature-length film, I shared the story with Belinda Fadlelmola and Adiyb Muhammad. These two magnificent humans showed such enthusiasm that it was soon transformed into a treatise for a screenplay. If you, like several of the test readers I'll mention below, found the book to have a strong visual element, that's why. While that treatise went into a COVID-induced holding pattern, it became the foundation for the novel.

And perhaps I should also give a tip of the hat to COVID itself, for it took my contracting the virus at the end of 2021 to free up the time needed to complete the initial draft. Perhaps more accurately, however—and certainly more importantly—I must acknowledge my wife, Patty. Editor, yes. Support therapist, yes. But above these, she took up the heavy burden of making life happen all those months when I was sequestered with a laptop, typing away.

Patty was not the only editor, however. I am thankful for the keen eye and experience of Maura Stevens, who did the early full-book editing pass, as well as Laura Smyth who was instrumental in the final polishing stages and getting the manuscript transformed into a final product.

A little more difficult to put into a timeline are the myriad of test readers who helped streamline the story with their insightful suggestions. Perhaps the earliest was my mother, Brenda Dunne, to whom this book is dedicated. She was reading it as the chapters were coming into existence, and her encouragement was boundless. Once the initial draft was completed, many other insightful and supportive people came to my aid. In alphabetical order (for there is no way to put everyone at the front of a list) are Shannon Dunne, Bruce Fenton, Jim Herczegs, Kathy Marshall, Greg Nelson, John O'Brien, Harvey Newman, Raederle Phoenix, Ann Pollack, Andrey Samode, and Rob Tuinstra—each of whom provided incredibly valuable feedback, and from a richly diverse set of perspectives.

There is one final group of people I must acknowledge, and I ask your forgiveness if this sounds a bit cliché. I want to thank you, the reader. You have, from the very beginning, been my motivation to transform the ideas in my head into the best novel I could craft. Were it not for you, all of this would have been pointless, and I cannot thank you enough for reading (and hopefully enjoying) this book.

Kickstarter Recognition

The last stage of publishing for *Nexus* happened via a Kickstarter campaign. It was an overwhelming success in every sense, and in large part thanks to the almost 150 fans who were not merely enthusiastic backers, but went above and beyond to support the campaign as Sponsors. While some prefer to remain anonymous, I do want to expressly recognize all of them for their kindness and support.

The highest level of support was entitled Worldstone Sponsors, and included five incredibly generous souls (who may just have to make appearances somehow in future books): **Michael H. Brobst, Kevin A. Moore, Joseph V. Morrow, Jay and Judy Sadowsky,** and **Brett William Steadman**.

The next tier of sponsorship was the Diamond Sponsor level. This group comprised nineteen people who single-handedly (well, thirty-eight-handedly) accounted for nearly a quarter of the overall project support: the **Bhaktivedanta Institute for Higher Studies, Arjun Baradwaj, Kiki Be, Yvie C., Adam Curry, Sanjeev and Leena Dev, John P. Finnegan, Jenifer Grundy Hollett, Rob Hopf, Matt Leyendecker, Lorelei Freyja McKelvey, Wyatt J. Nash, John O'Brien, Michael J. Slusser, Jeff Spencer,** and **Brenda Windberg**.

The center tier was dubbed Gold Sponsorship, and included these wonderful friends: **Jerome Anello, Alex Brady, Joseph Downs, Leslie and Rick, Pierino Gattei, Samuel D. Park, Paula Petry, Ph.D., the Preator Family, Zaza Soriano,** and **Rob and Julie Tuinstra.**

There were twenty-eight generous supporters in the next tier, named Silver Sponsors, including: **Jean and Jim Berard, Steve and Lori Bruun, Chris S. Carothers, Jeremy A. Clark, Michael Cornell, Shawn Fournier, Barb Gasper, Tatiana Glad, Julia Gritzbach, Neal Grossman, Terri Ann Laurino, Stephanie Lepchenske, Chris MacIntyre, Megan Millane, Richard Novak, Rocky Nunzio, Robert Paddock, Ellen Pilcher, The Poissants, Suma Raj, George Sapio, Melissa Stephens, Jason Stillwell,** and **Alex Wrigglesworth.**

The baseline Sponsor level—which I imaginatively named "Sponsor Level"—included an overwhelming collection of spectacular people from around the globe (at least I think they're all native to Earth): **Wagner Alegretti, Tony Amaio, Dave Baxter, Brian and Jeane Binney, Kat Binney, Ari Rapkin Blenkhorn, Mary Bonanno, Dana Bonistalli, Pierfrancesco Briganti, Karen Campbell,**

Ed Chapman, Clare and Gina, Cyndi Consoli, Lynn Ann Cornell, Kevin Cropper, Janet Daly, Frank and Karen Daly, Sam David, York Dobyns, Russ Donda, Sten Duncan, Rachel Earing, B. Fenton, Brian Flatley, Kerry Frater, Steve Freedman, Selena Renee Gill, Michele Glock, Dara Gold, Dan Goodrich, Dana Hall, Dr. Marilyn Hamilton, David Hanauer, Donna L. Hawkes, Tina D. Hoff, Robert Howard, Peter Jackelow, Jaime, Rich Kargher and Carole Capen-Kargher, Melissa Kleinberger, Sergey Kochergan, Robert J. LeBlanc, Jonah Sho Levinson, Hillary Leyendecker, Teresa Liberatore Johnson, Maia, Marlene May, Marge MdGugan, Dr. Peter Merry, Jason Miller, Pier Francesco Moretti, Pamela Morgan, Vlad Moskovski, John O'Hare, Carsten Ohrmann (CxO-Coaching), June Rachelson-Ospa, Terry Phillips, Ann Pollack, Julie Press, Robby Rose, Michelle Rose-Waller, Andrey Samode, Nora Silini, Sue Ann Staake-Wayne, Taylor Steadman, Analaura Trivellato, Nanci Trivellato, Gene Valendo, Señor Neo, Bob Singer, William Wills, and **Jacqueline Youm**. As an additional callout, I want to thank Michelle Rose-Waller for her incredible enthusiasm and support in creating the beautiful *Nexus* stickers that are soon to be making their way into the world.

I am immensely honored that these kind and generous people will be the very first to receive signed copies of the finished work that is *Nexus.*

About the Author

Jeff Dunne was born in New York City in the mid-1960's. A bunch of stuff happened over the next few decades, and one day he woke up with a fascination for the nature of reality, a Ph.D. in Physics, and a passion for writing. His interest in science fiction took root in the works of Roger Zelazny, his love of fantasy out of J.R.R. Tolkien, and his appreciation for the power of humor from Terry Pratchett. He has been writing for most of his life, beginning with poetry in high school, music in college, and stories ever since. Although he has written several books, *Nexus* is his first published novel.

Dr. Dunne is also a prolific playwright, a connoisseur of ursine collectibles, and occasional thespian. He lives with his family outside of Washington D.C.